DEAD GODS
(HM2)

Also by Ophelia S. Lewis

MY DEAR LIBERIA (Recollections)
JOURNEYS (a collection of poems)
THE DOWRY OF VIRGINS & OTHER STORIES
HEART MEN (a novel)
MONTSORRADO STORIES
LIBERIA UNSCRABBLED (a game book)

Children's Books

A IS FOR AFRICA
GOOD MANNER ALPHABETS
(how to be a super polite kid)

DEAD GODS
(HM2)

OPHELIA S. LEWIS

VILLAGE TALES PUBLISHING
NORCROSS, GEORGIA

ISBN: 978-0-985-36252-2
LCCN: 2014901053
eISBN: 978-0-985-36253-9

Printed in the United States of America

Dedication

To my readers,
with love and gratitude. Always.

Acknowledgement

It is God who makes it possible through the very challenging tasks of completing every book I write. May His name be glorified.

Prelude

A SMILING NEIGHBOR asked the old woman, "Where is the little boy, your handsome grandson?"

"No one has seen the boy since yesterday morning," another woman answered in hushed tone.

Who is not silent when a child is missing? There was not much talking. There was silence. Everyone was crossing his fingers and praying the child would be found sooner than later.

The old woman had survived much to get to this point. First, the coup during the eighties, then the civil war during the nineties. Her life had been marked by tragedy and pain, but nothing could have prepared her for such distress during peace time. They say everyone's response to life's buffetings and blessings depend on their spirits. But such tragedy leaves a loved one with a void that nothing can fill, like stealing the brightness of the sun itself. Cold emptiness froze the old woman's feelings with sadness and the only comfort she was able to get was lack of feeling. Unimaginable relief.

__**********__

Aided by the full moon, the fishermen followed the tracks from the white sandy beach, then high-stepping tall grass to the edge where the hard ground started. The bushes where the body lay had mud and blood. Barely thirty minutes later, officers from the Monrovia Police Department were approaching the dead boy.

Police Chief, Aaron Dolo, had seen human death before, yet he still felt something rising from his stomach to his throat. He knelt down and stared at the body. "Sonofabitch," he muttered.

Dolo got up, did a quick sweep of about ten feet of shoreline before coming back to the body. His gaze swept the surrounding area with the ease of someone accustomed not only to observe, but also to making accurate assumptions from what he observed. There was also an edge to his features that clearly demonstrated an internal anger. The stress of his occupation had hammered fine lines around his eyes. He questioned whether this type of murder could not have spared a child. "My God," he gasped, his gaze fixed on the dead boy.

Everyone who had even remotely seen the disturbing wounds sustained from body organ extraction already knew the boy had died at the hands of the heart-man. His chest cavity showed missing lungs and heart, while the incision on his back exposed his missing kidneys. The incisions were surgically clean, proving that the little boy's body had been carried to the beach after the extractions.

Some of the police officers had openly shed tears and cursed out when they saw the body. An onlooker watching a weeping white journalist looking at the body, quipped, "That's nothing. We see that too often around here."

"Officer Lonos!" Dolo called to his best detective. "Notify the family... now!"

His tone was curt, and Lonos understood why.

__**********__

Word spread quickly by the infamous, *They-say*, as to what had happened. Several neighbors and a few friends had stopped by to see the old woman, offering supportive words, puzzlement, and fear.

Two men hurried to the house, not running but not strolling either. Officer Lonos kept his eyes on the old woman's face while she sat on her porch with a worried look. He came slowly inside the porch, gaze settled on her, cautious and nervous.

She got up.

She was tall but bent, her spine had curved itself over the last decade, and that had reduced her height by four inches. Her hair was cut to low Afro, showing her face which had all the wrinkles and sun tan one would expect after living over seven decades under the African sun.

Navigating with the aid of a cane, her small hand clutched the handle of the cane as she walked over to meet the two men.

"Old Ma, sit down," Officer Lonos said, taking her by the elbow and steering her back to her chair. She sat. He crouched at her feet, settled his gaze on her eyes and said calmly, "We found your grandson. I... uh... I wish I had better news."

Cold fingers of ice gripped the old woman's heart and squeezed. It beat once, then stopped and beat again.

"How did he die?" she mumbled, her gaze sliding back and forth between the two men.

"The heart-man," Lonos said, not taking his eyes off her.

How else could he explain the little boy's missing body parts?

"The heart-man," she repeated, tears stinging her eyes. She wondered what it was like when her grandson drew his last breaths. Who were by his side when he left this world? "Mister, God is for me," she choked. "God is on my side because He has wiped away every tear from my eyes. He has collected every teardrop that has fallen and is saving it in a bottle. When the time comes, the person who did this thing will pay. Go now and find those people who killed Matthew, please."

It felt as though she had literally cupped her hands around Officer Lonos' heart. He sighed. "I will find the people who did this to your grandson," he promised.

What else could he have said? Lonos mumbled 'goodbye' and pulled himself to his feet. The two officers left.

Later that evening, the old woman's voice wiped away the quiet of the late night, wailing sorrowfully until morning.

__**********__

CeRue Manor was attractive in a dangerous kind of way, he was helpful in the eyes of many. The LJC gave praise to his monetary gifts to charitable organizations throughout the country and Africa. Everyone saw Manor's gift as the human side of him. Lonos, on the other hand, felt the man's presence was simply an affront to anyone with a shred of dignity and conscience. Lonos was always alert, always careful, always thinking like a detective. He'd suspected Manor made a living by ending the lives of others.

His stomach rolled and his chest tightened at the thought of CeRue Manor paying for the boy's funeral. Officer Lonos had been forced to do nothing to stop him. He could not afford this worthy undertaking based on his policeman salary.

The old woman would not have accepted Manor's cash, so he paid the total expense in person, what Turey's funeral home was charging for the boy's burial. As if he couldn't live with himself if he had left the old woman to pay the expenses. This generosity was an act of public bribery; poor people keep their silence no matter what is done to them, as long as incentives were piled on them.

Lonos felt sick at the repast, looking at Manor sitting near Matthew's grandmother.

CeRue Manor always seemed to wind up like a tightly coiled rope, full of tension and threatening to snap. He was as handsome as far as what money could get him. There were no dimples, no brown eyes, and no natural dreadlocks. He was all hard lines and no friendly eyes. Looking at the man, most people freeze in fear. The old woman did not freeze in spite of the distant, detached expression of sympathy on Manor's face when he entered her humble home.

Manor looked remarkably at ease, sitting next to the old woman like he was at home. Officer Lonos kept giving Manor warning glares. Manor, however, didn't seem to notice. Officer Lonos then turned his attention to the old woman. She met Lonos' gaze with a mixture of concern and curiosity. The officer need not worry. No matter how friendly Manor seems, she would not pretend, not even for the other sympathizers' sake. She wanted Manor to get on with whatever business he'd come to do and leave.

"I am sorry for your loss," Manor said, hesitantly.

The old woman smiled, but it looked like it took a lot of effort. The smile faded as quickly as it had come.

"My grandson was all I had. Both of his parents died during the war. They were killed inside the Lutheran Church in Sinkor," she said, sounding edgy, even irritated.

"That war was bad for all of us," Manor claimed. "Thank God, we have peace now."

The old woman sighed and remained quiet.

"I'm not sure what else I can do to help you," Manor said, steering the conversation away from the war.

As far as the old woman was concerned, Manor could not do less or more. "You have done enough," she said. "At least I know who killed my daughter and her husband. As for my grandson, only God knows. You've paid for his burial… you have done enough."

Manor was not a man easily shaken off. Anyone who truly did know him—and that number could be counted on one hand—he was a ruthless and highly capable killer. But he could see the old woman was a clever woman, and she would be okay if only he stop feeding her deceits. She wasn't afraid of him.

You need to be able to stay calm under pressure and not get flustered, especially when you're doing things you don't want people to know about. Manor felt as if he had lost his place in the conversation.

"I think I should go," he said and rose.

The old woman stared quietly.

Manor gave her a brief nod and walked out.

Indeed, why would he want to chat with her? He probably just wanted her to believe he was trying to be a part of their community when he wasn't.

Family members and neighbors came with food and drinks for the sympathizers. But the crowded house brought nothing but gloom to the host and mourners. People were sensitive to the facts of little Matthew's murder and how he'd been found. Silence crept into every corner and festered like an open wound. Some ate, but many never touched the food. The old woman's appetite had not been nearly to normal since her grandson had been missing, and later found dead.

Lynnette Vinton, a woman from the Words of Christ Church, brought some food on a tray for her and tried coaxing her to try a little of it. She drank a small amount of tea, pondered the good deed of the woman, and quietly admired this generosity. Then she put a piece of shortbread in her mouth and tried to forget the reason people had come to her home.

Chapter 1

THE WORLD CONNECTS at lightning speed, but things were still as if it was 1986 in Liberia. After 15 years of civil war and six years of an elected presidency, progress was painfully slow. Although the cellular phone was booming and substantially more widespread than fixed line telephonic transmission, technology was otherwise, creeping out of the Stone Age in Monrovia: a city police department without computers on every detective's desk, and a wish list of working fax machines and photocopiers needed for critical documents. Forget quick access to DNA technology. Some would admit fingerprint was still being matched by human eye. All this is hard to gasp in today's CSI effect, but it is what it is.

His pay is not the biggest pay, his job is not the easiest, but Officer Lonos is a man who would rather die for his principals than live without one. He accepted the occupation as an officer knowing the responsibilities and hazards involved. As far as he was concerned, hell was not large enough for heart-men. Based on the most recent crime scene, it was evident the heart-men had struck again.

Behavior science never changes, so criminal profiling is still a quick thinker's investigative tool. For the detective in such environment, criminal profiling is always brought to the forefront of law enforcement. For one thing, such crime involves co-conspirators who could keep secrets. Second, logistics, the means of transportation. Getting from point A to point B increases having to be neat and discreet. Then, lodging the victim. They had to put their victim where extraction is done without drawing attention. Disposal was the final and easier step, Liberia's shorelines, the beaches.

As far as Lonos was concerned, Aaron Dolo had only done enough for his conscience to feel as if he had done something. The police chief had not done nearly enough because CeRue Manor, the mastermind behind most of the mishap in Monrovia, was still a loose thread.

It was no wonder that some consider victims of the heart-man unlucky. Murdering for human parts is a peculiar wicked deed, but a heart-man does his job and not cares about his soul. Keep in mind: heart-men are serial killers. Everyone takes part in a crime and everyone knows it's a crime except for the mastermind. As immoral as it is, CeRue Manor saw it as a business and made sure to keep it that way, buying and selling human parts as commodities. Lonos had yet to prove it.

The Good Book teaches: 'For the love of money is a root of all kinds of evils'. It is through this craving that some wander away from their conscience and does not experience anything close to a sharp pang of guilt. They push God completely out of their life, and set their hope on the uncertainty of riches. These kinds of people always want more because greed strengthens their hands. Lonos saw Manor as someone insatiable.

CeRue Manor had the sixth sense to foresee the rich future. Now that Liberia was about to dip her foot in oil, he vowed to play a key role in it too. He was doing well, more than well. His wheeling and dealing concealed some of the biggest unlicensed business operations in Africa that made millions—the smuggling of diamonds, underage girls, and human organs. Since kickbacks and corruption turn a blind eye to regulations, smuggling paid exuberantly well, along with illegitimate private clubs.

If there was a place where people could meet with reasonable confidence that their deeds would not be exposed even in their world of ultra sophisticated matters of illegal, or even murderous, it was Manor's exclusive club, Le'Toit, (English translation-The Rooftop), a facility not for public. No one set foot in some areas and it was Manor who prescribed limits for his establishment. Even his trusted acquaintances went so far, and not further. Le'Toit was surrounded by hidden security cameras, and only Manor knew their locations.

'A fool's paradise', that's what Lynnette Vinton, aka Salvation Lady, calls the club, but services were premium all the way. "Satan is in the walls of that place," she often said.

Activities at Le'Toit was not limited to just a place where rich men met and drank, organized prostitution soared. Underage girls, barely teenage, were shipped in from neighboring counties to entertain these men. They had not come on their own, most being kidnapped. His assistant, an Ivorian native, handled all Manor's commodities, directing the routes of his precious freights—girls, human organs, drugs, diamonds, and weapons.

Inside the naughty housing of Le'Toit, amid the drinking, gambling and businessmen chatting their wheeling and dealing, the winding hall led to a place where a darker side of Manor's financial bloom lies, the top floor. Young girls are kept here to satisfy the men's lusts. The girls are forced to have sex with men for long hours, and are denied contact with anyone, family or others. Some were put into an international place-ment agency for mail-order brides. Human trafficking by unregulated placement agencies for maids, rather than prostitutes, was also a part of Manor's business. Demand for maids was increasing because in America and Europe, people would pay far less for what they would normally pay legal agencies for people to cook, clean, and look after their children.

Manor did not employ stupid people, and his employees were com-pensated very well. Over half of his staff was imported into Liberia and they all had one thing in common; convicted criminals. He made sure all his well qualified employees had salaries bumped way higher than their counterparts, paying them far more than they'd earned any place else. His medical team was structured with an Asian doctor, an Indian surgeon, a Jamaican bartender, and a head waitress named Peaches.

Peaches had worked Las Vegas five years before coming to work for Manor. Wild as hell, she had spent more time in the backseat of cars than she did in the classroom, could drink any man under the table, and always had a purse full of pills. Other than her legal documents, passport or driver license, Peaches didn't need a last name.

Cheah Boatswain, a Monrovia city police officer, ran Manor's personal security force. Once a war lord, Boatswain was one of those who tried to make a holocaust out of Liberia all at once, fueling the senseless civil war with acts of violence beyond wordy description. Most remembered the mad killer, a short man with a shaven head and bushy beard. Though Boatswain had grown his hair and shaved his beard, people remembered him.

A civil war had been ignited because a few Liberian men turned war lords, set their minds on reversing peaceful living to war time so they could take ownership of things they did not want to work for. To rule you must serve, but their mixed-up instincts, and sneaking urge to power, permitted them to rule and get fancy cars and big houses they did not pay for. They turned from being family guards to become gun smugglers' customers who turned them into dogs. They sold drugs along with the country resources, like timbers and diamonds. They put guns and drugs into the hands of their sons and taught them to be rapists and murderers. The assaults on women were inconceivable, as if these men had never clinched to breasts that nourished them.

Today, lawless killings were in the past. But like every place in the world, crime still soared in Liberia.

Chapter 2

ADRIANA LEROUX, MANOR'S key porter, is a gangster with the face of an angel. She's near five feet nine inches tall, with model features; long legs, shoulder length golden-brown hair, compelling light brown eyes, full breasts, flat stomach, and spotless skin most men longed to touch. The woman's voice held neither fear nor skepticism, just filled with cockiness. Very much a presence, Adriana never simply walks into a room, she strolls, which makes a man's heart beat faster. Her hand is soft and warm. When you shake hands with her, you get that jolt that goes through your body when you touch someone who has touched your heart. She is drop-dead gorgeous, the perfect package of a beautiful woman, but has the nerve and reflexes of a snake, and a soul to match.

Manor finished his work at Le'Toit and raced his car at a ridiculous speed to reach Kendejah Resort, where Adriana had checked in. He waited for her at the bar, while she thought of the American woman she had seen at the airport tonight. Afloat in an immense white tub, yellow rose petals surrounding her, scented oil smoothing her tired limbs, Adriana thought about Dr. Mellody Douglas.

An hour and a half later, clean and fragrant, relaxed and wrapped in a soft white cotton robe, Adriana sat on the sofa and waited for Manor to join her.

"The diamonds," she said, holding out her hand, shaking her fingers.

Manor handed her a drawstring cotton bag. She opened it, inspecting the stones carefully. Then she nodded at him and he left her, went over to the bar, fixed their drinks and walked back carrying two glasses.

"French," he said, holding out a glass.

"Thank you," she said appreciatively, and took a sip of the wine. It was cool, light and absolutely perfect for the flimsy way she was feeling.

Adriana lifted her eyes and inspected Manor's face. His eyes met hers. Criminals that they were, knew all the snitch signs of guilt; how the eyes challenge or avoided, keeping deep secrets.

"Sixty-five thousand is what I'm asking," she said, making that number sounds like an unbelievable steal.

"No problem," Manor said, then drained his glass and joined her on the couch.

He put one arm around her shoulder and slipped his free hand under her robe. Then he began drawing circles around her nipple with his finger. Adriana normally jumps at a chance to make love, but she suddenly felt tired. She nearly fainted at the thought of sex. The frequent journeys between the two countries was catching up to her; dealing with charter contracts, security checks, and too many persons to bribe at the airport. Once she starts flying her own plane, there would be less middleman to deal with.

"Perhaps later," she whispered and got up. "My father may get me that plane. I know how you feel about charters. Flying my own should ease your concerns, as well as the pesters. Even a *nobody* wants a bribe," she criticized.

Manor smiled widely, as if genuinely amused. "Your own plane?"

"Of course, why not?"

"I have to tell you, Adriana, most women wouldn't want their own plane or fly it."

"I'm not most women."

Manor's eyes met hers, "No." Then they slowly lowered, then went back up, covering every inch of Adriana, up and down, before meeting her stare again. "No, you're not."

Adriana smiled mischievously.

"I want to touch you tonight," he muttered. He got up, stepped toward her, stood in her face, leaned in and whispered, "Adriana, I want you," his lips tickling her ear. Then he told her where he wanted to touch her.

Manor's lust was muted by her thoughts on the doctor at the airport. *Who is she? Why is she in Liberia? How could she get to meet her again?* "Not tonight, Ce," she replied.

Manor did not show his disappointment.

Manor and LeRoux were the perfect couple, both loaded with cash and up to no good. They enjoyed the finest things in life, especially those things ordinary people cannot afford, and the respect money bought. She was as ambitious as he was, and as ruthless. It was her beauty that had taken his eye the first time he'd seen her at Kendejah Resort in Monrovia.

The beautiful hotel had greatly improved Monrovia landscape. Everyone who is anyone, and those in Liberia on business or for pleasure, dines at Posh, the hotel's modish restaurant, and frequented the pool bar that offers light fare in a luxurious, yet relaxing atmosphere. The best bodies flaunt the best designer bikinis there; beach shirts and sandals you would see anywhere in the world. This is where Adriana stays, conveniently located just twenty-five minutes from the Roberts Field International Airport, booking a presidential suite for her three-day stay every other month.

Her two-year relationship with Manor had started with him sitting at the bar waiting for his lawyer to arrive, sipping on his drink when he spotted her, dark olive skinned, long legs and knockout gorgeous. She was wearing a simple black suit, a skirt three inches above the knee, obviously a designer. Her only jewelry was a pair of large diamond studs. The woman was wearing a six-inch heel black suede almond peep toe sandals with gold leather trims, just an added attraction. Rich girl was written all over her. Adriana reached the bar, purposefully stopping next to his bar stool and asked the bartender for a pen. Like a hound rising to the scent, Manor's sexual antenna reached out to her. She turned her head toward him and looked deep into his eyes.

"Hello," she said in a soft and seductive Afrikaans accent. Then she placed her hand on the back of the empty chair next to him. "Is this chair taken?"

Manor looked at her, mouth hung open, almost drooling, and replied, "I'm alone."

"That's not what I asked you," Adriana teased.

They both laughed.

Holding out her hand, she said in a voice like slow-poured champagne, "I'm Adriana LeRoux."

"CeRue Manor," he introduced himself, taking her hand. Her hand felt soft and warm. He held it up to his lips and kissed it. Electricity flickered between them.

"Well, Mr. Manor, care to join me for lunch?"

Manor drained his glass and winked his satisfaction at the bartender. Then he paid his tap, totally forgetting about his lawyer. The bartender had placed the pen on the bar, but Adriana ignored him, her attention to

Manor. She didn't bother taking the pen she had asked for, and the two slipped away straight to her suite.

Electricity played no part in their lovemaking. Bait-casting would have been a more suitable word to describe it, his exploring hands doing magical things to her inner thighs and her explicit satisfactory screams. He discovered the tiny red diamond tattooed on her shaved pussy, a hair-breadth from the top of her inner labia, and kissed it. CeRue Manor had never had a woman like Adriana. She had never had a man like Manor and she wanted to keep him if he was truly the shark she'd checked him out to be. He thought it was just the dumbest luck to have screwed this beautiful stranger without an ounce of effort on his part.

Lying naked on the rumpled sheets, they both spent, still shining with sweat, Adriana said in a sexy voice, "It's very simple." And then she explained how simple it was; she, soon to become a licensed pilot, can easily transport merchandise, critical medical merchandise for instance, to any part of the world if he had customers buying and, or, supplying them. They will make a lot of money while helping people get organ as quickly as possible, without the waiting list. "If you have the money to pay for something you need, why not," she justified.

That's why she can afford a presidential suite, Manor thought and smiled. Their meeting was more of the devil's luck than God's blessings. Adriana did not care about how or where the merchandise were obtained, she only cared about taking them from point A to point B, as long as they were willing to pay her what she was asking. They became instant partners in the aftermath of their love play.

"Now tell me about your wife," Adriana baited, staring deep into Manor's eyes.

"No wife."

"Out of sight out of mind?" she coaxed, knowing Manor was still married to his Nigerian former fashion model wife, Omolola Sanusi. His gaze dropped to the floor and she chuckled. Then she slipped her hand down his crotch and gently stroked him. "Let's do it again," she whispered.

Besides money, sex was an addiction. The woman's addictions were obvious and CeRue Manor fell for her like a ton of bricks.

Time had not stood still for those two, things were accelerating. Unswerving transportation became relevant as persuasive demands for certain merchandise grew, especially in the US, Europe, Johannesburg, and Abuja.

Chapter 3

THEY SAY 'DIAMONDS are a girl's best friend', but not for Dr. Gia Ricciola; her husband is. And as for RJ Douglas, it's always about the family. With his lawyer life, Douglas made sure he wasn't always at the office toiling away his life. He made time for his clients, his aging grandmother, his daughter and his wife. He had a marriage so typical and yet uncommon.

RJ always shows his wife how much he loves her by all the unexpected gifts he pampers her with. He had called Gia's office before heading home to see how her day was. Paola, Gia's office manager, informed him it was a shitty day at the office, and at Spelman College too. Especially the irate divorced husband and his combative ex-wife Gia had to deal with all week. That night he stopped by Carithers Flowers in downtown Atlanta and purchased 15 long stems pale apricot roses in a chic modern glass vase, a European style bouquet. The roses were fully opened, revealing perfectly arranged petals nestling in the heart of the bloom. He took it upstairs to their bedroom as soon as he got home and placed the bouquet on the nightstand on Gia's side of the bed. An idea came to mind as he was about to walk out. RJ took a long look at the roses, pulled one out, and brought it to his nose, inhaling it with his eyes closed.

"I hope my baby love you half as much I do," he whispered.

Then he palmed the rose petals, plucked them off the stem and sprinkled the petals on his wife's pillow. He sniffed the air again. There was a very light tea fragrance, offering a feeling of warmth and romance in the bedroom. Pleased, RJ smiled and walked out. He wasn't done. He cooked dinner, fed Kitty and got her ready for bed.

By the time Gia got home she took all in stride with a gracious appreciation for what her husband had done. She savored the delicious soup

RJ had kept warm, kissed her daughter good-night and when she got upstairs to their bedroom, Gia looked RJ in the eyes, and for a moment, just a moment, her eyes twinkled. A slight smile formed on her lips.

"You are beautiful, honey," she said, and kissed her husband's lips.

— ✱✱✱✱✱✱✱✱✱✱ —

After seeing her last client late Thursday morning before lunch, Gia was anticipating whether to leave the office for lunch or order in, when her cell phone rang.

"I'd like to tell you a secret," RJ said before she said anything.

"A secret?" she said, smiling as if he could see her.

"I'm in love with the most wonderful woman in the whole wide world."

"Yeah? I'd like to meet her," she teased.

"Honey?"

"Just kidding, baby, as if I don't already know. That's the only reason you're calling? You tell me that every day."

Gia loved this man so much and knew he was up to something. Their third wedding anniversary was two days away.

"When I woke up this morning with you in my arms, I knew I was wrong."

"Wrong about what?"

"I never thought I could love you more than I ever did. I love you a whole lot more than a billion times. I woke up thinking… lying next to me is the most beautiful, and the smartest woman in the world. How the hell did I manage that," he laughed.

"Oooh, honey, I am the lucky one," Gia said. "But, Mom would say *blessed*, not lucky. I am blessed beyond words."

"So," RJ continued, "how about us turning into Big Apple refugees this weekend?"

"You mean a change of scenery? Escape Georgia fresh air for the crowds, hectic pace and real excitement? That's what you mean?"

"I told you you're smart," he laughed. "That's right, honey. We are going to New York tomorrow morning."

"Tomorrow? The three of us?"

"You mean the two of us," he corrected. "Mel will baby-sit Kitty. She's flying in tonight from Rhode Island."

"Honey, I'll have to check my schedule and see if I have any clients tomorrow or… if I can find someone else to see them if I can't."

The phone still at her ear, Gia walked out of her office into the lobby.

"You don't have any appointments for tomorrow," RJ assured. "No clients tomorrow."

"How do you know?" she asked, then turned her gaze at Paola, who instantly looked away. Paola was in on this, she realized.

"I asked Paola not to schedule any appointments for you," RJ confessed.

Gia smiled and nodded at Paola. "Well, even if that… I don't know what to pack," she nitpicked. "I don't have enough time."

"Honey, we will travel light and buy what we need when we get to New York."

"Tell me something, Flaky… did you book us at one of those hotels where clothing is optional?"

RJ laughed.

"Baby, you are the most lovable… adorable… man I've ever met. And, you're crazy."

"That, I am," he laughed. "I'm crazy about you."

__**********__

Airlines insist that first-class customers have always been, and always will be, special. Those sitting in first-class seats typically pay higher fares. If, that is, they did not upgrade for a few more dollars. RJ booked two first class tickets to start the weekend.

Flying first class on Delta, their early morning flight from Atlanta to Newark was flawless and the scenery divine, a sunrise over the Atlantic, an eyeliner-thin trace of pink over an unmade bed of clouds. Then, they rode in style from Liberty International Airport to Kimpton Boutique hotel in a luxury Lincoln Town Car, chauffeur-driven.

After checking in, RJ and Gia walked into their hotel room that featured the largest arrangement of fresh flowers she had ever seen. It was bursting with colors, perfectly arranged, and its fragrance was just amazing. Gia stopped in her tracks, and lingered for a moment to admire the beauty.

"You like the flowers?" RJ said, embracing his wife in a bear hug.

"I like you," she said, freeing herself and then kissing him.

The abundance of beauty that captured her eyes felt the same as the abundance of her husband's love that had captured her heart. She was also ready for everything RJ had planned for their trip, a honeymoon they were not able to take when they got married, and for a good reason.

Romance barely blooms when there's morning sickness, mood swings, abdominal bloating, frequent urination, and fatigue. Gia experienced every pregnancy symptoms carrying their daughter. Most nights she suffered some of the common discomforts of the pregnancy which made it more difficult to get a good night's sleep. For all his wife had to go through to carry his daughter, RJ had prepared an extravagant getaway—first class flight, then deluxe accommodation in midtown Manhattan at Kimpton Boutique hotel, embracing the grace and energy of Park Avenue itself. The personal concierge service he'd arranged included peach rose petals on their bed, chilled champagne and chocolate covered strawberries upon arrival, Broadway tickets, a private helicopter tour of Manhattan, breakfast in bed, in-room massages and spa services, dinner reservations at the Russian Tea Room, and a shopping spree at Goodman; all with chauffeur-driven Lincoln Town Car for the duration of their stay.

A New York shopping spree is something that the average Joe would only dream about, but everybody should do this at least once in his or her lifetime, by planning ahead. On Friday, Gia was treated to a shopping spree that would make a bit of a dent in any pocketbook, but her husband had planned their budget accordingly for the high-end shopping spree in terms of awesomeness.

Real bargains were found on the sale and clearance racks at Barney's, Bloomingdale's, and Saks. Gia shopped at all of the quintessential New York shopping spots without having to pay typical New York shopping prices. She hit the thrift stores too. The thrift stores in New York are what boutiques are in most other towns and cities. She bought more fabulous fashion pieces and filled shopping bags with assorted choices at the thrift stores.

Then lunch at Skylight Diner had plenty of options.

After more shopping, they headed back to the hotel where the bellboy escorted RJ and Gia to their suite. He set down the shopping bags, RJ tipped him, and when he left, RJ place the *Do Not Disturb* sign on the door knob.

Gia unpacked what they would need for the night, then they took a long hot shower together. Soon they were under the smooth cool sheets. Sex was fast, they talk a little and drifted off to sleep. Four hours later, Gia woke RJ and they made love again, this time slowly and tenderly.

Surprising her, RJ spoke a few *bedroom* Italian and she loved that.

Seven o'clock Saturday morning Gia woke to a kiss, feeling the soft cotton sheets tangled around her bare legs as they spent the second morning of their get-away still sequestered in midtown Manhattan.

"Morning," RJ whispered and smiled.

The scents of chocolate and strawberries on his breath lassoed Gia and pulled her even closer to his heart. She nestled into him, wanting to keep close. And then she rubbed his bare chest, kissed a nipple and looked up at his eyes. They were smiling. RJ had been recapping last night's episode of their lovemaking in his mind.

"Happy Anniversary, honey," he whispered.

"I love you," Gia replied, lifting her head, reaching for his lips.

"I love you more," he said, then lowered his head and kissed her. The pleasure registered on her face.

"More?" Her smile turned impish.

After breakfast in bed, the driver met them at the entrance of the hotel and drove them to the downtown Manhattan Heliport. Holding hands, Gia followed RJ through a door that led out to a large landing pad, and a large, sleek helicopter. Once they were belted in, the helicopter lifted quickly, causing a minor rebellion in Gia's stomach. She frowned.

"Are you okay, honey?" RJ asked.

She nodded, but swore to herself.

"We're going to have fun," he said, patting her leg. "Don't be nervous."

Soon they were soaring over the most captivating city in the world, and nothing else mattered but the breathtaking scenery of Central Park, Empire State Building, Statue of Liberty, the new Freedom Tower, and other iconic landmarks located throughout Manhattan. The private romantic VIP tour lasted nineteen minutes, satisfying RJ's flying desires.

"Wasn't that great, honey!"

"Unforgettable," Gia replied, rolling her eyes.

"Were you scared?"

"I was thinking. Maybe we both can't be suicidal at the same time. We have a daughter. Remember?"

"You were scared," he teased, then kissed her. "I did check their safety records, unparalleled." RJ hugged her close.

Gia dismissed the thoughts of more shopping and wanted to chill the rest of the morning. At 2:30 p.m., they both enjoyed the musical *Chicago* at the Ambassador Theatre. Later, after dinner at the Russian Tea Room, they'd taken a carriage ride through Central Park, and then returned to the hotel for champagne cocktails and fruit plates waiting for them.

After a long hot shower together, RJ made love to his wife, pressing his forehead to hers, watching her, reading every note with pleasure etched on her face. He picked up the rhythm and she directed their pace. When she gasped and arched her back into him, he felt the first jolt of his climax.

RJ lay on his back afterward, one leg over Gia's. She curled into him, warm and soft. He kissed her forehead and listened to her breathing until it became even. Soon she was asleep. RJ took a moment to admire her before drawing the covers over them.

If the romantic conversations with her husband was the lyrics, their laughter was the music, making the time spent together in New York a melody that could be replayed over and over without getting stale. Plus, every single day RJ woke Gia in bed with three presents; a small but expensive piece of jewelry, a hand-made greeting card with funny jokes, and an extravagant bottle of French perfume.

Every present came straight from his heart.

Chapter 4

NANA TURNED NINETY-SIX last summer and her physical capabilities were fading. She could still move around with her walker, but she needed someone to cook her meals and help her with other personal tasks. Beulah, Katharine's youngest sister, had moved in with Nana to take on those tasks. Wanting to help in some way, Katharine flew from Liberia every other month to help and spend time with her aging mother.

Besides her practice, Gia had also taken on the position of associate professor at Spelman College, a historically Black college in Atlanta. Katharine and Beulah were both aluminum of this institution, a global leader in the education of women of African descent. After work, Gia went to pick up Kitty from school and RJ went to visit with Nana.

Nana was wearing a short light pink satin nightgown and the robe in matching color, featuring lace trimming intended for subtle beauty and elegance.

"Nana, you look beautiful… as always," RJ said, kissing his grandmother's soft smooth cheek.

"You know who give it to me, don't you?"

RJ nodded.

"She's a good woman, RJ," Nana said, smiling. "Gia is caring too… so you treat her right, hear me?"

"I know, Nana. I'm a lucky man," RJ answered and sat in the chair next to her.

No matter what age, a woman must always feel like a woman, sexy and young at heart. That's what Gia said to RJ when she bought Nana's birthday present. The one she was wearing.

"See, Nana, you don't need an excuse like a honeymoon to look sexy," Gia teased when she'd handed her the gift. It was as lovely a gift and sexy too. Gia knew Nana loved it because her eyes twinkled when she opened the gift box, and then said, "I sure don't." Then she gave Gia a close, affectionate embrace.

Although the Bible says a man has a lifespan of three-score and ten years (70 years), or more, Nana had lived passed ninety-eight years and a few weeks. Her body had made it close to a hundred, now it was falling apart; steady erosion on the inside and at her joints, failing kidneys too. Her heart rate was decreasing every week and RJ was worried about that. Nana wasn't. She told him she had no time for worry in the twilight of her life.

"Every day, everybody dies little by little from life blows," Nana said. "Finally, when you're worn out, but not necessarily so with everyone, you rest. You sleep, you know... die. That's the gift of dying."

"What is?" RJ asked.

"Rest. A good long sleep," Nana replied. "The good Lord's own pre-scription."

"Of course, Nana," RJ whispered. He tried his best to look brave, but a knot twisted in his stomach. He dared not to think the worst. "Nana, you'll be fine. You'll live to be a hundred... I hope to pass a hundred."

"Child, I'm tired," she chuckled. "Who wants to go pass a hundred?"

"Well, Nana... I want you with me for as long as I'm around."

"Now, you know that's not possible," Nana said, her voice soft and gentle. "No need to live that long. That's not how the good Lord wants us to think."

Tears welled RJ's eyes.

Nana lived until ten weeks after her ninety-eighth birthday. Her death was a good death.

— ********** —

The call had come from Beulah Thomas, who informed Bohn that Luverne Thomas had passed away. Bohn called a florist and arranged for a delivery, then booked a flight out of London for six days later.

He stood in the slow-moving line at the crowded airport and waited until a spot opened at the counter. Bohn showed his ID and answered the basic security questions before being handed his boarding pass. The direct flight took him to Atlanta, and once he landed, picked up his rental car and headed for Macon, Georgia.

Until he merged onto I-75 South toward Macon, via Exit 58, Bohn had not realized how long it'd been since he left home. Thirty-five years to be exact. Most of the people he'd grown up with, and he was sure of this, had moved on to bigger towns and lives. People like Eugenia Harris, now Senator Harris, and Carl Hoffman, an African-American Republican candidate for Governor. Macon sons and daughters also made it on to the rosters of NFL, MLB, and NBA teams. Well known actors, musicians, politicians, as well as war heroes, hailed from Macon too. But experience had taught him that what matters is not where you grow up, but how you grow up.

Sharing your life stories with others help, but not in the case of Rufus Bohn. It isn't easy to explain his life. Not everyone can say this about his own life, but do not be misled. The man is as common as it gets, nothing special. However, Bohn had never led a simple life. Like everyone else, time doesn't make it easy to stay on course. And, life paths may seem straight as ever, but it can be strewn with rocks and gravel that accumulate over a lifetime. Having graduated sixth in his class of two hundred from the U.S. Marine Corps, Bohn learned that bad things do happen to good people. At the tender age of eighteen, he had been whisked off to Vietnam.

He earned many young Vietnamese girls undying trust and friendship who were being sexually molested by several South Vietnamese officers when he and other U.S. soldiers chased those officers from the villages. Bohn had spent much of his tour living in 56 of the 114 Vietnamese villages and hamlets throughout the I-Corps area of South Vietnam. His six month tour was extended to thirteen months, which established strong ties and close relationships beyond those boundaries. Bohn toured Vietnam ten times, between 1965 to 1970.

After he returned from Vietnam—a chest full of medals, including a Purple Heart and a Combat Bronze—he had problems with his personal and professional relationships. He didn't recognize he had symptoms of depression, until Katharine Thomas left him for a tall, handsome African named, Robert Jenkins Douglas II. They dated for two years, an engagement was an expected conclusion, and a few weeks after she'd finished her masters degree, Douglas married Katharine and took her to Liberia. Bohn joined the Secret Service agency and was able to add meaning to his life, turning things around.

Rufus Bohn was the best at developing strategic and tactics from scratch. His focus was placed on crimes and investigations, which had been used in the past, from which ideas would be worked on. After retirement, he created a small unit of about ten men by which professional protection service, and combat-oriented missions would be conducted. On many contracts, he used his high level connections of world secret agencies, like the CIA and the IBA, he referred to as joint forces.

There was something that kept a distance between him and any woman who started to get close. He was sure that he did not want to be miserable or want others miserable around him. Bohn never married, and made sure he never fathered any children. He had followed Katharine's path throughout the years though, all the hurdles she had to go over, good and bad. Not once, did he build up the courage to see her again, not even after her husband's death. Bohn needed an opportunity, but not one that would make him seem desperate. He was glad Beulah had called him and he was looking forward to seeing Katharine Thomas, for sure.

On the way, Bohn settled into the hour and a half ride thinking about Kate. He always thought she was pretty, but he wasn't alone in that, boys vied for her attention. She was beautiful and caring. Throw in the fact that she was smart too. Katharine Thomas was not just the senior class president, but also valedictorian.

He knew he was in love with Katharine because she would touch his arm to get his attention, and the feeling would linger for hours. They talked about their favorite books, the movies they enjoyed, their secrets and dreams for the future. He admired her honesty, an honesty rooted in the fact that she cared more about others than about herself. Katharine loved Africa and was always interested in learning about the *homeland*, that's how she called it.

When Bohn told Kate about him going to Vietnam, she heard something almost like fear in his voice.

"Your faith is in the wisdom of man… mine rest in the power of God," Katharine told him. She let the words hang, and when he didn't say anything, she did. "I always want to be part of your life, Rudy."

For some people, you cannot preach about God to them and you cannot describe God. These people have to be able to set their eyes on miracles to believe. Not Katharine Thomas, who lives each day allowing God to help her demonstrate her faith, not only by words, but actions. Bohn had treasured up all those things about her in his heart.

It was during Bohn's second year in Vietnam when Katharine received her notice of acceptance to Spelman College, a dream of hers since she'd been a little girl. A degree in Sociology would intensify her desire to spend much of her time in the *homeland*, mainly, Liberia.

The female voice from the GPS announced, "You've reached your destination," which was First Baptist church.

Bohn pulled into an empty space and turned the engine off. He stepped out of his car and surveyed First Baptist Church, marveling at more than a hundred mourners going in for the service, and the stained-glass windows he'd always admired. It felt good to stretch his legs. The tension in his neck and shoulders remained. Or was it guilt, feeling excitement at a funeral. Thinking about Kate brought a smile to his face. He put on his dinner jacket, matching his black pants, straightened his tie and marched in.

The message given at Luverne Thomas' funeral was about another kind of reunion, especially for those who know and love the Lord—death's parting is temporary. The pastor told them to believe in God's promise and that one day Nana and her family will be reunited forever! Then, RJ and the rest of the family were comforted by the pastor's reading from the Holy Book, First Thessalonians 4:13-18:

But we do not want you to be uninformed, brothers, about those who are asleep, that you may not grieve as others do who have no hope. For since we believe that Jesus died and rose again, even so, through Jesus, God will bring with him those who have fallen asleep. For this we declare to you by a word from the Lord, that we who are alive, who are left until the coming of the Lord, will not precede those who have fallen asleep. For the Lord himself will descend from heaven with a cry of command, with the voice of an archangel, and with the sound of the trumpet of God. And the dead in Christ will rise first. Then we who are alive, who are left, will be caught up together with them in the clouds to meet the Lord in the air, and so we will always be with the Lord. Therefore encourage one another with these words.

The minister blessed the church right before the funeral procession: "May the Lord bless you and keep you… may the Lord make His face shine on you and be gracious to you. May the Lord turn his face toward you and give you peace."

Bohn felt a sense of sweet calmness come over him.

The gathering for the repast occurred at the church, directly after the burial. Food and condolences seemed to go hand in hand, ironically, grief is better digested on a full stomach. But the meal allows family and friends time to catch up on each other's lives. Bohn was talking to an old schoolmate he hadn't seen since he left Macon, when Katharine walked by, his back turned. She was walking around, greeting and thanking people for coming, and thought she'd recognized a familiar voice.

"Rudy?" she said, but wasn't quite sure.

The six-foot-two gentleman turned, his body carrying about 210 pounds of fairly hard muscle under the Armani suit. An older man, hair speckled with grey, about sixty-something. It was Rufus Bohn, and aging had tilted in his favor. She smiled an incredible smile.

Bohn felt his breath catch as his heart hammered in his chest. Katharine Thomas still took his breath away. They embraced for a long time, holding each other close. When they finally pulled apart, Katharine could sense his unspoken emotion.

They exchanged greetings and wondered, in their minds, about the things that each other had gone through over the years.

"I had to come, Kate," Bohn said with a cheery voice.

"I'm glad you did. I'm so happy to see you."

Katharine talked about her three children and a granddaughter that she spoils. Bohn did not say much, only that he spends more time in London than he does at home.

"London," Katharine said, incredulously.

To which he replied, "Mostly business… only business."

Bohn stood in front of her. For a long time, he was silent. Finally he said, "Regret is a painful thing, Kate."

Katharine touched his arm. He smiled to himself. He was glad, because the feeling would linger for a while.

"Rudy," she mumbled.

"Yes."

"You are still handsome," she said, looking at his eyes.

He sighed. Then he smiled and purred, "Thank you."

With an understanding that Katharine had other people to talk to, Bohn promised he wouldn't leave Macon until they'd spend some time together to catch up. Katharine assured with another touch, and told him that she was looking forward to it. As Bohn walked away, she took in her breath and let it out slowly.

Only magic between two people would make a woman react that way.

RJ walked up to Katharine. "Mom, who's that?" He wanted to know.

"Rufus Bohn… an old friend."

"I know all of your childhood friends, how come I've never heard of him?"

"Well, you'll get a chance to meet him, RJ," Katharine said. "He wants to meet my children."

Chapter 5

GRACE PUPOH HAD been a brilliant case manager for Amadou Law Office. In her mind's eye, Diallo Amadou, her longtime boss and the man who had given her a chance, was truly a lawyer, slash, liar. As good a lawyer he is, his only defense for the senator was based on ethnic prejudice; hatred for a successful Congo man and a desire to make the heart-men lineup a diverse one. Diallo's theory made sense then, but not anymore; like a football player not trying his best because he'd been paid off.

Throughout law school, Grace had gone over the evidence files of more than fifty pictures and hundreds of pages of documents. Senator Douglas had no connection to the crime, it seems. Zero. And, all the evidence that could have proved his innocence had been deep-six by Diallo and Aaron Dolo; a video surveillance of Tamba Wumah meeting with Duo Boley and Charles Sarpo, snap shots of Wumah and Boley leaving Le'Toit Club, Charles Sarpo's confession of never meeting the senator, and the doctored Court records. The firm's number one client, CeRue Manor, made a lot of things happened then, and now. Grace could not get past that.

"Diallo, I've been dying to ask you something," Grace started one morning.

Diallo caught her gaze.

"How did you manage to get the Senator's body to his family? I mean, that has never been done before. I know you have connections, but that's better than a golden touch… that's platinum," she smirked.

Diallo sighed. "You've asked a lot of questions lately, young lady," he forced a smile. His smile faded as quickly as it had come. "What's up?"

"You know what they say, a clean conscience makes a soft pillow,"

Grace shrugged. "After a long day's work, I like a good sleep at night."

"You're in the wrong business then," he chuckled.

"Being a lawyer?"

"Yeah… you don't mix law and conscience. You don't know that?"

Fresh out of law school, and perhaps naive, Grace had gone into the business of law thinking it is a higher calling to fight injustice and social ills, and do all sorts of great things because she's a lawyer. She wanted to make a difference. Her greatest fear was not letting a guilty person go free, but sending an innocent person to prison.

She stared at Diallo. A few seconds passed.

"Don't look at me like that," Diallo laughed. "I did not become a lawyer to be a crusader. I like to test the law."

"Well, I like to test the law too," Grace said. "We didn't argue that case, Diallo. We did not test the law, and that's what lawyers are for. Isn't it?"

Diallo remained quiet.

"Not testing the law in your client's best interest is one thing, but… sending an innocent man to his grave is something else."

"Wait a minute. What case?"

"Senator Douglas."

"An innocent man?" he frowned. "What do you think criminal law is?" Before Grace could speak, Diallo answered, "Crimes and their punishments. You win some, you lose some. The most important thing is, you make sure you get paid. You make *damn* sure you get paid, either way. Why you think I can afford to pay you so well? You do like your new big house, don't you?"

"It's honest money and I work hard for whatever I get."

"Exactly."

"I wasn't talking about my paycheck."

"Oh?"

"I'd like to know, Diallo. Really. Was it your connections to Manor?"

"We both know about my connections to CeRue Manor… he pays our salaries."

"Yeah, and I've really been thinking about that too."

"Are you asking for a raise?" Diallo joked. When Grace didn't laugh, he said, "You are due one anyway."

"I've already told you, it's not about my paycheck."

Now Diallo was staring. He ought to know better because stares never bothered Grace Pupoh. She stared back. During law school she had learned to dig deep and discover secrets. This thrilled Diallo and at the same time unnerved him.

There is a breed of men out there who are attracted to strong women. The problem begins when they don't know what to do once they win these women over. Diallo's feet suddenly felt like bricks, and his knees were weak. He sat down.

"Grace," he said her name carefully. "Have I done something to offend you?"

"I've been going through the Douglas files," she confessed. "I came across a few evidence I had missed. I swear those were never among the files I worked on."

"Evidence? What evidence?"

"Detailed confessions of all the accused, including Senator Douglas, witness interviews, even a specific police report indicating the senator had no interaction with other suspects at any time other than one person's borrowing his car. Some videos," she added, "and don't pretend you don't know about the videos."

Diallo frowned. "Oh! Those?"

Grace stared.

"I got those videos long after the trial and the...."

"The hanging?"

Diallo sighed. "Yes. After."

Grace sighed.

"I have done nothing wrong, Grace, I swear. I did nothing wrong. I came across the videos six months after the execution." He paused. "I didn't show them to you because... well, what else could we have done?"

"Tell his children that their father was never a heart-man," Grace quipped.

"So, you want to sue the Liberian government for wrongful death?" Diallo said with a smirk. "Good luck with that."

Grace's body and mind had different reactions. Her shoulders slumped and she let out a slight gasp. But her mind fought back instantly. "You don't need luck when you have evidence."

There was a long pause.

Diallo studied her, his mind was spinning. Then he got up, took two steps closer, and hissed his tough-guy speech, "Don't you go pulling some harebrained stunt, Grace Pupoh. You take one piece of property out of here and you'll find yourself in shit so deep, you wouldn't dare open your mouth. If you want to play the smart-ass brilliant lawyer, try me."

Grace didn't blink.

"It's one thing to win Douglas over, just remember one thing though… the life you've planned so well will be pretty much shot to shit. Do you really want that?"

Oh, what the hell, Grace thought. *A smart woman knows better than to enter a pissing contest with a dick. If I overreact now, the outcome could be a disaster. Why take the chance? Not now. It is what it is in Liberia. That heap of evidence might never see the light of day.*

She rolled her eyes.

"I thought so," Diallo muttered. "I don't want to have this conversation again, Grace… understand?" His eyes never left her.

"We won't," Grace answered quickly, "because I quit."

She'd spoken with an air of confidence that surprised even her.

"I'm walking out of here right now with what's mine… briefcase and handbag."

—**********—

Grace got home, the front door slammed behind her, and she paused for a second before walking into the living room.

"How was your day?" Alex asked.

"Great."

"Well, that's good."

"I quit."

"You what?" Before Grace said anything else he said, "You'll be alright. You don't need me anyway."

She blew out a soft sigh. Alex was doing what he does best, killing her *high*. She stood for a moment, silent and thoughtful. Then she walked from the doorway toward the chair Alex sat in. Grace placed a knee on each side of his legs, held his hand to her lips and kissed it. "It's not about our income, isn't it?"

Alex remained quiet.

"I do not want to keep hurting you," she whispered. "You are a good man, Alex. You deserve something I am just not sure how to give to you."

Grace remained close to him. Alex closed his eyes and breathed her in, hurting and happy at the same time. He wanted to hold her, beg her, and convince her he was still willing to give her space, even more time until she'd seen the whole picture. He loved her so much he was willing to protect her from herself and RJ's world.

"All I want is for you to let me love you… protect you," Alex started.

"I'm not yours to protect," Grace corrected quickly. "Oh, I know what this is… no man wants to think his woman can be as independent and as clever as he is, is that it?"

Alex gazed at her. He'd learned the hard way to be careful when dealing with her.

"Don't they?" Grace asked.

"It's bad to make generalizations," he waved a finger slowly at her. She shrugged.

"I'm not like most men," Alex said. "We have a history together. Fifteen years is a long time, Grace. Three years ago I could have walked away, I didn't."

She sighed and stared.

He saw Grace as a different woman, one who stands on her own and does not need a man or anyone to prop her up.

Crazy as it seemed, the rejection was a sour seduction. The more Alex had professed his love for Grace, the more he seemed to have murdered his chances of being with her and building a life together. After so many straight talks, mostly her rejecting him, Alex was still trying to hold on to her. He was treading on the blade of rejection once more; attempting to change her mind, with the help of Yassah. He didn't mind pawning his pride. Grace is worth losing his pride.

"Loneliness is a sad thing, you know," Alex baited.

"I am not lonely," Grace quickly corrected.

"But you'd rather settle for a lonely life while that man moves on with his wife?"

"Don't be ridiculous," she snarled. "RJ has nothing to do with this."

"I know there is no future there for you and him," Alex went on. "You do know that, don't you? You are a very smart woman."

She hated it when he accused.

"Look, Alex, this has nothing to do with RJ Douglas. As far as I'm concerned, about my work, I do not claim to be ahead of the Liberian feminist movement. I just always felt I should earn my way into the world without the help of a man. I am entitled to be recognized by my own life, am I not? I am Grace Pupoh now and I intend to stay just that."

"Well, good for you," Alex said with a grin. Impulsively, he reached out and took her hand. "I am not asking you to change. I wouldn't mind sharing that life with you."

"You love me but you don't love my son," she finally said it. "It is a challenge for you, Alex, and we both know it," she finished and slowly pulled her hand away.

"Have I not been there for Peace?"

"You are there... but you do not show that you care."

"I don't understand."

"Alex, you hate it when my son wants my affection... it makes you jealous. You complain when he needs me to hug him. And your excuse is, he's a boy. Boys don't need to be hugged? You only take up time with him when I ask you to... that's the only time you're there... when I ask."

"The point is, I am there," Alex stressed.

"The point is, you don't care. Look, I'm not asking you to."

"Okay, Grace... how many men do you see pamper boys? Just answer me that."

"I've seen many Liberian men toss ball to their sons... horse around with them, you know... play fight. That is not pampering. They are bonding with their sons. You, on the other hand, can't even look at Peace. I know the situation is painful and I've always encouraged you to move on with your life... without me. I know you love me very much, but you cannot bring yourself to love my son. And, I understand."

"Oh, you do?"

"Yes. I don't know about the rest of Africa, but I've noticed most Liberian men do not know how to love other people's children... especially boys. Why is that?"

Alex shrugged. *Because they are other people's children*, he thought and chided himself. Finally he said what he'd thought all along.

"Our real problem is, no one is up to your standard except for RJ Douglas."

Chapter 6

THE WOMAN DID not know whether it was out of jealousy or spite—she had not given him a child, and age had made it impossible—but her husband had changed over the years. As would in a marriage, a husband protects, promotes and provides for his wife. The man did the opposite. He'd never given her enough money for the groceries, but expected her to make hearty meals with very little. When she couldn't, it annoyed him immensely. She often wondered whether her husband was even human, since the cruelty seemed to be his sole purpose.

Their neighbors did not see him for the man he truly was. People had no reason to think he treats his wife so poorly, him being polite enough. However, he said the most awful things about her to friends, family and the neighbors. He kept her confined in their marriage as a prisoner. She tried to have some good days. She tried very hard. But over the years exhaustion imprinted itself into every deepened wrinkle on the poor woman's face.

The woman was so ashamed of her weakness that she did nothing. Not one complaint passed her lips, until one day she found the courage to tell him to stop. He got so angry, when he gripped his wife's shoulders, she expected him to shake her until all the teeth in her mouth loosened. He did not. But he told her she was weak and ugly, and was a pathetic wife, "As dull as dog shit," he had put it.

When introduced to the woman, Grace extended her hand and the woman shook it. "My name is, Grace. I'm a lawyer."

Grace had always wanted a stable life, and she wanted to be dependent on no one for it. She'd experienced God's goodness whether things were good or bad, and her life had been used in ways she'd never thought possible. So to Grace, her life told a story.

Grace took her role as being the servant. Qualified to serve, the lawyer was the great woman among them, the mark of true leadership, not power nor privilege, but humble service. She had become the type of lawyer who before ordering her case in front of any judge, filled her mouth with arguments. She knew the words of defendants before hand, and understood everything he, or she, would say in or out of court. The rookie lawyer had soon developed oratorical skills like no other person in Liberia's courtroom.

Of late, if men in Liberia thought violence is their heritage, they had another thing coming. More women were done shouldering the blame, and here on out these women that Grace Pupoh represented would no longer have to struggle to explain the violence as if it were their responsibility. She had become the women's community sponge, soaking up their troubles, beatings, and rape. She'd become someone the women could say, because of her their lives will never be the same. Like a Swiss Army Knife is associated with equipment for survival in the wild, so was Grace to the women who were depending on her for the survival of their human rights. Depending on the model of the knife, it may have several blades; a saw, a scissors, a magnifying glass, a ruler, a can opener, a screwdriver, a toothpick, an ink pen—all in one knife!

God had put compassion on Grace's heart to be an *activist-knife* for their rights. They needed someone who had compassion for them and the law to survive in a world too often cruel to women. Laws to protect their rights are given blind eyes because those in charge of upholding the laws were the main law breakers.

A mentor to the women in finding new freedom of self-love, not only had Grace invested time in their troubles, but she had taken risks by giving them advice and representing them when she had no license to do so. Many saw her as God's perfect instrument, giving them a shot at a better life. They came with burdens that put their spirits down and Grace tried her best to lift them up. Many lives were changed, and they were thankful. The women collected money, quarters, dimes, dollars, and those who could give more did, to cover her tuition at the law school. She did not need the Douglas' money after all.

Grace and her clients knew the truth, their bruises and broken bones were proof. But the abusive husband's lawyers were never interested in the truth. They wanted to deny the women the pain their clients were responsible for. It was one thing to use the law to negotiate her client's compensation for their suffering and another to seek justice. One important thing she had learned, law on the books is never about the truth, it is about negotiation.

Out of law school, not only was Grace Pupoh a good lawyer, she was a better person. Her heart was broken mostly for the women she represented; at times providing their needs and soothing their bleeding wounds, feeding hungry mouths, giving a cup of hope here, or a loaf of self-worth there.

Many of the women were cursed with the dreadful disease of ignorance. For most of them—every woman Grace represented so far—there was the confusion of the court system. Also, when they needed the law to protect them, they did not have money to pay for proper defense. Their abusive husband used the family money, most earned by the woman, to hire a lawyer to eventually win the case against her. The bottom line, the court was not interested in hearing their case. There was also a legitimate complain about the amount of time the formal proceedings took.

Grace took her time to explain it all.

"If you have no money, there's no justice for you," one woman had pointed out in an earlier meeting.

Another woman said, "All paths to the court require some backing, money or an influential person, like Grace, to plead for you."

"You are right," another woman agreed. "If you look at the Temple of Justice building, it says, 'justice for all men'. It makes no mention of us women."

"Then we all have to start wearing pants," another woman said, gesturing as if to put on a pair, sending the gathered women into fits of giggles.

"When they say 'men', it means women too," Grace corrected.

Another woman asked, "Why didn't they put *and women*?" When Grace did not reply fast enough, she said, "Because there is no justice for us poor women."

"Then together we must fight for our rights," Grace encouraged. "We will demand justice. The main thing is, for things to change, we must all be willing to work hard."

A temple, by most definitions, is a sacred place. Justice; fairness and rightfulness, according to Webster's. Put the two words together, Temple of Justice should mean a sacred place where fair reward or penalty is deserved. But the women's view of Liberia's Temple of Justice had been nothing but failure for many.

But not just for women, Grace recognized. For many others as well. Senator Douglas, for instance. She might not have used the Douglas' money for law school, but she felt the need to fight for their justice too.

Chapter 7

IT WAS 7:00 in the evening without a cloud in the sky. RJ had asked Bohn to meet him at the Cassava Patch about an hour before Gia would arrive. Bohn arrived on time, saw RJ, and stepped forward for a polite handshake. Bohn was a big man yet his hand fitted into RJ's hand like a child's. He looked at RJ's fingers wrapped around his. They were big. Very big.

"You played ball in college?" Bohn asked.

RJ nodded.

"Quarterback?"

"I get that all the time," RJ chuckled. "I played wide receiver at UGA."

"How come you're not in the NFL? I mean, with those hands. If you don't mind me asking."

"I enjoyed sports, but I was never interested in the NFL. I'm doing what I've always wanted to do, which is law."

"Smart man," Bohn praised. "One is a lawyer… one is a doctor… and one is going to be an engineer. I guess the apple didn't fall far from the tree. Your mother is a very smart woman."

"She is. So was my dad."

"I never knew your father," Bohn shrugged. "He must have been a special man to have caught Katharine's eyes."

"You could say that."

"Well, I'm here now… I'll be looking after her."

"She's very good at looking after herself," RJ said, trying his best not to be impolite. "Besides, she has me, Mel, and Razaq. One of us is always around."

Bohn chuckled. Like any of them could stop him. He didn't need their blessings, he had *claim*. When you've had something you've loved more than anything else, and then loses it, it leaves a massive hole dead center in your chest. Then life gets funny sometimes. Not funny like when you get a clean bill of health one day and drop dead the next. But funny in the way you get another chance to fill that hole, and everything falls into place so easily that it seems unreal.

"RJ, your mother is a very special person," Bohn said. "No amount of words can ever express how."

"She is. Anyone who knows Katharine Douglas wouldn't think otherwise."

Bohn flicked a victorious glance.

"So what do you actually do, Mr. Bohn," RJ asked. "Since you've planned on spending some time with my mother."

"I own a small security agency," Bohn replied. "I have an office in London and Atlanta. I provide private army in nasty places," he said, of himself, proudly. "I'll even say, my words have actions behind them."

"Huh. Some way to earn a living," RJ interjected. "Like, a mercenary for hire, offering your services to the highest bidder, whoever that might be? With no allegiance to any man or country?"

"Nothing like that," Bohn laughed. "It's more like protect and serve, but not like the cops. It's part private investigation and part bodyguard service. It depends."

"Personal bodyguard?" RJ asked. He hoped there wasn't a hint of disdain in his tone. He wasn't telling Bohn he was an assassin.

"You can say that, but at a much higher level," Bohn replied. "All within limits," he added. He idly glanced around the place. "How often do you come here?"

"Quite often," RJ replied. "Osei and I were college roommates. He's like a brother… a brother from another mother."

Bohn smiled. "It's always good to have one of those."

RJ managed a weak smile. He was more concerned about Katharine than Osei.

"Sounds like a dangerous business," RJ suggested. "Your agency, I mean."

"It certainly can be," Bohn said, turning his gaze at RJ. "Technically, yes, but I am never in danger or anyone else connected to me. I match the client to the service provider, I strategize, my staff carries out the action, and everyone is left happy. RJ, believe me, your mother would never be in harm's way. I would take the bullet for Kate any day. She's the love of my life. I've lost her once, and I don't intend to lose her again."

For a moment this simple confession of fondness the man had for his mother pleased him. "Well, I hope it won't have to come to that," RJ replied. "God knows my mother deserves the best there is, even served on a platinum platter."

RJ had spoken in a wistful faraway tone that was oddly both hopeful and tragic. Katharine had left America for Liberia and had lived with a womanizer husband whose illegitimate son she'd adopted and come to love like her own. Then the man's life had ended tragically in the worst conviction in humanity, a heart-man, killing a human being to sell his vital organs to the highest bidder. He didn't know how his mother had held up so bravely.

Regardless, he loved his father, a unique man in his own right. Robert Jenkins Douglas II provided well for his family. He made a lot of money, hired people to serve Katharine and bought her many beautiful things. He just wasn't the wonderful husband who loved her enough not to look at other women. RJ wondered if the nut had fallen far enough from the tree.

RJ always knew that the Senator was innocent, now he had proof—thanks to Grace. He just wasn't sure how to go about clearing his name.

"I want to clear my father's name," RJ said, assuming Bohn knew everything about the hanging. "I'd like to file a lawsuit against the Liberian government for wrongful death, demand official clemency, and a well publicized apology."

Bohn almost laugh. He came so close to telling RJ, Do you know that is sort of impossible! A smile still eased across his lips.

As their conversation petered out, RJ alternated between looking at Bohn and then toward the door, expecting Gia to join him any moment. "So would your agency be able to help me?"

"We are not international lawyers, RJ," Bohn replied. "But we can do something with the proofs that you have."

RJ looked at him stubbornly. "I want clemency, if anything at all," he said in a voice straining with emotion.

"Let's take it one step at a time. I want to look at all the evidences, see who's involved, and who worked the case. I won't disappoint."

A private investigator, RJ thought. *I expect the cost to be brutal. We might be able to manage, between Mel and Me.* "We can discuss cost later," RJ suggested. "I'd like to have Mel and Gia there when we do."

"One step at a time," Bohn reminded.

"Fair enough."

"Whatever you have, get it to me as soon as possible," Bohn suggested. "I want to start right away... like yesterday."

RJ stared at the man, something close to cockiness in his eyes. He opened his briefcase and pulled out a five-inch thick manila envelope. With a heavy heart and steady hand, RJ handed it to Bohn. "I can't tell you where I got that, but they are authentic."

Bohn admired RJ's no-nonsense boldness. He had his mother's spirit, otherwise he would make a damn good defense attorney. "Thanks for the confidence," he said and took the package.

Bohn clearly possessed the appetite to pursue the matter. RJ had been sore displeased with the Liberia justice system. Now seeing the brutal truth, reality was bugging. His heart did a small leap. Truthfully, it concerned Bohn how corruption in high places had continued to hinder the achievements of the world's poor, especially in Africa. He couldn't wait to try out a new scheme he'd invented himself, to fight Africa's gangsters. To some it may seem cruel, but he thought it was beautiful.

Bohn left the Cassava Patch shortly before Gia arrived.

—**********—

Juanita Sherman had perfected the art of attention seeking, especially when it came to RJ Douglas. Mel always warned something was off with them, but was hard to pinpoint it. Maybe it was the absence of enthusiasm when Sherman talked about RJ while he on the other hand, was crazy about her. Then she ended the relationship when he decided not to pursue an NFL career for law school.

Juanita entered the Cassave Patch, saw RJ standing next to Gia and ran over toward them, smiling warmly. She had not seen him for a long time, and each time she ran into Osei and asked about RJ, the man deliberately changed subject.

"RJ," she exclaimed and embraced him, ignoring the woman standing next to him. She'd caught RJ by surprise. It was obvious she wasn't wearing a bra, and the hug seemed designed to drill her bare breasts into his chest. The embrace linger a bit, passed *just* friends. RJ kept his arms away from her body and waited for Juanita to let go. She didn't. He shoved her away slightly, trying not to be obvious.

"Juanita, this is my wife, Gia. Honey, this is Juanita," RJ introduced the women.

"No wonder you've been in hiding," Juanita giggled, hiding the shocking news, extending her hand to Gia, yet gazing at RJ.

Gia shook her hand, giving the woman an unfriendly gaze.

She was fashionably thin with curvy hips, a round firm bottom with long slender sexy legs. Juanita also possessed an endowed proportion set of breasts. They were real, not one of professional work.

RJ put his arm around Gia's waist and pulled her closer.

Juanita's eyes slowly shifted to Gia. "Good to meet you, Gia," she said in a soft voice. Then she shifted her attention back to RJ. "Well then congratulations are in order, Counselor."

"Thanks, Juanita. It is."

"Well, I better get going. See you around," Juanita excused herself and walked off.

"So," Gia began slowly as the woman walked away. "You are going to tell me you two dated." It was more of a statement than a question. RJ looked at her, still shock. "You don't get a hug like that from just a friend."

"Honey, it was a while back. So far back, I don't even care to recall... as long as there's breath in my body."

"I see," Gia muttered.

"We broke up years before I met you. Honey, it was a long time ago."

"I'm not sure she got that message," Gia shrugged. "Looks like someone forgot to tell her."

Chapter 8

IT'S HARD TO realize your only child can become invisible in your life; worst, if the blindness is mutual. But not in Pieter LeRoux's case. A friend of a friend of Pieter LeRoux had asked a favor: Could Bohn find a bodyguard for his friend's daughter, who travels and takes care of his cement business in several African countries. Fortunately for Bohn, Liberia was one of those countries. Perfect. He contacted his number one agent and put him on on-call status.

A rock-solid 6-foot-5, 228 lbs with broad shoulders and narrow hips, Jay Cowan was a three-time All-American wrestler before he received his SEAL billet from the Academy. The test is administered by the United States Military Entrance Processing Command, and used to determine the qualification for enlistment in the United States armed forces. Cowan honed his athletic skills in high school wrestling, a sport known to be among the most mentally challenged of all athletic pursuit. His love of wrestling is an indication of the dedication it took to finish his SEAL training. He had also trained in taekwondo, a second dan senior, second degree black belt.

__**********__

The phone rang at around three in the morning and Cowan knew it was the call he'd been waiting for. He didn't have to look at the cell phone screen to see his caller.

"Cowan."

"Ready for the job?"

"When do I start?"

"Now."

Cowan waited for details.

After a pause the caller said, "You'll be flying out of Atlanta to Johannesburg, South Africa this evening around six. See you at the check-in desk one hour before takeoff."

The call ended.

Cowan had no one to pump him for information of his whereabouts. Nagging questions like, "Where did you go? Why didn't you call me? What happened to you?" He was a free bird. He didn't talk about anything to, or with anyone; what normal people do. The only person who knew when he was or wasn't around was his 20-year-old house-sitter, a responsible college sophomore with big dreams. Hawah Camara took care of his one bedroom apartment while he was away, making sure the place always looked as if someone lived there. If it wasn't for junk mails he wouldn't have needed a mailbox key. She collected his mails to prevent any pile ups. Hawah took better care of the 2003 4-Runner than Cowan did. In fact, having a one bedroom apartment and a good used car saved him a lot of hassles. Spending more time away than in Atlanta, Cowan didn't want too much to care for.

Still young, he could have retired with a good pension and other benefits after his military life and have a pretty good life. He didn't have a death wish or anything like that. But Jay Cowan wanted something exciting, new and often. Settling into a quiet life was never part of his plan and forget sharing old army stories. Honestly, the man never dwindles on the past.

Cowan consumed his breakfast at six, which was a one day-old donut and some black coffee, while he packed his bag. He always kept his Cabela duffel bag under thirty pounds, and carried it in hand by its strap handles.

Cowan boarded the Delta flight to Johannesburg at six, scheduled to arrive 4:35 p.m. the next afternoon; fifteen hours and twenty minutes nonstop. He didn't care. The trip cost him nothing and he had a nice escape from normal life in Atlanta for one year.

He arrived at the Oliver Tambo International Airport and spotted a man holding up a sign with Cowan's named printed in large black block letters. The man politely offered to take Cowan's bag but he declined. The driver escorted him to a black Bentley Arnage and opened the back door.

"Thanks, but no thanks," Cowan said and smiled. "I think I'll get a better view of the road up front." He opened the front passenger door and got in.

"Sir," the driver said courteously, closed the door, and boarded.

The driver went over the speed limit all the way, increasing the speed as much as the traffic allowed it. The twenty-mile trip took them twenty minutes.

Their final destination was a 1.2 million dollar baronial masterpiece, a private sanctuary located in Atholl, overlooking the river, one of four homes Mr. LeRoux owns in South Africa. The luxurious cluster sat on 1700 square meters of land with no expenses spared. The attention to detail was exceptional; a soaring foyer, lofty ceilings, stained glass windows, marble, wood flooring, wall paintings, marine fish tank—all there. It had an exceptional main bedroom suite with private study, plus three additional bedroom suites. The gourmet kitchen had its own greenhouse.

A female domestic staff dressed in black formal uniform with white apron and headpiece greeted Cowan at the front entrance and escorted him to LeRoux. After a brief, but cordial greeting and handshake, Pieter LeRoux talked while looking intensely at Cowan to see if he would maintain eye contact. Cowan did not blink.

"Mr. Cowan, I like what I know about you," Mr. LeRoux said. "That's why I'm putting my daughter's life in your care. Adriana wants her own plane, so the deal is, she gets one only if she agrees to have a bodyguard. That's where you come in."

Cowan nodded.

"One hundred eighty thousand a year with no time off. Seven days a week. All you have to do is look after my daughter, you sleep when she sleeps. We will try it for one year and see how things go. You've already been brief with the conditions?"

Cowan nodded.

"Absolutely no emotional ties with my daughter," Mr. LeRoux confirmed his conditions anyway.

"If you're going to own me for a full year, make it an even two hundred thousand and we've got a deal," Cowan coaxed.

"Done. And, you answer to me, not my daughter."

"When do I meet Ms. LeRoux? I'm supposed to be her shadow, right?"

"Tomorrow," Mr. LeRoux replied. "She's returning from a business trip from Liberia. The chef will prepare whatever you like. And, take this time to rest. It *was* a very long flight from America."

__**********__

What type of adults do spoiled children become? A spoiled child acts the same way he or she acts as a kid, except according to the new limits in his, or her, new environment.

Pieter LeRoux's spoiled daughter expects the whole world to respond to her demands whenever she complains or asks. Adriana expects the world to adjust to suit her instead of trying to adjust her ways to suit the world. He would have protected his daughter with his own life in keeping her safe. However, Pieter LeRoux overprotected his only child with his wealth by giving too much too often, without realizing that this parenting style had severe effects on her. As a result, Adriana turned into a rebel who refuses to take orders from anyone and never accepts *no* for an answer. She had not learned that every relationship involves both give and take. An adept manipulator, she boasts of her disrespectful and defiant stance. She had been so spoiled, she tends to believe that being alone makes her unhappy, and thus the source of her happiness is other people rather than herself.

__**********__

Adriana was up early to meet the bodyguard she'd bargained with her father in exchanged for the private jet. Pieter LeRoux had promised his daughter a 2.5 million dollar Citation Mustang as long as she'd have a bodyguard twenty-four seven.

She knocked softly on the bedroom door. No answer. She quietly walked in, looked around. Everything was in its proper place. Either the man had made his bed or he'd not slept in it.

It's easy to wonder why the heck the military would make such a big deal about how a soldier's bed is made. Perhaps it develops a soldier's discipline and attention to the smallest details. The military drills its recruits over and over again in the skill of bed-making. Then the moment of truth comes when the sergeant pulls a quarter from his pocket and bounces it off the bed to see just how tightly it's made. If it doesn't bounce, the soldier usually has to do it again and do fifty pushups as reparation.

Adriana admired the bed as she walked pass it, and then noticed the bathroom door ajar. Cowan, his back to her, was in the process of undressing to take his shower. She could have looked away or alerted him of her presence but she didn't. She watched as he removed his shirt. She'd never known a man's back could be so magnificent. His dark chocolate skin looked smooth, stretching tight over muscles across wide shoulders, and down to his narrow waist. Only dedicated athletic rigid excises could have enhanced such magnificence, the way intricate carvings turns a plain piece of wood into a beautiful one. Cowan pulled at the waistband of his shorts, pushed down, slip one leg off, and then the other. He was entirely, quite splendidly, naked.

Oh my heavens, Adriana thought. She started to leave. But how could a girl not look at all that hard, smooth flesh when it was put in front of her? And those buttocks! Was it wrong to want to sink her teeth into them because they belonged to an employee? She'd done it before. Anything that delicious had to be tasted.

She watched Cowan grabbed a washcloth off the rack and held her breath. If Adriana had any concern she would turn away, but it seemed all concerns had fled and her mind was empty of every thought except one; any woman, and perhaps some men, would pay dearly to have a front-row seat at this show. Cowan climbed into the shower and drew the curtains close.

Adriana pressed her palm to her rapidly beating chest. She was suddenly thirsty. Parched. A few drops of water would do. She was about to turn when the shower curtains opened. A small, strangled sound gurgled up from her throat as she spun around and ran out.

She heard his low rumble of laughter and stop. Then gently splash of water, followed by slow drips, confirmed he had resumed washing. Adriana closed her eyes, but that didn't help. The image of the water sliding over his muscular back, down to his buttocks and thighs, danced in her mind. She wanted to turn around and take another peek, but ran instead.

Cowan finished his shower, got dressed and hurried to Pieter LeRoux's private study to meet his principal. Adriana was there waiting.

"Darling," Pieter LeRoux said, "I'd like you to meet Mr. Cowan."

Adriana was much too distracted by the thought of Cowan's bare ass and shoulders to hear anything. All those muscles gently rising and falling across his shoulders and down his arms. Thick and powerful. She had a strong urge to trace them with her fingertip, especially the one that disappeared beneath the waistband of the briefs he wore.

"Adriana?"

"Yes, Papa," she sighed.

"This is Jay Cowan."

Adriana's gaze met Cowan's. He smiled.

__**********__

Conduct is the best indicator of character, proven by consistent actions. Cowan did not quite know how to take it, his boss staring at his manhood like it was an exotic creature. She seems a delicious woman, positively delightful, but no sexual tension there. Not for Cowan, at least. Maybe because men don't appreciate what women give so willingly. It's all about the *chase*. Men love to chase.

Then again, the hands of the persons near your principal are always the greatest threat and as such, the bodyguard should always watch their hands and plan defensive countermeasures. Cowan wondered if he would be watching Ms. LeRoux's hand rather than that of suspicious persons. He might have made a good first impression.

Chapter 9

"**ARE YOU TIRED** of the abuse!" Grace shouted at the start of the first Frisky Women's meeting.

"Yes!" A chorus of voices exclaimed in Words of Christ Church meeting hall.

"Are you ready for change!"

"Yes!"

"One woman is weak!"

"But two or three together are strong," the group exploded!

In Liberian colloquial English, *frisky* is a slang term for someone who is characterized by the ability to make lively, clever remarks in a sharp amusing way. Many husbands used it frequently when referring to their wife's clever disparagement when standing up to them, or to a challenge, especially during a fight. Thus the women decided to name the club, Frisky Women.

People just don't understand the power of the weak, those who are feeble and poor, or those kept backward and ignorant by individuals in power to use them as pawns. There's power in numbers. The effective, fervent efforts of a group for liberty avail much. Being in a group you become bold, strong, and persistent; warring to win the strife. Chance favors the prepared mind, so Grace took the chance to form an organization for the women to have as an anchor for their emotional, social, and legal needs.

In Monrovia those who were suffering under the hands of abusive spouses or adult children, came. Those who were harassed by corrupt tax collectors, came. Those who were forced to bribe government workers, came. Those who were molested by male bosses or foster parents, came. Those who were raped and then intimidated, also came.

Then there were those who cheered others and comforted them.

There were those who prayed over the broken hearted and consoled those without hope, and even anointed those cursed with oil in the name of the Lord. In that gathering, shattered dreams stood the chance to be mended.

One woman responded with a thought-provoking question. She asked if being a member was about paying dues, or if Grace wanted anyone, especially those without skills, to be involved at all in the organization.

Grace pointed at the woman and said, "You are necessary." She pointed at another woman sitting across the room, "You, too, are necessary." She pointed at a dozen more and said the same thing, "You are necessary."

Then Grace asked Yassah to read from the Bible, 1st Corinthians 12: 14-26, which Yassah had suggested for the meeting, and she did.

The body does not consist of one member but of many. If the foot should say, "Because I am not a hand, I do not belong to the body," that would not make it any less a part of the body. And if the ear should say, "Because I am not an eye, I do not belong to the body," that would not make it any less a part of the body. If the whole body were an eye, where would be the sense of hearing? If the whole body were an ear, where would be the sense of smell? But as it is, God arranged the members in the body, each one of them, as he chose. If all were a single member, where would the body be? As it is, there are many parts, yet one body. The eye cannot say to the hand, "I have no need of you," nor again the head to the feet, "I have no need of you." On the contrary, the parts of the body that seem to be weaker are indispensable, and on those parts of the body that we think less honorable we bestow the greater honor, and our unpresentable parts are treated with greater modesty, which our more presentable parts do not require. But God has so composed the body, giving greater honor to the part that lacked it, that there may be no division in the body, but that the members may have the same care for one another. If one member suffers, all suffer together; if one member is honored, all rejoice together.

The reading had to be interpreted for most, so when Yassah ended the reading Grace said, "The Bible is saying this, not us," meaning Yassah and her. "We must be one, like our body which is made up of eyes, ears, hands, feet, nose and mouth. Each of us is necessary for the change we're all looking for."

There was group agreement after this explanation.

"Every woman plays an important role in our organization, so no one person is more necessary than any other person," Grace continued. "I am a lawyer, but I am not the most important person here. We are all equally important."

"Some of us can't read," one woman pointed out. "Those of us who cannot read, what can we do?"

Another woman said, "I do not make enough money to pay the dues. What can I give that can help any of us here?"

Grace said to each woman, "You have a role here. You have a significant part to play and FW need you to make the organization successful."

"Are you going to pay my share of the dues?" the woman asked Grace.

"No," Grace answered. "I will pay my own dues... you will pay yours."

This brought out a burst of laughter.

"FW is here as one and each person will bring something special to make the organization strong," Grace continued. "We will unite to fulfill the purpose of the organization, which is to help each woman make her life better for her and her family. When each member is committed to doing what she can do better, the organization will be successful."

"That's true," the woman added.

"I want you to know that whatever happened to each of us has really happened to advance women's rights for our daughters and younger sisters... for our nieces... and for our friends," Grace continued. "Our efforts will be known throughout the whole country."

"And other places like Guinea!" another woman shouted.

"Yes! Guinea... Sierra Leone... and other places," Grace added.

The women applauded.

"Other women will have confidence and become much bolder to say 'no' to the abuse," Grace encouraged.

There were more group agreement noises.

"My husband is good to me," one woman said.

The woman sitting next to her asked, "Then why are you here?"

"Because my husband told me it would be good for me to be a part of this," she explained.

"Men are not our rivalry, only the abusive ones," Grace interjected. "I did not become a lawyer to fight men in the courtrooms. God has blessed me with this education for the defense of people's rights, everyone. Women, children, and men. Anyone."

The women applauded.

Yassah raised her hand and Grace acknowledged her.

"I know that through God's help and with education, this group will turn out for many women's deliverance," Yassah encouraged. "We have to be willing to learn."

"That's true," Grace added. "I hope that we will all try our best. It will take courage and hard work for women in Liberia to be respected. If we are to bring change to our homes and to our country, we cannot be afraid or lazy. We cannot remain ignorant either. Education is important too."

One woman raised her hand and said, "Men who suppress the poor and weak are afraid of an educated woman."

Another woman added, "If you are not educated, but practice common sense, they are afraid of you too."

This brought out a burst of laughter.

"So we cannot let fear or laziness hold us back from change," Grace encouraged.

"We are not scared," one woman shouted from the back. "Many of us here were also among the women who prayed the devil back to hell. Where is he now?"

"In hell where he belongs," Yassah replied.

The women applauded.

When the applauds died down Grace said, "So let's help the organization by reminding each other what we've all spoken here today."

The lawyer prayed at least some of her message, if not all, would take root in their minds.

Chapter 10

RJ WAS CERTAIN that this was the year he would be made partner. He was perfectly capable of achieving it. At Crane & Morton he played it tough and fierce. They were amazed by his confidence and how impressive he was with every case.

RJ explained to Bohn how he'd expected to be offered partnership but instead, Crane & Morton handed him a bonus check made out to his name in the amount of $75,000. It was a big chunk of change, half of his yearly salary, but it wasn't the magic word he was expecting. He wasn't confused, though amazed at the generous bonus to pacify a would-be disappointment. He was hurt, he was mad, and he was silent. They had the nerve to tell him they would be appointing three lawyers the following year and his name will be at the very top.

"I told them that the bonus was generous and reassuring. But I don't think they recognized the sarcasm," RJ chuckled.

Bohn admired Kate's son. He smiled.

"I deserved the money, but I would have prefered partnership."

"I Know a guy who's looking for a partner," Bohn baited.

"Law firm?"

"Nah… sports."

"Sports?"

"His name is, Sayon Dortu. He's Liberian."

RJ began shaking his head *no*.

"Now hold on," Bohn interjected diplomatically, "wait until you hear me out."

RJ frowned, slightly nodding. He'd never heard of the man his entire life, Rufus Bohn, his mother's first love, now the epitome of fatherly concern. He was taking care of Katharine, (without RJ's approval), protective of Mellody, (didn't matter to Mel, she thought he was interesting), now he was trying to be fatherly to RJ and Razaq. Katharine seems so happy since their reunion, maybe the man was more than happy to claim the family he'd never been able to have with his type of business. He was even helping to clear the senator's name.

"Okay," RJ said slowly.

"Dortu's firm has quadrupled it's worth in a few years, secured dozens of million-dollar contracts and is becoming one of the primary names in the business," Bohn informed. "Of course he wants to grow bigger, but he needs a solid partner to do so."

"I'm a lawyer," RJ interjected. "If he has made so much money, sure he can afford the best lawyers out there."

"He needs a partner, not a lawyer. Well, you know what I mean. A young, smart partner. How old are you? Thirty-one, two... three?"

RJ stared.

"Anyway, I've recommended you," Bohn said straight face.

"I'm not a fortune soldier," RJ chuckled. "I'm a family man."

Bohn laughed a soft laugh. RJ had sounded like the typical defiant son, not wanting to follow his father's footsteps.

"RJ, it has nothing to do with my business," Bohn said. "I'm just making use of my network. I think this will be a good opportunity for what you've always wanted. Being a senior associate is not the same... Crane & Morton is not exactly dangling 'partnership' before your eyes, are they?"

RJ furrowed his brow, thinking. It didn't take an ingenious person to figure that out.

"You'll have more time for family... still practice, do your two pro bono cases a year... and make real money," Bohn added. "You will be your own boss, in the office at nine and on the golf course by three."

"I don't know about being on the golf course by three. I have to pick my daughter up from pre-K."

"Just a figure of speech," Bohn corrected.

"Anyway," RJ took in his breath and let out his breath slowly. "You're going too fast here. You know so much about me, how much does this... *Dortu* person know about me?"

"It doesn't matter."

"If he's Liberian, it does."

"Okay," Bohn nodded. "Dortu is about fifty, or just turned fifty. He has been married to his wife, Toine, for over twenty years. She's about forty-ish. I'll say around forty-five or forty-six, but not more than that, and one heck of a chef. They have a son, seventeen or eighteen. Get this... the kid wants to be an astronaut. I think Dortu knows he's not going to be taking over the family business... you know, negotiating contracts. He needs a partner who's young, smart, and if he's lucky, a brilliant lawyer," Bohn ended with a smile.

Nothing else got RJ's attention except for the boy's aspirations. "Astronaut?"

Bohn nodded.

"That's interesting."

"The kid graduated high school at fifteen," Bohn supplied. "One of the first graduates of GSMST."

"You mean Gwinnett County's prestigious charter school?"

"The one and only... Gwinnett School of Math, Science & Technology."

RJ was impressed. "An astronaut?"

"The Dortus are famous for their dinner parties. Like I said, Toine is one heck of a chef. She hosts so many dinner parties on her husband's behalf. And, Sayon Dortu is a great guy," Bohn nodded.

RJ acknowledged it was something to consider and promised to discuss it with his wife. This pleased Bohn.

__**********__

Dortu's sport agency handled mega-financial deals and he needed a partner with money management skills. Equally important, a mediator which his pro athlete clients can get advice and action that calls for considerable finesse. If there was one thing RJ Douglas loved even more than negotiating terms was renegotiating terms. The lawyer was definitely not the kind to run from a challenge. At Crane & Morton, Douglas loved his job and was best when wrestling with multi-million-dollar settlements.

Bohn got RJ an interview with Dortu and he showed a quick-witted intelligence to forever hold Dortu's interest. A couple of weeks later, his wife hosted RJ, Gia, and their three-year-old daughter.

Antoinette Dortu was welcoming and gracious, like Bohn had painted her to be. She had created a home that made people feel comfortable as soon as the door was opened. The entire time spent at the Dortu's home, Toine made sure her guests were comfortable, especially their little daughter.

Early Monday morning RJ walked into Crane & Morton office building with the same swagger they had come to like. He tapped on Morton's office door, got a "Come in," and walked in. Morton, sitting behind his big executive-style desk, on a large chair beneath his own portrait, smiled.

"Morning," RJ greeted. "I didn't expect to see you here this early. I saw your car, so I decided to check your office."

"Now you can buy your wife that dream car you always talk about," Morton joked, referring to RJ's bonus check.

RJ politely smiled.

"My unfailing insight tells me that you're disappointed that you weren't made partner," the man guessed correctly. "Douglas, we're glad to have you at the firm, you are a terrific lawyer. You've helped built this firm to where it is. You work hard…." He paused for a phony-sounding chuckle. "Maybe… maybe it was a little too much distraction with the situation in Africa. That's over now, right?"

It's been three years, RJ thought.

Morton expected RJ to say something. RJ said nothing.

"You are definitely on the top of that list," he assured.

"It is a disappointment after all those efforts," RJ said politely.

Morton rose and slowly walked around the desk.

"Douglas, to tell you the truth, my own bonus wasn't much more than that," he said, gaze planted at RJ's eyes.

"Glad to know that," RJ smiled.

Morton's gaze softened.

"Actually, there's something I came to tell you," RJ said, looking at Morton directly in the eyes. "I'm leaving Crane & Morton effective immediately."

Morton furrowed his brow.

"You don't believe me?"

For a split second Morton looked confused, totally off his game.

"It's true. Effective immediately," RJ repeated.

Morton knew it was true, if the words came out of Douglas' mouth.

—**********—

Two weeks later, and with a sixty-forty partnership agreement, Sayon Dortu led RJ to his new office, an expansive corner suite with light wood-paneled walls, a stunning downtown Atlanta view, and its own leather sofa. Definitely some money in the sports business. *For all the room's luxuries, how much time would I have to spend here*, he thought. An office at a law firm looking this good meant you'd be spending many hours in it.

"This is to impress our clients," Dortu said as they walked into the room. As if he'd read RJ's mind, he said, "Not the place to work, work, work. Other than meeting with our clients, you can work from home if you prefer."

RJ liked hearing that. Dealing with morning rush hour and driving to downtown Atlanta every morning would be a pisser.

Chapter 11

Two a.m. Lonos couldn't sleep. He had nothing against a good night's shut-eye, but tonight a long investigative task lay ahead and occupied his thoughts. Why the little boy? Why were all his internal organs missing? So far the theory of the case *has* to do with financial gain, though a murder case.

CeRue Manor sprang to mind. The man carried a high level of cash and greed, making him suspect number one—hard to argue with that. He had more people in his pocket than the city of Monrovia. Manor had a lot of inconspicuous means to easily conceal crimes.

The more he thought about it, the more challenging it seemed. Challenge after challenge, after challenge, after *damn* challenge. Lonos didn't like it. Two a.m., to three a.m., to four a.m., to five a.m., still awake. *Why a little boy?* He thought and ached in his heart. Sleep. Who needs it?

Lonos rolled out of bed at five-thirty, bathed and changed into a clean uniform. Lead or no lead, this was the all-pain-no-gain phase of his investigation and he'd better be ready.

He headed to the Monrovia Police Department, then checked in Aaron Dolo's office. Deserted. Looked like the man had not stepped foot in his office. *Police Chief a no-show again*, Lonos thought. He peeked at his watch, seven fifteen. *Fair enough, it's still early.*

An officer, passing by the office as Lonos closed the chief's office door, informed, "Chief Dolo called. He'll be here around noon… said he had to check on something."

"About the case… the little boy?" Lonos asked.

The officer slowed down and replied, "I don't know."

"Did he say where he was going?" Lonos asked, keeping his voice down.

The officer shrugged and continued walking. Lonos grunted.

Lonos went to his office, sat at the small desk and waited. Didn't know what for, but waited. With Chief Dolo out of the office, there was no one around to worry about prying eyes or keen hearing. *Game plan for the day*, he thought. That's what he was waiting for, orders. *Aaron Dolo normally dumps everything on me... except this case*, Lonos thought. *Why stick around and wait for orders?*

"I don't have a choice," Lonos mumbled. "Heart-men will start throwing more bodies at us and then what? What the hell? I'll start with my gut suspect."

"If the Chief ask for me, tell him I'll be right back," Officer Lonos said to the receptionist and headed over to the Manors residence.

Manor took extra precautions to keep his life private after his very lavish wedding to the formal super model, Omolola Sanusi. The new large five-bedroom house was perched on well kept grounds of a neat landscape, long and high walls surrounding it, about seven feet high and topped with jagged chunks of broken glass bottles to discourage anyone considering climbing over it. Large gates prevented intruders.

The Manors' residence was also closely watched, a HS08CS-PRO complete 8-camera surveillance system packed with high performance modern features; four vandal proof infrared dome cameras with thirty-six infrared leds lens and 700 TV lines resolution, and four weatherproof (lightning-proof function) bullet cameras with forty-two infrared leds, adjustable vari-focal lens and 650 TV lines resolution. The cameras combine with a 8-channel H.264 DVR, a 500GB hard disk drive, and HDMI output, providing high resolution recording.

Besides the ten twenty-two-inch monitors bringing the cameras, the DVR and security teams together, Manor monitored the DVR videos from the cameras himself, in the palm of his hand on his smart phone.

"What do you want, Officer Lonos?" Manor barked over the intercom speaker before Lonos even touch the bell button on the side of the gate.

"I'd like to talk with you."

"About what? We are not friends and you cannot afford anything that I sell."

"About the boy," Lonos ventured. "I need to talk to you, now."

"Don't go knocking on death's door, Officer Lonos," Manor snarled. "Just ring the bell and run off."

Aware of Manor's surveillance, Lonos did not crack a smile. "Are you going to let me in, or not."

"Um... not," Manor chuckled. "Definitely, *not!*"

He watched Lonos' face burned with frustration. Lonos sighed.

"Death hates that," Manor continued the joke. "I mean, you, running from death. You want him to catch you next, right?"

What Lonos wanted to do was to wipe the smugness out of the man's voice with his fist. "You did it, didn't you?" he provoked. "You had that little boy killed so you can sell his organs to the highest bidders. That's low, Manor, even for you."

"You think I did what?" Manor shouted. "Do you have evidence?"

"I do, actually," Lonos lied.

A flash of red flared before Manor's eyes. It would have been nice for the officer to see it. "Do you realize accusing me wouldn't make you a hero? I'd like to see you prove it."

Lonos imagined the twisted smile of satisfaction on Manor's face. He'd never felt so powerless. He hated it. "I promised that little boy's grandmother that I'd catch his killer and damn if I don't."

"I told you... I'm not the one. Know what you are, Lonos? You're not even a police officer. I don't know why the hell Dolo got you thinking you are. You're nothing but a cadet, wet behind the ears with a chip on your damn shoulders. So back off me, boy!"

Lonos looked up at where the iron gate meets the high wall, guessing correctly the location of the hidden camera. He daringly waved his finger. Manor smiled quietly and continued to monitor Officer Lonos as he jumped in his old beat up Toyota Corolla and sped off.

__*********__

Lonos did some more snooping around the different communities near the Sinkor Old Road area; Key Hole, Chugbor, Fiamah, Lakpazee, and Duport Road. Tomorrow he'd planned on snooping around the communities across the bridge; Logan Town, West Point and New Kru Town. He meant to keep pressure on Manor, so around three in the afternoon he drove his jalopy to Le'Toit Club.

"I'm afraid I have some bad news for you," Lonos said, entering Manor's downstairs office.

"What the hell?" Manor jerked his head back as if he had been insulted.

Lonos had slipped by his temporary help. The downstairs office was opened to the community, but not just anyone. Manor's private office on the second floor by no means was opened to the public.

Manor furrowed his brow. He did not stand or offer a hand, or extend any courtesy that might indicate any type of respect.

"I'm not going away, Manor," Lonos shrugged. Then he caught sight of the man's desk; freshly-oiled, darkened-polish mahogany. The graceful curve of the legs displayed hand-hewn craftsmanship of each, hours of meticulous painstaking labor. Definitely imported and would cost three times Lonos' yearly salary.

Manor stood up. "Know what you have, Lonos? Plenty of nothing!" he snarled. "You *will* die poor." He'd put emphases on *will*. "If you know what's best for you, you might just have a bright future." Manor took the five-inch stack of bills out of the inside pocket of his blazer and slapped it on the table. "If you use this wisely, you would never have to lift a finger to work."

Officer Lonos' eyes went from the stack of money lying on the beautiful desk, back to Manor's eyes. "There's a thin line between love and hate," he said. "I love my conscience. I hate you. That is the thin line," he pointed at the stack of cash. "Blood money you're trying to bribe me with? You see, I love my conscience more… so I'm saying 'no' to your fucking bribe!"

"You can't be serious," Manor said incredulously. "You have no idea how much that is."

"Doesn't matter."

Manor picked up the money and stuffed it back in his jacket pocket.

"Lonos, you are a fool. You will never be able to hold that amount of money with your lousy paycheck."

"Maybe. But this fool is going to nail your rich ass. I promise you that, Manor."

"No, Lonos… you're the one who's numbering his days," Manor chuckled. "Just wait and see."

"See what? Most people are afraid of you because of your connections, but I'm not part of that public. I'm not afraid of you or any of your connections. Your demons are meant to chase you, not me."

"Well, let's see what tomorrow has for you," Manor promised. "When you have the dough, they don't say 'no.' And, Officer Lonos, just so you know… I have a lot of dough. There's plenty where that came from," he patted the spot where he'd put the stack of cash.

Lonos nodded and marched out.

Manor got his phone and frenetically punched some numbers.

"He wouldn't take the bait," he barked into the phone. "Dolo, get him off my ass! I don't care what you have to do!"

Chief Dolo was quiet.

"I care about nothing other than my business. And, Dolo," Manor barked, "make me look bad and *you* will disappear."

Dolo's Adam's apple did a hard barb.

"Are you there?" Manor yelled.

Dolo cursed under his breath, and answered, "I'm here."

"You want to go swimming at night? If you didn't drink so damn much they'd find your ass on the beach too. Don't fucking test me!"

The phone went dead.

Dolo stared at the phone. "Not my ass," he muttered, shaking his head. "Your ass would get there quicker, you bastard. You want my liver too? Not a fucking chance."

Dolo put the phone in his pocket and check his watch. It was still early, but a head start at the bar was far better than thinking about Manor. He headed to Sugar Shack.

Chapter 12

HER HUSBAND HAD hit her before, shouted so loud that the neighbors heard her cries. He'd ground her down a little bit every day for years with insults aimed at undermining her. He'd slowly sucked the life out of her, a piece at a time. The woman was so close to losing all her strength and will, but she'd hung on for the sake of the marriage, and fear.

Tomah had anticipated another fight. She heard her husband entered the house mumbling, a sound that had become distressingly familiar. That is because every time Cheah Boatswain went to Sugar Shack to drink with friends, rottenness entered into his bones. He came home at 5:00 a.m. and started the argument, beginning with a slap. His wife had refused him sex because his breath and clothes reek cheap liquor and cigarettes. The next blow was harder, knocking her off the bed onto the floor. Tomah's screams alerted Boatswain's eighteen-year-old nephew sleeping in the room next to theirs, and he ran to their bedroom. The nephew tried to intervene but Boatswain denied it.

"I will kill you if you come between me and my wife," Boatswain threatened his nephew. "Get out of our bedroom!"

A third blow followed, sending Tomah unconscious for a minute or so under this battery. Then Boatswain ripped his wife's clothes off and pulled down her panties as she came thru. She fought him, but this only energized her husband. Tomah felt his hand on her privates, then soon after, he penetrated hard. She stared at her husband like a mouse at a black mamba. In his eyes, she could see that he did not care about her and she began crying, calling out for help. Boatswain rebuked his wife, telling her to be silent.

Tomah cried out more, "Don't do this thing to me! Please, Cheah, stop! You are hurting me."

The man did his business while continued hitting his wife. If it wasn't for some neighbors butting in to stop the beating, it would have been a dead ending for the woman.

Following the terrible humiliating rape and beating by her husband, Tomah ran into hiding to escape her embarrassment. Crying uncontrollably, she had hardly noticed that a small group of women, mostly elderly women hearing the commotion, had come to find her. One old woman took Tomah's hand and said, "Come, my daughter, let us hide you from that monster. He's sure to find you here."

Tomah lifted her face and the woman saw blood and tears. She held out her other hand and Tomah took it. The old woman pulled her in a close embrace. Tomah struggled for a moment, and then became calm like a child. From her throat came the kind of helpless cry that comes from abused women. The old woman comforted Tomah, and she was good at this because she knows the shame and pain. Tomah begged to be left alone, but the old woman did not.

Not only did Tomah need a doctor, she needed a lawyer like the woman-lawyer people were talking about; Grace Pupoh. The old woman told Tomah that God had sent Grace to respond to the hurt and needs of women like them. What Grace was doing for them—opening their eyes to see the abuse and finding self-worth—can only be God's doing. They needed someone who understood and cared, and Grace had opened her heart to help them. They were now learning their self worth and self-respect.

A short time later, the old woman's house was packed to overflowing with other women from the neighborhood. They had phoned Grace and she was there promptly, ready to help. Grace's commitment to the women's needs is a daily calling. Her aspiration to help them had always been fueled by the belief that kindness picks others up when troubles weight them down.

Tomah Boatswain was somewhere around twenty-nine years old and her story was moving. She finished explaining her ordeal and ended with, "I am ready to stand up to my husband."

They all gazed at her with amazement. Tomah's eyes were red, but no longer crying. She seemed to have already become a different person.

"If I don't, he is going to kill me," Tomah continued. "What choice have I got?"

"What do you want me to do for you?" Grace asked.

This is always the specific thing she says to her clients. Most of the women do not like that kind of specificity when they first meet their lawyer. It is because they do not know what exactly they want, or what could get done for them. There are times Grace would talk to the client poetically and there are also times she would say things bluntly. Being specific was a sign of trust for her clients because right then and there, they would acknowledge what can be done and what cannot be done. She does not need to impress the women by a flurry of far-fetched words of false hope. This shows she is actually listening to what their heart feared.

"Divorce him," Tomah asserted.

Grace liked what she was hearing and decided right away to take on the case. "Okay," she approved, "that will happen later. First, let's get you to the hospital."

__**********__

Doctor Douglas was walking out of the emergency room and into the waiting area when she saw Grace with a grumpy little boy in hand among the small group of women. She was talking to the women, instructing them to organize. They moved toward the back of the room walking hurriedly, moving too fast a pace and the little boy's legs couldn't keep up. The child abruptly stopped and his hand slipped out of Grace's grasp. He burst into tears. Grace gathered the child in her arms and lifted him.

"Here's that woman doctor," one woman said, referring to Mel as she reached them.

Grace turned and sighed, seeing who the doctor is. "Dr. Douglas," she said softly, "I didn't know you were still in Liberia."

"I'm in and out," Mel said, her gaze going from Grace to the child, then back at Grace. "Who's the handsome little guy?"

"This is my son," Grace sighed.

Mel pulled a clean napkin out of her coat pocket, mopped tears off the child's face and wiped his running nose. "Can he have a lollipop?"

"Sure," Grace replied.

Mel returned the soiled napkin to the other pocket and exchanged it with the candy. "I hope you like red," she said, handing him the candy.

Grace said to the child, "What do you say when someone gives you something."

"Thank you," the little boy uttered shyly.

"You are welcome," Mel said, smiling. "That face of yours is just too cute to have tear stains on it," she added, not being able to take her gaze off the child. She recognized familiar features.

"Thanks for the candy," Grace said.

Mel said nothing. Grace thanked her again, this time it startled Dr. Douglas.

"Sure," Mel said, forcing a smile. "Who's sick?"

"One of my clients," Grace said, and explained the young woman's ordeal.

"Is there anything I can do to help?" Mel asked.

"She's already with the doctor. Thanks."

"I don't think I have your number," Mel baited. "Can I get it?"

"Sure," Grace replied. She pulled a business card out of a black case and handed it to Dr. Douglas. Grace suddenly had the feeling it wasn't just to give her updates.

Chapter 13

RJ's **FIRST BUSINESS** in London was to negotiate a four-year contract for their client, 21-year-old Oko Azusa, a six-foot, 190-pound all-around mid-fielder from Ghana, who is brilliant in every video recording advertising his performance. Azusa reads the game well and does a lot of unnoticed defensive work when he has to. Combining creativity, power and pace to great effect, he will get better.

In the course of this day RJ had gotten a contract that pays a $250,000 signing bonus, plus $125,000 the first year, $150,000 the second, and $200,000 for an option year. He wants a deal shorter than four years because he knows his client would be a big star, and soon they would be commanding more money.

For an African athlete to start a soccer career in Europe with a three-year paycheck for $725,000 isn't bad. RJ's fee of 5% brings him a little over $37,000. He would also be helping Azusa with investments to secure a solid financial future.

If his clients had questions or concern, RJ would find an answer or an expert promptly. "Call me if you need anything," he said to Azusa, after the big signing.

After bending a few more ears on the phone, then studying more potential contracts, RJ called it a day. It would have been a glamorous day had he had the time to call his wife before collapsing into bed, except that he did not have that luxury. He was meeting with Bohn to discuss how they would handle the case in clearing the Senator's name.

Bohn had made reservations at IL Baretto, an Italian restaurant located in the heart of central London. The maitre d' welcomed Bohn like an old friend and ushered the pair to a private corner table. The décor was authentic Italian, deep mahogany tables, banquette seating and a glass faced wine cellar cutting a fashionable line against traditional Italian dining experience. They ordered drinks and perused the menu for a moment. As RJ studied his menu, Bohn studied him.

"I was just thinking," Bohn said to RJ.

RJ looked up from his menu. "I'm listening."

"If you go ahead and file a lawsuit against the Liberian government, you'll find yourself on the flip side of a mountain impossible to cross over," Bohn advised.

"What mountain?"

"The international community of the big boys club," Bohn replied. "The case will move so slowly, you'd be a great-grandpa before anything comes to light. The only thing will happen is you've gotten things rolling. Some hot shot would... you know... car block you."

"So just leave things alone? Don't clear my father's name?"

"I didn't say that."

"What are you saying?"

The waiter returned with their drinks and they gave their orders. Bohn worked on a glass of Andrea Oberto 2005, while RJ nuzzled a glass of Alteni di Brassica, 2008 Piemonte.

"Hear me out," Bohn said and straighten up. "Sandbag Manor into something solid and let one of the big boys, like a foreign government agency, nail him. Something that will stick... something solid. The FBI or CIA can flatten that bastard like a damn cockroach. Feed him to the Russians if we have to. Know what I mean?"

"Feed him to the Russian? Or the CIA?" RJ said incredulously.

"I'm neither a spy nor a magician, RJ. I'm a business man with a lot of experience in intelligence planning. I use my connections to the fullest. I will lead the battle from a distance."

RJ listened, but he was thinking, *The Russian? CIA?*

"Let's just say we are the good guys when you're in a bad situation," Bohn assured. "That's what I've obtained for serving my country... proudly served my country in Nam. "

Bohn was always quick to admit what he did for Uncle Sam was because of pride. Pride in himself and in his devotion to his country.

"Vietnam, uh?" RJ acknowledged, gauging his capability. "I know our military is the best, but...."

"This is not a war?"

"I didn't think of it as a war."

"It is," Bohn nodded. "Them against us."

"Them? You don't mean the Liberian government, do you?"

"Those responsible for your father's demise. And RJ, we will win the war," Bohn said, staring into his glass. "I already have a number of irons in the fire. It's only a matter of time. Where there's bait, there's always hope."

Bohn knew enough agents to play the roles needed to send Manor's thoughts into a tailspin. Without official channels of course. Pretend operations in the world of espionage where no classified information is ever improperly disclosed. With the right sort of bait, they could coax Manor into paranoia and break down. Lie to a liar.

Bottom line, the mission would not be successful without the supplementation of powerful forces such as the CIA and other international big name agencies. His connections were his ace. Bohn's plan was sound in principal and effective in execution. His tactic, he hoped, would prove to be a viable resource for the future when dealing with African war lords. How else to deal with scumbags who have the resources to scorch their own country? These bastards suck the life right out of the poor women and children. And, the only way those poor people get rid of the insidious infestation is to replace one with a different one.

Such operations cost a lot of money, perhaps close to half a million. Who has that kind of money to spare? Why use your money when there were other people's money? The bad guys' money. Bohn didn't want this to bleed Katharine's children financially dry either. Instead, he wanted Manor to bleed financially while being defeated.

"RJ, you would be saving yourself a whole lot of headaches if you just hear me out," Bohn said, drumming his fingers against the table. "Have you heard of The Box?"

RJ looked up, curious. "No."

"Most African leaders never think about things beyond their lifetime," Bohn started. "They forget about beyond their children's lifetime when it's their number one duty. The rule of law in their so-called open society falls on deaf ears. Too many of them are in a psychic state where integrity is unreal. They don't understand that as you help others, you're helping yourself. I don't know how or why, but at this level they are deeply conflicted. They keep taking bribes and stealing the country resource for their personal gain in the name of leadership. In fact, it is for greed and womanizing. Will it ever get to the point where they know that they are not doing right?"

RJ smoothed out his napkin, remaining silent as the waiter delivered their food and left.

"No," Bohn answered his own question, then went on. "Taxi drivers, for instance, making an honest living. They are stopped by police officers, not for traffic violations, but to be hassled. The argument is usually about collecting bribes. The whole country is bribed to the nickel. It seemed every public office is for sale."

As if RJ didn't already know that. He shrugged, wanting Bohn to please tell him what he did not know.

Then Bohn went on to explain *The Box*, the annoying way that bureaucracy prevented things from getting done. When a new person comes to Liberia to start a business, scores of opportunists compete for the chance for you to bribe them. The nest is the office and they are like baby birds opening their beaks for their mother to drop a crumb into their mouths, only to swallow it and demand more.

"You think things slowly get done by our government in America, in Liberia government foot-dragging is far worst. Here's the thing, growth is extremely slow because of the burdensome hurdles it erects, or there isn't any at all. Every effort falls far short of accomplishing any goals."

"To be fair, bureaucratic red tape is in every government in the world," RJ challenged Bohn.

"Of course. But elsewhere stuff gets done," Bohn interjected, "Not in Liberia. The Box is hindering people's access to making a better life for them and their children. Companies can't go there and build factories to offer employment. That's what I'm talking about."

"If there was one truism in corruption in high places, it is that it continues to hinder the achievements of the Liberian people," Bohn continued. "Not only is it morally wrong, it is stupid."

"If Liberians can get on their feet, the economy would be moving in the right direction," RJ offered. "I've met a lot of young people with big dreams. They want to do well. All they need is a chance to do so."

"That's what I'm talking about," Bohn exclaimed. "Legitimate businesses with export and import opportunities will create jobs there."

Through dinner Bohn talked about Africa's trouble, being the richest continent and yet had the most poor people because of disgusting greedy leaders. RJ offered what he believed to be the problem, lack of education. Then the conversation went to small talks and the men began their good-byes.

__**********__

RJ hadn't realized how tired he was until he saw his bed. He wasn't sure what time it was in Atlanta until he looked at his watch. It read, 10:00 p.m. Now he remembered he'd not set his watch to London time, which was four hours ahead of the US Eastern Time. Gia would be up, and Kitty should be sound asleep. Knowing his wife, she wouldn't go to sleep until he'd called her.

"I better call home before I even hit the shower," he muttered.

The loud house phone ring would wake Kitty so he dialed Gia's cell.

"Baby," she answered on the first ring with a happy, but sleepy voice. "I've been waiting to hear from you. A minute more and I would've been sleeping. Kitty's asleep."

"Sorry I didn't call earlier. I would've liked hearing her voice."

"You sound tired."

"I am," he mumbled.

"Why aren't you in bed?"

"I would, but not after hearing my wife's lovely voice… so I'm calling first."

"Baby, we miss you too," she whispered.

"How's my princess?"

"She follows you like a puppy when you're home," Gia chuckled. "You can imagine how she gets when you're away. She wanted me to call you. 'Mommie, lets call Daddy, pleaseeeeees'. And this time, honey, that plead was just too pitiful."

RJ chuckled. "Can you wake her?"

"No, I won't wake her," Gia laughed. "I won't be able to get her to go back to sleep."

He wanted to continue their conversation but his eyes had other ideas. "I'll call first thing in the morning to talk with her. Kiss her for me… I love you both."

"We love you more," Gia said and hung up.

The second RJ placed his phone on the night stand, it rang. He picked up.

"RJ," Mel said as soon as she heard the phone turned on.

"Hey, Mel."

"Did you know Grace has a son?"

"No. Why? Am I supposed to know," he giggled.

"Well... maybe."

"And, why's that?"

"He looks just like you."

RJ was quiet. Tiresomeness left him.

"Hello? RJ?"

"I'm here," he answered slowly. "I still don't understand. How old is he?"

"Same age as Kitty."

He felt his heart sink. "Fuck!"

"That's what happens when you do," Mel said.

"Mel, are you sure?"

"I wouldn't be telling you this if I wasn't. They came to the hospital today."

"Something's wrong with the boy?"

"No. Grace brought a young woman in and she had her son with her. I don't think Mom has seen him though, she would have said something. I don't know why she's been hiding him. The kid even walks like you. Maybe I should do a DNA, but I bet he's yours... same fingers, nose, eyes... I mean the kid looks like a mini you."

"Maybe you need to do a DNA to be sure," RJ said. He wasn't sure of himself for thinking that. "I'm not about to jump the gun here. Could you, please?"

"Well... I could, but it's a touchy matter. If you ask Grace to prove it, she might be resentful."

"So what am I suppose to do, Mel? Accept it?"

"I'm not saying that. I'll think of something," Mel blew out her breath. "RJ, you have really screwed up if it turns out this kid is yours. You know your wife."

"Thanks, Mel... that's what I really need to hear."

"Well... I'm just saying."

Chapter 14

SEVERAL WEEKS AFTER the body had been found, the LJC lead story was still about the body of a little boy found with missing vital human organs. A headshot photo of Matthew Seekey smiling from ear to ear had been used, and under his face were the ominous words: WHO WOULD STEAL AN INNOCENT HEART?

The story was long and thorough. It began with the discovery of the body on the beach, and all the results of the autopsy detailing his missing vital organs; heart, lungs, liver and kidneys. It mentioned no suspects, no arrests. People started to wonder why, when the MPD had claimed to be working very hard. Not a word from Police Chief, Aaron Dolo, and they wanted to know. It appeared as if the reporter had made efforts to contact Dolo, but to no avail. They hoped someone, anyone, working on the case would say something.

Paranoia had set in and everything made Dolo suspicious. One thing was for sure, whatever Officer Lono's intensions were, he wasn't playing around with the investigation. He was going after Manor tooth and nail, tagging him to Seekey's murder was close and personal. Dolo was not feeling much comfort after the call from Manor.

Officer Lonos had been overworked due in large part to the fact that his boss, Aaron Dolo, sat on his ass while he took care of a majority of the duties of the Monrovia Police Department. Lonos was in charge of everything Dolo did not want to do. Overly ambitious, Lonos completed the extra tasks Dolo threw his way, aware that the man had every intention of going to his house, while Lonos was at work, so he can fuck his wife. Lonos was a detective, a very good one, and was completely knowledge-able of the facts.

The moment Lonos walked into the MPD building, the receptionist greeted him with an order from Chief Dolo. He was to report to Dolo's office as soon as he'd gotten there. He knew it wasn't to plan a surprise party. Lonos went straight to Dolo's office. The door was open, and Dolo waved him in.

"Close the door," Chief Dolo said.

Lonos did.

Dolo walked from behind his desk and stepped toward the officer. "Officer Lonos," he said, "I know you've been handling this investigation from the beginning. I understand your difficulties in pursuing this case and gaining witnesses." Then he paused for a moment, seeming to select his words with great care. "Your approach is hardly effective," Dolo continued. "And the fact is, a child is dead." Then, he coldly ticked off the points on his fingers, "Missing lungs, kidneys, his little heart, you name it. And, not so much blood. Put it all together and I'm looking at a ritualistic killing here." Chief Dolo sighed and said, "Tell me something. Since when do we go around harassing law-abiding citizens? Liberians who support poor people? Who the hell gave you permission to interrogate Mr. Manor and his wife?"

Lonos took a long breath. He had been expecting this repercussion from the moment he had visited the Manors' home.

"With all due respect, sir, I don't see how that could be the case. I've interrogated no one."

"Did you not go to Mr. Manor's house?"

"Well, I did… but I did not interrogate anyone. I did not go beyond the gates."

"You went without my permission," Dolo snarled. "You went over the line."

"Sir, you appointed me to the case from day one. Here is my observation. I don't think Matthew Seekey was killed for ritualistic purposes… it was the heart-men. I think they stole his organs for medical reason."

Dolo raised his eyebrows to emphasize pretend-doubt to the obvious point.

"I intend to find his killer," Lonos continued. "I'm not going to be quiet about it."

"Killer?" Dolo said, incredulously.

"Or, Killers," Lonos assured.

The thought itself was nearly paralyzing to Dolo. Officer Lonos' approval rating with his boss went down sixty points. These reprimands,

Lonos knew, were designed to get him off Manor's ass. Dolo could add the appropriate mumbo-jumbo to deter his officer, still Lonos saw in Dolo's past, as well as his own future. Now Lonos wondered. This is more than a simple bout of analyzing evidence and suspects.

"Besides Manor, who else have you talked to?" Dolo wanted to know.

Lonos pulled the small notepad out of his shirt pocket. "A couple of people," he said, flipping the pages.

"Let me have it," Dolo ordered.

"Their names or my pad."

"Pad."

Lonos handed it over.

Dolo flipped the pages, reading quietly to himself a list of names. "I thought you said a couple?"

"A few," Lonos shrugged.

"Which is it? You have a full list here," Dolo said, and counted. "Ten."

"Sir, those are just names thrown at me," Lonos said, his voice tight and edgy. "I haven't had the time to check them out yet."

"I don't like this," Chief Dolo said. "You have a shit load of people to interrogate and you're chasing one man?" He put the pad in his pocket.

"I need that," Lonos said, looking directly at his boss.

"Not any more. If we have a shot finding the killers, I'm not going to have my officers running after the wrong suspect when we already have a list."

"Those are not suspects."

"Call them what you will," Dolo snarled. "Suspects… material witnesses… I don't give a shit. They signed that boy's death certificate and they must pay."

Lonos was quiet for a bit, studying his boss. He had signed ten death certificates by putting their lives in Dolo's hand. "All right, I'll start interrogating them."

"No. I'm pulling you off the case. Someone else will investigate Seekey's murder."

Lonos knew Dolo was protecting Manor, and getting rid of him would be his first tactical choice. But he needed those names back. "Why take the pad? Rip the sheet out and give me back my pad," he suggested.

"Fair enough," Dolo sighed, and he did.

Officer Lonos put the pad back in his pocket. His first plan of action would be to see whether there are imprints on the page that was beneath the page the list was written on. Then give those men fair warning. Everybody and everything associated with them would be subject to intense scrutiny. That was all he could really do. Depending on how this turns out, they might not have many tomorrows left. And, they better be praying men.

Dolo was fidgeting. "You know, we cannot keep you on the force, Lonos," the Chief made known his decision.

"What?"

Chief Dolo's gaze said what his mouth didn't. It wasn't a legit way to end the employment, Lonos could fight it all he wants, but it would be a waste of his time. Corruption was more rampant in high places (who knows you) and Dolo knew a lot of higher-ups.

"Who's firing me?"

"I am," Dolo said. His tone was one of contempt. "Let's just say I have a better person now than I did a few days ago. You're wasting the government's money and time, chasing a myth… among other things."

Lonos rubbed his temples. He tried not to think about the man fucking his wife, the irritating tricks he'd used to keep Lonos busy, as if he could not tell, and especially him and Manor, pot-pissing buddies that they were. He wanted to punch the living shit out of his boss, but he let out an enormous breath instead.

"See you around," Lonos said, and walked out.

Aaron Dolo had expected a strong reaction from his officer, but Lonos had taken everything calmly in stride. He went back to his desk, cleared most of his belongings, turned in his badge and said goodbye to some of his coworkers.

Chief Dolo waited until he was sure Lonos had left the building. Then, he got his cell and punched in some numbers. "He's gone," he said into the phone. "This case is closed."

—✳✳✳✳✳✳✳✳✳—

"Sonofabitch! " Lonos grumbled. "What a morning. How the hell I did not see it coming?"

There's never an hour too early to see a lot of people at Sinkor Circle. He needed someone to talk to and he needed a drink, but with some food. As he drove within the painful commute of the city heavy traffic, he thought to call Grace. Lonos dialed her number and wanted to know if she could meet him at Sinkor Circle. Grace told him she would try to get there within an hour.

Lonos sipped on his beer and munched on an order of fried plantains while he waited.

Forty minutes later Grace arrived at Sinkor Circle in a taxi. She scanned the room, saw Lonos sitting at the bar, and walked over. Lonos grabbed his beer and escorted her to a table for two. The eating space he selected was in a small niche, private because of the wall.

As she and Lonos sat at a table, Grace said, "If I haven't thanked you before, I'm thanking you now. I wouldn't have known for sure that the senator had no proven ties to Johnny Bono's murder."

Lonos flicked a gaze at her. "I'm glad to help," he said dryly. "I'm not into helping criminals, that's why I did what I did. People make mistakes, but once you find out your mistakes you must correct them. I tried correcting mine by giving you the evidence when I found out we had sent an innocent man to his grave. There was nothing else I could do."

Grace stared very deliberately at him and said, "What could you have done? It's hard to be the good guy in our society. There's so much greed and corruption among those who control the Liberian Government's purse strings. It's crazy."

A waitress came over and took their order.

As soon as the waitress left, Lonos said, "Aaron Dolo had squeaky clean hands during the first two years. Then the waters got a little murkier as his relationship with Manor went further. Manor's bribery had started out cautiously at first. Police Officers are not wealthy, and providing a decent home for your family is not cheap. At one time Dolo also believed in the change Liberia needed. He was okay his first few years as police chief, then he became a real hard-ass after Manor had dangled enough carrots before his eyes."

"CeRue Manor," Grace said, nodding in agreement. "What a monster. Some people would say, a bogeyman."

"You mean, heart-man."

Grace's eyes widened. "Lonos, how would you know he's a heart-man? As a lawyer, I can tell you that is a hard thing to prove, especially when those in authority are blocking your efforts. Senator Douglas lost to Manor, not the Liberian Government."

"What do you mean?"

"The man's own lawyer, and the people investigating him, teamed up against him. How could he have proven anything? Why did they set

Senator Douglas up? That's what I'd like to know."

"I don't know," Lonos replied. "But I intend to find out."

"How? You no longer work at MPD."

"I don't know yet, but I will. The evidence is there. I'll just have to keep digging."

Grace didn't say anything for a long moment. Then the words somehow came easier. "You cannot go after someone based on rumor or hint," she said. "If you go after important people, you better be damn sure. Don't target someone like Manor unless you're loaded to hunt an elephant." She looked at him and asked, "How's your gun?"

"Empty," Lonos replied. He'd said it so softly Grace could barely hear him. "And I'm not sure where to go to reload."

"Then think this through, Lonos. I wish there was something I could do to help. Sorry," she shrugged.

Several people came up to greet Officer Lonos when they walked by, not just to say 'hello', but also asked about the case. Lonos told them they were still working on it.

"You're popular," Grace remarked. "Just think if you were running for office."

He chuckled. "Maybe I'm popular, but I have no interest in politics."

The waitress delivered their order and left.

"I bet Dolo wish he could put Boatswain on the case, but he can't."

"You mean, Cheah Boatswain?"

Lonos nodded.

"I'm representing his wife," Grace informed. "I would be happy for any information on that man. Boatswain thinks he's above the law. When I'm done with him, he's going to put his nuts on the table to bargain his freedom."

Officer Lonos barked out a laugh. People turned and stared. "And if he does?"

"Oh, he's going to lose that little peepee of his," Grace chuckled, winkling her pinkie finger.

"Do you know that they call him, Big Tiny?"

"Big what?" Grace threw back her head with a delight laugh. A few customers turned and looked. "He's an ass," she muttered.

"Grace, I didn't know you cuss," Lonos chuckled.

"Everybody does. I do occasionally... when I have to."

The food was excellent and the service attentive.

Lonos vented about his ex-boss, a little about the case and his personal challenges. Grace listened and when she could, encouraged

"Excuse me, Grace," Lonos said and stood. "I need to use the men's room."

He left.

After doing his business, Lonos went to the sink to wash his hands. As he stared in the mirror, the image of little Matthew came at him in flashes. "Matthew, they may have kicked me off the force but there's no way I'm going to abandon you," he muttered.

When Lonos returned to the table, Grace obviously sensed something was wrong. "Are you okay?"

"Yeah," he nodded. "I was just thinking about Matthew Seekey."

"What a shame," she said. "I have a son, so I can't even imagine what his poor grandmother is going through."

"Grace, I can't let her down. I have to continue the investigation."

"For what it's worth, here's a little advice for you, Officer Lonos," Grace said. "CeRue Manor never goes through channels, he goes direct."

"I know… and he brags about that," Lonos confirmed.

"So be careful."

Lonos nodded.

"I paid the bill when you went to the men's room," Grace informed.

"But, I invited you to lunch."

"I know."

"Thanks. Next time, lunch is on me."

"Okay," she said and smiled.

"I'll be fine," he said convincingly. It was for him, more so than for Grace. The fact is, he would be without a paycheck in the awful economy and he didn't know for how long. "I'll run my old Toyota for taxi during the day. I'll get all the information you need on Boatswain," he assured.

Grace rose from the table. Lonos did too.

"Good," Grace said, looking at her watch. "I can be your first customer. I need to meet with Mrs. Boatswain, and then go to Temple of Justice."

Chapter 15

TOMAH UNDERWENT A series of crucial exams; genital, oral, and rectal. The young male doctor was gentle and sympathetic. He checked her vagina for injury and documented that. His notes included physical damage—bruising, bites—all of which were documented and photographed for evidence. Grace requested and got all Tomah's medical reports, including the rape test she had insisted to have done.

Grace explained to her client that when someone files for divorce, he or she will have to state a valid legal reason or grounds for the divorce. There are faults and no-fault grounds, she explained. She prepared a petition for the dissolution of Tomah Boatswain's marriage to her husband on the grounds of cruel and inhumane treatment that endangers the physical and mental well being of her client, making it unsafe or improper for Tomah to continue living with him. The Court was to look into the matter and rule accordingly:

There was force, menace, and duress in the marriage; adultery during the marriage; habitual intoxication; cruel treatment, consisting of willful infliction of pain, bodily and mental, upon Mrs. Boatswain, such as reasonably justified apprehension of danger to life, limb, and health; spousal rape; and the marriage is irretrievably broken.

As far as Grace was concerned, the court need only to pronounce judgment in keeping with the law and there were reasons for justice to be done. Nowhere on earth is justice negotiable, why should Liberia be different. Grace wanted justice for her client and it was not negotiable.

__*✱✱✱✱✱✱✱✱✱✱*__

After the meeting with Grace, it was like bravery and hope had kissed each other. Tomah felt the desire to seek justice. She decided no matter what, she'd go after her husband, even force his steps to the courthouse if she had to, and seek justice.

"It won't be easy," Grace told her. "Poor women in Liberia just don't file for divorce because they were beaten."

"It is not just the beating," Tomah said shyly. "He forced me to have sex with him so many times. I cried and begged him to stop, but each time he had this way anyhow."

"I have the medical report from the last one," Grace assured. "We will use that in court."

The thing is, both men and women seemed highly skeptical of the idea that forcibly imposed sex with a spouse should be viewed as raped. They understand rape to be when any man who is not your man forces you and have you. Grace thought things over and attempted to explain to Tomah what rape is. She was not ready to tell Tomah defending her rights would be a lengthy legal process, likely to be traumatic and demoralizing. What matter is they would be looking for justice.

"Even when you're married and your husband asks you for sex and you don't want to have sex that day, he has no right to force you. If he does, you have the right to take him to court for rape," Grace advised. "Tomah, Cheah is your husband, but you were raped."

"I know that I was raped," Tomah confirmed. "But that's not how people see it."

"It's not what people think," Grace said. "We are going by what the law says. He's a police officer, isn't he?"

Tomah nodded.

Grace pulled out a clean notepad and clicked the top of her pen. "Tell me about him," she said. "I want to know everything… every detail."

"What do you mean? Tell you about my husband?"

"Every detail," Grace repeated, ready to write.

"I met him at the taxi depot at Red Light junction," Tomah started. "It was after the war."

"Had you met him at any time during the war?"

"No," Tomah shook her head. "It was after. Right after the war, when everyone was showing a better side than what had been shown during the war. I heard rumors about him being the kind of man he was during the war, but I did not believe it. I thought it was hearsay. The truth is, I was stubborn. I did not see Boatswain as a predator then, but as a man. After all he was a policeman."

"I understand," Grace said. "Go on."

Tomah did.

It was in the intense dry season heat, the noise and clamor at the busy depot, when she met Boatswain. The police officer had come to her stand to buy cold water, but later discovered he had lost his wallet. He was old enough to be her father, soft-spoken, and friendly. So Tomah gave the man some water for free.

She had not seen him for months, until she'd needed a taxi. It was late and getting dark when Tomah realized she had not heard from the taxi driver that takes her home every evening. Taxis do not leave the main road to take passengers to their homes. But this driver made Tomah his last run so that he helps her with her water container, from the road to her house. It was at that precise moment that a man approached her from the side, dressed in blue dungarees and a white T-shirt. Tomah did not recognize him out of uniform, but Boatswain had not forgotten her.

Before the marriage, he treated her as if she was a precious treasure. He wooed her with whatever she asked for. Then when he proposed marriage, the word curled around her like a feeling of safety. After the wedding, she discovered her husband's web of deceit. That first deceit, when he'd claimed to have lost his money, begun a pattern, a trail that had led to this moment.

Boatswain was a man of strong influence and even stronger emotions. She lost all her independence little by little, until finally he stripped her of all freedom. Over the years, she had tried to appear cheerful in front of neighbors and friends to hide the shame of rape and beatings. But all could see how the young woman wore hard times on her beautiful face; sad, sunken eyes and empty smiles. For some time she accepted her life, the rough with the smooth. Overall, it filtered the strain of exploitation and abuse.

"I am ready to take back my life," Tomah finished. "It is worth something now. Isn't that what you've told me?"

__**********__

Three weeks after the beating, Tomah needed her spirits uplifted. Grace decided the woman needed to undergo some pampering and discussed a plan with Irene Zarway and Yassah Johnston. Four hours later Grace and the women had updated Tomah's hairdo from simple cornrows to shoulder-length extension braids, applied makeup for the first time in her life—mascara, eyeliner, eye shadow, blush and lipstick—and fitted her with a different wardrobe too, jeans and a blouse. The change was dramatic because not long ago she thought of herself not fit for human company. All the women gasped when Tomah stepped out of Yassah's house and into the yard.

"Bring the mirror from my room," Yassah instructed one woman.

Tomah took a look at herself in the full-length mirror and was too shocked. She kept staring at the image before her, looking to find proof that it was really her. Her former self became evident as she tried walking in shoes she had never worn before. She laughed along with the others, at her clumsy walk. Grace thought the transformation was only the beginning. With this new start, God will have to do the rest for the woman. She hoped that Tomah remembers she is special like every other human being.

Tomah just stood still, smiling. This was something she'll have to work hard at, this new change of giving up the way she allowed her wife-beating husband to abuse her. She liked the way she was walking, leaving as much of the dark past behind. What Tomah saw in the tall looking glass was a woman learning to love herself, the beginning of a better life.

Chapter 16

"OSEI, I AM in deep shit," RJ said as soon as Osei picked up. His voice had a nervous tinge to it. "I'm so deep... I mean... I'm up to my eyeballs in it. I can smell it, hear it, see it... I can even taste it. Somehow, I've managed to screw up my life."

"RJ?"

"I wish I was dead, Osei. I wish I was."

"Where are you?"

"On my way to you," RJ said and disconnected his Blackberry.

Osei called back, but his call went unanswered. He did this for almost an hour. No answer.

RJ reached the Cassava Patch, parked, and waited in his car for an hour before texting Osei that he was outside.

Osei ran out to the car. "Come in, let's have a drink while we talk," he suggested.

"I can't. I don't want Ama to see me."

"Okay," Osei nodded. He opened the door and sat in the passenger front seat. "This sounds serious."

"More serious than a heart attack," RJ replied. "I wish the world would end today, I swear."

"Now you're scaring me. Is it that bad?"

RJ nodded.

"What's going on?"

RJ hesitated, then said, "I cheated on Gia and she's about to find out...."

He broke off when Osei slapped at his arm. "You didn't!"

"I wish I hadn't."

"But why?"

Before RJ could start again, Osei said, "Forget why. How could you? When? Where?"

"Liberia."

"Liberia?" Osei took in his breath and let it out slowly. "Damn, RJ, are you sure she hasn't already found out?"

"She doesn't know yet."

"And, you feel the urge to tell her? I don't understand. When did this happen?"

"Three years ago."

"When you went home for the trial," Osei concluded.

RJ nodded.

"So, now you feel guilty and wants to confess?"

"No," RJ snapped. "Mel called me the other day while I was in London."

"Mel found out, and she's gonna snitch on your ass?" Osei joked.

RJ made a point to cross his arms, he wasn't laughing. His mouth had a tight pinched look. Osei could tell that he was hurting.

"You are not making any sense here, RJ. Talk to me."

RJ thought for a moment, long enough to work himself up steels for nerves. "There's a boy as the result," he muttered.

"Holy jumping Jesus!" Osei screamed.

Both men instantly turned and looked at each other; Osei, trying to hide the shock and RJ, hoping to hide the shame.

"Who's the woman?" Osei asked.

"Grace."

Osei's eyes widened as he said, "The one who helped with the trial?"

RJ nodded.

"Damn," Osei said, and turned away. "Why you had to go and make the same shitty mistake I did?"

Osei's own extra martial affairs had come to light after the tragic accident of the woman he was involved with. Six months into the affair, the woman had gotten pregnant. Having an affair with a married man, pregnancy is always a woman's problem, but Osei took full responsibility. The affair ended, and when the little girl was born Osei spent as much time afforded him without his wife knowing. His confession came after the car accident. Now that the child's mother was dead, her relatives, strangers to Osei and the child, were threatening to take the toddler to Africa. With RJ's help, Osei petitioned the court for legal parental rights and the DNA tests proved he is the little girl's father. Four years later, he and Ama were still working on their marriage; trust, in particular.

"You'd have to tell her before someone else does," Osei urged. "Let this come from you."

"I'd rather die."

"Oh, you won't die. Death only comes when the Man upstairs says he comes. But you'll beg and beg and beg some more. Then you will pray that your wife loves you enough to give you another chance. Women don't forget, RJ," Osei put his hand on RJ's shoulder and sighed. "They have long memories."

"All I know is, I don't want a life without Gia in it."

"Then be the one to tell her, and not someone else."

RJ rubbed his forehead, processing the confession, how he would tell it. He had a long way to go and no map to get there. One step at a time, right? "I'll tell her tonight," he said, and turned the key. The engine jingled to a start.

—**********—

RJ reached home and quietly walked in.

"Today I bought me a new Victoria's Secret nightie," Gia greeted her husband with a smirk, then a kiss. "I'm wearing it tonight to see if you're still paying attention to me, or whether I have to compete with your new job."

Her words filtered in slowly. RJ smiled when they finally registered, an unrehearsed turn-on from his wife. Being on the receiving end, even with a confession planned, he'd tried to respond without a trace of desperation. Maybe he should confess tomorrow.

They had gone a full week without lovemaking, since he'd returned from London. The pressure of her husband's new job, she thought. Gia enjoyed making love to her husband, or him making love to her, or them making love. Whichever way they did it, she loved it. He joined her in bed, naked butt for his shorts, and pulled her into his arms.

Their lovemaking is like dancing the fox trot; RJ's gentle one-step, two-step slow dancing, and Gia saying '*more*' in the voice of a woman who wants her pleasure to last. Tonight RJ seemed a little aggressive, not rough, just a little more enthuse than usual. This was no fox trot. He was doing the jitterbug and soon enough Gia protested. Her moaning receded two minutes into the dance. She lowered her arms from around his hip and turned her face away from him.

He sensed it immediately. "What?" he whispered into her ear, his nose pressing hard against her head.

"Just finish," she said.

Her request made him unable to. All his desire drained out of him. RJ pulled out, then off, rolling to his side of the bed. He stared at the ceiling and felt her watching him.

"What?" he said, still staring up.

"What is it with you tonight?"

RJ heaved. "I thought… let's start over," he said, touching her shoulder.

"That's not making love, RJ. I don't know what's wrong with you," she said, turning her back. Gia pulled the covers up to her shoulders.

"I'm sorry, honey," he whispered and lay closer. She didn't move. "It's okay, we can start over tomorrow. Okay?"

__*********__

Hoarding a secret for a long time sometimes becomes a larger offense than the original sin. RJ's troubles came like the sun, shining in full strength, hot and showing everything. His deceit was now seeping into their lives. The burden of conscience kept him up every night and he'd stopped reaching his wife, naked soul to naked soul. Gia could find out from someone else, or sooner or later, simply recognize his behavioral changes. Telling her as soon as possible was practical.

Another week passed. He was running out of time.

Ordinarily it would be a cheerful greeting, but RJ had come home later than usual. Gia had not heard from him all day, and he had not returned any of her calls.

"Where have you been?" she asked a split second after RJ walked into the living room.

"Do you love me?"

She could tell something unpleasant had happened. Her eyes were trained to read emotions like a weepy voice and eyes red from crying. The man's hands were shaking.

"Of course I do. You know that," she replied.

"Then promise me you're not going to leave me," RJ said, staring.

She flinched. "Why would I want to leave you?"

"Just promise me."

Gia let out a nervous chuckle. "Well… at least I need more information and… you're scaring me. Honey, what's going on?"

RJ held his wife's hand.

"You are shaking," she said, staring down at his hands.

"I've got something to tell you," he muttered. His heart pounded between his ears, his legs felt weak.

At times, even the best of us find ourselves drawn to someone who isn't our chosen one. But unprotected sex is not smart, neither is throwing caution to the wind. Admitting to doing something painful to someone you truly love is the hardest thing. Gia is that person that he loves and wants to be with forever, and she's the only person that gets his heart beating. His throat muscles would handle the huge amount of pride he'd have to swallow. It didn't matter how much it would hurt.

RJ had to be in his best composure and be himself. He did not know where the important part of the story should begin.

"Three years ago, before we got married, I had a… a… an…," he swallowed the rest of the sentence.

"You had an affair?"

Gia had been joking, knowing her husband wouldn't dare.

He nodded and he wasn't smiling.

"You had an affair?" she repeated and pulled her hand away slowly.

RJ remained still, staring at her.

Hurt and anger came over her. Gia took in her breath and let it out slowly. They stood for a long time and neither spoke a word. To limit the pain he had caused her, he would answer only what she asks, he thought to himself. He wondered what she was thinking, staring shamefully at his wife. She looked wounded with the hurt that comes when something special is taken away. He knew a storm was raging inside her.

"You've waited three years to tell me this," she finally spoke. "There has to be more."

"There is," he sighed.

"Well?"

"There's a little boy involve," RJ mumbled. Whatever else he had wanted to say died on his lips.

Gia knew not to explode. Angry words, or even unintentional verbal abuse, can do immeasurable and even lifelong harm. The proofs were before her but she would guard carefully what comes out of her mouth, and rightly so. Cheating always lead to divorce, a void so many of her clients' lives had disappeared into. She looked up at her husband with tired eyes, wearied from deep thoughts. She stared at him until he dropped his eyes.

"Grace," she said the name as if she'd known all along.

RJ nodded slowly, barely moving his head.

She thought for a moment, forehead wrinkled, eyes serious. "You did not think about your health, my health or our daughter's. You could have screwed around using a condom, but you didn't. The first pussy you saw available, while I wasn't around, you grabbed it. Is that it?"

RJ said nothing. His heart pounded wildly in his chest.

"Have you been tested?"

"Yes," he confessed, embarrassed. "Every year since the incident."

"You called your little escapade an incident?" She cut her eyes. "And?"

"All clear," he said and heaved a heavy sigh.

She said something in Italian. She spoke it fast. RJ furrowed his brow. "What a mess you've gotten us into," she translated.

His gaze fell to the floor.

"I'll have to be tested. I mean, I can't trust you anymore," her voice quivered.

Gia couldn't bear looking at him. One time she thought their marriage was paradise compared to so many of her clients and a lot of their friends. So long paradise. That impression of her marriage was lost. She gave RJ a sad smile, more than any words spoken, ran out of the living room, then up the stairs to the bedroom. RJ ran after her, but she shut the door in his face. The beautiful aroma of her perfume lingered in the hall. He heaved a deep prolong sigh, breathing her in.

"Mommy," he heard Kitty cried and ran to her room.

The slammed door had wakened her.

Gia climbed into bed, got under the covers and her fury turned into tears. What had happened to their love? The love she'd expected to have when their youthful looks fade and bend with age. The love she feels when they hold hands. The love she sees in her husband's eyes when he gazes at their daughter, the product from their beautiful lovemaking. She was thinking of her daughter now, it was not only about her or the marriage. All things boil down to Kitty who would be caught up in the middle of this storm. Their love would suffer from mistrust and she didn't know if it would handle all the hate she was feeling at the moment. Could her heart survive all the hurt that hate was sending? She had always trusted

RJ and hoped their love never dies. Now, she wasn't sure of anything.

The tears couldn't stop. They trickled from her eyes into her ear, soaking her pillows. All the tears did not soothe her badly aching heart one bit. It did absolutely nothing for her. Her world had tilted, and she needed to hang on or she would slide off. At that moment she hated RJ, and couldn't feel any love for him. Finally Gia closed her eyes, shutting out reality.

Chapter 17

Lonos went to buy cigarettes, and by luck, the peddler had the same name matching one on his list of witnesses that Dolo had confiscated. A friend from across the street had yelled the peddler's name and asked whether he could change a ten.

Lonos knew how to get the man talking. "You would think the heart-man business will stop, just how the war stopped," he baited. "But they continued to do that wickedness."

"I know," the man agreed, nodding. "Da shame what happen to da boy. I think da ley heart-man who did it."

Lonos looked at him. "You really think so?"

"Uuh-un... yeah."

"How? From the papers?"

The man did not seem like he knew his ABCs, much more read a newspaper. Lonos could bet his last dollar that he was illiterate. His simple English had the twang and sloppy grammatical habits.

"Paper?" The man's brow creased, he chuckled. "Da from people talking. I no ree paper oh."

"I see," Lonos said. "What are they talking?"

The man started to say something, but hesitated.

"You can tell me," Lonos coaxed.

"I see some-tin on da beach one night," he said, after giving it a moment of thought. "But I no tell nobody."

Lonos knew why the man had gone to the beach. Sadly, parts of Monrovia shoreline were used as latrines, especially those areas near the slums.

"Did you see people?"

The man nodded.

"How many?"

He showed three fingers.

"What were they doing? Walking? Talking? Were they carrying anything?"

"I no see them carrying some-in oh," he said. "I bend down in ley tall grass so they must not see me. Small time pass, then I hear car noise. I get up."

"Did you see the car?"

He eyed Lonos and cleared his throat. "Not car. Bus."

"A bus?"

He nodded and replied, "Renault bus."

"What color?"

"I not sure. It was night time."

"Was it a light colored van, or dark colored," Lonos asked pointedly. "White, you think?"

"Not white, but not dark."

"Maybe tan," Lonos suggested.

The man shrugged, looking agitated. Lonos was keeping him from selling his cigarettes.

"Give me one more pack of cigarettes," Lonos said, putting his hand in his pocket. He pulled out a ten dollar bill and handed it to the man. "Keep the change."

The man's eyes widened. "For true?"

Lonos nodded and said in a serious tone, "Don't repeat this to anyone. Not even the police."

"Uh?"

"Hold your tongue, save your life."

"I no tell nobody da thing."

You just told me, Lonos thought.

Lonos spotted Chief Dolo's shiny blue Ford in traffic as he got in his jalopy. His decision to continue the investigation was no longer of concern to the police chief. But not waiting for things to cool off before pursuing Manor again would only cause unnecessary trouble. It wasn't his job to pacify anyone. He had to fight smart. He could wait a few more days before confronting the man.

—✳✳✳✳✳✳✳✳✳—

Manor and his wife enjoy scheduled sex and had just finished a section when they saw Boatswain's car drive up to the front gate. He got out of his car and stared at the iron gate as if it was a camera.

"This better be good," Manor said into his phone. It came out loud and clear over the gate speakers.

"Mr. Manor, it's me," Boatswain said, looking around.

Manor stared at the man and smiled. Standing five feet tall, looking at the man, you wouldn't think a man that small can make a woman happy. But a lot of women said Boatswain did make them happy, a five-foot man with six-foot ideas.

"I know it is you," Manor replied. "What the hell do you want?"

"Mr. Manor, my wife has hired that woman lawyer, Grace. I need your help. Can I come in?"

"Wait."

Boatswain forced a fake smile and said, "Thanks."

Manor is the king of his little empire, with the expected ego of one who rules by his decree or thinks he should. The granting, or denying, of a simple request with a *yes* or *no* answer should take a few minutes, but that would be too easy for anyone asking. An hour passed before Manor informed Boatswain that he is to report to Diallo's office at nine o'clock in the morning.

—*********—

Diallo was gathering proper paperwork for the case when Boatswain walked in at nine o'clock sharp, unannounced. When Grace worked for him, no one passed her desk without him knowing. Manor had talked him into hiring one of his girlfriends who did not know her head from her ass; a beauty with absolutely no brains.

"Mr. Manor sent me," Boatswain said in a simple bold tone when he walked in. "Did he call you yet?"

"Did my secretary said it was okay to come in?"

Boatswain studied his fingers as he thought of an answer.

"I don't allow people to just walk into my office without me knowing they are coming," Diallo said. "Do you understand?"

Boatswain face lit up. "Oh, I see," he said, smiling. "You don't want your wife catching you with a woman here, is that it?"

Diallo stared at the dark circles under Boatswain's eyes, the eyes of a drinker. "That's not *it*," he said, but did not give the reason. "Manor called me last night and asked to represent you. I told him I would."

Boatswain thanked Diallo profusely for taking on the case, and did not care that he got only a nod.

Diallo searched in the desk top drawer for a pen and pad. "I need to get some information from you," he said.

Boatswain nodded, his eyes darting around the office. Diallo hadn't asked what information he needed, so Boatswain said to him, "I thank God that I was not born a Congo man, or a woman."

Diallo wondered why the man had said that, but remained silent. He resented Boatswain and wished to strike back at his meanness, but he was determined to get richer and Manor was paying him well to represent his watchdog.

"A Congo man is less than a dog," Boatswain went on, "and a woman is, well, you know." He laughed a long high-pitched laugh.

The laugh itself could be the source of much humor, Diallo did not laugh.

Ignorance is the most terrible disease in the world. It is the most painful, the most destructive, and the most contagious disease. It causes people to suffer all their life, and Africa is plagued with it.

Boatswain had no idea Diallo's wife was so-called Congo, although she wasn't. She was not an Americo-Liberian, but her ancestors had migrated to Liberia from the Caribbean, the West Indies. He was convinced Boatswain did not even know who was Congo and who wasn't. Most people didn't and he wasn't sure of himself either. Anyone who did not speak a Liberian native language, or ancestors had migrated from overseas, was Congo. According to history, the Congos were recaptured Africans rescued from intercepted slave ships and taken to the colony, which later became Liberia after becoming an independent state.

Diallo forced himself to draw tolerance for his miserable client without forging some form of relationship, not even an uneasy friendship.

"You compare someone who is Congo to a dog? Why?"

"Because they stole Liberia from the native people," Boatswain said. "They kept us as servants after stealing our land."

"I don't think being Congo makes you a dog. I am grateful I was not born a woman though," Diallo laughed. "That would be too great a burden."

Boatswain slumped back in the chair and picked his nose with a thumb. Based on his client's demeanor alone, Diallo knew they wouldn't be walking into trial with a reputation for reasoning, responsibility or calmness. Being legal counsel for a formal war lord was like walking a tight rope through fire.

"When we go to court, do your best to make a good impression," he said to Boatswain. "Do not show emotion or make threats. Talk in a relaxed tone."

"Why?"

"Because you stand a better chance of winning a request if the Judge is happy with your behavior."

"He's just another human being," Boatswain argued.

"He has the power to make decisions for you and for your wife," Diallo explained. "The Judge decides the outcome. He will listen to everything and take notes. He will ask questions, so remember to answer in a calmed voice, no shouting."

"I thought Mr. Manor said we might not go to court. Where is all this advice coming from?"

"We might not have to go to court if we can get things settled," Diallo replied. "Maybe we can get Grace, or your wife, to drop the charges, especially the rape charge."

"They will drop it," Boatswain said with confidence.

In a hurry to get the man out of sight, Diallo hurriedly got all the necessary information he needed; his and his wife's personal information, their property and Boatswain's medical history.

Later that morning, he filed a temporary order for custody of the Boatswain's family house and their business.

Chapter 18

FOR ALEX MASSAQOUI, not being part of the men's legendary unfaithful club suited him just fine. He cared about his students at Tubman High school and idolized his girlfriend more than she cared to recognize. He'd accepted her only mistake and had forgiven her for it. The problem you see is, it's so much easier to fall in love and so much more complicated to fall out of it. Alex had fallen in love with Grace.

Falling in love is, the both of you laugh, you cry, you share midnight feelings and eventually have tender sex. To Grace, nothing had changed. As far as Alex was concerned, it had. Things between them were fundamentally good, but slightly different since meeting RJ Douglas.

They had nurtured the same hopes and dreams, assuming they would do better than most couples, and had actually managed the complicated and lonely period during her pregnancy with the other man's child. Grace had cheated on him, but she had never lied to him. His love for her had concealed, not dissolved the pain of betrayal that he needed to go away. Thankfully, they had passed the "working on it" phase of their relationship and moving into their new home together. Grace wasn't *ready* for marriage, while Alex waited for *magic* to happen.

Grace had purchased prime property in Sinkor and she and Alex reached a verbal agreement to build their home together. The blueprint detailed three bedrooms with full baths, one half bath, a laundry room, a family room, living room, dining room, a home office, and a full-size kitchen. A garage attached to the house had a two-bay arrangement. One parking slot for their slightly used silver Toyota Corona, while the other side would be used for a meeting place and storage.

Alex came up with a reasonable budget for a modern house, and from start to finish, they decided on furniture, decorations, floor tiles, appliances, windows, doors, arts, interior and exterior paint colors, and draperies; their home, joint decision. While they show off the latest progress on their home, Alex rubbed her back showing pride and satisfaction.

For safety, they wanted to make sure the noxious smell of fresh paint would no longer be in the house when they move in.

__**********__

Their new office was also ready for business, serving as Alex's accounting office and Grace's law office. The entrance was covered by a black canopy bearing the name of the firm—Law Office of Grace Q. Pupoh, Esq.—in large white block letters. Seven-thirty a.m., Grace stood in front of the building hungry to satisfy the needs of her clients. She closed her eyes tightly before putting the key in the door of her new office and offered a short, but sincere, prayer of thanks. Grace unlocked the door, turned the knob and stepped into her new world.

Lawyers are slaves to precedents because that's how they are trained. The arbitrary way in which they charged clients, the billable hour practice, that is, bears no clear relationship to the service clients are paying for. They never have an understanding of the legal fees and the actual value of that service received. How long their lawyer takes to provide that value has always been irrelevant. Naturally, Grace moved away from the billable hours to a value-based model.

Her legal services would be faster, cheaper and better. She modeled her practice in a way where she would be more of a consultant, rather than a "law" technician selling results, not time. She recognized, being proactive and interactive with her clients would provide maximum value to them at minimal cost to the firm.

No matter who the client is, Grace always gives detailed information on legal services and billing practices. They would be getting good representation, but not unreasonably priced. Most of the litigations coming in were simple and well-defined; wills and uncontested divorces, for instance. She charged a flat fee with an understanding of exactly what that fee will and will not cover, such as filing fees.

On a contingent fee basis in certain types of cases like plaintiff's counsel in automobile accident lawsuits, medical malpractice, personal injury and debt collection, she would take no fee from the client up-front, but would get a percentage. Typically, one-third of the money upon judgment.

Grace had a few clients that fitted in the hourly rate arrangement.

Under this arrangement, an agreed-upon hourly rate between $50 to $200 was paid for the hours worked on their case or matter, until it was resolved. Less than fifteen percent of her clients made up this group.

The Law Office occupied the first floor of a new building on Clay Street, a side street intersecting Camp Johnson Road and Capital Bypass. The office suite consisted of two office spaces with lockable doors and paralegal space, a semi-private interview area with visual access to the reception area. This was created through the use of a glass vision panel in the workstation, utilizing full height panels. There was a room used for a break room and as a copy/printer/fax/file storage room, a small library with lockable door, which doubled as a conference room and workroom for trial preparation, a private bathroom, and the reception/waiting area.

In addition to stationery, office equipments, filing cabinets, and furnishings, Grace stocked supplies: staplers, paper clips, scissors, two-hole punch, three-hole punch, telephone message pads, rubber stamps and inking pads, scratch pads, legal pads, paper cutter, felt-tip markers, staple removers, Scotch tape, desk calendars, pens and pencils, manila envelopes, Rolodex files, coffee cups and equipment, check protector, a large fireproof safe for wills, documents, receivable records, et cetera. Telephones, computer lines, fax lines and internet lines were all ready, completely installed.

Grace determined positions need and put her hiring process into motion. She and Alex developed the key requirements needed for each position; special qualifications, traits, characteristics, and experience. After salary range was determined, the positions were posted under the *Job Opportunities* section in the LJC classified.

Over a hundred interested candidates filled out applications. Selected applicants' resumes and cover letters were screened and interviews scheduled. Grace was clear about each position and their role at the firm; culture fit, technical qualifications, customer responsiveness and knowledge. A Job candidate evaluation form was filled and a second interview was scheduled for sixty qualified candidates against the prioritized qualifications and criteria established. Candidates also participated in different testings required for the positions.

Grace and Alex filled out the candidate's rating forms, checking credentials, references and other qualifying documents and statements. Anyone who had stated qualifications dishonestly, or who had failed to pass the checks, was eliminated as a candidate. Through the entire interviewing process, Grace stayed in touch with the most qualified candidates via phone calls and emails. When that round ended, thirty finalists, people whom they were considering offering the positions, were invited for a third interview.

After informal talks with the candidates about whether he or she was interested in the job at the offered salary and stated conditions, an offer letter was sent to each of the four candidates Grace believed viable; Lutee Andrews, a second-year law student to fill the position of personal assistant to her and Alex, Gbomai Sirleaf, hired as paralegal and office manager, Weyatta Pratt, hired as receptionist and legal secretary, and a 20-year-old freshman studying political science at the University of Liberia, Kaifa Grimes, office boy.

During a lengthy orientation, Grace and Alex assured the staff they would be working hard, but not with the office clock wrapped around anyone's throat. It was extremely important to meet the clients' expectations, a generous compensation was guaranteed and brown-nosing strongly disallowed. They spent the last hour going over the rules; phone use, lunch breaks, office protocol, overtime, et cetera.

Around 9:00 the following Monday morning, a lawyer and her staff were on time and ready for the parade at the Law Office of Grace Q. Pupoh, Esq. A steady stream of excited clients met with their lawyer and toured her new office until 5:00 p.m. Each person received a business card and a pen with the business name and number imprinted on it.

Chapter 19

GIA HAD COUNSELED more couples in their shaky marriage because of cheating than anything else. The person who cheats doesn't easily fit into a particular mold. There are those who will cheat once, feel badly about it and never repeat their mistakes. Some will continue the cheating pattern again and again until they are caught. Others make a lifestyle out of being unfaithful. She'd always advised her clients that if they have a need to know just how to handle a cheating partner, they must first decide how likely it is that their partner will repeat the same behavior over again. Then they'll have to think about whether they trust that partner enough to take their word for it when they say they are sorry. Finally, it takes hard work to build trust that has been damaged.

Considering the sincerity of the person who betrayed you when they ask for reconciliation is not the easiest thing in the world to do. Unless you know your partner very well and can account for their actions, you will probably not be able to reassure yourself that it was a one-time event. Once you get past all of that, move the spotlight onto yourself. Gia tried to do just that.

To forget the betray should not be expected, but the willingness to forgive is important because you have to mean it. The cheater must understand the kind of irreversible damage they have committed. And, once you start mending the relationship, it is like going back to square one. So be sure the conditions that may have caused, or allowed for the betrayal, are eradicated.

The advice Gia would have given her client is that the person who your partner cheated with has to be out of the picture. No friendship, no once in a while gathering; no contact whatsoever. However, if a child had come into the world because of the affair, that's another story.

RJ was afraid that things between him and his wife will never be the same again, but with hard work it can still be good. He checked their chances; Kitty was their common ground and would always be the bridge between them. Strengthening the love he hoped that had remained was up to him. He'd do whatever it takes. Thirdly, he prayed Gia will support him in saving their marriage half as much as he intended supporting her in every way possible.

—***********—

Weeks after finding out about the affair, there had been no tears left to cry but Gia could not face their daughter without crying. Kitty's open laughter and innocent play only heightened her despair of her husband's affair. As she got her daughter ready for bed, choking back tears, she thought. She had to talk to someone. No. Not her parents, even if they adore RJ. They would be overly judgmental. She'd advised her clients not to report every negative thing about their spouse to family. They might be forgiving, but relatives would hold it against that spouse long after they had forgotten.

She should tell Paola who had been a terrific friend. She was all heart, loyal, and had a generous amount of common sense. After all, people are their best when true friends get behind them. An opportunity was at hand as Paola was stopping by the house to drop off some papers from the office.

When Paola got there, Gia let her in and went to finish reading Kitty her bedtime story. Paola walked into the living room and noticed the bronze picture frame on the fireplace. She wondered how come she had missed it before. It had a popular bronze finish with floral and scrolled vine and leaf design. Its base was accented with light pink jewels and pearls. She picked up the frame to admire it. Rather than a photograph, it complemented a wedding prayer:

Dr. Gianina Ricciola & Robert Jenkins Douglas III
Heavenly Father, hear our prayer as we bow before you as a couple. Bless the life we are about to share. Be our guide in all we do and let love shine within us. As we pledge our love today before your altar, may our hearts stay toward you and each other. May our marriage be the reason for tomorrow. Amen.

Paola finish reading it and smiled, quietly admiring the relationship Gia and RJ shares.

Gia walked in a few minutes later and she handed her the papers.

"Thanks," Gia said, forcing a smile.

Paola could easily see that her friend was not herself. Gia had smiled absently while greeting her at the door and answering questions with little thought. They conversed on less serious matters until it was almost time for Paola to leave.

They were quiet for a moment.

"The other day I found out that RJ cheated," Gia's voice broke.

Paola looked at her, surprised. "What!"

Gia's eyes held sadness and she could not repeat it. She fought back the tears, but her hands were shaking. She could not steady them.

"RJ did what?" Paola asked. "Cheated? Are you sure?"

Gia nodded. She couldn't repeat it, and Paola was afraid to ask if the marriage would be over. It couldn't. Not for them. The thought was disturbing.

"How do you know? I mean, who told you?"

"He did."

Paola took in her breath and let it out slowly. She said, cautiously, "Do you know what she looks like? I mean, have you seen her?"

"Yes," Gia replied. "She's a lawyer. She's pretty. A Queen Latifah look-alike, you might say. Do you know the actress, Queen Latifah?"

Paola nodded and said, "Isn't she one of those women comedians? The queens of comedy?"

"Don't tell me you're one of those who think all black people, or all Asians, look alike. Or, is it because her name is Queen Latifah."

"Of course not," Paola smiled with chagrin. "She's not a comedian?"

"I don't know if she's a comedian, but she's an actor. She once acted in a comedy show. Queen Latifah is a musician too. She's done it all. Rap, jazz, and now she's hosting her own TV show. RJ is a big fan."

"Okay, Gia. I do not know the lady," Paola confessed. "Maybe I don't want to know this Queen person, if the woman looks like her."

"Actually, the woman is a Liberian."

"Is she here in Georgia? Have you met her?"

"No, she's not here," Gia rolled her eyes. "She lives in Liberia. And, yes, I met her when we went for his father's trial. Grace was the second chair of the defense team and she wasn't even out of law school yet. She's a smart woman."

"My God! You even know her name. How long did they see each other?" Paola's voice was quiet but firm as she'd begun fishing for more details.

"He told me it was one time. One night. Nothing planned. It just happened."

"Do you believe him?"

"Yes," Gia shrugged. "And, I think I know when it happened."

"It happened while you were in Liberia with him?"

"No."

Paola sighed. "Did you ask him? Or, did he confess," she baited.

"He told me, but it was also based on intuition. I had no evidence. He'd just gotten to Liberia. I called one night, this one night, and he'd not picked up his phone. It was late, past midnight. I'd called the house first, and Mom told me RJ had not come home from the lawyer. I just thought…," Gia couldn't finish. "Well… it doesn't matter. That was the only time I'd called and not reach him. Then I went to Liberia, and we were always together. I always knew where he was. My husband had never given me a reason to suspect him of anything like this. That wasn't something that would cross my mind. I trusted RJ."

"Then it was a mistake," Paola pleaded. "Gia, he made a mistake. He loves you. There's no doubt there."

"It gets worse," Gia whispered.

"Worst?" Paola scowled. "What on earth do you mean, worst? Is he leaving you for her?"

"No. No."

"I don't understand. Are you…."

"That night my husband fathered a child with her," Gia interjected coldly. "A son. Same age as Kitty."

"Oh my god," Paola slapped a hand over her mouth. "I am so sorry," was all she could say.

"The smoke is out of the bottle," Gia said sadly. "Once the smoke escapes the bottle, you cannot get it back. I found out my husband not only had an affair, but fathered a son. I felt like someone had kicked me in my stomach. My heart stop beating. I wish there was a pill I could take that makes love go away. The sad thing is, I can never trust him again."

Paola's response was immediate. "Are you going to leave him?"

"Damn if I know," Gia said in a far away voice. "I'm a marriage counselor and my own marriage is a sinking ship. I have a problem, Paola. I don't know how to be angry with my husband without hating him."

Gia's legs could not hold her up, she sank into her chair. Paola looked at her with filled comprehension and remain standing.

"Our marriage has never been crowded," Gia continued, "but our relationship has. There's no difference. We had a commitment. We were engaged, committed."

The comment had left Gia's eyes dead. They appeared as if she'd cried every tear inside of them. Paola waited, wondering anxiously whether there were other things Gia had found out. She wanted to ask, but knew that being direct was not the proper thing to do. It was appropriate to allow the venting to continue.

"I remember something," Gia whispered, as if a light bulb had come on in her mind. "The day RJ introduced me to Grace, this was at the house after the funeral. I saw Grace gave my husband a certain look. I've always looked at RJ that way. He's that type of man, Paola. I've seen other women look at him that way."

"Gia, he made a terrible mistake," Paola said, as if pleading. "I know for sure that he loves you. RJ is a good man. He loves you very much."

"Love has nothing to do with it," Gia said and got up. "People don't cheat because they no longer love you."

Before Paola could ask what that meant, RJ picked that moment to get home. The door opened and he emerged. Gia caught his gaze and crossed her arms, creating a wall between them. But his pleading eyes won, and she conceded a kiss on her lips. Then RJ went to greet Paola with a friendly kiss on the cheeks, but she could not meet his eyes. And he knew why.

"I was just leaving," Paola excused herself. Then her voice drifted toward Gia. "I would like to take Kitty to the park tomorrow, if you don't mind."

Gia flashed a grateful look.

"I'll see you tomorrow then," Paola said.

RJ watched his wife's best friend walk out of their home and prayed all the respect she had for him had not suddenly been shelved. Even if it comes to that, he hoped of solving that problem. Paola was like family.

Chapter 20

MEL HAD TWO stops to make on her way home; one was to drop off expensive fabrics at the tailor shop and for measurements, and the other was Sophia's Ice Cream Shop to pick up some ice cream for Tapee.

She reached the tailor shop and went inside, but had to wait while the apprentice went to get him. Mel had not heard the person sneaked up behind her when a whispering voice said into her ear, "Where can I buy a smile like that?"

The accent was neither Liberian nor American, but the luxury fragrance of Chanel No. 5 branded the prowler to be a woman of substance. Chanel is synonymous with that of the elite. Turning to see her intruder, Mel said, "And, you are?"

Mel had no idea who she was, but the woman had the grace to blush. She looked elegant, wearing a simple black skirt suit with a lovely string of pearls, everything just so perfectly displayed. Her beauty burned with an inner fire. She was so beautiful, it hurt anyone's heart. Mel's heart lurched and her smile widened. *I've got to use that line*, she made a mental note.

"I saw you at the airport the other day, but wasn't fast enough to reach you. I'm Adriana LeRoux," the woman introduced herself, smiling.

At the same moment, both women said, "What do you do in Liberia?"

"You first," Mel chuckled.

Eyes fixed, Adriana replied, "Business."

Her eyes were sparkling. Mel waited for more but the woman said nothing. She was only smiling, or was she flirting?

"Just business?" Mel asked. "What type of business? Or is it a secret? I could find out."

"Oh yeah?"

"Yes."

They were both flirting.

"Of course I will tell you," Adriana said, teasingly. "I manage my family's cement business. We export cement out of South Africa to Liberia, Ghana and Senegal."

"Business must be good," Mel said. With all the rebuilding," she added.

"You can say that," Adriana charmed.

"I can see that."

Adriana chuckled and said, "I detect an accent... you are not Liberian. So what's an American girl doing in Liberia? I'm sure you are not anxious to tell me anything about yourself either."

"Well, there's nothing to tell. I don't have any secrets. I work in the health business with WHO."

"You're a nurse?"

Mel laughed.

"You are not a nurse?"

"I multi-task... I'm an ER physician."

Adriana looked embarrassed and impressed. "That's quite a job, playing god for the needy."

"Not playing god... I'm one of those who like dealing with desperations and the emergency room suits me."

"I see," Adriana murmured.

Silence hung between them as the two women studied each other, admiringly. *How gosh damn cute she is*, Mel thought, then chided herself. *Nothing but trouble for you, Dr. Douglas, some old habits are just hard to die.*

"How do I call you," Adriana asked, breaking the silence.

"Dr. Douglas, like everybody else," Mel said, knowing the woman was asking for her phone number.

"Okay, may I have your number?"

"Of course," Mel said, and right away pulled the pen out of her bag. She jotted the number on a napkin. "That's my phone number in America, but you can reach me no matter where I am. If I don't pick up, leave a number... I'll call you back the first chance I get."

"Thank you, Dr. Douglas," Adriana mimicked, taking the napkin. She pulled out her phone and punched in the numbers off the napkin.

"It's real," Mel said, sensing what Adriana was doing.

"I know. I did not want to lose it. And, now you have mine."

Mel's Blackberry chirped. She did not answer. The Blackberry stopped.

Moments later it rang again.

"Not me this time," Adriana assured. "Must be someone important."

Mel looked at the phone. "Excuse me," she said and turned away for privacy. She pushed the button and said, "Hold on," and then turned back to Adriana. "It is an important call."

"Of course," Adriana said. Then she gave Mel a smile that said more than words, and walked away. Had she been a puppy, she would have been wagging her tail in delight.

"What is it, honey?" Mel said into the phone as soon as Adriana was gone.

Tapee reminded her about his ice cream. She assured him she had not forgotten, but was running late because she had to stop by the tailor shop.

"I'll soon be home," she said, ending the call.

The tailor returned, his apprentice in tow, and apologized for having kept Mel waiting. He instructed her to hold out her arms for measurement, bringing a tape measure around her waist, then her arms, then across her shoulders and finally her bust size.

"Your measurements have not changed," he noted, marking the numbers on a pad. "Most of my customers won't come for measurement every time they need something new made."

"I like my suits properly fitted."

"I know," he said, laughing.

"What's funny? Why are you laughing?"

After a moment of thought, he said, "Dr. Douglas, you are the only customer who doesn't mind me taking measurements when you come to have something new made."

"Is that right?"

"Yeah," he nodded. "The women bring their garments for me to go by and the men are always in a hurry."

"Ask her," the apprentice said unexpectedly.

"Ask me what?"

The tailor hesitated.

"Ask me what?" Mel repeated.

"The boy wants to know why you don't have me sew you dresses... just pant suits."

A soft smile fluttered at the edges of her lips as she looked at the apprentice. *Maybe because I don't wear women's clothing*, Mel wanted to say. Instead, she asked, "You don't think that women should wear pants?"

The apprentice spoke his reply in Mandingo, his native Liberian language.

"What did he say?" Mel asked the tailor.

He gave a rueful grin and said, "The boy think you are too pretty to wear men's clothes. He said that you are much prettier than the girls in the movies."

"I will tell my husband that," Mel teased.

The boy eyed her warily.

"I'm joking," Mel confessed.

He let out his breath and hurriedly walked out.

"Why is he running?" Mel wanted to know. "Is it something I said?"

"It is because of your husband," the tailor said. "A man can kill another man for woman business."

Mel half-smiled. "Well, tell him no one is going to kill him because of me, that's for sure."

The tailor stood in silence, processing the designs of the Prada and Gucci suits Mel had shown him. Exceptionally talented, but Mel was the only client that paid him an outrageous amount of $300 for a suit. The man had no idea that in the world of luxury tailoring, the suit he'd pirated so well would have cost this client $2,600. The dinky sharp-needle establishment made outfits that fitted so perfectly, Mel's suits impressed just about everybody.

When the tailor finished, he said, "Bring the boy so I can take his measurements. I will make him a suit with whatever material remains."

Mel didn't know what to think. Was he offering to make Tapee a suit? Or was he adding up a tab? She could afford it and wouldn't mind him making a suit for Tapee. She waited, rather than jump the gun.

Her silence had its effect.

"I would be doing it for free," the tailor offered.

Mel smiled, just thinking of Tapee wearing a suit that matches hers.

Chapter 21

AT ONE TIME, just before and mostly during the war, it seems as if laws were looked at as mere suggestions. Liberia has never been lawless, yet most criminals don't see it that way. There has always been provisions of Magisterial Courts located throughout Monrovia and the various counties in the country. These Magistrate Courts have civil and criminal jurisdiction. However, in very serious cases, including rape, murder or burglary, the Magistrate Courts must refer to the Circuit Courts after preliminary hearings are conducted.

With law in place, even the most commendable, clear cut, or scandalous cases made absolutely no progress unless an often bewildering succession of "fees" and costs were continuously being paid. To pursue the case through the police or court of law, victims ended up spending more money than what was owed them. This made them to be the loser in the process. At the Temple of Justice, those employed in civil services were there only to make money, mainly from taking bribes; from office to office, up to the top.

Nowadays, rebuilding efforts were also in the justice system.

The law says that when you sue a person, you must give formal notice to the other side that you have started the legal process. In the same way, when you are already involved in a case and file papers with the court, you are required to give the other side notice of the paperwork you have filed. The legal way to give formal notice is to have the other side *served* with a copy of the paperwork that you have filed with the court.

The divorce case would not move forward until documents were served. Grace prepared the Service of Process, the formal court document that notifies all parties involved in the lawsuit. The court document could have been served at Boatswain's attorney's office or his residence, but Grace chose to serve his attorney's office as well as serve him at his workplace, the main office of the Monrovia Police Department. Rather than have Kaifa take it to Boatswain, she would take it herself.

No one has ever had the nerve to oppose Cheah Boatswain until now.

"Are you Cheah Boatswain?" Grace asked, standing within normal speaking distance of the man.

Boatswain laughed. "Why? You don't know me? You've been in my face several times and you still don't know me? You should ask my wife. You are her lawyer, she can tell you if I'm Cheah Boatswain or not."

"I'm serving you a summons for a lawsuit, Mr. Boatswain," Grace said sternly, handing over the court documents in front of several police officers and office workers.

One police officer standing near saw it and sighed, blowing out a low whistle. Boatswain had never been sued, to anyone's knowledge.

Boatswain opened the envelope, unfolded the document and read it. He looked up from the papers and the expression on his face had changed dramatically.

"I have witnesses that I served you those papers," Grace said to him. "Your lawyer has copies too."

Boatswain mumbled something and waved her off.

"See you in court," Grace said and walked out of the office, then through the corridor, like Moses in the Bible walked the parted Red Sea. Police officers and civic workers going about the day's business scurried out of her way.

She was out the door and heading to the court when her phone rang. Grace picked up without looking to see the caller.

"Hello?"

"You are in serious trouble, young lady," Diallo's voice came over the receiver.

"You know something I don't know?"

"You're heading into deeper waters. So here's a little advice for you. CeRue Manor never goes through channels, he goes direct."

"Good," Grace replied. "Because I'm heading back to the court to take the Proof of Service document." She hung up.

__**********__

It was obvious there was something in the served documents to get Boatswain fired up. He left his office as quickly as his feet could take him to Judge Amos.

"That woman, Grace," Boatswain vented, shaking his head, "is nothing but an attack dog. She is not a real lawyer."

"I don't care what she is," Judge Amos replied. "We will wear her down and break her will. Man was never put on earth to be made shame by women. Don't worry, Boatswain... don't worry."

Boatswain vs Boatswain had Grace smack in the middle between the mighty and the weak, facing tight spots, meager resources, a vast army of problems and seemingly dead-end solutions. What they did not know is, what made Grace different is she did things what other people only talked about. And, when she decided to do something, she'd do it whether anyone wanted her to do it or not. Once a brilliant law student, fiercely determined and blessed with enormous stamina, the woman was intellectually sharp so she could easily cut arrogant men down. Sometimes it took time and sometimes it did not.

Court matter is not a short procedure, but it's appalling when the magistrate postpones a hearing giving a reason on the perpetrator's behalf; a tactic to discourage the victim when he's taken a bribe. The dance goes on for months while the victim suffers financial struggles, even for bus fares to go back and forth to court. And those who continued to pursue justice, the Magistrate suggests more strongly, there is little or no evidence against the perpetrator.

As far as Grace was concerned, Judge Zee Amos was a pathetic and a dishonorable judge. For as long as people can remember, he sat on the bench like a god, taking from the poor their civil rights with a flagrant disregard for the law. Judge Amos was among a handful of judges who were bought off cheaper than a five cent bread.

Everyone knew Cheah Boatswain was a nasty police officer. He'd been accused of cracking the head of several handcuffed suspects, beating juveniles, hiding evidence, stealing from suspects, defying direct orders, lying and falsifying police reports. It seems in spite of all his misconduct, there was nothing Boatswain could do to lose his badge.

The country had a long history of influenced peddling and corruption, stretching back decades. Politics had been eating away at the police departments for so long it seems impossible to tell what was the norm. Government leaders had been accused of taking bribes, accepting illegal campaign contributions and covering up criminal wrongdoing.

Boatswain basically bragged about all the things he'd done and how he got away with everything. He joked about his misconduct and those overly ambitious 'women' authorities who have been unable to get him fired. He was proud of being called a thug.

Cheah Boatswain challenged his wife's lawyer to name names and show what she had on him. On the next court date, the lawyer did. Grace presented as matter-of-fact reality of power and the influence Mr. Boatswain had on the entire magistrate system; how it went hand in hand with corruption.

As expected, Judge Amos ruled there was no evidence against the perpetrator and that Tomah wanted to use the new rape law falsely against her husband, probably because of some other dispute.

"First, she accused him of having plenty girlfriends," Judge Amos reprehended. "Now, rape. Rape? Only someone who's stupid would say that, not a wife. What is expected to happen between a man and his wife is not a crime."

"The woman is a victim, she's not stupid," Grace argued. "Next court hearing, I will have more evidence."

At the next hearing, when Grace ended the introduction of evidence in the case, Judge Amos blasted so much bullshit about the lack of evidence that the courtroom had to be fumigated after he had finished.

Chapter 22

A HEARTBREAKING UNDERSTANDING had come between them. RJ could not bear to hear his wife's accusation although it was the truth. Gia was speaking of characters he shrugged; a cheater, a liar. What he was being accused of spoke out those characters, as his love for her had called him from a world of lust. She was more than enough to fulfill all his wants, wishes, and desires, but he had found relief in pressure of his father's trial in a one night affair and had fathered a child. Grace had been too much a temptation to escape. She was a special woman he'd admired.

Now RJ must petition the woman he had hurt for understanding and forgiveness. The only hope he had was her love for him, and he wasn't sure it could stand the blow of distrusts or deceit. Her heart was no longer eagerly waiting to love him. It was broken and RJ had to find a way to fix it, then he would beg for forgiveness. He must make it possible for her to believe his words again, trust him.

Heaviness in the heart of a person makes it stoop, but a good word makes it glad. Gia's heart weighed heavily on her husband's affair. She wasn't sure of any word, good or grand, that would lift her spirits. She heard his car drive into the garage and drew in her breath. The back door opened and closed, then she heard footsteps.

"Hi, honey," RJ greeted and moved in for a kiss.

Gia immediately made an evasive maneuver and his suspicion was confirmed. She wasn't waiting like before, for his presence to light up the room and lift her heart. It did not. She had the skills to make her husband feel he was the most important person on earth, as much as the skills to freeze him out.

"Why the old duck and roll?" he teased, luring his wife.

She drew a deep breath. Gia felt hopeless and she had not felt hopeless ever in her entire life. She saw her husband's affair like a porn movie, loose women without morals, who have sex and look like they are the only people in the world who enjoy it. This made her heart heavy.

"I… ah…," she turned away and lowered her head. A few deep breaths later, she looked at RJ. "I can do nothing for us at this point, but I can do something for myself," she said.

RJ took her by the elbow and steered her into the living room. "Sit, please," he indicated the chair nearest to the entrance. She sat with her hands in her lap. He got down on his knees, settled his gaze on her eyes and clasped her hands. "Now, let me explain it again," he said calmly.

If what her husband had done wasn't so awful, she could have looked at him. It was impossible to. Gia held back the tears pricking her eyes. If she allow herself to give into them, she would not be the calm woman he wanted. They both understood the seriousness of the situation and RJ had reacted with the appropriate amount of guilt and remorse. Very well then, if he must make her understand it by explaining it again.

"No need to explain it *again*," Gia said, sarcastically.

"Honey, I made a terrible mistake, that's all it was," he pleaded. He sounded as if his doom was imminent. "I swear."

Since the confession they'd slept in their bed together, but now Gia sleeps with her back toward him. She says 'Good morning' only to be polite, and barely says anything after that.

Although there was no one at home beside them, Gia glanced around out of habit. Kitty was spending the night with Paola. They had every reason to keep her out of their edgy moments. They'd tried keeping things as if everything was normal, yet their marriage and family could be destroyed by the affair RJ called a mistake.

He took both her hands in his. It was what she'd expected. They performed a short tug-of-war until she gave in.

"I'm begging you, honey," he said with half a smile. "I made a mistake… a terrible one too."

She shrugged.

He leaned forward and did a forehead kiss. "I am so, so sorry. I love you," he whispered, squeezing her hands and massaging the knuckles with his thumb.

It was a soothing motion, but there was nothing reassuring in his sad expression. The thought of her husband making love to another woman made her gut churn. Gia couldn't bring herself to look up at him. She forced herself to turn her face away and stared over his shoulder instead.

"Honey," he pleaded.

Gia made a quick glance at his face.

Forehead lined with concern, his eyes met hers. "I want to fix things like the way it was," he pleaded.

"That's not possible, RJ," she muttered.

She'd finally spoken, but it was not what he wanted to hear.

Gia leaned forward, slightly so that she looks at his eyes. "You can't un-ring *that* bell, RJ. Can you?"

Her voice sounded strong. She'd hardly ever called him by his name. It was no longer, 'honey' or 'baby'. She was actually calling him by his name, *RJ*, every time she wanted his attention. The dreadful thing was, she hardly wanted his attention lately. He attempted a smile, smiles were a good way to make the other person feel comfortable. Not that Gia was uncomfortable. RJ was worried. Not quite afraid, but certainly apprehensive.

"The important thing is, I will try… impossible or not," he replied.

Gia made a sound of protest, except it came out a whimper. Their future was very much uncertain.

__**********__

Mel had flown into Atlanta to surprise them. That's what she had told Gia, but the woman knew better. Mel had come to her brother's rescue. After dinner, she and Gia remained sitting at the table while RJ got Kitty ready for bed.

"I've always believed it was possible for a couple to stay with each other all their lives. Now I don't. Do you think that is even possible?" Gia asked Mel.

At first Mel didn't believe she, of all people, had been asked that. "Of course," she said, incredulously. "It's possible."

Gia chuckled. "Quite frankly, I don't know which hurt more, the affair or the secret. If Grace hadn't gotten pregnant, I would have never known my husband cheated. Your brother kept that from me. What scares me is, RJ was so comfortable doing it."

"RJ didn't confess because it was something that meant nothing to him, that's all."

"Yeah? Is she the only one?"

"I'm sure she's the only one," Mel said, stressing *only*.

"Well, how do we know this? He's good at keeping secrets. And, don't tell me he was protecting me. That's bullshit!"

"I know my brother, that's why I can bet my life. Grace is the only one and the only time."

"I know my husband too, or I thought I did."

Mel furrowed her brow.

"Tell me something," Gia challenged. "Since when did his respect for women changed?"

"It hasn't."

"Well, if Grace meant nothing to him, then it has," Gia disagreed. "That night simply meant having four bare feet in bed? Is this what you are telling me?"

"No."

"Or, was it a pussy he was just passing through? Opportunity came knocking? The RJ I thought I knew would have gone around it."

"You know RJ doesn't see women that way."

"Then she meant something to him!"

"Gia, you mean more to my brother than any other person in the world. You two have a bond so special, there's nothing to compare it to... not even two peas in a pod."

"It had nothing to do with me, Mel. Men cheat for so many reasons. It's my job to make sense of why they cheat on their wives. I deal with that sort of thing every day. Every man knows, at some level, that cheating is wrong. But they do anyway. The number one reason why some men will opt to shed their devotion and cheat on their partner is because they can get away with it. To me, that's the worst."

"Why is that?"

"To do something just because you can get away with it is too damn selfish... what the eyes don't see, the heart doesn't feel. One of my patients actually told me, as long as his wife didn't know about the affair, he wasn't hurting her. He really believed that. Another guy told me men cheat because, 'Women let us... they are quick to forgive.' They cheat and place the blame on their spouses. He's right about the forgiving part. Most women are too willing to forgive men for their unfaithful behavior. Maybe it's their fear of being alone. But not every woman, I told him."

"What happened to that guy?"

"His wife divorced him."

"Ouch!"

"Look, Mel... we are not talking about one of my patients here. RJ knows me and what I stand for. He made that choice. Trust has never been an issue with us. Everything about my husband draws me towards him and keeps me wanting more. I was falling in love with RJ while he was falling in love with me. That's what has always made our relationship special.

"We understand the motivation of each other's character, good and bad. The wonderful sex doesn't just exist in service to the romance in our marriage. Our personal desires immutably intertwine, creating a plot that is constantly compelling. Do you know what my husband gave me on our second anniversary?"

"What?"

"A simple black plaque with gold writing that says, '*Always kiss me good-night*.'"

"That's my brother," Mel smiled. "Sometimes I wish I was as thoughtful as he is. I know he loves you very much."

"Why the hell did he cheat?"

"Maybe it was only a quick escape from his problem, Gia," Mel suggested. "You know… maybe an anesthetic he thought he needed because of the pressure from Dad's trial."

Gia gave Mel a look that said, I know you can do better than that.

"Okay, Gia," Mel said, correctly reading into her sister-in-law's raised brows. "I'm not making an excuse for him, I'm just thinking out loud here. I used to cheat because I was afraid of commitment. But, RJ has never been afraid of that. He is Mr. Commitment itself. I can't answer for him. I don't know why he did it. Maybe loneliness, I guess. I don't know," she shrugged. "I know it wasn't love. Please, Gia, don't mistake loneliness for love. He loves you."

Gia sighed and shrugged.

"Look, whatever happened, happened," Mel continued. "RJ screwed up, okay? I mean… he really fucked things up. It can be fixed, right?"

Gia remained silent.

"Right? Come on, Gia… that man loves you. He adores you. I've seen him show you more than he tell you. I don't know of too many guys who makes sure his wife's car is cleaned and gas-up every Sunday before the week starts, checking the oil, tires pressure, or even vacuuming the inside. He does that every Sunday, football game or not… without you asking him to."

"Oh, isn't that just dandy," Gia interjected. "Mel, that's what a man suppose to do for his wife. I make sure he eats healthy, don't I? Don't you think I'm just as tired as he is when my day is over? Between my practice at the office and teaching at Spelman, I am shit tired. But I get home on most nights, tired or not, and make him home-cooked meals. And as far as taking care of our daughter, we are both her parents. He is suppose to help bathe her, make sure she eats, get her ready for bed, like I do. He's not doing me a favor when he does that. We both work out of the home… we both should work in the home. I don't get brownie points, he gets no brownie points. We are responsible for Kitty. I don't want you telling me RJ is special because he gives his daughter a bath or read her bedtime stories or wash my damn car. Those are his responsibilities."

"Okay," Mel raised her hands, surrendering. "I see your point," she said, then muttered, "although most men don't see it that way."

"Really?"

"Either way, my brother loves you. I want you to keep that in mind. Okay?"

"Uh-huh."

"Pleaseeeeeee," Mel pleaded.

Gia gave an impish smile. "Most men? That includes you?"

"I see you still have your sense of humor."

Gia laughed. She sounded good.

"Keep me out of it and let's focus on my brother here," Mel playfully scolded. "RJ doesn't want to lose you over something he did," she said, seriously, then added, "not something so meaningless."

"He's afraid I'm going to divorce him, that's why he asked you to come. Didn't he?"

"He didn't," Mel lied. "I missed y'all."

Gia raised her brows again. She knew how close the siblings were, as if they were twins. RJ condided in his sister, everything. "You missed us?"

Mel responded with a smile.

"I thought so," Gia muttered, then said, "We've missed you too."

Mel's smile continued.

Gia had counseled enough couples to know the ugliness of divorce. There is something pitiful about a person when they are about to get divorced or is already going through a divorce. No one likes the formal dissolution of their marriage—the big D, DIVORCE.

Divorce is like a disease, something one might not get recovery from. Some cry, get depressed, overeat and gain weight or stop eating at all and lose weight. Some sleep into a macho mood that fails them. At times it's so obvious, it's pitiful. She understood the deep seated fear of divorce.

"Wipe that smile off your face," Gia said, cutting her eyes. "He's not going to get off easy.... if he gets off."

Mel sighed. "Want some free advice?"

"Do I have a choice?"

"No," Mel said. "You and RJ do the family a favor. Keep the lawyer-cap and doctor-coat, off."

__**********__

The following afternoon, strolling thru Stone Mountain Park, Mel's arm looped around her brother's arm, she told events of their childhood and checked to see a smile on his face. She was desperate to cheer him up. They talked about friends and family, and regrets they each had from the past.

"What were her exact words?" RJ pressed. "And, don't give me no gibberish."

"If you want Gia to forgive you, you must forgive yourself," Mel said. "Move quickly before she even thinks about divorce."

RJ felt his stomach twist with fear as he held her gaze. "Divorce?"

"Isn't that what cheating husbands get?" Mel teased.

RJ's face reeked with misery.

"Oh, RJ, your wife isn't going to leave you," Mel playfully shoved him. "Gia loves you too much. But I don't know if she can forgive you. Not anytime soon, I think."

"Whose side are you on?"

"You cheated on your wife!"

"Well... isn't the pot calling the kettle black."

"I don't have a wife," Mel poked at his arm. "Ah! It had to be the powers of breasts," she chuckled. "Is that why it happened? How can you not know this?"

"Know what?"

"My dear brother, everyone knows what they do *to* a man, and what they do *for* a woman, especially under the right touch."

RJ stopped, un-looped their arms, and gazed at his sister.

"What?" Mel asked innocently.

"I'm serious, Mel," he protested. "I'm damn near close to losing my wife and you're acting crazy here. Be serious for once."

"I'm not crazy, RJ. I'm serious. I was going to say… everyone knows female nipples are the devil's work. If you touch one and don't pray enough, you go straight to hell."

"What!" RJ said, trying to keep a straight face.

"I swear," Mel said, raising one hand, also trying to keep a straight face. "Ask the Salvation Lady… Mrs. Vinton."

Two seconds later, they were both laughing; RJ in stitches, holding his stomach.

Chapter 23

MEL RETURNED TO Liberia and Rufus Bohn arranged dinner for the two at Posh. He was waiting at the entrance when she arrived.

"Hope I didn't keep you waiting long," she greeted him with a hug and kisses on the cheek.

"I just got here," he said. "I saw you parking and waited so we can walk in together. Let's go to the bar, I'll buy you a drink. I certainly need one before we sit."

Inside customers crowd the restaurant and bar area along a wave of cheerful busyness. Conversations echoed everywhere as the scent of wine and liquor hung heavy, complimenting the aroma of gourmet cuisine. They walked up to the bar. Bohn ordered a cosmopolitan from the bartender and asked Mel what she was having.

"Whatever you're having," she answered.

"Two," Bohn said to the bartender who nodded.

They waited for their drinks as the bartender crushed some ice, added a couple of measured grey goose vodka, a hint of Cointreau, and a measure of cranberry juice. Shaken and then poured into two large chilled martini glasses, a squeeze of lime, and their cosmos were ready.

Bohn tasted his first and give the bartender a thumps up.

"It's good," Mel said, after tasting hers.

They settled on their bar chairs.

"So, how does it feel to get away from human's moaning and groaning for a change," Bohn asked.

"You sound like Katharine," Mel said, meaning motherly. "She's always so worried about me working a lot of hours. That's my job. That's what I enjoy doing, helping sick people."

"But a little break wouldn't hurt, will it?"

"No, I suppose."

They were almost finished with their drinks when the maitre d' came to escort them to their table.

"Excuse me, sir, your table is ready," the man said with a rhythmical Liberian accent, smiling. He escorted them to a table for two. Handing each a menu, the man said politely, "Someone will be here shortly to take your order," and excused himself.

"We forgot to tip the bartender," Mel reminded Bohn.

"You mean the mixologist," Bohn corrected.

"The what?"

"These days they are called, *Mixologists.*"

"Who are? Bartenders?"

"Yes. It's just not a fancy name for a bartender, you know. When you can whip out twenty well-made popular drinks, often featuring your own creations, and over fifty draws of beer before the customer knows what happened… while keeping a crowded bar happy, you are a *mixologist.*"

"Well, if you put it that way," Mel nodded.

"And, yes… I tipped him nicely."

"Good, because that was the best damn cosmopolitan I've ever had and I can use another one," Mel said. "I'll order another when the waiter comes to take the order."

Bohn read the menu. "What are you going to have, Dr. Douglas," he asked, looking at her.

"Let's see," Mel said, running her finger down the list. "Any suggestions? I don't come here often so I don't know what they have that is good."

"I like their steak."

"That sounds good. Whatever you're having, order two."

Bohn signaled the waiter and put in their order, "Grilled beef filet steak and continental salad."

"Don't forget my cosmopolitan," Mel reminded him.

"Two cosmopolitans from the mixologist," Bohn added.

The waiter furrowed his brow.

Bohn said, "From the bartender."

The waiter nodded. Mel smiled.

"Would you like some soup, sir?"

"Do you have goat soup?" Bohn asked.

"Yes," the waiter replied.

"Is is spicy?" Bohn asked.

"Not too spicy," the waiter replied.

Bohn looked at Mel to see if she'd like some.

"I'll pass," Mel shook her head.

"One order of the soup," Bohn said to the waiter.

"Anything else, sir?"

"Two bottles of water," Mel said. "We'll let you know if we need anything else later."

The waiter wrote it down, looked at Bohn and waited.

"That's it," Bohn said to him.

"Yes, sir," the waiter said and walked away.

"I hate a damn chauvinist," Mel snapped as soon as the waiter was out of hearing distance.

"What are you talking about?"

"The waiter. He was only interested in getting what you wanted."

"Come on, Mel. I think you're just overly sensitive."

"Whatever," Mel shrugged. "Anyway, aren't you going to tell me about this woman," she baited. "This mysterious South African woman I told you about?"

"Wow. We've gone from chauvinist to curious George?"

Mel chuckled.

"She's rich," Bohn announced.

"How rich?"

"Very rich. In other words… prosperous and with affluent ancient family credentials."

"Umm, sounds interesting."

"Ever heard of Lichtenburg," Bohn said, eyebrows raised.

"Yes, that's where my assignment is… General De La Rey Memorial hospital. It's located in Lichtenburg, South Africa. Don't know much about the place though."

"North West Province, South Africa."

As if speaking to James Bond, the movie spy character, Mel said with a grin, "Well, Mr. Bohn, tell me what I have to look forward to."

Bohn chuckled and said, "Lichtenburg is about 230 km west of Johannesburg. The climate is reasonably comfortable. Frost occurs in the winter, but the days are pleasantly sunny. It was established in 1873 by Commandant H. A. Greeff."

"I'll say," Mel chuckled, thinking *grief*.

Bohn also laughed, getting the joke.

"So, Mr. Good Grief found his way to Africa and found himself a town. Go on," she said, still laughing.

"Lichtenburg means *Town of Light*," Bohn informed.

"Town of Light," Mel repeated. "I'm sure black people didn't see it that way."

"It gets better," Bohn went on. "On March 13, 1926, a man named Jacobus Voorendyk... not sure I'm saying his name right, discovered a diamond on his family farm. Within a year or so, there were over 100,000 fortune seekers on the scene."

"Africa and diamonds," Mel shook her head. "It's like a blessing and a curse."

"Yep... diamonds! Anyway, that diamond rush lasted ten years. Within that time, 1927 to be exact, the largest pure red diamond was discovered there."

"Red diamonds? I never thought there were red diamonds. I know there are black, yellow and pink diamonds, but never heard of red."

"Oh yes, there are blue, gray, chocolate-brown... there's even green diamonds... lime green. Red diamonds are extremely rare... maybe the rarest and most exotic diamonds. There are many jewelers that have never seen a red diamond. The one found in 1927 was flawless and pigeon blood red. The stone was about 33 carats rough, and sold for £66."

"Speak American to me, Bohn. How much is that in our money?"

"About $104."

"A hundred bucks?"

"It was sold for that, but later valued at $150,000."

"Well, somebody got their lips ripped off," Mel laughed. "That's highway robbery."

"That's a tragedy," Bohn agreed. "But get this, today, it's worth about $6,000,000 or even far more. It is the purest red diamond in the world."

"Don't tell me Ms. LeRoux's family owns it."

"No, they don't," Bohn laughed. "But their family is one of the earlier settlers in Lichtenburg. They participated in the diamond business during the ten-year rush. That's the root of their wealth. Pieter LeRoux, her father, now owns the largest cement production company there, and she's daddy's little girl... what she wants is what she gets."

"Bohn, I hear the woman flies her own plane," Mel said, impressed. "Does she really?"

"It's true. She owns a Cessna... let me see... yes, a Citation Mustang.

It cost only 2.5 million US dollars."

"The bitch is rich," Mel laughed. *And, beautiful too*, she thought.

The waiter arrived at the table with two steaming entrée platters and two salad bowls on an over-size tray. He placed an entrée dish in front of Mel first and smiled. The beef filet steak was grilled to her preference, well done, served with stir fried vegetables and garlic roasted potatoes, finished with green asparagus sauce.

Mel thanked him.

"Still a chauvinist?" Bohn baited.

Mel knew what Bohn was getting at and smiled.

"Enjoy your meal, ma'am," the waiter said and put down the salad bowls.

Mel stuck her fork in hers and fed her mouth. "Mmmm… the salad is good."

The greens were fresh, flavorful and anything but bland. It was a mixture of local garden greens tossed with tomato, cucumber, onion and croutons with French dressing.

"You did not answer me," Bohn baited.

"About what?"

"The waiter."

"What about the waiter?"

"Is he, or isn't he."

"Oh, you mean being a chauvinist? He is."

Bohn laughed.

"What's funny?"

"He isn't," Bohn argued. "You see… he assumed, I, being the guy, is going to pay for the food. And you, being my date, would suggest a sizable tip, that is, if you are happy with the service."

"So, you're telling me he just played us?"

"That's not *playing* us, that is simply business."

"Can't argue about that, I intend on leaving him a good tip. The food is good… I got just what I ordered… and he was friendly, I must admit. I almost forgot that you read people."

Mel's last sentence got a laugh out of Bohn. "Then stay away from Ms. LeRoux," he murmured.

Mel put her fork down. She looked up and caught Bohn's stare. "You've been spying on me?"

"No," Bohn answered quickly. "I'm only suggesting."

"She's cute," Mel shrugged. "And, the best way to eliminate temptation is to succumb to it."

"She's dangerous," Bohn warned. "A strong minded woman like Ms. LeRoux is a different kind of animal. She has something that's undiscovered."

"I was only making a joke," Mel chuckled. "Quite frankly, I have no interest in the woman. She just held my curiosity."

"I'm glad to hear it's just that, Mel."

"Well, it is."

"Enjoying your dinner, I hope," Bohn changed subject, then signaled to the waiter, who was there in an instant with the check.

Chapter 24

CHEAH BOATSWAIN CONTESTED his wife's divorce petition and Diallo had thirty days to file a response. Diallo responded on day twenty-nine. To state his client's position in the plaintiff's case, he wrote in the Answer to the Complaint:

Mr. Boatswain denies the allegations made by the plaintiff and also files a counterclaim in conjunction with the Answer; the plaintiff should be denied a divorce, but he is granted one.

During the period of discovery, Grace and the staff gathered enough information to form a file seven inches thick. The documents included any and everything relevant to the case or that may lead to further discovery of information that would be relevant to the case. Documents on the behavior of the defendant, his finances, property owned, medical history of both parties, photographs of the plaintiff's injuries; the list went on and on.

__**********__

Alex thought that when they moved into their new home, he and Grace would have more time together. At least they would be sharing a bed, but sleep was about all they did. They actually went twenty-one days without sex. Alex counted.

Grace office hours went from sixty to seventy-five hours a week after she'd moved into her new office. Her client lists grew by the minute. Nearly every woman in Monrovia that needed a lawyer came to Grace Pupoh. There were more lawsuits with people trying to reclaim lands that relatives had sold illegally—the same property was sold two or three times to different people—and hundreds of appeals by those who had lost litigation more than twenty-five years ago. While she tried to make everyone happy, Alex was very unhappy and had often started their quarrels.

Massaquoi's eleventh grade class was bugging the shit out of him also. They were all so good at figuring out how to get great grades, that they essentially ignored actually studying their books.

Mr. Massaquoi walked into class lugging his heavy briefcase. He stood behind his desk, studying his students. The students were settling down as each sensed his presence. One student raised his hand and asked, "Is there going to be a make-up quiz, Mr. Massaquoi?"

Alex remained silent. He looked at a girl slouched over in the back of the class. Another student looked like he was texting. Alex slammed the book bag on the desk and jolted everyone to full attention.

"Pay attention, because we will never have this discussion again," he dove right in.

No small talk. No "Good morning, folks." Their teacher stood in khakis, a denim shirt and dark blue tie, talking in a tough confident voice.

"Listen. The war has stolen about twenty-five years of your life and its already tomorrow, the day you are preparing for. That's to show you how fast it happens. When you have no future, you will be forced to live in the past. If you're not studying with your heart as well as your brain, you will definitely be one stupid grown-up."

"Stupid grown-up?" they mumbled among themselves.

He had his students' attention.

"The highest mark on the test is a seventy-three… thirty is the lowest. How's that?"

Silence.

"Are the lessons that boring?"

Again, silence.

"Be obsessed about education, whether it's college or trade school," Alex's voice got deeper, and the rhythms got faster. He was passionate though. "Seize the life given you… seize what has been handed to you. Seize the opportunity and make smart decisions." Then he said his words slowly, intending every word to be absorbed, "Because life is a temporary situation. Go and ask the tens of thousands Liberians that lost their lives to stupid adults because other stupid adults allowed it. Education makes a difference. Smart people don't' do stupid things." Then he asked, "Who asked about a make-up quiz?"

The student raised his hand.

"Why should I give a make-up quiz?"

"Mr. Massaquoi," he stammered, "because I know that wasn't my best on the test. I can do better."

"Who else feel the same way?" Alex asked the class. "Be honest."

Half the class raised their hands.

"Who feel they were just not ready?"

Over half the class raised their hands.

"Well, no. I'm not going to give a make-up quiz," he said in the tone of a patient professor.

"Ahaaaaa," grumbling noises roared from the class.

"I am willing to give you another opportunity though," he offered. His voice was barely audible over the blaring disappointment cries. "Did you hear me?"

The boy who was texting, asked, "Opportunity?"

"Yes. And, glad to finally get your attention," Alex chided.

"What opportunity?" The boy asked. "We all know that when the teacher gives a hard test, it is because he wants everybody to fail. Then that's the *opportunity,* so we can pay for better grades."

The class erupted with laughter. Alex furrowed his brow.

The accusation had merit. Some teachers were actually selling good grades, but definitely not Mr. Massaquoi. They weren't helping the students, those teachers were *stupid adults,* depriving the youth of their education.

"Not Mr. Massaquoi," yelled the boy who had asked about the make-up quiz. "Nobody pays for grades here!"

All Massaquoi ever wanted was to teach economics, or at least try to make the students love learning ways to improve their lives. The war had robbed them of all expectations and he'd promised himself he wasn't going to let that happen to them again, not under his guidance. Not even in the middle of his personal life crisis.

Alex held up a copy of *The Richest Man in Babylon* by George Clason.

"What's that, Mr. Massaquoi?" one student asked.

"Your assignment," Alex replied. "This is your make-up quiz."

Grumbling noise again.

The book teaches the primary principles of paying yourself first and living within your means, important knowledge needed to improve one's finances.

"You want us to read it besides our textbook, so you can test us?" the same student asked.

"No," Alex shook his head.

The noise calmed.

"I'm surprised this book isn't part of your textbook… it should be."

The class made disappointment noise again.

"It's a small book, so I don't know what you're all afraid of," Alex provoked.

"We are not afraid," another student challenged. He looked around the class. "Who's afraid? I'm not."

A lot of "I'm not" followed.

"Good, because I don't care," Alex announced.

Laughter erupted.

"The book has a terrific collection of stories of what was written in the early part of the 20th century. It will help you with your money."

With that, he got their attention.

"Tell us how it will give us money," one student challenge.

"You have to read it for yourself," Alex said. "Here's what I would like you to do. Read the book and write a one-page report. And I'm not talking, half a page. I expect a full page. Grades will be scaled on originality. I have only ten copies, so the copy can only be borrowed for just one week. That way, all thirty students will get an equal opportunity to borrow it."

"That's the opportunity?" one student asked.

Alex said, "Yes," and explained the book was an easy read, and no one would have difficulty understanding it. He hoped his students understand they needed to learn how to improve their finances, saving and not spending more than what they'd earn. They would discover how Arkad, the richest man of Babylon, achieved his wealth and hopefully, they can achieve their own wealth. Poor people do the best they can under the circumstances, but give anyone an opportunity and let it be their choice whether to take it or not. Alex was giving his students a chance in the form of knowledge.

The events of the day could not have put Alex in a needier frame of mind. It definitely was more of an emotional overload than anything else. He needed to be needed, to be stroked, and to be told that someone cares. He fumed and pouted all the way home.

__**********__

Alex showed up at the house around seven. Grace had just gotten there herself. She'd given Peace a bath before getting him into his pajamas. Afterward, she showered, lingering under the spray and enjoying the lavish feeling of soap rinsing the sweat from her body after a very busy day. She made Peace peanut butter and jelly sandwich and warm milk, and after supper, read him the African folktale about how greediness is the reason for the spider's tiny waist, his favorite character.

The people of two villages, opposite each other, had invited Spider to a feast. Although both banquets were on the same day, he accepted both invitations. In order to attend the festivity in both villages, he tied a rope around his waist and gave one end of the rope to the people in each village, instructing them to pull the end of the rope the moment the party started. That way, he would join the festivities in one village and wait for the other village to pull their end and join them later. The party started at the same time, and the people in both villages begin pulling at the same time. Both villagers really wanted Spider at their party, so each group tried to pull the hardest, not wanting to let go of the rope. Thus, leaving Spider with a tiny waist.

After the story, Peace crawled into bed without complaint and Grace lie beside him for a few minutes. As soon as he fell asleep, she kissed him before tiptoeing out of his room.

Alex quietly grabbed a bottle of cold beer from the fridge, went to the living room, turned on the TV set, sorted through the collection of African movie DVDs, selected one without much thought and pushed the disk in the player. Grace joined him in the living room and collapsed on the couch, tucking her legs up under her. She watched Alex struggled with whatever it was on his mind, while he watched the movie. He wasn't talkative at all and the room felt suffocating, as the implications weren't clear.

Halfway into the movie, Grace leaned to the side and playfully nudged at his shoulder, wanting his attention. He grunted before looking at her.

"Hard day at school?" she asked.

"Hard day at life," Alex whined, then he yawned.

Grace lay back and continued to watch the movie, an hour to go. Alex stared at the screen, a frown tucked on his forehead. He was quiet, she was tired. Her eyes stayed closed a fraction longer with every blink and she began to melt into the cushions. "Alex, if you're tired, why don't we go to bed," she suggested.

"I didn't say that I was tired," he argued, staring at the half-empty bottle of beer he was nursing. He drank, hardly working on finishing the bottle.

Sensing a fight, she sighed. Communication had not been easy. He'd accused her of drifting and now they were no longer snuggling on the couch or laughing while the cheating spouse got caught on the screen. Rather than fight, she wanted to lie down and go to sleep.

"Well, I'm tired," Grace yawned. She rose to her feet. "Coming?"

"No," he mumbled.

"Are you really watching that movie?"

"I am," he answered without looking up.

Grace said "Good night" without waiting for a response and walked away. She climbed into bed. Her eyelids, no longer heavy, stared.

Listening to the sound of the television fade, Grace lay on her back in darkness wondering what Alex had been seeing in her all along. He had always liked the fire in her, not only when she challenged things, but at all times. Not anymore. It had become smoke in his nose, a fire burning all day, every day, all the time.

Fire. It purifies and condemns. Fire is powerful, the weapon of heroes. Now he seems tormented with the same fire he once admired. The thing is, aspirations, resembling gasoline, is constantly being pumped through her veins as she resiliently fight for the rights of others and work hard at providing her son with the best life has to offer. Grace liked nothing more than the flammable fluid feeding her fire. Busy, busy, busy minding her dealings. Other than being their financial wiz, she wondered, had she given any thought as to where Alex fitted in that life of hers?

Chapter 25

THEY USUALLY FALL into a rhythm of small talk, but it was not today. After a very quiet family dinner, while RJ was getting Kitty ready for bed, Gia jumped into the shower, shampooed her hair and begun scrubbing her scalp vigorously as if to stimulate her brain back into neutral. Twenty minutes later she got out of the shower, wrapped herself in her pink bathrobe and twisted a bath towel into a turban over her wet hair. Gia looked in the mirror and noticed her eyes. Were they bloodshot from the long shower or really because of all that crying, she wondered. She quickly got the bottle of eye-drops out of the medicine cabinet, dispelled drops in both eyes and patted her closed eyes dry. All in time before RJ returned to their bedroom.

"Kitty is tugged in," he said, walking into the bathroom, trying to get his wife talking. "She was already snoring by the time she hit her pillow," he chuckled.

"That's because she's tired," Gia muttered.

"I see you're all ready for bed too. I'll take a quick shower and join you," he said and begun taking his clothes off.

"I'm going to Florida to Mom and Dad for a few days and I'm taking Kitty with me," Gia said in one breath.

Shirt in hand, RJ stopped and furrowed his brow.

"I'm not trying to take your daughter away from you," she added in a flat voice and sighed. "It's best she goes with me. We'll be gone for a few days, that's all."

"A few days," RJ repeated, his voice worrisome. "How long exactly?"

"A week," she shrugged. "A little distance between me and our problems can do us both some good."

RJ continued frowning. After giving a moment of thought, he said,

"Okay, as long as you don't see *me* as our problem."

Gia gave him a matter-of-factly stare.

"I can take a week off and the three of us go," he suggested.

"I need some *alone* time. It may put a different prospective on things."

"A whole week?"

"I need some *alone* time," Gia said again. "I'd rather take Kitty away than one of us leaving the house for a week. Don't you think this is better?"

"What would be *better* is, if the three of us go."

"That's not giving me *alone* time, does it?"

RJ attempted to put his arm around her, she flung it away and quietly walked out of the bathroom. He rested his head back against the wall and closed his eyes.

__**********__

Gia was happy to see her father waiting at the arrival gate. Kitty ran into Valentino's stretched arms.

"Ciao bambina," he greeted, scooping her up.

"Ciao nonno," Kitty replied and kissed her grandfather. "Dovè Abuelita," she said, looking around for Elodea.

"She's at home making you dinner," Valentino said proudly, impressed that his three-year-old granddaughter was learning Italian. "You are very smart, Kitty," he kissed her again, before putting her down.

"Hi, Dad," Gia greeted, and kissed Valentino on both cheeks.

"Hi, Nina," he smiled, "how are you?"

"Fine."

"Just fine?"

"Dad… I'm not here to cry or pout or complain…."

"Okay, Nina. I'll stay out of it," he interjected before she'd finished. "I just wanted to let you know that Robert called."

"Of course he would," she replied. "I don't want to talk about it, okay Dad?"

"Okay, Nina," he nodded, smiling at his daughter with caring eyes.

"Let's get the bags," Gia said. She held Kitty's hand and they walked to baggage claim.

After a quiet dinner of chicken enchilada filled with corn and green chilies, topped with cheddar and jack cheese, a favorite her mother had specially prepared her, Gia read Kitty a bedtime story and tugged her in bed. She took a hot shower and went to the guest bedroom across from

Kitty's. Elodea had changed the bedcovers with a fancy floral patterned quilt—Martha Stewart's Hydrangea—another surprise to lift her daughter's spirits. The set featured blooming flowers in an array of pink, purple and blue hues for a look full of nature-inspired charm. She'd also piled the bed with pillows in case Gia wanted to read. Gia loved every bit of it.

In this very cozy room, curtains drawn, light rain spattering against the window, with the duvet pulled to her chin, Gia felt safe. But loneliness, like a disease, overtakes you in weak moments. She was still mad at RJ and disappointed too, but she missed breathing the familiar man scent of her husband. Loneliness wrapped around her like a damped blanket. Curled up in the comfortable bed, her head on soft pillows, she thought about her life and marriage. She wondered what had made RJ do such a thing, making love to another woman. Didn't he see it as something that could end their relationship? Was the woman or the one night affair, he had carefully put it, worth losing her? Did this woman mean nothing to him? She could think of no answers, only that now she can never trust him. *One bad apple spoils the whole bunch*, she thought. He did it once, he could do it again.

—__**********__—

The next afternoon, Elodea handed Gia a package the FedEx man had delivered to their door. She had ordered a copy of *Man, Woman and Child*, a novel by Erich Segal. It details the lives of Robert and Sheila Beckwith and their daughters Jessica and Paula. Out of the blue, Robert is contacted one day by a friend in France who tells him that Nicole, a woman with whom Robert had had an affair with years ago, has died. Jean-Claude, the son Robert never knew he had, is now an orphan. That evening Robert explains the situation to Sheila and they agree to take Jean-Claude for the summer holidays. However, they also agree to keep Jean-Claude's true identity a secret.

Later that summer, Sheila, a journalist, is tempted by the possibility of an affair with an author she has been interviewing. Unlike Robert, she doesn't cheat. At the same time, Jessica and Paula discovered Jean-Claude's true identity through Davey Ackerman, Robert's friend's son, and the girls refuse to speak to their parents.

As the Beckwiths are bringing Jean-Claude to the airport to return to France, he suddenly falls ill and is hospitalized. After surgery, during which the Beckwiths become closer again, he makes a full recovery. At last the whole family comes to terms with Jean-Claude and would like him to live with them. However, Jean-Claude refuses politely; he rather go to the school in France which his mother had chosen years before.

"Gia, that book must be interesting," Elodea said, staring at her daughter. "You haven't put it down since it got here."

"It is, Ma."

"What is it about? Is it for your students?"

"No," Gia answered, not looking away.

Elodea waited, but Gia continued to read.

"Aren't you going to tell me?" Elodea finally asked. "I like to know."

Gia sighed. Turning the page, she said, "It's about a cheating husband, Ma," and went back to reading.

"Does it tell you how to catch him... or give the reasons he cheated?"

"No, Ma," Gia said, placing a bookmark between the pages. She closed the book and looked up at Elodea. "Most affairs are with someone the man knows... usually a co-worker or a close friend," she explained, lifting a finger for each word, "proximity, availability, opportunity, the come-on, and no consequences. I am a shrink, Ma, remember?"

"Not a shrink, a consoler," Elodea corrected, smiling.

That was the word Gia had used to explain to her mother what their hard-earned money had paid for, sending her to Stanford. The doctor she had become comforted people, heal them emotionally, not physically.

Gia nodded and said, "The story is about a man, his wife and their two daughters. They learn that the man has a son. It seems a few years ago while visiting France, he had an accident and he had an affair with the doctor who treated him. Now he has learned that she just died and is informed of his son. He tells his wife and she suggests they bring him over to America. Now that the boy is with them, all sorts of tension begin to take place."

"Oh, Gia," Elodea gasped, "RJ has not asked you to bring his son here, has he?"

"Ma, this is not our story, it's just a book. Besides, I'm not about to discuss my marriage crises with you... if anything, it will be with RJ." Then she mumbled, "And, I don't intend to lick my wound publicly either."

"Okay, Gia, you are right," Elodea agreed, only hearing the first part of her daughter's comment. "Just don't let a book tell you what to do."

"Believe me, Ma, I'm not looking for answers in a book. This is not just about extending the circle of our little family's love."

Elodea gazed at her daughter and collected her thoughts. "Nina, listen to your mother," she said, almost pleading.

Now she was *Nina*, the name her father calls her when he's pampering. Gia was listening.

"Do you love your husband?"

"What does love have to do with anything?"

"Oh, but it does," Elodea said. "Love is bearing and forgiving... even with the hurt that disappointments cause."

Gia heaved a deep prolong sigh. She said nothing.

"Do you want a life without RJ in it? Is that what you really want?"

Gia said nothing. Elodea's eyes never left her.

"Then stop running away from your husband while he is trying to fix things," Elodea said, staring. "He made a bad mistake and yes, punish him if you must. You may not see it right now, but you and RJ are good together. Don't let things simply fall apart because you are angry. Listen to me. When you have a man who shows you he loves you, never let him go. When it comes to love, this is true, Nina, you will never find again what you have right now."

Chapter 26

RJ CAST THE blame on the right person, himself; then planned to pray and wait. He wanted that prize again, his wife's heart. He will cast on her an everlasting promise to love her though he'd compromised his loyalty. Left to face his regrets alone, the realization that his cheating had pushed him away from Gia, his truest and dearest friend, hurt. He also felt deep in his heart, together they will make it through.

Gia had been gone for two days and her Blackberry had thirty missed calls, all came from RJ's cell and the house phone. He had left a message each time, all ending with; *Don't forget about us, I love you,* or *I'm not giving up on us.* Running out of patience, the message before the last one said, *You're alarming me, honey. I love you.*

After getting no returned calls, RJ's last message said: *Ok, honey… you wouldn't take any of my calls on your cell and I'm tired of that. Dr. Ricciola, I want my wife and our daughter on the first plane to Atlanta tomorrow. I've email you the ticket information, flight number and time of departure. I will pick you up at the airport. If I don't see you on that plane, or hear from you, I'm flying down to Florida. I love you.*

Gia did not bother returning that call either. The following morning, RJ booked an early flight out of Atlanta.

He arrived in Florida, got a rental and drove straight to the house. They had just finished breakfast and sipping coffee, when out in the driveway a car door slammed. No one was expecting RJ. Gia did, knowing her husband did not bluff. Moments later he was embracing his in-laws and kissing his daughter.

After pleasantries, it didn't take RJ long to get down to business. He walked over to Gia, took her hand, palm up, and lifted it to his lips. She barely looked at him. He sensed the invisible wall was still between them.

"Please, baby, let me tell you how sorry I am," he pleaded.

"Come with Abuelita, let's go out to the swings," Elodea enticed her granddaughter.

Kitty happily ditched her parents for the seesaw.

Gia's mind was empty, her body drained and emotions numbed. She still would not look at him. She wasn't watching him, but she could feel his gaze on her.

"Honey, our marriage is withering. Don't you care about that?"

Gia did not answer.

"Marriage like ours just doesn't disappear," he continued. "And, an empty future is the scariest thing. I don't want that. I'm not accepting that."

He wasn't pleading. This was a simple statement of fact.

Gia's hand gripped his hand, and he let out his breath.

"No," she mumbled.

He wondered if she meant their love just wouldn't disappear, or their marriage.

"I know this guy who misses his wife so much he has not slept in weeks. I've missed you," he whispered. He wanted to put his arm around her and kiss her, but her body language was not encouraging.

Gia smiled at him sadly, pulled back her hand and said, "We need to talk."

His eyes considered her for a long moment. "Okay, honey," he sighed.

Gia got up and walked away. He followed her.

The silence between them was thick as they walked to the den. RJ understood hell will freeze over before Gia let him off the hook, and rightly so. She was angry with him. He'd never seen her like this before, like a small intense storm ready to burst. He gave up the thought of apologizing and thought of begging instead.

They entered the den, Gia did not sit. She folded her arms across her chest, caught RJ's stare and said, "When you asked me to marry you, I said something to you that night. Do you remember what I said?"

"Yes, I remember," RJ said. "You told me, 'There's room for only two people in a marriage.'"

"That's what I said," she said in a softer whisper. She couldn't believe he'd remembered every word.

He stared at her in a long moment of silence, hoping for her smiling pupils to assure him everything will be okay. This time it wasn't the happy Gia waiting to love or nurture. Her eyes had turned from light to a dark greenish hazel color. They still had their tiny blend of gold in them and she still looked beautiful, even when fuming mad.

"Honey, I've never cheated on our marriage, I swear," he pleaded, staring at her eyes.

"No, RJ, you did not cheat on our marriage... you cheated on your commitment. Fidelity is not a feeling, it's a decision. When you engaged me, you were telling me that of all the billions of people in the world, I mattered most. I was the woman you will always make feel special, more special than any other woman. That's how I felt when I agreed to be your wife."

"That hasn't changed."

"Oh, yes, it has. You lied to me."

"I've never lied to you."

"You used the oldest trick in the book, RJ... omission."

That was a fact. A lawyer knows there are various ways of not telling the truth. He sighed.

"You gave yourself to her. Another woman. Her."

It felt painful when Gia said this. RJ closed his eyes.

"You made love to another woman while you were committed to me. At that moment, you took a piece of yourself away from me, and gave it to her. Your heart was torn from me and given to another woman, whom you thought was a better fulfillment than me at that moment."

"No! It never was like that," RJ grasped. "I can't even breathe without you, Gia, let alone have anyone lured my heart from you." He took her hand. "I love you. I've always loved you. I always will. I'm not looking for forgiveness right now. Honey, I'm pleading for another chance to do right by you."

His eyes were filled with both pity and fear.

"You and Kitty... ya'll my life."

"And Grace?" Gia asked, her eyes probing.

"Grace," he sighed. "She is the mother of my son, Honey. I am not the senator. I will not turn my back on a child that I... I...."

"You helped bring into this world?"

RJ held his breath and let it out slowly. "Yes," he hesitated, barely audible. "Peace is my son. He is a part of me too. Only Peace. Not Grace."

Gia pulled her hand away.

She understood RJ could not promise he will never see or hear from Grace again. However, he could never be in Liberia alone. He understood that.

"Honey, Grace is helping me with Dad's case. We need her help... there in Liberia. I can't do much without it. That's important... while we're trying to clear his name."

"It is. We owe it to Dad... and I want that as much as you do."

RJ smiled.

Gia wanted to cry, but she didn't.

"I won't stand in the way of you meeting your son," she said sadly. "But, you are not going to Liberia alone... ever."

"I hadn't planned on going there without you."

"You won't," she said, and walked away.

RJ thought about suggesting they go for counseling, but he was looking at the best marriage counselor, his wife. Then he thought, *love trumps everything.*

Chapter 27

GRACE WORKED FOR a couple of hours returning some calls, opening files, pulling up some half-finished contracts on her computer, and going over notes she had taken from clients. She was checking emails when Lutee knocked softly on her office door.

"Yes, Lutee. Come in."

Lutee poked her head in and said, "I wanted to remind you about your meeting with Mr. Manor. He just called."

"Thank you, Lutee," Grace said, and rose from her desk.

__**********__

Grace entered Le'Toit through the private entrance, per Manor's instructions, and was greeted by Peaches, who escorted her to the door and left. She listened for a moment, heard no voices, then shoved it open. Manor was at his desk smoking a cigar, sipping Cognac and wearing an annoying grin on his face. That's how his ego went.

"Look at you... so pretty," he greeted as Grace reached his desk. "You take care of beautiful things and they take good care of you. Listen Pupoh, you are too pretty to be those damn market women guard dog."

"I am nobody's guard dog," Grace defended and sat down. "I'm hired to defend their rights."

"I see," he nodded. "Well, I wasn't looking for an argument." Manor picked up his desk phone and held it against his ear. "What can I get you to drink? A glass of wine?"

"No, thanks," Grace said. "I'm on the job."

Manor nodded. "Where the hell have Amadou been hiding you?" He said and put the phone back on the switchhook. "I sure could use you on my team. I could use more attack dogs, you know... get certain people off my ass."

Grace got a momentary vision of Diallo with a dog collar around his neck and chained to a leash that went from him to Manor's hand. *So, I'm a dog? A bitch? I'm nobody's bitch.* She gave the man a prolonged stare and then looked away. Her look finally softened and she shook her head.

"What," he asked in a deferential tone.

"The thing though, Manor," she said and turned, "you don't have what I require in order to represent you. You *could* use some."

"Some of what?" A big smile broke across his features as he said this. He looked Grace over and winked.

"Compassion," she cited, wondering if this was the man's best pickup line.

"That's true, I don't have compassion," Manor admitted. "But I think I have enough money to buy some. I am rich and money can solve many problems. How much of it would I need," he asked and smiled broadly.

Grace chuckled. She knew of his reputation with women and he had enough money to fuel that ego of his, and keep it hungry too.

"I'm serious. I'll pay whatever you ask."

"I'll rather have an empty purse," she jeered. "There's always hope in the little things in life, but you'll never get it."

Manor shrugged and said, "Well Ms. Pupoh, sometimes you have to put that good girl away. Do you know what they say about good girls and an empty purse?"

"What?"

She was dying to know. Not because Grace was naive. She knew a lot of women that a hard life had driven them outside the line of integrity. Now they were trying to outrun their past and would be doing so the rest of their life.

"An empty purse makes a good girl go bad," Manor explained. "Like I said, put that good girl away for a moment."

Grace said nothing. She held his gaze intently. Her stare was like a gut punch because Manor didn't look so confident now.

"Did you say you're from Grand Bassa County?" he asked.

"No."

"Where did you say you're from?"

"I didn't."

Manor's eyebrows rose. "Damn," he chuckled, nodding his head. "I like you, a girl with attitude. No, I love you," he corrected. "I love a woman with chills that has nothing to do with the temperature."

But it was Manor who had ice water running thru his veins. When you think he's giving a compliment, his words are actually ugly and cold. The last thing Diallo said to Grace before she left his office for good was, "Challenging CeRue Manor is a suicide mission."

Grace simply stared.

"Come on, throw a little smile my way," Manor coaxed.

Still, gladness made no mark on the woman's face.

"Why are you so tough on me," Manor continued. "Everybody got something wrong with them."

Manor actually felt he was every woman's wet dream. His way of getting attention from the ladies was a habit of tonguing his lips, trying his best to look sexy. He did this lusciously. Grace also remembered Diallo saying that Manor is a dog and he would screw a rock if it breathes.

"I'm sorry," Grace said, her tone honest. "I'm one of those women who understands she has something better to offer the world than her body."

"I see," Manor nodded. "You're one of those hard to get women." He'd quoted *hard to get* with his fingers. "Who's your boyfriend, by the way?"

Grace chuckled and said, "Are you this persistent with all the women, or am I just special?"

"The question should be, are *you* this tough with *all* guys?"

"I asked you first," Grace challenged.

"You're not a lesbian, are you? You know it's against the law in Liberia. Oh, yeah… you are a lawyer, you should know."

"You still wouldn't answer *my* question."

"Well… you don't have to tell me if you don't want to," Manor played it off. "I can find that out."

"I'm sure you can."

"Grace… Grace… Grace," Manor chuckled. "Don't ever let people know you have a softer side."

"Too late for that," Grace said, "you are seeing my softer side."

Manor smiled admiringly.

"What's the real reason for this meeting, Manor? Why am I here? I'm sure you're not looking for a lawyer."

"Are you really taking Boatswain to court on a rape charge? Or, you're going after him just for the sheer fun of it?"

"Do people go to court for fun?" Grace jabbed. Actually, she thought it would be fun when she get the opportunity to ground Boatswain's face into the legal dirt. "Mr. Manor, like you, I have a business to run. I'll let you get to it while I get to mine."

"Sure you don't want to join my team? If you do, then you wouldn't have to take Boatswain to court."

Grace Pupoh was sure of two things; (1) indeed there is a heaven and (2) Manor would never make it there. She put up her hands in mock surrender and headed for the door.

"I hope you at least think about it," Manor said. His gaze trailed her until the door shut. *Now that's an ass I would love to ride*, he thought. His mouth edged into a grin.

Chapter 28

TEMPLE OF JUSTICE parking lot was less than half-full before two o'clock on Thursday afternoon. As Diallo walked out of the building, he spotted Grace walking to her car.

"Grace!" he called out to get her attention.

She turned, watched Diallo run to her and slowed.

"Grace," he said, trying to catch his breath. "I've spoken with Cheah Boatswain and advised him how serious the case is. The man is very sorry for what he has done to his wife. What man does not care about his wife?"

"The ones that beat them," Grace replied sharply.

"People make mistakes, Grace. Cheah says he's sorry and I believe him. He is willing to beg Tomah for forgiveness. He's even willing to pay you for your services, you name the price. Quite frankly, for what it's worth, it's better you do not push this case."

"Or what?"

"Nothing," Diallo said quickly. "Nothing."

"Is that why you waited this long to respond? Hoping you can talk me into convincing my client to drop the charges?"

"No. I've been busy, mostly traveling. You know I have clients in other countries other than Liberia."

"Look Diallo, I know you're a busy man. Under any other circumstance I would have negotiated, but this is different."

"It's a simple divorce case," Diallo chuckled. "What's so complicated about it?"

"It's not so simple, your client…."

"Hold on, Grace," he interrupted.

"He raped her," Grace finished anyway.

"It's her word against his," Diallo challenged. "Who's to say?"

"Really? He told you that he didn't rape his wife?"

"He said he doesn't remember doing anything like that. He was drunk."

"He can save that sorry-ass excuse for the judge. I don't intend on dropping anything."

"All the woman wants is to divorce her husband. He'll allow the divorce… isn't that what she wants?"

Grace stared and waited.

"He will not put up a fight as long as she drops the rape charge."

"I thought he didn't remember," she chuckled. "I bet he remembers everything about that night. When we get in front of the judge, I'll have my chance to jog his memory."

"Grace, spend your time wisely," Diallo advised. "You are a damn good lawyer. Leave the cat fights to the other women lawyers, let them fight over the few loose change. Come to the dog pound, that's where the big bones are. I can teach you more than what you've already learned. And, Grace, you can earn more money than you will ever need, I promise."

"You fired me, Diallo, remember? And, Mr. Manor already offered me a job that I turned down. You see, I've already turned down that invitation into the dog pound."

Diallo folded his arms and stared.

"Don't get me wrong, Diallo," Grace continued. "This case has nothing to do with my relationship with you. I appreciate all that you and your wife did for me. Had it not been for you, I wouldn't have thought of law school to begin with. You gave me a start."

"Then give me a break, Grace."

"My loyalty is to my client, Diallo, not to you."

"How much *do* they pay you?"

"Not half as much as Manor is paying you to represent Boatswain," she replied, and then added, "You don't think I know? Boatswain can't afford your service. He owns a few houses and taxis, but he doesn't have that much money to pay for your service."

"Okay," Diallo mumbled. "Can't say I didn't try."

As he turned to leave, Grace said, "I will enter that dog pound on my own terms."

---********---

Being her number one fan, Alex loved watching his girlfriend perform in the courtroom. War is not a business of women, but Grace goes to court marching as if to war. When she's cross-examining witnesses, it is an anxiety-filled experience for anyone not on her team. One lie, or one unintended testimony, can change the case outcome. He feels a constant tension as the court drama unfolds. That is part of what makes Grace Pupoh better than a damn good lawyer. Good lawyers win every other time, a great lawyer never loses.

A divorce case is calmer, unlike a criminal trial where there are shocks and surprises, frustrations and fears, because everyone is unsure of the outcome. Both sides already know the outcome, except for when the couple's property is being divided. Boatswain had full knowledge of this and planned on keeping as much, if not, all, of their property he claims to be all his.

__**********__

Alex's phone startled him. He checked the screen, but it wasn't anyone he knew. After five rings, he pressed the little green phone image and held the phone to his ear.

A man's voice said, "Massaquoi?"

"Who wants to know?"

"This is Boatswain. Cheah Boatswain."

Alex started to ask how Boatswain got his number, but instead said, "What do you want?"

"Let's talk over a beer at Sinkor Circle later," Boatswain invited.

Alex considered the casual invitation to discuss what he suspected to be something involving Grace. At least he was anxious to know what was on the man's mind. "What time?"

"Can we meet at five?"

"Four."

Boatswain agreed.

Boatswain arrived first, then Alex.

"Thanks for coming," Boatswain said, as the two men shook hands.

They sat on bar stools at the far end, away from the crowd. The conversation would last at least for as long as it takes to drink one glass of Club beer. Boatswain was careful not to use the tone he's used when giving orders, an oratorical tone of intimidation. They talked about soccer, politics, then the new rape law and what he and most Liberians thought of it—an increase in false accusations in order to achieve leverage against the other party for some other reason. He explained that his situation was a clear example of a consequence of the new law.

Boatswain raised his beer in salute to a few guys that knew him when they entered the restaurant. He paused and waited to see how things were going so far, and found it satisfactory.

What a conspirator, Alex thought. Looking at the sly smile on the man's face, he understood the power game too often played. Those with power, or money, think they can get any or every thing their heart desires.

"That case should not be in court," Boatswain started.

"What case?"

Boatswain looked at Alex. "My wife is suing me and your wife is representing her," he said, incredulously.

Alex nodded. He did not bother correcting Boatswain that Grace was not his wife.

"If anything, we should have gone to our old people to settle whatever my wife is accusing me of. Don't you think?"

Alex shrugged.

"The charge must be dropped and this is for everyone's own good," he said with a dismissive flair.

One thing was certain, it would require a miracle to talk Grace into dropping the rape charge. He had never witnessed a miracle. Quite frankly, Alex wouldn't dare ask Grace even if he could talk her into doing so.

"When Grace has decided to do something, she has decided to do it," Alex said.

"But you are her man... you can change her mind."

Alex wondered if the man actually knew Grace Pupoh at all. He wanted to say, it's like asking a hungry cat to not chase the mouse. When Grace goes after something, stay out of her way.

Alex caught Boatswain's gaze and chuckled.

"Tell me, who wears the pants in your house?" Boatswain provoked.

Alex took a sip of his beer and put down the bottle. "We both do," he replied.

Boatswain furrowed his brow.

"Haven't you seen Liberian women wear pants?"

"I'm not here for jokes," Boatswain cautioned. "I will not be charged with rape because I fucked my own wife. You think that is funny?"

Alex took in his breath and let it out slowly. "You already know this, but I'll tell you anyway. Boatswain, you are a mean man," he articulated coldly.

This remark caught the police officer by surprise. Perhaps Alex had forgotten whom he was talking to. Boatswain had the means to do whatever he chooses to convince the man, but he had come to ask a favor.

"Yes, you heard me," Alex continued, staring directly at Boatswain's face. "You are a mean-spirited human being. People aren't afraid of you any more. The war has been over for years now. Liberia is changing whether y'all like it or not."

Boatswain sighed. He drained his bottle, sat it hard on the table, and jumped to his feet. The conversation was over. He pulled several bills out of his pocket and slammed them on the counter. The bartender collected the money and counted more than the total owed. "Keep the change," Boatswain told him.

"Thank you, sir," the bartender replied.

"Alex, I will remember this," Boatswain threatened and walked away.

__*********__

During dinner, Alex reached into the serving bowl without interest, dished out some rice and piled his plate. He added some stew and put down the spoon.

"What's the matter? No appetite?" Grace asked.

"Not really," he replied irritably. "All I can think about is us."

"Us?" Grace leaned back in her chair.

"You are amazing," he said, his statement more accusatory than praise.

"Why? Because I don't carry our relationship like a burden?"

That didn't help his mood. Alex wanted to say, 'Because you love like a man, and men don't have mushy emotions,' but he forced a smile instead. His chin dropped, then he took a breath.

Grace wasn't having any of it tonight.

"I fight every day, Alex," she said calmly. "I fight in the courtroom. I fight with the women so they can learn to take better care of their selves. And, I fight off bullies. I certainly don't want to fight in our home. This is where I exhale. This is where I keep calm, for my son and my man."

Grace was direct, as usual. Their argument starts the same; Alex opens his soul to her and leaves his balls against the wall. What Alex wanted was a guarantee, something Grace gives no one. Her relationship with RJ made him insecure, the women she worked with made him insecure, her son made him insecure, her career made him insecure. It seemed everything Grace did made Alex insecure. She knew he was in that zone again and didn't care why.

Grace put down her spoon and folded her arms across her chest. "What do you want from me, Alex?"

"You know what, I... I can't do this anymore," he said, hesitantly.

Grace frowned. "Do what?" She unfolded her arms and sat up straight in her chair. "What are you talking about?"

"I'm tired being last on your precious list," he asserted. "I'm just... tired."

Every word came out of his mouth in slow-mo as Grace tried to hush her thoughts so she could clearly hear them. She, too, had grown tired of his pathetic cries.

She took in deep breaths and let out a small sigh. "Okay, let me tell you once more. Alex Massaquoi, I love you. I'm with you."

"You love others *more*," he accused right away. Then very quietly, almost mouthing the words, he said, "Maybe we should break up."

Her eyes widened. "Did you say 'break up'?"

"Maybe breaking up is for the best," he bleated.

Not that he didn't like where he was and wanted out. Neither did he need change. This request he had spoken had become the root language of his inability to change Grace. He almost regretted saying it, but it had already escaped his lips.

"For the best? What good can come out of our breakup?"

"It's just that... I've had enough," he mumbled.

Grace remained silent.

"You understand why, don't you?"

"Understand what?" She gave him a withering look. "You, leaving me?"

Pride crept up, but the guilt of selfishness began clouding her mind. She tried combating it with logic, reminding herself that there was nothing more she could've done to convince Alex how much he meant to her. Still, she battled within. She would concede this victory to him, if he'd consider it a victory, and allow herself to regret the loss, if she'd consider it a loss.

"You want the only human being on earth that makes you second best," Alex accused. "You want to be second best?"

Grace stared. She said nothing.

"It is not your face that man wants to see," Alex continued. "You know that deep in your heart."

Grace stared.

"He'll make you feel insignificant like you've made me feel ever since you met him. I love you, Grace, so I don't mind. Not you. No one makes you second-best and you accept it. I know you."

She stared.

"It's not lack of love, you see," Alex continued. "He loves her first… you, he loves second."

What the hell did Alex know, she wanted to say. Grace heaved a heavy sigh.

"You will desperately hope to move up in RJ's heart to earn first place," Alex went on, "it's not going to be easy. Or, it's never going to happen. Even if it did, it will be a slow, slow move."

Alex Massaqoui always talk with straightforwardness.

Grace stayed calm.

"I'll be moving out on the weekend," he informed.

This surprised her, but she shook it off quite well. She wasn't about to beg him to stay. The erosion of the relationship had been slow, but certain. Grace frowned, then rolled her eyes and bit her lip. She would find some way not to blame herself.

"What about the office?"

"I'm not leaving the business."

"Just me?"

Alex shrugged.

She hated being blindsided. Grace got up. "Take whatever you want," she said, and walked away.

Chapter 29

GOING TO MEET your illegitimate son, and taking your wife and child along, can sour a long international flight. RJ booked their seats, making sure away from the exit row because of their small child. Gia prepared for her daughter's long plane ride, her first trip to Liberia, West Africa. She packed entertainment for Kitty—a Kindle Fire and a Nintendo DS with extra games—and for everyone, three travel pillows, some snacks, protein bars, hand sanitizer, and the latest edition of *Psychology Today* magazine for her.

The gate was packed with travelers and it seemed every plane that came and went held at least two hundred passengers. After fighting Highway 85 traffic, the check-in procedures, and the crowd along the concourse, everyone seemed ready to board. The flight would take them from Atlanta to Accra, then on to Monrovia.

Stressed gate agents came to life and the passengers began inching forward. The first announcement was made, asking those who needed extra time, and those in first class, to come forward. Gia clutched Kitty's hand.

"Let me hold her," RJ suggested and pick his daughter up.

They joined a long line and inched away. Gia handed over their boarding passes, then looked at RJ. They stared at each other for what seemed a long time, a second or so. She sighed and forced a smile.

The psychologist knows an important step in managing anxiety involves facing feared situations, places or objects. It's normal to want to avoid the things you fear. However, meeting her husband's love child was inevitable. She couldn't have stopped him from meeting him any more than she could have stopped the rain from falling. The sooner they get to meet the boy, the less anxious she'd feel about the idea of having another child they had not planned for.

Gia had the magazine opened but the pages weren't turning. She stole a glance at her watch and prayed the long trip would be quick. Returning to Liberia this time was a struggle. Here she was supporting a cheating husband, while one of her clients was happily scorching her husband's ass because he had been caught with his pants down. In her mind, Gia smiled at the woman's exact words, "Hell, I always knew he had zipper problems, couldn't keep his pants on." His excuse was, an evil voice came from nowhere and he listened to it. He swore, each time it happened, he did not want to. But he was weak, a victim to the voice. That *voice* cost him his Senate seat and over $160,000.

RJ had cheated only one time, so he claims. But once you've been cheated on, you never forget it. The anger slowly goes away but the scars remain deep, raw. You stay hurt. Maybe because some sins cannot be forgotten, and cheating on your wife is one of them.

She stared at RJ, his eyes closed. She knew he wasn't sleeping. Before his cheating days she would kiss him and tell him to stop faking sleep. Not today. Gia took in a deep breath and let it out slowly, then turned back to the pages. One thing was for sure, she definitely did not want his ass scorched.

Eyes closed, drifting pleasantly to their wedding day, RJ played it in his mind. Joy is the only word that describes their marriage ceremony. A three-piece string band played Keiko Matsui's *Forever, Forever* in the clear warm June air as two dozen guests, family, and friends crossed the threshold into the Ricciolas' backyard in Florida. Gia looked stunning in an antique white dress strung with a hundred luminescent pearls, no baby-bum yet, as Valentino Ricciola proudly walked his daughter down the aisle. RJ was incredibly handsome in a jazzy black tux, his eyes bright and shining, his beautiful smile more radiant than the sun. It was magnificent.

As they stood before the altar, RJ leaned toward his bride and whispered, "You look incredibly beautiful. How in the world did I get so damn lucky?"

She blushed.

A second after RJ and Gia pledged their love, everyone stood and yelled as planned, "Congratulations, Mr. and Mrs. Douglas!"

They kissed and held each other.

"Are you as happy as I am, Mrs. Douglas?" RJ whispered.

"Oooh, Flaky, I've never been happier," Gia replied, rubbing her abdomen.

RJ skipped meal and snack until they landed in Accra, picked up more passengers and were soon on their way to Monrovia.

From Ghana to Liberia could be nerve-racking to say the least, that is, if RJ let it. A little over two hours flight would be enough time to calm his nerves, but he would rather have happy thoughts than watch the minutes drag on. RJ sat back and closed his eyes, wondering what he'd missed about his son's birth. He had not been there to welcome his other child into his life and wondered what had it been like. He looked at Kitty snuggled against Gia, sleeping and holding on to Mono her favorite stuffed monkey. His heart melted.

RJ drifted to the day when they returned home from Liberia after the trial—a long and grueling emotional trip—and how Gia had kept the news until they were off the plane and standing at baggage claim waiting for their luggage. She left him for a moment—thinking she'd gone to the restroom—and returned with two balloons, one pink and the other blue.

"Where did you get those?" he asked.

"Mel left me a message while we were on the plane."

RJ furrowed his brow.

"I'm not sick, honey… we are pregnant."

RJ's expression went from weary exhaustion to squint-eyed bewilderment, then to dawning happiness, followed by absolute adoration. He swooped Gia up, with balloons in hand, and they laughed, then cried.

"I'm going to be a daddy!" he announced and released the balloons.

Everyone in hearing distance applauded as both balloons went floating slowly toward the high ceiling.

That night when they got home, RJ made love to his wife with his eyes focused on her face and on every sigh coming out of her mouth, every undulating moves of her body, as if he was memorizing her.

Happiness flooded their lives as their baby grew inside Gia. They wanted to experience natural childbirth, so they attended Lamaze classes. Gia and RJ couldn't wait to meet her.

A guest bedroom was converted into the perfect nursery, gathering things they thought a little girl would love. Elodea had saved the same crib Gia and Dante had used when they were babies, but had made new pink and white quilts that hung over it. They jammed the shelves with a colorful assortment of stuffed animals, dolls, books and more books. Gia read to her unborn child every evening before going to bed.

Just over six pounds, Katharine Elodea Douglas entered their world with a distinct and mighty cry, announcing her arrival like an opera singer. She looked right at Gia and RJ, strong and alert. RJ began to cry, so did Gia. After the doctor's care, Gia got to hold her baby, they counted ten little fingers and ten little toes and then, RJ got to hold her in his arms before Kitty was taken to the nursery.

From the moment RJ held his daughter in his arms, she seemed absolutely perfect. When they received the birth documents, he painted his lips with Gia's red lipstick and kissed his daughter's birth certificate, leaving an imprint of his lips next to Gia's name.

"Thank you, honey," he whispered and handed her the document.

"For what?"

"For loving me, marrying me, and especially for this beautiful little girl. My whole world is right here in this room. I love living my life with you."

When they took their baby home, RJ was first one up to see what was the matter when they heard the baby crying. He loved it when his baby gurgled and cooed in his arms. She'd look up at her daddy with expressive little eyes and he would look to see if she needed changing. Big job or little job, RJ happily changed diapers. If it wasn't that, he would check to see if she was hungry. When it was neither, he would lift her up and sit with her in the rocker next to her crib. Then back and forth they went, until her little eyes slowly close and the tears dissolved into a beautiful dream. RJ would put her back in the crib and watch her little tummy rise and fall.

One time he had not heard Gia come into the nursery.

"How is she?" she whispered.

"She just wanted Daddy's company," he replied, and put his arms around his wife. "Honey, she is gorgeous."

"She is," Gia smiled and her soft hazel-green eyes were full of joy.

Watching his baby grow before his eyes was a glorious thing. RJ loved every moment, every smile, every hug and kiss, but hated those dreaded baby shots because he cried more than Kitty did. He bragged about Kitty's first tooth, then her first step, and after she said her first word, RJ taught her a new word every day. By three Kitty was actually reading, although she was not old enough to block-letter her name.

For RJ, reading his daughter a bedtime story became the high point of his day. Kitty loved every moment of it, sitting on his lap and listening to every word. She would examine the details of every picture and wait eagerly to hear what was on the next page. RJ did not only communicate the story through words, but also through actions as the characters responded to whatever they encountered.

Two nights ago, before they left Atlanta, he sat holding his daughter on his lap; book in hand, and tears rolled down his face.

"Daddy, are you crying?" Kitty asked. "Are you sad, Daddy?"

"Yes, honey," he said softly, "Daddy is sad."

"Why?" her gentle voice whispered.

"Because Daddy did something bad. And, Daddy is very sorry for what he did."

"Don't cry, Daddy. I'm not mad at you," she hugged his neck.

The pilot's voice came over the intercom announcing their arrival. RJ's mind slowly rocked free from his thoughts. He opened his eyes and saw Gia looking at him. He read nervousness and hope competing for space on her face.

"I'm in love with *you*," he said, then tenderly patted her hand. "Thank you so much, honey. I love you more than you will ever know."

—***********—

Katharine and Bohn were waiting at the arrival gate. Kitty spotted them and went running to her grandmother's opened arms before Gia could stop her. Bohn assured RJ he'd take care of their luggage, which he did. Soon he was stuffing their things into the trunk of a new full-size SUV Toyota Sequoia, which was parked illegally at the curb in front of the terminal.

"Mom, I didn't know you bought a new car," RJ baited as they headed home.

"It's not mine, honey... its Rudy."

RJ and Gia turned and looked at each other.

"Rudy," RJ's lips moved, barely a whisper. Only Gia heard him, she shrugged.

"I still have my Land Cruiser," Katharine continued. "Since Mr. Tom retired, Cecelia uses it to run errands and to go to school. I'm glad she's here with me. She's a nice young lady."

"I feel as if I know her... from talking on the phone with her," Gia added. "She seemed nice."

As they drove into the yard, Katharine turned around from the front seat, stared at her children and smiled. Her thoughts showed through so clearly on her face, *No matter what brought y'all to Liberia, we will remain a family.* She could tell RJ had a whole lot on his mind.

A cheer went up when Bohn slowed the SUV in the front yard, a loud 'they are here' from some people waiting on the front porch.

"My goodness," Gia gasped, "what a crowd."

They made their way from the yard and onto the porch. RJ and Gia smiled and said "Hello" before making their way into the house. Another cheer went up when they entered the house, RJ holding Kitty's hand. The living room was packed with people, a different sort of crowd for Kitty, not that it mattered. Mostly Katharine's church members and the women who'd heard Gia speak at the first DOC meeting were there. They all wanted to see RJ's beautiful daughter, especially Mr. Tom, Ma Teete, Cecelia and Lynnette Vinton.

Ma Teete rushed to embrace Gia, a big welcoming smile on her face, arm stretched out completely, and wearing every piece of apparel Gia had ever sent to her. "So happy to see you, my child," she boomed.

Gia smiled, amused at being called Mama Teete's child. She understood *my child* is simply a Liberian expression. "I'm glad to see you too, Mama Teete," Gia embraced tightly. "I see that everything fits," she chuckled and let go.

"I loved everything... thank you plenty yah!"

"I'm glad you liked them," Gia smiled. "I bought you some perfume... the one you like."

"White diamonds?"

"I remembered, " Gia said, nodding 'yes'.

Everybody waiting to say 'hello', and those around the living room, was looking with admiration.

"Now, we all know who she likes," Lynnette muttered, staring from across the way.

Ten minutes later, RJ and Gia had introduced their daughter to everyone. The polls showed Kitty had her father's eyes and her mother's stunning beauty.

"Da lil' girl too fine," one woman said in simple English.

Chapter 30

THE FIRST MORNING in Liberia, Bohn and RJ were out on the beach jogging before 8:00 a.m. Ten minutes, and sweat was already forming on their necks and backs. Perspiration was dripping down from Bohn's face, burning his eyes. A little extra muscle never hurt and keeping in reasonably good shape was a necessity in his line of work. Bohn kept up with the much younger man.

"I've been dancing around something," Bohn said to RJ as they came to the turnaround point. "Maybe we should hire Lonos."

RJ stopped. "Officer Lonos?"

Bohn continued jogging, but had slowed. "Yeah," he replied, still moving.

RJ started back and caught up.

"Did I just hear you say, Officer Lonos? The same guy who helped send my innocent father to the gallows?" RJ's voice carried a little hurt and a little anger. The Senator had stubbornly maintained his innocence and his lawyer had not made enough effort to show proof of this.

Bohn stopped.

He wasn't doing this just for Katharine's children, but for Katharine Thomas, his first and only true love. She needed closure on that part of her life so they can move on with their's.

"He no longer works for the Liberian Government," Bohn supplied. Then added, "I doubt he miss his paycheck enough to be loyal to them. A ridiculous pay... chicken shit, really. A good paycheck, that's the trade-off. He knows everything that we *need* to know. A source of information, actually."

"As far as I'm concerned, he's an enemy," RJ said, sounding a little pissed.

"Frenemy."

"What?"

"Frenemy," Bohn repeated. "That's someone who's an enemy, pretending to be a friend. In our case, he's someone who really is our friend."

"Our friend?"

"The enemy of my enemy is my friend," Bohn recited.

RJ gave it some thought. "Then I'd like to be there when you meet with him."

"Not a good idea."

RJ flinched and frowned.

"It's my job to be the detective. Right now, your job is to take care of your family."

RJ remained silent. Bohn was right. He had no idea how he would set up his meeting with Grace or Gia finally meeting his son. How would all this reunion affect his wife?

"Do you trust me?" Bohn wanted to know, he was serious.

"Of course I do," RJ replied. He seemed edgy; thinking, worrying, afraid of something. Who wouldn't be afraid of a past that has caught up to the future.

"I'm good for the long haul, RJ and my gut tells me Manor is the finish line. What's important now is for you to go and take care of your family. I'll take care of this. Trust me, I know my job."

RJ nodded, he liked the fact that Bohn always seems sure of himself.

"What that sonofabitch needs is for someone to clamp down on his ass like a ferret on a cobra," Bohn said. "No courtroom in Liberia would be able to do that. It would be an enormous waste of time and hugely ineffective. I know what I'm doing."

RJ stared as a number of potential strategies rolled through his mind. Obviously, he wouldn't have the support to carry any out. "You think he set my father up?"

"Somebody did."

"And, you think it's Manor?"

"Could be. One way or another, I'll find out. And, when I do, the man needs to be stopped. I'm doing this for Kate too."

"Do it. Thanks, Bohn."

Bohn smiled a conspiratorial smile. A second later, the men were footracing back to the house.

__**********__

At quarter past ten, Officer Lonos met Bohn at Sugar Shack, a hole-in-the-wall saloon where the young and hip crowd shook their stuff to the latest grooves until the wee hours. Bohn had arranged to use the bar while all the night crawlers had disappeared until darkness fell. Lonos showing up meant he'd accepted the job offer, before the formal interview.

Rufus Bohn saw potentials in the man. Tightly disciplined, Lonos had integrity for the most part, compare to many others he'd secretly investigated in Liberia. He liked that the officer's sense of dedication was of the highest degree.

"Tell me about Dolo," Bohn said. "And, I mean every single thing."

Lonos explained how the Justice Ministry had established a system for both investigation and prosecution of serious crimes. Crimes defined as crimes against humanity, ritualistic torture, murder and sexual offenses. The SCIU, or Serious Crimes Investigation Unit, made up of the CID and MPD, who were under the supervision and direction of the Attorney General's office.

"We were given access to foreign resources and expertise to perform our job," Lonos supplied. "This structure, in my opinion, was just what Liberia needed to bring about the kind of justice system that can be trusted."

"Transparency had also been in place, right?"

"Yes. And, those cases the criminal justice system tried were all open to the public."

"Right," Bohn concurred. "Don't get me wrong. I like hearing all that good stuff about justice and human rights. But I want you to get to Dolo."

"Chief Dolo is a fine police officer," Lonos started. "He, too, showed frustration about the heart-man murders like all the other officers and law enforcers. He had us working day and night on the last case… the Bono case. We got our conviction and then, the sentence we all wanted. Then…."

"Get to Dolo," Bohn urged. He had heard enough about the Bono case. He knew more than he'd let on. "You ever spend time with him while off duty?"

Bohn wanted to know how much Lonos actually knew about is former boss.

"A few times," Lonos answered. "Sometimes we watched the European soccer league games on TV at his house. He has the satellite dish."

"How many government employees in Liberia can afford such luxuries," Bohn mumbled. "What did he talk about?"

"What do you mean?"

"Besides work or the game, what did he talk about? Women?"

Lonos crunched down into his seat. He wasn't sure he should tell Bohn about the affair Dolo had with his wife. "Isn't that what most men talk about while they're hanging out and drinking?"

"I was asking about Dolo in particular, not most men."

Lonos stared.

"Is everything okay with you and your wife?" Bohn kept on hounding with questions.

Lonos frowned heavily. He wanted to ask, When did this line of questioning go from my boss to my wife?

"No," he admitted, instead. But Lonos couldn't quite get out the whole truth. "I no longer have an income. If you know my wife, you would not be asking. She's the type… no finance, no romance."

Bohn chuckled. He knew Lonos' wife and everything about the woman; her affairs, not only with Dolo, but other men. What a shame. While a lot of Liberian men were exploiting their women, here's a guy who loved and supported his wife faithfully. Rotten apples were in both barrels after all, barrels labeled *men* and *women*.

Lonos had some military training in the US, and in his fifties, appears to be in good physical condition, which was good. Knowledge of self-defense techniques was important. There were still more traits of equal importance for the job. Bohn needed to know Lonos' degree of duty consciousness and his fearlessness and courage to fight back. What was his expertise in hand-to-hand combat technique and firearms usage? Did he have a strong eye for suspicious people and movements?

"What about Manor? Do you think he's part of the current mess," Bohn asked. "Is there any connection?"

"Number one suspect, in my opinion."

"Why's that?"

"I don't have any proof just yet," Lonos said. "And, even if I did, there are too many hands in his pocket. Big hands."

Lonos said it like there was deep enough grudge for the man. He had what it took to be Manor's Achilles' heel. No justice system in Liberia could hold CeRue Manor. Near impossible to do, but burning all of Manor's bridges in Liberia meant he wouldn't survive there. Bohn thought of hiring him at Level Clay with a starting salary of $24,000 a year, and two months of training with IBA in Johannesburg. His first assignment would be a surveillance on CeRue Manor.

"You now work for me," Bohn said bluntly. "And you will go right on doing what you are doing until the net is as strong as steel."

That remark struck Lonos like a bullet to the brain. It was quite clear to him that Rufus Bohn was no small potato. He wondered if the man was CIA. He dare ask. What Officer Lonos wanted to ask was, What am I doing to keep doing? Instead, he asked, "Net?"

It had slipped out.

The Net Bohn had set to get Manor was to end Manor's activities outside the legal arena, and completely destroy his empire. If Manor fled from Liberian authority, he would fall into the hand of whatever country authority he fled to. If he manages to get out of the hand of any foreign government authority, he would be taken into the hand of a big named agency. There would be no place on God's green earth the man would be able to stand. When you are no longer standing in life, the only other place you have to be is six feet.

"I'm sorry if I wasn't clear," Bohn said. "In this business you don't ask questions. You follow orders."

Bohn was deliberate and focused.

"I'm sorry."

"No need to be," Bohn said. "You are a special type of public servant now. You would be working in extremes, but you won't be breaking any laws or committing murder. Still want the job?"

"Yes… yes," Lonos answered quickly. His new salary was unbelievable. He had never made even half of that a year. "My job is to become Manor's shadow and report to you. That's it?"

"That's it. And Lonos, I want you on Manor like ugly on a pig's face," Bohn said, straight face. "I don't care what you do or how you do it. Crawl through garbage, but you better come out smelling like a rose. In our business, we make sure we're never in a position to answer questions. And, you answer to no one but me."

"Yes, Sir."

The American had funny ways of using words. Lonos wished to giggle at the inclination to the pig, but didn't.

Chapter 31

BAD HABITS ARE like a comfortable bed; easy to get into, difficult to get out of. While Grace was trying to soothe the woman's broken spirits, her husband had other plans. Cheah Boatswain's heart seems buried six-foot deep in arrogance because he showed no concern that his wife's lawyer had every intention to drop his ego to human heights. He had failed to convince Alex, so he warned Grace with countless phone calls to advise her client to withdraw the case from the court, otherwise he will. If he was smart, he would have been trying to heal his wrongs.

Grace addressed the man with raw and honest words, "I don't know what evil spirit has possessed your mind, but don't be fooled by it. I will not tell your wife to drop the charges and I will not let you do so either."

__**********__

After their meeting Boatswain drove into the yard like a maniac, to where Tomah was staying. He hurried into the house with an unsettling presence, not knocking or greeting.

"Tomah! Tomah!" he screamed as he searched throughout the house, from room to room.

He reached the kitchen and saw his wife sitting on a low bench against the wall, opposite the door.

"Why can't you open your mouth while I'm calling you," Boatswain snapped. "Didn't you hear me? Uh?"

Tomah got up slowly, staring at his face. She didn't say anything.

"Are you challenging me now? Is it because you've worn jeans? Wearing pants will not make you a man."

Boatswain had interpreted his wife standing up as a challenge. More of an excuse, one would agree, based on their past fights.

"Let's go," he ordered.

Tomah silently walked before him, slowly from the kitchen, then through the back door. Boatswain shoved his wife's back as they ambled toward the middle of the neighborhood in front of the small group of neighbors, mostly teenage boys and men, now merging from their yards to see the man's intention.

The crowd stood in a semicircle, staring at Tomah as Boatswain stood proud to display the bullying style of most cowards. He pressed down on his wife's shoulders and kicked at the back of her knees until she knelt.

"You've all witnessed how my wife has tried to disgrace me, accusing me of being a rapist," he addressed the crowd. "Is sex not part of a marriage? How can a husband not be allowed to pleasure his wife without getting arrested? What is this world coming to?"

The crowd made group agreement noises and this encouraged Boatswin's speech.

"If I look to other women for sex, she'll accuse me of adultery. Her people will come to me for long talks. I cannot let that happen. I have to do this thing against my wishes… teach my wife as if she is a child. I have to teach her to respect me, and I will do so until she begs for forgiveness. Tomah, are you going to drop the charges?"

"Cheah Boatswain raped me even as I was a good wife to him," Tomah cried out defiantly. "Many of you were witnesses. Most of you were there!"

Boatswain raised the rattan, a bamboo stick about three feet long, split at the end, and angrily strike his wife across the back. The pain was stinging, worst than breaking bones.

Involuntary scream issued from Tomah's mouth, then she hollered, "Cheah Boatswain, you raped me!"

The next blow fell.

Tomah called out the same sentence after each of the next six blows, until the power to speak deserted her. She howled like a dog as the blows continued. Boatswain stroked her ten more times.

Seeing that Tomah had nearly fainted, an old woman threatened, "If that girl dies, we will all talk."

This stopped the blows from falling. Boatswain looked up, heaving, trying to catch his breath.

Many people had joined the crowd and the women outnumbered the men. The women were angry that no one had tried to stop Boatswain from treating his wife like a common criminal. The men were more afraid of the women than of Boatswain and some men had personal reasons to intervene and look good in the women's eyes. Women carry their own news and these men are aware that the women know everything that happens in the neighborhood. They know all the men who secretly fuck boys and those men who can't get it up in the marriage beds. And for this reason, women should never be allow to escape the iron grip of their men. They would tell all.

Boatswain Looked at the old woman, heaved a heavy sigh and dropped his shoulders, looking ill at ease.

"Cheah Boatswain, I *will* see you in court," Tomah sobbed. "You cannot hush me, I will talk. I will tell the judge how you've raped me many times."

"Go to hell," Boatswain yelled. "You are a witch!"

"I am not a witch," Tomah yelled back. "But you… you are a rapist! I will tell the judge that. You raped me against the law in Liberia! You did this thing during the war and you want to continue. Cheah, you are the one who's going to hell, you hear me?"

"No," Boatswain snarled. "You, are the one going to hell for your lies."

"You are not going to touch me again, Boatswain… I swear," Tomah sobbed.

Boatswain stared at his wife angrily.

"I forgive you of this crime against me, but you are going to pay for this in court."

Boatswain gestured a cuss with his middle finger and walked away. The men scurried along in a group. As they were leaving, he argued with those protesting the beating.

"I'm not afraid of a few women," Boatswain contested, waving his hand as if shooing a fly. "Because we have a woman president? That don't mean shit."

Only the women were left.

The old woman who stopped the beating said, "It is almost over, my child. But try not to come back here again, no matter what. We will call Grace Pupoh."

Tomah nodded and tried to stand on her own, but she collapsed. Then, supporting her by the arms, two women helped her to her feet.

"Thank you," Tomah murmured.

"How do you feel?" one woman asked.

"How do you think?" Tomah replied.

The woman shrugged.

That woman, Tomah remembered, is the same one who thought it is a crazy thing to do, accuse your husband of rape. "What is the man to do," she'd asked. "I'm just a woman as you are. I don't say no when my husband asks. He's my husband."

__*********__

Dr. Douglas was heading into the exam room to see her last patient when a woman walked by. She looked familiar, but Mel could not remember where she'd seen her.

"The patient that just left, what is her name?" she asked the nurse.

The nurse looked at the chart she was putting away and answered, "Professor Moore."

"Is there a first name that goes with that?"

The woman looked again. "Nàjma."

"Is there a phone number on the chat?"

The nurse furrowed her brow.

Mel studied her eyes. "Never mind," she said. "Just give me the chart."

The nurse handed Dr. Douglas the chart and waited.

"I'll put it away when I'm done," Mel promised and the nurse walked away.

Mel's phone went off as she was walking out of the building. She recognized the number, "Grace?" There was no answer, just background murmuring noise. "Hello? Grace?"

Grace waved to quiet the noise. The crowd calmed and she said, "Dr. Douglas, can you hear me?"

"Yes. Is something wrong?"

Grace explained the woman's ordeal and Mel agreed to meet them at Tomah's friend's house. She lived in a paint-faded ranch-style house on a gravel road in Fiamiah community. The yard was crowded, but Grace had managed to keep everyone outside except for Yassah and the house owner.

Mel arrived thirty-five minutes later and was directed to the home. She requested a basin with soap and clean water to wash her hands. She lifted Tomah's blouse, exposing her back, and let out a soft gasp.

"Is it bad?" Tomah asked.

"It may look worse than it is," Mel said, opening her doctor bag. "The skin didn't break everywhere. I need clean water," she requested.

The woman returned moments later, carrying a basin of clean water and a cloth.

Dr. Douglas carefully removed the dried blood, then washed Tomah's back with antiseptic solution. Her touch was professionally gentle and her movements soothing. She smeared ointment on some torn sores and Tomah twitched.

"I'm sorry," Mel apologized. "That shouldn't hurt, but I see you do have some opened wounds."

"What is it?" Tomah asked.

"Neosporin," Mel replied. "It's an antibiotic cream so you don't get an infection. I always keep a tube on hand, you know kids," she added, looking at Grace.

"Dr. Douglas, I'm so glad you're home today," Grace said.

"That makes the two of us," Mel replied. "Grace, call me, Mel, please. None of that *Dr. Douglas* stuff. We got a deal?"

Grace smiled. "We've got a deal."

After a frozen moment, Tomah busted into laughter.

Grace, Yassah and the house owner joined in. Then Grace asked, "Why are we laughing?"

Mel caught Tomah's gaze, she seemed to want to cry. And she did cry.

"I cannot believe I just stood there and let that man beat me like this," Tomah sobbed. She turned her face away from them.

Mel and Grace exchanged looks.

"Don't blame yourself, Tomah," Grace said. "You are the victim. Men like Cheah Boatswain look at women as second class citizen. They see us as weak human beings and does not value our rights."

"Grace is right," Mel assured. "Isn't the case in court?"

"Yes," Grace answered.

"Good," Mel said. "Men like that has to be challenged, if not, there wouldn't be any change. When do you go to court?"

"Next week," Grace said.

"Let me know if you need me for anything," Mel offered. "If I can testify to the abuse," she pointed at Tomah's back, "I would. Even if I'm in South Africa, I'll come back."

"It may come to that," Grace said. "Thank you, Dr. Douglas."

Mel gave Grace a reminder stare.

"I meant… Mel," Grace corrected.

An opportunity at hand, Mel asked, "Grace, do you know a Professor

Moore? I think she teaches at LU."

"Yes, she goes to Words of Christ Church… your mother might know her," Grace informed.

"I never thought of that," Mel chuckled.

"Well, I do have her number if you'd like to call her."

"Thanks, Grace. I might just give her a call."

Chapter 32

GRACE NEVER WITHHELD critical information about her son's biological father from him, even at a very young age. She was glad to introduce him to RJ, but promised herself she would make certain her son's life would not go from normal to insane, meeting his biological father for the first time. There was no future with RJ other than planned visits, and she wasn't even sure of that. He had a wife and child, and she wasn't going to leave any kind of false hope in her young son's lap. Alex had walked out of their home, but not out of her life. Fact is, she would never be anyone's mistress. Grace had too much spirit to remain one. Making love to him, then watching him return to his wife would remove a piece of her heart each time. Desires always pass. Sooner or later there would be nothing left but regret and bitterness.

First she plans on talking with RJ, and then he would meet their son. Grace arranged their meeting at her office for 10:00 a.m., and instructed her staff she was not to be interrupted unless a life depended on it. When RJ arrives, Lutee was to escort him to her office and run things until her meeting was over. She had also asked Yassah to drop Peace off at the office thirty minutes after RJ had arrived, giving her enough time to evaluate his consideration of the situation. They had to be on the same page.

This is what happens to a couple when one is married to someone else, it mutes the laws of attraction.

RJ walked through the door to Grace's office at 10:01 and looked at her. Her face had lost the softness of youth and faint lines around her eyes had deepened. There was a new edge to her. She seemed less innocent and more cautious. He stepped back, trying to compose himself.

The affair had not triggered any obligation, like the way tomorrow forces itself upon the calendar. However, since that night, their greeting kiss always seems to trigger an incredible emotional connection. For Grace, getting RJ's attention was easy; getting the passion was the challenge. Things could be different, if only love could be whipped into the heart. He'd never said that he did not want Grace, he showed that he couldn't.

RJ clutched at the hand she extended and gratefully received her hug. He focused ahead and did not dare try breathing her in. His heart hurt with the effort while he enjoyed the ease of meeting an old friend. "It's good to see you again," he said, when she released him. RJ stepped back.

He fastened his eyes on her with an intense stare. Grace wasn't sure why. Habit? Or was something there lurking deeper now, but nevertheless, a part of her that had never completely left him? That night he had lost control with a woman and taken a virgin. The scene came to him easily. He hadn't thought of that night in such detail until Mel's phone call. And although Grace had far less flesh on display today, the effect was still distracting.

Suddenly Grace was uncomfortable with the stare as RJ was comfortable with it. "I've prepared Peace to meet you," she broke the awkward silence. "Yassah is on her way to drop him off here."

"Good," RJ said, smiling. "I'm anxious to meet him." He really wanted to know why she'd kept their son a secret, but chose not to ask.

"Have a seat," Grace pointed at the chair across from the desk, then slid into the one behind it.

RJ didn't take his eyes off her. The look was guarded, but the charm, or was it power emanating from him, punched her heart. It seemed impossible to breathe.

"I can't thank you enough for what you've done for my family," he said. "This has brought such relief to my mother, Katharine can breathe easily."

"I wish we had uncovered the facts before it was too late," she said, forcing herself to look away and breathe normally. His eyes made her feel unbalanced when he stared so intensely.

"Important thing is, since Mom lives here, she can move on without the stigma."

"That's good," Grace said, and got to the point straightaway. "My only concern is Peace. If we both keep things real, everyone will benefit."

RJ's steady gaze faltered.

"Of course," he said, "the welfare of the child will always come first. Peace is more important."

You just can't let circumstances derail your dream. What Grace was making sure of was that her son would have a better life than she did. She had stronger opinions than most women.

Grace told him only things concerning Peace, from the moment she delivered to his third birthday. She detailed how Peace raised his head at one month old, at three months he listened to her voice and stopped crying as soon as she smiled at him. He was rolling from stomach to back by five months, crawled at eight months, and walked with help at eleven months. He was able to undress himself at eighteen months, form clear sentences, and used the toilet at twenty-four months. RJ didn't interrupt once.

"At two and a half, my son used the toilet by himself, all I had to do was wipe him," Grace said proudly.

"Does he like sports?"

"He loves to play catch," she praised. "Peace has been throwing a ball since he was two. And he catches so well," she added. "I don't know where he gets that from."

"He got that from me," RJ chuckled. "If he started catching ball at two, he's sure going to be an all-American."

"My son will never become an American citizen," her voice rose to almost a shout.

Her outburst seemed to take RJ by surprise. Obviously she did not know what he meant. All-American athletes are college players voted the best of the year in the US. He knew a determined woman when he saw one, and arguing with Grace Pupoh would be a waste of breath. He chose not to go into excessive details. Another time, maybe.

Grace regret raising her voice. She knew better. For your words to sink in, they must be whispered, not yelled.

"I'm sorry," she sighed. "I didn't mean to raise my voice at you."

"What are you afraid of? Do you think I'll take your kid away from you?" RJ spoke quietly.

"I wouldn't let you if you could," Grace said matter-of-factly. "And, no, I didn't think you wanted to."

"Right," he nodded. "I'm not that mean spirited."

They heard a soft knock on the door. *Save by the bell*, RJ thought. He was very good at covering his thoughts.

"That must be Peace," Grace said softly, her irritation suddenly gone. "Come in."

His energy went from blissful to fear, that quick. Whoever opened the door remained out, Peace walked in alone and the door closed behind him. RJ drew in a deep breath, along with a solid dose of courage.

As his *Secret* ambled toward him, RJ searched for all the paternal evidences Mel had talked about. Same nose, ears, lips; even his eyes. The little boy looked much taller than most three-year-olds, his hands were larger too. RJ's heart sank and rebuild itself in that instant. "Good Lord, the kid looks just like me," he mumbled, beaming at the child.

Apparently Peace was happy too, he stretched his small arms out and ran to RJ, who took him. The little boy wrapped his entire body around the stranger and hugged so tightly, Grace thought they would never separate. She glanced back and forth between them, smiling.

It was reveling in many ways; to feel his son's body in his arms, feel the connection with this little boy, the *happy ending* for all his troubles. RJ always shook hands with his father, even as a young boy. His father had never pampered him. In fact, Robert Jenkins Douglas II never hugged another man in his life, not even his sons.

"Daddy," Peace said with a glad smile. Then added, unexpectedly, "You my daddy."

Grace furrowed her brow. She hadn't expected that.

RJ laughed. "Yes, I'm your daddy... and I'm glad I'm your daddy," he said, jiggling the boy in his arms.

"Okay, Peace, you can get down now," Grace coaxed the child, arching a defiant eyebrow.

The boy clung tighter to his father. RJ closed his eyes, breathing deeply to empty his mind of the raw and real challenges ahead. The overwhelming fear of Gia's reaction when she finally meets him. The potential threat against his desire to love the reality of this young boy. What was important was keeping his family together, and he would be the strongest dad ever, protecting both of his children. RJ opened his eyes and said, "We'll do what Mommy says, okay?"

Peace nodded and RJ put him down. The little boy's hand found RJ's fingers and tightly wrapped his tiny, but large, hand around one. He clung on, happy his daddy was there with him.

"Uncle RJ?"

"It's Daddy, remember?"

Peace nodded and said softly, "Daddy?"

"Yes, son."

Trying his best to keep three fingers up, Peace said proudly, "I'm three."

RJ gently held down the boy's thumb and pinkie, and the other three fingers extended nearly perfect. "That's three," he coaxed. "You're a big boy."

Whether Grace liked it or not, RJ picked up his son again, held his cheek against his face and talked softly to him. Peace nodded occasionally, grinning at times.

Grace's brows drew together, wanting to know what he was telling her son. If she didn't ask, she'd never find out. It was worth a try at least.

"What are you telling him," she asked.

RJ didn't stop talking, and she knew she wouldn't get her answer.

Chapter 33

NOW SPLITTING HER time between the US, Liberia and South Africa, Dr. Douglas had been a physician in Africa for five years. She felt incredibly lucky, a workaholic whose life had become hectic with rounds, research, overtime, overwork and double shifts. There were challenging moments though, dealing with the system of government and the hopeless inadequacy of the continent's poor healthcare provisions. There were also moments she absolutely cherished; seeing patients get well, and even being with some when it was clear they wouldn't recover.

Mel had just come off a twenty-four-hour rotation at JFK Medical Center, tired beyond anything imaginable. It was late Friday afternoon, the weather was nice, and the air sweet and crystal clear. It was the kind of day she lived for while in Monrovia. She took a quick shower, changed into a pair of shorts and tees, and headed to the hammock on the front porch. She hoped to luxuriate in the peacefulness for a few moments before fading into nothingness, a quiet nap.

A yellow Datsun taxi pulled into the yard and came to a stop. Cecelia must have just left, leaving the gate open. The car door opened, then slammed. This woke Mel as she had began drifting. She lifted her head, saw the taxi drive in reverse as Ma Tarloh walked to the house. Mel sat up.

Apparently Tapee's mother had chosen a life she'd imagine for her son. Dr. Douglas had shown care for the boy from the moment they first met, the kind that fitted all of the hopes and dreams she has for her child. She would be placing Tapee into the arms of a special woman who loves him as much as she did.

The reality is, birth mothers do not *give up* anything when choosing adoption for their child. They are choosing life, one complete with all of the things they desire for the child. It is not the easiest route, but the reward is nothing but pure love for their child. Gone are the days when a birth mother simply handed her baby over to an adoptive family, never to see or hear from them again.

"Doctor, I see how you've cared for my son," the woman said. "I've come to ask you to adopt him."

Mel's eyes widened, then she let out a sigh. "I didn't expect that," she mumbled. "Ma Tarloh, I don't mind helping Tapee financially... taking care of his medical needs. But asking me to adopt him puts my relationship with him at a different level. Do you know what you're asking?"

"I know," Ma Tarloh said and sat down. "You love my child as much as a biological child. God gave him to me first, but I'm not able to care for him. Now, He's giving the boy to you. God has put this in my heart. I'm giving him to you, Dr. Douglas. Please, take him as your own. There will never be an ounce of regret in this decision."

By the time the woman was finished pleading, Mel realized there was nothing else of value in her life besides work. She earns about $130,000 a year, saves most of it, and spends the rest on clothes and other things she didn't have much time for. She had not wanted children in her life, but she has been without a significant other since the breakup with Shakari and with Dr. Cho. Not that Mel was lugging the baggage of her past. Until now, there had been no plan or prospects to change any of it.

Since as a little girl, Mel had chased her dream to be the kind of doctor, and the kind of woman, she wanted to be. Odd as it was, *Mommy* resonated with a wonderful sound for her, like recess bells of an elementary school. Mel already loved the kid and spend as much time with him as she possibly could. *Wait a minute*, she thought, *I would have to spend more time with him. The Lord might be getting even with me for not being fruitful.* She smiled. It wasn't a bad deal after all. She was getting a kid of her own without nature's way.

Maybe it's the sound of it, the silly rhythmical flow of the tune; Mel's whistling always sent Tapee into fits and giggles. Blind since birth, the boy was incredibly alert, checking everything out with his other senses.

Mel had spoiled him with things. She took him a present from every trip, specially made toys, watches and electronics for the blind. As the boy matured, she had gotten him a soccer ball with jingling bells inside, wooden blocks with print and Braille letters, Braille math blocks so he can learn about numbers and math, 3D paint pens that he could make lines he will feel. She even bought him a Braille UNO card game and taught him to play.

As Tapee outgrew the games and toys, Mel donated them to the MaryMartha Orphanage. The boy had no problem parting with those things, except for his tub of play-Doh, which he shaped and molded into every imaginable thing. Mel quickly discovered the boy's passion for art and bought him tons of Play-Doh.

"Okay, Ma Tarloh," Mel said. "If you are sure of this, I'll be happy to be Tapee's mother. I will check into the legal side of things, then take it from there."

This was for Mel. Every part of her, body and soul, knew she'd made the right decision. There wasn't an inch of the boy she didn't like. Even her workaholic side was in agreement. She was already experiencing motherhood. In fact, it made her feel she would be needed more. Working between Liberia and South Africa, she would take Tapee with her sometimes, but the rest of the time she'd have him stay with Katharine and pay Cecelia to take care of him while she was away.

__**********__

After she'd given Ma Tarloh a ride home, Mel checked her timepiece and saw that she still had moments to spare. The route had taken her passed the university and the thought hit her. She spun the steering wheel hard in the direction of LU entrance. The Land Cruiser came to a stop in an empty space in front of the administration building.

Mel stood against the driver-side door, pretending to be exhausted and making it seem to passersby that she was waiting for someone. Finally, the woman walked out with a nice, easy smile. She was kind of laid-back. She looked at Mel as if there was something familiar about her. Nàjma wondered if she had met her at church or maybe at the hospital.

"Are you looking for someone?" Nàjma asked. Then she remembered who the woman is and said, "Dr. Douglas?"

"Mel," Mellody said. "Please, call me, Mel."

Nàjma laughed. a nice laugh. "I was almost sure it was you."

"The other day at the hospital… I wanted to talk to you but you seemed in a hurry."

"I was late for class," she explained. "We can talk now."

"How about lunch? Late lunch."

"Aren't you waiting for someone?"

"Actually, it is you," Mel admitted.

Nàjma looked surprised.

"If not now, some other time, perhaps… but *soon* I hope. I'll be flying to South Africa in a few days."

"Uh… today is fine," Nàjma said. She had an endearing smile. Mel noticed. "I have a better idea," she said. "How about you come to my house for dinner tomorrow… Saturday?"

"I would love to, but I have an all day shift tomorrow at the hospital."

"All day?"

Nàjma seemed a little disappointed. Mel noticed.

"I get very little time outside of the hospital. This is one of the negatives being a doctor," Mel said, then baited, "But how does Sunday morning breakfast sound?"

"Church," Nàjma replied. "I try to make it to church every Sunday."

"Hmmm," Mel mumbled. She playfully threw up both arms.

"Why don't *you* come to church?"

"There are two forces I don't mess with… God, and Mother Nature."

"Now I see why it took a moment for me to recognize you," Nàjma chuckled. "I've been thinking, where have I seen this person? At first, I thought it was church."

"And, you sound just like Katharine," Mel laughed.

They remain standing in the parking lot. Mel and Nàjma talked about work, changes in Monrovia, Ellen's government, successes, struggles, and disappointments. Nàjma had spent most of the civil war years living in London, Paris, and New York, eventually earning a Ph.D. at Teachers College of Columbia University before moving back to Liberia after Ellen Johnson-Sirleaf won the elections. She was happy to move back home and help with the progression Liberia needed.

The afternoon was quickly turning into evening. They'd talked for a while and time had flown. Mel noticed they'd been standing longer than either had planned and Nàjma looked tired.

"I can't believe how fast time has flown," Mel laughed, looking at her watch.

"You know what they say… time goes by fast when you're having fun."

"We could have had dinner," Mel said.

"Or you could have told me why you're here," Nàjma chuckled. "Anyway, why don't you call me when you get back from South Africa… I'll make you dinner. Nothing fancy. I'll throw some fresh barracuda and plantains on the grill… and we can talk."

It had a nice feeling to it. "I'd love that," Mel said.

Nàjma handed her a business card.

"Tomorrow is a hospital day for me," Mel said. "I might not get home until Sunday... then I fly out on Monday afternoon."

"You have my number now," Nàjma said.

"And I plan on using it." Mel felt her heart skip a beat, and thought, *My... my... careful, Dr. Douglas.* She already had the woman's number.

It felt so good talking; a nice getting-to-know-you moment for both women. Mel loved it. Damn it, she liked Dr. Moore. She liked her a lot. They might as well become friends.

It was late when Mel got home, but she wasn't tired. If anything, she was overwhelmed with excitement. She hadn't expected any of this to happen, talking easily to Nàjma. She was singing and dancing on the inside. She felt lucky and hoped it rub off on this new challenge of adopting Tapee. Mel shared the adoption news with Katharine, RJ and Gia, then called Grace to arrange a meeting.

Chapter 34

SUNDAY MORNING WAS quiet. While Peace was spending the day with Uncle Moses, Grace was putting more documents in order for the court hearing, which she had spread out on her couch and on the living room floor and even on the polished coffee table. She would serve two clients today out of her home office, Mel and Tomah.

Mel arrived mid-morning. After a mini-tour of the house, Grace escorted her to the study. Two cheap metal folding chairs had been temporarily placed in front of the desk covered with the evidence of busy work; thick files, large envelopes and several notepads. A laptop was open and on.

"Have a seat," Grace said, waving at the folding chairs.

Mel did.

"Sorry, it's not the most comfortable chair," Grace apologized. "We use those for our meetings. I usually don't meet clients here."

"I'm fine," Mel assured. "You have a beautiful home."

"Thanks," Grace said pleasantly, then added, "Let's go over this."

Mel nodded.

"I don't mean to be in such a rush here, but I have another appointment," she explained. "I have to prepare Tomah for court, so she should be here," she looked at her watch, "in another hour."

"Oh, I understand *rush*," Mel said. "And don't hesitate if you need me during the trial. That offer still stands."

"Thanks... I might need you to testify," Grace said, and looked at the laptop screen.

Next to it, on top of a stack of yellow legal pads, was a fresh white pad, a black pen on it, waiting. Grace took the pen and pad.

"It could take up to three months... four, tops, and cost up to twenty thousand dollars," she informed Mel about the estimated cost and time to expect for the adoption, and wrote on the pad. "There are a lot of huddles here, Mel. I cannot guarantee anything because in life nothing is, but I can promise to do my best. My best is meeting my client's expectations."

Grace handed the pad to Mel.

Mel knew about the needy. A street lawyer can hardly make enough money to sustain a decent lifestyle working for minimum earnings protecting the poor, the oppressed, or the abused.

"I'll pay twenty-five," Mel offered, taking the pad. "Believe me, I know how legal expenses are. The rest can go to helping those women that can't afford to pay for your time."

"Thanks," Grace said, and let loose a deep satisfying sigh. "I'd like you to jot down on the pad answers to these questions… information I might need. I'd rather have everything now while I have the chance. I can't even tell you about *busy*," she chuckled.

"Sure," Mel replied, then softly recited as she wrote 'This is my life' on the pad.

Grace laughed, then launched into a series of quick questions about family members, marital status, education, jobs, addresses, hobbies, interests, church affiliations, even politics. She did not ask about lifestyle because homosexuality is a crime in Liberia. Mel thought Grace could have asked the question. If she really wanted to know, Mel would have answered truthfully too.

When they finished, Grace lectured on the government basic policy regarding non-Liberian adoption.

Liberia had been closed to new applications since January 2009, and an Ad-hoc Central Adoption Authority was created to process adoption applications submitted before the suspension. The biological parents (or mother, if the child is born out of wedlock) have to submit a statement of relinquishment, and the Ministry of Health and Social Welfare has to provide a case summary proving that adoption is in the best interest of the child.

"DNA testing has to be done in order to establish a blood relationship between Tapee and Ma Tarloh, since she is relinquishing her child," Grace informed.

"That's fine. I know she *is* his biological mother. *She* was the one who brought him for treatment when I first met them."

"Well, it could be proven she's not. In Liberia, people take on as caregivers for relatives without any legal proceedings. Say, a woman cannot afford to feed her child and she gives the child to her sister. That sister becomes the legal guardian without anyone going to court."

"Really?"

"Yes," Grace nodded. "Let's just pray that the DNA matches."

"And if it doesn't," Mel sighed.

"We'll cross that bridge when we get to it."

"After we've filed the adoption petition, how will the adoption process affect him traveling with me?"

"Usually that will require an exit clearance," Grace explained. "But he has been traveling with you, right?"

"Yes. I take him to South Africa for school because they have a better program there for the blind. And, I've taken him to the States several times for medical purposes... also while I'm on breaks."

"That shouldn't change, as long as it's an open ticket."

"I've always bought round trip tickets."

"Then there's no problem."

With that, Mel hired her attorney with a contract for twenty thousand dollars, but a verbal agreement of twenty-five. Fifteen would be deposited within three business days, and the balance when the adoption is finalized. Mel left and drove home hopeful, with heavy traffic crawling as commuters retreated into the communities of Key Hole, Fiamah, Lakpazee and Chugbor.

—✱✱✱✱✱✱✱✱✱—

Tomah arrived on time for her meeting with Grace and they got started.

"You are bringing the action to court so you will be known as the plaintiff," Grace explained. "Your husband is the defendant."

Grace wanted to make sure her client would do everything to score points with the judge, being the powerful figure. Making a good impression is vital, given the fact that a judge will determine her client's fate.

"Tomah, when we are before the judge, avoid making wild gestures with your hands," she advised. "The judge might not remember the issue raised up until the trial, but if you've already made a spectacle of yourself before him, he might remember it. I know it would be hard to stay calm when you know your husband is lying, but you have to stay calm."

Tomah nodded.

"Remember to follow all the court rules," Grace continued. "Do not talk at all unless I tell you to, or the judge asks you a question directly. If you think I've missed something important, bump me gently on my arm and ask, in a very low voice, if we can talk."

Tomah nodded.

"Remember, do not overreact to anything, no matter what your husband or his lawyer does."

"I must remain quiet?"

"I would be doing all the talking, Tomah," Grace said. "That's why I'm your lawyer."

Chapter 35

GIA HAD BEEN in challenging situations many times, but this was different. Before coming to Liberia, the situation had seemed like a bad dream. They were now in Liberia and everything was real. While RJ and Bohn were out working on the investigation, she would be meeting his love-child in a few hours. Something flashed before her eyes, blinding at first, then clearing so that her mind was empty of everything except disappointment and anger, so intense it hurt. *Seeing is believing*, she thought. The events of the day proved that. Gia wondered if meeting the boy without RJ around had been designed this way.

It was one of those incredibly beautiful mornings; perfect temperature, light breeze, and not a cloud in the blue sky that stretched without end. Kitty had finished eating all her breakfast and asked if she could leave the table. She wanted to go out in the backyard to play.

"No," Gia said softly. "Honey, you can't go outside by yourself. You need to wait for me to finish my coffee and go with you."

"See Mommy, I'm three," Kitty cooed, holding three little fingers up. "I'm a big girl. I can go by myself."

"I know, honey," Gia said, encouragingly. "Mommy's almost done. I'll go out with you."

Two minutes later Gia called her daughter with a ready smile to take her out. As soon as they walked out the door, Kitty ran in her eagerness to get to the swing set Bohn had installed, made out of an old cutout tire on chains, and demanded a push. After about forty-five minutes of squealing, jumping and skittering around, it was time to head back in the house. Kitty whined but Gia brushed away her plead, avoiding long exposure to the sun.

Gia left Kitty in the kitchen with Katharine and was walking into the living room when a familiar voice snapped, "Don't run."

Peace came running ahead of his mother. He ran through the front door before she could stop him. Gia saw the boy, and her eyes widen. The world stood still. She stared at the little boy, feeling the heat craw up her back, then stinging her face. She was looking at a miniature image of her husband; same eyes, nose, the shape of his face, his smile. The little boy was smiling at her. Grace finally caught up and held his hand, and Gia's eyes went from the boy to Grace. It was awkward. Grace felt Gia's eyes burning into her and ignored it.

Of course Gia's chest hurt. It's because that is where her heart is.

Despite all efforts against it, her heart sped up. "Excuse me," she whispered, then turned and walked out of the living room on legs that trembled. She didn't know whether to start running, or scream, or just hit RJ when she finds him. Her fists were balled and ready. How could he have made love to that woman? Totally humiliated, Gia walked to the bedroom and shut the door.

Katharine heard the bedroom door slam and rushed out of the kitchen.

"Oh my God!" she gasped when she saw the child. She stared at the boy and the child stared back, not blinking one bit. He looked exactly like RJ, her own little boy not so long ago. Katharine humbled down and took the boy's chin in her hand, lifting his face so she could see him properly. "Hello, honey," she said gently. "I'm your...."

She could not finish.

"Say hello to Mrs. Douglas," Grace said to the child.

The little boy lowered his head, overcome with shyness.

Katharine looked at Grace, smiled and look back at the boy. "You are a very handsome young man," she coaxed. "What's your name?"

Shyness made Peace unwilling to speak. He stood quietly.

"She asked for your name," Grace said, encouragingly.

"Peace," the child said softly.

"Peace?" Katharine repeated, and looked at Grace.

"I get that look every time my son is introduced," Grace said.

"You named him, Peace?"

"Actually, I named him Solomon, which means peace. But I use Peace instead of Solomon."

Katharine thought about King Solomon in the Bible. "I like that," she said, standing. The shock faded from Katharine's face, and in its place was a beautiful smile.

Grace sighed in contentment. "I promised RJ that I would be leaving Peace for a couple of hours," she said. "I hope it's okay."

"Of course I don't mind," Katharine said. She turned to the boy and said, "Peace, would you like to stay and play with Kitty?"

He nodded.

"Say 'yes,'" Grace encouraged.

"Yes," Peace mumbled, looking at Kitty.

"Come," Katharine said, drawing Kitty and Peace closer. The children rested their heads against her and she ran a hand lovingly over each. "He will be fine," she said to Grace. "You're welcome to call to check on him."

Grace thanked Katharine, promised Peace that she would pick him up later, reminded him to be on his best behavior and left the house.

Gia waited for a long moment to be certain Grace was gone. She peeked out the bedroom door, making sure the coast was clear, and walked out.

"Where is Kitty?" Gia asked Katharine, who'd walked out of the kitchen, and into the living room at the same time.

"There," Katharine pointed at the children sitting on the floor playing with toys. "They'll be friends," she said, about the children. "The way I see them look at each other."

Gia said nothing. She did not look at Katharine to show what effect her words had. But her expression, or lack of, was a window to her feelings. Perhaps the silence was a protest of the children getting along too easily. Katharine understood the disappointments, fear, and sorrow of a cheating husband.

"Gia," she whispered and touched her daughter-in-law's hand. Gia raised her head and curled her fingers around Katharine's hand. Her eyes confirmed her disappointment, her fear, and her sorrow. "He's a good man who made *one* mistake," Katharine went on, her voice soft and thoughtful. "Now, I'm not saying this because RJ is my son. I know y'all can be happy again."

People can't be talked into happiness, Gia thought, although that was her job to talk people into finding happiness. But deep down she knew RJ was the best of people. He is everything she wants in a man—caring, thoughtful, and utterly selfless. He is a good father and husband. It went without saying that he felt guilty about what had happened, he'd expressed it. Guilt is the cornerstone of any good marriage. It meant that a conscience is at work.

"I know, Mom," Gia whispered. "I just wished he hadn't done what he did. It changed everything."

Change is one of the unavoidable laws of nature, demanding its toll on people's lives. Mistakes are made, regrets formed, and all that is left are consequences. She wanted to breathe and cry and laugh all at once, but it came out a choked sob. She loves her husband. And he loves her. There were just too much to swallow. Acceptance of his love child, in particular. How could they be happy again?

"There are more reasons to stay together than to do anything else," Katharine went on. "I just know it." Then she hugged Gia. "Y'all will find a way to make it work."

"Thank you, Mom," Gia said, then whispered, "You know I adore you."

"I love you too, honey. Everything will be all right."

Katharine left feeling everything was going to be okay, despite hearing a hint of hopelessness in her daughter-in-law's voice.

Kitty belched. Peace snorted. The children laughed, their voices high and cheerful. They were getting along like two bundles of happy energy, taking turns chasing each other. Gia shut out their chattering while they engaged in different recreations. Every now and then, Katharine went out on the porch to check on the kids, preventing them from teasing or accidentally hurting one another. The children played on the porch, then in the yard, as the afternoon light faded.

Grace called to check on her son, and because the children were getting along, she agreed that Peace could spend the night.

The children each had a few tearful moments because of falls. Interesting enough, each helped the other up. Then, a little after six, when Kitty had her second temper tantrum in a fifteen-minute span, Katharine took both children by their hand and brought them into the house. It was time to take their baths so they could eat dinner.

The air was still warm, but a light breeze had picked up. The stars spread across the sky in random intricate patterns. Gia stayed on the porch lying in the hammock, gazing at the half moon like a diamond brooch in a midnight blue sky. She wished she would think of something astronomically inspiring, but her thoughts traced back to her husband, whose betrayal hurt so badly tonight. Gia was angry as hell at him, feeling the tug of ache on her heart string. She thought about Grace, her body and RJ's claiming each other's rhythm as they made love. She thought of the child he'd fathered with her and wondered how will he fit into their life with their daughter. How would she compete with a young boy who needs his father? Wasn't her love enough? Was it love or infatuation? Does he know the difference? The questions kept on rumbling.

The front door opened and RJ stepped out. He looked toward the hammock, saw Gia and walked over.

"Honey," he whispered as he came near.

She looked up without answering. Gia didn't want to cry, or did not mean to, but when she caught his eyes staring from his concerned face, stupid tears rolled out of her eyes and slid down her cheeks. She did not sit up to make room for him. She simply did not want him there.

"I should have known," Gia whispered tearfully. "A woman always know, or at least suspicious."

"There has never been a woman or cause of suspicion," RJ corrected. "This was something that just happened. One time, I swear. Honey… I swear."

Gia got up and stood face to face, her eyes only inches away from his. "Well, it did, didn't it? I don't know if I can get pass that."

RJ's heart plunged. He gazed at his wife as tears filled her eyes and rolled down her face. Her tears tore into his heart.

"Right now I resent you for putting me in this position," she said. "And today I am really feeling it." She sighed and said, "RJ, please don't follow me," and walked away.

RJ thought to hold her back, but his hand felt too weak to move. That skill of hers, to make him feel he was the most important person on earth as much as the skill to freeze him out. He watched her disappear through the front door, the screen door closing right after. RJ plopped his backside in the hammock and sighed. "I'm so sorry, honey," he whispered. "What can I do?"

Chapter 36

EVERYTHING ABOUT THE Douglas's reunion in Liberia was intense, and intensely frustrating—RJ's affair with Grace, Gia's seeing her husband's love child, Bohn's hiring Officer Lonos, Grace's handling of Tapee adoption petition, Kitty's dislike of sharing her Daddy with Peace, and Razaq feeling left out while he's away at college. An uplifter would improve everyone's frame of mind.

Mel told Katharine she was a *mastermind*, even if Katharine didn't believe her, because she had a brilliant plan that would bring the family together. Since it was Tapee's thirteenth birthday, she was certain to pull it off. A festival with silly games, party bags, ice cream, candies, cookies, sugary drinks and a birthday cake with thirteen candles.

"What is better than a birthday party?" Mel challenged Katharine, with a conspiratorial smile.

"Oooh, Mel," Katharine chuckled. "Besides a *master*-doctor, you are a *master*-something-else."

They both laughed.

Planning a totally awesome birthday party for becoming a teen and officially ending childhood can be challenging. The thing is, there would be more three & four-year-olds than pre-teens. Not a problem for Dr. Douglas and her team. Armed with packs of party favors for girls and boys, Mel, Katharine, Cecelia, and Gia got balloons, streamers, hanging decorations and a huge *Happy Birthday Tapee* banner to hang over the front door.

"We will use nothing pink," Gia warned. And when they wanted to know why, she said, "You don't want my daughter thinking it's her birthday."

That got everybody laughing. Mel wanted laughs, the *mastermind* that she is.

Sixteen boys and girls, mostly eight and under, arrived at the Douglas' home. The party started around four o'clock. Bohn was surrounded by the older children while he twisted and turned long slender balloons into different shapes animals. While many younger children rushed to RJ for the top spot—his back—Kitty pushed and block off their paths. A few rodeo riders went away crying, but most pouted. Gia explained to Kitty that nobody was there to take her daddy away from her, then threaten with time-out. Kitty settled instead, to take charge of the long line while the children competed to see who would last the longest while RJ horse around.

When Grace drove into the yard, she heard the laughter and joyful screams of children. Music was playing in the living room. She entered the house quietly through the front door. No one had noticed her, except for Gia, who was walking out of the kitchen toward the front door. Luckily Peace spotted her, because it would have been awkward to start a conversation with the woman whose husband she'd had a love child with.

Peace abandoned the group of children watching balloons turned into animal figures, and ran to meet his mother.

"Momma," he shouted as Grace folded him into familiar arms. "I want to go with you."

"Not now," she coaxed. "After the party… right?"

He nodded and asked, "Can Kitty come too?"

"I'll have to think about it, honey," Grace said, and got up. She was face to face with Gia.

As Gia's eyes drifted over the woman's face, her mind drifted back in the thoughts of her affair with RJ. She felt the pain that had shamed her marriage and crushed her spirit. She was thinking, *Somebody needs to teach you a lesson on how to stay away from another woman's man!* But Gia mustered up her best fake smile, and insincere words began coming out of her mouth.

"Thanks for helping us with Dad's case," Gia began to converse.

"You're welcome," Grace said, forcing a smile. "I am happy to help. I was on the wrong team and didn't know it."

Gia nodded, barely.

"Here," Grace handed her an envelope. "This is for Tapee. I didn't know what to get him for a present, so I put some money in his birthday card."

"I think you should give it to Mel," Gia suggested. "She's in there somewhere," she added and stepped out of the way.

Grace said, "Thanks," and walked away.

Gia still had a deep root of bitterness hidden within her, twisting around and strangling her heart. But for Peace's sake, she'd have to let go of the bitterness. Whether she liked it or not, he is just as well a part of their family as Kitty is. Her husband had planted his seed inside of another woman, and a precious little boy was the result. Forgiveness on the other hand, is a different story. She didn't know how to set her husband's affair free.

Mel saw Grace and drifted her way to say 'hello'. They hugged, Grace handed her the birthday card, and the conversation turned to the children having fun, chasing one another.

"I'm not staying," Grace informed her. "I'll come back after the party, if Peace wants to come home."

"Then have some cake," Mel offered, and led the way to the kitchen. Grace followed.

__**********__

Nàjma walked through the opened front door and felt out of place, didn't know exactly why. It was Mel's world, and she had insisted Nàjma come to the party. The best thing to do, she planned, was float through pleasant-enough small talks, then make up an excuse to leave before the party is over. Some women from Words of Christ Church acknowledged her presence with quick waves and nods. No one expected her there. It wouldn't seem odd if she had brought a child to the party. That made her feel awkward, maybe a little scared.

Mel spotted Nàjma, took Tapee's arm, and walked with him to meet her. "I'm glad you made it," she said, smiling. "I'd like you to meet my son."

Tapee put his hand out. Nàjma noticed the hand at the end of his shortened arm was missing three fingers. Other than a scar that suggested he'd had some type of surgery, no one could easily tell he had been born without eyes or nose. She reached out, and warmly shook it.

"I'm Tapee," he said, and explained, in a very grown-up way, how he had been blind from a birth defect called Amniotic Brands Sequence.

Nàjma gaze went from the boy to Mel. She smiled, admiring his wit.

When Tapee was still waiting to be born, his forming face fused to the membrane lining of the amniotic sac. Normal development was stopped, resulting in the large clefts in his mid-face. Part of the amniotic membrane ruptured, and the sac that was supposed to protect him, instead, entangled his developing limbs in shriveled fibrous amniotic strands. Decreased circulation to the limbs caused multiple deformities and amputations. Incredibly, normal intellect, and normal emotions, were framed in a twisted blind body.

"I think I'll go and help Uncle RJ," Tapee excused himself and took off before Nàjma could say anything.

"Does he always tell people that?"

"Yes," Mel replied. "That breaks the ice. He wants people to be comfortable around him. In a way, he's giving you all the answers to why. Most people won't ask, they just stare."

"He's smart."

"He is," Mel chuckled. "Very smart."

Nàjma sighed and looked around. "I feel out of place here, really."

"Why? Because it's a kid's birthday party?"

She shrugged.

"Well, I know that's not it," Mel said. "There's more to life than always following the rules, you know."

"What about consequences?"

"Choices, you mean."

"Consequences," Nàjma rolled her eyes.

Mel laughed. "Come with me to the backyard so we can get you some adult food. Bohn is managing the grill."

Nàjma instantly inhaled the scent of charcoal, burgers, and chicken wafting toward her, mixed with the sound of children's joyous screams echoing throughout the house and yard. Suddenly, she liked being there.

__**********__

RJ noticed Gia walking in his direction and he half-turned. She'd been too busy to say two words to him. "You are busier than the host," he joked and caught her around the waist as she walked past him carrying a tray full with party bags.

"I am," she said. She tried to put a laugh into her tone but her words still sounded forced.

He kissed the back of her hand. "You were never too busy for me," he whispered. And with that, helped himself to a party bag from the tray.

She looked at him. It felt like the light had gone out within her. She had shown coldness to him since the confession, even on days when he thought things were getting better.

"Hey! Love birds! The kids are waiting for their party bags," Mel hollered from across the room, hands on hips.

"I'm coming," Gia called out.

"Don't let the kids mob you for that tray," RJ joked and offered a smile, which was wasted because she didn't look at him. She walked away.

Would she be forever undecided between her anger and her trust in me, he thought.

RJ prayed every day their love was still alive. There were no doubts that everyone at the house noticed the tension between them. Everyone had. Even Grace.

Chapter 37

CHEAH BOATSWAIN CHALLENGED his wife's lawyer to name names and show what she had on him. On the next court date, the lawyer did. While Grace attended the Boatswains divorce hearing, Lutee interviewed new clients and Gbomai worked on the Douglas adoption documents.

Grace wasn't afraid of power, great or small, when it came to a challenge. Not having an ounce of fear put strength in her. She presented the reality of power and the influence Mr. Boatswain had on the entire magistrate system; how it went hand in hand with corruption. Judge Amos looked steadily with squeezed eyes at the attorney, but the gray-haired judge did not scare Grace like he did everyone else.

"Your Honor, we respectfully request that the case be referred to the Circuit Court," Grace requested.

Diallo objected to the motion, condemning Grace of a deliberate use of opportunistic forum shopping, in which she was choosing a formal system primarily because it would give her client advantage over their opponent.

"Your Honor," Grace interjected, "my client is not a friend of any judge. Mr. Boatswain is."

"Enough!" Judge Amos roared. He gave both attorneys stern gazes. "This is just a hearing for Christ's sake. You two settle down." As both lawyers took to their seats, the judge mumbled, "I can't believe I'm sitting here on a marital rape case."

Grace said very quietly, almost mouthing the words, "You would rather him drink himself into liver failure to enable her an escape from his abuse?"

"There's no rape, Your Honor," Diallo implied. "Mrs. Boatswain is bitter because her husband stays out late with friends drinking. She's using the law out of bitterness. First, she accused him of having affairs and could not prove it. Now this. We ask the court to drop the rape charge because there's no evidence."

Grace turned to her client, eyes downcast but looking at nothing in particular. Then she turned to the judge and said, "We have evidence, Your Honor. I have physical evidence and eyewitnesses."

"To the rape?" Diallo challenged.

Grace looked at Diallo, and said, "Several, actually."

"You don't bluff, Ms. Pupoh, do you?" Judge Amos asked.

"No, Judge," Grace replied. "I don't find that useful at all."

"Good," Judge Amos said, "Because I'd like to see the evidence and hear from your eyewitnesses. At the last hearing, you did promise more, right?"

Diallo snickered. Boatswain laughed. Grace stared.

"I believe the case can be tried in my court effectively, so I wouldn't recommend this case be referred to the Circuit Court," Judge Amos ruled.

—************—

Grace couldn't stay late at the office because she was meeting RJ at Sinkor Circle to discuss the future of their son, so she took some paperwork with her. Her session at the Magistrate court had filled her mind with dire predictions of the case, and it made her mood somber. She drove into an empty parking space, opened the door, and decided to take the pile of folders with her. She would look them over while waiting for RJ to arrive. Grace got out of the car, closed the door, and was about to turn when she saw him coming from the opposite direction.

"Let me carry that for you," he offered.

"That's not necessary."

"I know." RJ held his hand out and she gave him the pile of folders. "I like to be of some use."

Grace gave him a questioning look.

"What? Boys never carried your books for you during school," he joked.

She stifled a giggle but a little snort escaped.

RJ cocked his head to the side, a half smile tugged at his mouth, and asked, "What's so funny?"

"Nothing."

"Were you laughing at me?"

"No," she said and hurried ahead.

He easily caught up to her. RJ had a stride twice as long as hers. "You were," he said.

She glanced at him, he was still smiling. The man had manners and that cheered up her mood. When they reached the entrance RJ opened the door, Grace walked in and led them to an empty table for two. Even though Sinkor Circle was filled with diners whose mouths were occupied with tasty Liberian dishes, it was still noisy.

"Do you mind," Grace said, holding out her hand for the files.

He gave her the files and immediately pulled out her chair. She took the files, put the pile on the table and sat. He sat down. What else could he do? RJ signaled for a waitress. "What would you like?" he asked Grace.

The waitress arrived, Grace ordered fufu with goat soup and RJ order fried chicken wings. A bottle of Coke, with ice, was added for Grace and RJ wanted a bottled water.

They both could think of many things to say to each other, but just didn't know how to tell them. Everyone's throat went dry and tongue grew fat. Speaking had become torture.

"You've done a great job with Peace, thanks," RJ said, breaking the silence.

Grace was careful not to treat him like a stranger. She would have said to anyone else, *parents don't get thanked for taking care of their responsibility*. Instead she said, "That's what mothers do, don't they?"

"Not all mothers," RJ replied. "Carrying papers around and raising a boy on your own is no small task. I know what it's like being a lawyer… and balancing life outside the courtroom."

"You're not thinking a woman can't do both, family and career?"

"Oh no, I wasn't thinking that. I'm all for equality, no matter whose."

The waitress brought their food, it smelled delicious.

RJ said to the waitress, "There's always a wonderful cooking smell coming from your kitchen when I come here."

Offering an admiring comment is always an effective way to get good service. She gave him a genuine smile and walked away.

"Peace can't stop talking about you," Grace said, looking at him.

"I'm his father," RJ said, proudly. "Boys love their dad."

Grace smiled the oddest smile. She didn't seem to know what to make of that statement. He wasn't thinking about taking her son to America, was he? The thought crossed her mind twice. The question burned in her brain and she even formed the right way to ask, but just couldn't do it. What if she was wrong and he got offended? He couldn't take Peace anyway because he is a Liberian citizen.

"A little boy needs his mother," she implied. A bubble of laughter burst out before she could control it, but not loud enough to disturb the other patrons.

RJ straightened and the curious half smile played on his lips again. He kept looking at her with heavy curiosity. Then the curiosity became something else. It wasn't desire, but he didn't know what exactly it was. His heart skipped and his face grew hot and tight.

Then an incoming message tone on his phone buzzed, startling him. RJ looked at the screen and saw Gia had sent him a text. It took several heartbeats for him to begin to think clearly again. "Excuse me," he said and read the message. Gia reminded him to take home some milk after his meeting with Grace.

Merriment slowly died away, as well as the smile, off RJ's face. Grace correctly guessed the message had come from the man's wife. She'd seen men behave like that before, men who managed to switch emotions at the drop of a hat for whatever reason.

"I understand Peace needs his father too," Grace went on. "I'm sure we can come out with an arrangement. That's why we are here."

"Thank you, Grace," RJ said. He wanted to add that he was grateful, but bit his tongue to hold on. "I am available for Peace for whatever and whenever he needs me."

"I know."

"It's also important that Peace and I spend some time together. I live in America, and you live here," RJ said, sucking in his breath.

Grace nodded.

So far, so good, he thought.

"He's only three, but that's three years I've missed," RJ continued. "I want him to get to know me."

"My son is not going to become an American citizen, RJ, we've already discussed that."

RJ pressed his lips together and swallowed hard. "I... uh..." He rubbed the back of his neck. "We don't have to go into that now."

Grace rose her brow. "That's important to me," she muttered around the rim of her glass. She sipped and put down the glass.

RJ said, "It will sort itself out later."

"It might, and I hope it'll be in a way that will be good for the three of us."

"It will," RJ said before he'd thought it through. Perhaps that was a good thing. He would be a fool to fight Gia and Grace at the same time.

"Very well," she said cautiously. "My son means the world to me… *everything* and *everyone* else come second to Peace."

RJ flashed a quick smile and nodded. He was already very much aware of that. He seemed pleased.

"And, there's another man in my son's life," RJ said with a mock disbelief.

"There is."

"How is that working out? I'm just curious," he added.

"Peace knows that Alex is not his biological father."

"I meant, how is he around Peace?"

Grace couldn't resist. She knew how to read people and adapt accordingly. "I've not turned Peace against Alex because he's not the boy's father," she jeered. "They like each other."

RJ's face grew tight. "I would never question how you discipline Peace, but as far as Alex, I have concerns."

"No need to, RJ, Alex has always…."

"Not any more," RJ interjected.

"Discipline?"

"Discipline. Okay, punish. I would rather Alex does not punish my son."

Grace sighed. "It takes a village, you know."

"Grace, I mean it. That's a big deal for me," RJ said, his tone laced with seriousness.

"Okay."

"Thank you."

They discussed charges and costs met within the child's needs; daycare, food, clothing and other benefits. RJ offered a child support agreement of $21,000 a year, making $1,750 monthly payments. A thousand dollars would be sent to Grace and the balance $750 would be invested in mutual funds for the boy's future; to pay for college, and anything else.

"If he needs anything, please let me know," RJ added. "That has nothing to do with those payments."

"I've been managing, RJ."

"You no longer need to manage, Grace," RJ said softly. "I'm not offering you help. He's my responsibility."

Grace nodded. "Okay," she said, taking in the quiet assurance in RJ's voice.

She couldn't deny that RJ's support would get Peace into a better private day care without putting a strain on their finances. And, there was Alex. She wasn't sure how he would deal with the fact that his salary wasn't even half of what RJ had offered for child support. Would he feel challenged? On the other hand, did it matter? Of course not, she thought, while simultaneously thinking, it would to Alex Massaquoi. Women have to sometimes give in to the stupidity of some men. She would cross that bridge at a later time since he still wasn't speaking to her.

For an awkward moment, they faced each other silently.

"Would you like anything else?" RJ offered, flashing his way-too-familiar smile. "Another Coke?"

"No Thanks. I couldn't take in another ounce," she shook her head.

RJ felt a mixture of relief and disappointment. "I know you're tired from work and wants to get home," he went on.

"Yeah, I am bushed. Besides, I need to go over some papers tonight before I go to bed."

Checking his watch, he saw that he had a few minutes until he had to leave. "Anyway, I need to get to the supermarket before it's too late."

Grace nodded and began assembling her files and other belongings to prepare to leave. "Listen," she said. "I would rather Peace not go to the airport to see you off. It would be too heartbreaking for him. I don't know when he'll see you again."

"Soon," RJ interjected. "I'll make sure he sees me as soon as possible."

"RJ…."

"Soon, Grace," he assured. "In the mean time, I'll leave a phone with him so he can call me any time."

"Okay," she said, feeling a little foolish.

"But how about this," he said. "Can you bring him by the house to see me before we leave?"

Grace swallowed. "Sure," she shrugged.

"Thanks."

RJ smiled at the thought of having a friendly relationship with Grace, before it gave way to a frown, wondering how would Gia fit into that triangle. It would be innocent, mind you, but it had a vaguely unfaithful feeling about it.

That pretty much summed up Grace and RJ's plan for their son. They both liked it. There was nothing like two parents, living in separate homes, come to an agreement so easily.

Without his help this time around (he offered; she declined), Grace piled her files in her arms and was ready to leave. As they headed toward the exit, she felt everyone's eyes on them. RJ held the door open for her and she walked out. A young couple, holding hands, walked past. RJ smiled at them and followed Grace out to the middle of the parking lot. There, they parted to their own cars. He waited until she got into hers.

Grace pulled out of the parking lot, eased toward the road, then turned right. In the distance, she waved at him out the window. Watching the red lights fade as the car rounded the corner in traffic, RJ waved, though he knew she couldn't see him.

Chapter 38

RJ SAT IN his home office listening to the rain dance on the roof. He looked at pictures of both kids, Peace and Kitty. The thought held him; his children would grow up apart not knowing each other. That possibility hurt him. But thoughts of his daughter made his heart dance. When he is with Kitty, all the lawyer business goes out of him and he wants nothing more than to stay on the floor at her level discussing whatever his daughter directs their talks to.

"Come on, Daddy, have some tea," Kitty handed RJ the tiny teacup.

He loved her voice, so peaceful and reassuring. He lifted the teacup to his mouth and pretended to drink it.

"Drink it, Daddy," Kitty encouraged. She wasn't easily fooled.

"What is it?" RJ ventured.

"Tea."

"No, really. What is it, Honey?"

"Apple juice," Kitty confessed. "Mommy gave it to me."

RJ tilted his head and tasted it. Thankfully it was what she'd said it was. "Ummm, the apple juice is good," he complimented.

"Tea," she corrected.

"The tea is good, Honey," RJ smiled. "Can I have some more?"

"May I?" Kitty corrected. "Mommy says to say, 'May I' when you want something."

"May I have more tea, Miss Katharine Elodea Douglas," RJ played along.

Things had changed with his daughter since the affair came to light. Kitty almost never threw temper tantrums when things weren't right. But since they had met Peace, she got frustrated easily, and now temper tantrums were the norm. On those nights when RJ was away on business trips, Kitty would whine until Gia put her in their bed, and then until she fell asleep, cried the saddest words, "I want my Daddy" over and over.

He thought how selfish he'd been to jeopardize everything he cherish and pressed his lips together to bite back tears. Will his wife ever be able to forgive him? Perhaps she would be forgiven as long as he doesn't stop asking. He would simply have to think of a new way to beg every day. So creative, she would have no option but to give him another chance.

After getting caught up with the paperwork, he went to the living room where Gia was. She had slipped off her shoes, sitting up on the couch. RJ thought of rubbing her feet, thinking they were sore after spending all day standing. That's what he used to do. She loved it when he gently rubbed her foot, and would say something silly like, 'I'm crazy about your feet', just before giving a surprise tickle. She'd laugh and tug her foot away.

"Honey," RJ said, reaching for his wife's hand instead.

A small ache lodged in her chest, she withdrew it out of instinct. His fingers closed on empty air, and he let his hand fall. She was still treating him with coldness. With all he'd tried, she couldn't bring herself to completely set aside her anger.

"Aren't you ready for bed?" He asked.

"No," she sighed.

"It's late," he suggested, rebutting her short awkward response.

"You can go on... no need to wait for me."

"I want you to come with me," he coaxed.

"Oh?"

He gave her that cute half smile, the one that made him look needy. She wasn't watching him, but she could feel his gaze on her.

"Honey, what's wrong?"

"N-n-nothing."

RJ blew out a breath. "Can I get you anything, a hot cup of tea?"

"No, thank you."

"Or, a warm glass of milk?"

She said nothing.

With mock horror, he asked, "I can't even get my wife to look at me?"

"RJ, I'm not tired," Gia said, still not looking at him. "I'm not thirsty either."

His admirable attempt to soften the tension with jokes had fallen flat. RJ laughed softly.

"Thanks, anyway," Gia added.

"Ah. You're dismissing me," he joked. He made no move to go. He touched her cheek with the back of his hand. She flinched and jerked back. "Gia," he whispered, "I want my marriage... I want you. What scares you?"

"Nothing."

A long silence stretched painfully. RJ drew a breath several times, as if to speak. Finally, he whispered, "You don't think I can be trusted?"

She couldn't swallow, couldn't speak; her throat hurt.

"Honey." His hand swept her hair off her shoulder. She sat very still. "I'll prove to you that I can be trusted. Okay?"

All she could offer was a shrug and a mumbled, "Trust you?"

He sighed, then held her chin and gently lifted her head to see her eyes. Her gaze met his. "You never look at me any more. You recoil when I'm near you, and you bite your tongue rather than say what's on your mind." He paused, perhaps waiting for her to speak. She said nothing. There was nothing to say. He was right, but she wouldn't even acknowledge that. "I would never hurt you again... I swear."

He sounded as convincing as the first apology after the confession. And yet she couldn't reassure him that she was going to forgive. Not that she would forget. She tried very hard not to think about the way her husband made love to another woman. She did anyway, and frowned. RJ had failed on all counts.

"Why don't you go on to bed," she suggested.

"You coming?"

Clearly he wasn't going alone.

"Yes," Gia answered and sighed.

He gently released her chin. "Come on," he held out his hand. She took it.

Gia got up from the couch and turned off the TV.

They hit the showers at different times; Gia, first. While RJ took his, she checked on Kitty before settling in.

RJ climbed in bed beside his wife, very close, then wrapped one arm around her and pulled her gently to his chest. Gia tensed, yet wanting the warmth of his body next to hers. She could feel his warm breath in her hair and against the back of her neck. He just couldn't leave her alone. Gia shifted away and tugged the comforter high up under her chin.

RJ wanted to tell her to stop brushing him aside. He wanted to unlock her heart, know what she thought and how she felt exactly. He only hoped he'd not hurt her even more by keeping asking for forgiveness. From now on, he definitely would not mention anything close to what their marriage was facing.

"Honey," he whispered.

A long silence stretched and he gently shook her.

"What?" she answered sleepily.

"Could we go to the Cassava Patch tomorrow? Please?"

Finally, after another long silence stretched, she whispered, "I suppose so."

The room reeked with an air of desperation. Gia was still too annoyed with him.

"I'll meet you there after I drop Kitty off."

"Okay," he said, softly. "Thanks."

The heartbreak was physical. Gia had actually felt her heart crumbled, as if someone had pulled it out of her chest, slammed it on the floor and stomp it. When a woman's heart is broken, most of the time she does not think properly. So Gia had put ice around her heart to protect it, and in doing so, forbidden forgiveness to break through. She still saw goodness in her husband though, the man who she'd loved with all her life, but somehow had broken her heart. Her soul would have to be renewed in order to forgive him and it wouldn't be easy, to say the least. She didn't know how to forgive him.

__**********__

RJ was grateful for the embrace, surprised Gia hugged him when she walked into the Cassava Patch. They followed their regular routine, greet Ama and Osei with hugs and kisses, order food and drinks, and sit in their favorite seats.

"You need to learn to forgive," Osei playfully scolded Gia when he embraced her. She playfully hit his arm.

This was the closest his wife had come to touching him without being coaxed. Which was good. Employees took over the service and Osei and Ama joined them. Actually, Osei sat at the bar with RJ and Gia and Ama sat at a table, a good distance from the bar.

"Look at them," Gia pointed at RJ and Osei sitting opposite each other on bar stools. "Our husbands... the wanderers."

"They look pitiful, don't they," Ama added.

"Sometimes I don't know if I want to slap him or kiss him. I am so mad at him, Ama. I love him though."

"I know the feeling, Gia. For a year, I never wanted to kiss Osei. I just wanted to slap him most of the time."

Both women chuckled.

"But," Ama went on, "they are good men. Fools, you might add, but good men. We have to admit it."

"Yeah," Gia agreed. "That's why I'm depriving him of what he'd given away so freely."

Ama gave Gia a conspiratorial smile.

"Yes," she confirmed, nodding. "No goodies for four months and I might go for six or even a year."

"What?" Ama exclaimed. "Six months? One year? Osei would never survive that."

"Oh yes he will… if he hasn't got a choice."

"Too bad I didn't think of that."

"You have to hit them where it hurts the most… goodies deprivation," Gia said. "I know it's killing RJ because my husband is a virile man. Every time he thinks he's finally getting some, I changed my mind."

The two laughed so loud people turned to look. Not only had they gotten the attention of other customers, Osei and RJ turned their gaze toward the women at the same time.

"They are talking about us," Osei accused.

"I think you're right," RJ agreed, and then added, "I bet I know what is being discussed."

"What?"

"My wife has been holding out on me for four months," RJ confessed. "Last night when I thought we were going to make love, finally, after countless weeks, she changed her mind."

"What?"

"Yes… she's very good at that. She dangles carrots before the rabbit and yang it away as soon as he touches it."

"That's wicked, RJ," Osei said, straight face. "You're a lawyer, I'm sure it's against the law for a wife to do her husband like that."

"No, it's not. It's against the law to let my snake play in another woman's yard," RJ admitted, with remorse in his voice. "That serves me right… it hurt like hell, but I guess I deserve it. I just hope she gives me a damn break soon."

Catching Gia's gaze, RJ did a cute, slow finger-wave. She turned to face Ama without waving back.

"I guess no break for you tonight lover boy," Osei teased.

"Shut up, Osei," RJ scolded playfully and chuckled.

Chapter 39

HOW CAN THERE be progress? The universal lack of integrity in the country made progress impossible. It seemed more Liberians in general, refused integrity and structure. Corruption was being committed at every level, personal and civil. Laws written to govern the country were soaked in bribes, and it seemed the people love to have it so. What country or city in the world does not have corruption? Corruption is in every human society. But a ninety percentile of corruption in any society is insane. Too many people had taken to bribing, in very special ways, certain key office employees for their assistance. It worked wonderfully.

Most employees move slowly, stopping to talk to each other over personal matters because in most government office, time means little. They sit behind desks, reading magazines, or filing nails instead of filing documents. They clock in late, take extra long breaks, and clock out early. They are stone-faced and oblivious to those not bribing. They... they... they.

Many things could go wrong at the government office. For instance, delays of a dozen varieties could be crafted, that is, until they were bribed. Paperwork gets lost, but in this case, paperwork gets found.

A quick game plan was devised. Health and Social Welfare office kept a record of every adoption application, local and international. On Monday morning, a secretary would check the computer files against a list of 2009 applications and would create a match, properly indexed into the files, leaving no trail. There was an element of relief because it was finally happening.

Five o'clock was approaching and a crowd was forming at Sinkor Circle. Gbomai simply ignored the line at the door and walked directly in. The dining area was a little noisy, pleasing aromas wafting from the kitchen, the crowd a mix of young and middle-aged variously dressed in suits, jeans, traditional clothing, and high heels. She scanned the room and saw her friend waving. She walked to the table where the three women were waiting for food they'd ordered.

"I'm not late, am I?" she greeted and sat down.

The waiter came over and Gbomai ordered jollof rice for her, and a bottle of *Goats do Roam Rosé* wine for them.

When the wine came, the women clinked glasses and Gbomai said, "Here's to us girls." She took a long slurp of wine before setting her glass down. The entry on her palate was slightly sweet and fruit-driven, finishing on an intense, yet refreshing note. "Forget Italian wine," she said, savoring the taste. "I rather South African wine."

The four friends met once a week for girl's night out. The women had been friends since the ninth grade and had kept each other in the loop for more than twenty-five years. One woman works at Health and Social Welfare, one works with Chevron Corporation, one at Liberia Maritime Authority, and Gbomai, gainfully employed by the Law Office of Grace Q. Pupoh, Esq.

During the war, while most were looting and shooting, these women managed to escape Liberia and sort opportunities in Europe and North America, where they stuffed their brains with intellectual competence. The war had been over for ten years now and life had become better. In fact, life was better than good.

They ate their fill and sat back. Each woman put some cash down for the meal.

"Don't look now, but here comes Mr. Liberia," one of the women said, referring to CeRue Manor.

They all turned to watch Manor marching in with his wife.

__**********__

Mel and Nàjma were finishing a late lunch when Manor walked in with his wife. Mel knew Omolola Sanusi on a business level because she frequented the woman's boutique to keep up with the latest trend in women's fashion while in Liberia. Molola's, the sleekly modern boutique known for exquisite women's clothes, accessories, handbags, fashion jewelry and perfumes, runs in four major cities in Africa; Accra, Cape Town, Lagos and Monrovia.

Wearing dark blue jeans, sneakers and a white shirt, (the top buttons of his shirt undone so that his bare chest is partially visible), Manor escorted Omolola to the table across from Mel's table. This was on purpose because the waitress was taking the couple to another table when he abandoned the waitress by pulling on to his wife's elbow, and directing her in another direction. Omolola sat with her back turned to Mel, while Manor sat facing Mel and her guest.

Manor kept staring at Mel's breasts, making sure she was aware of this. His eyes danced from her breast to her face. When his gaze met hers, he smirked.

"My face is above my neck, dirt bag," Mel said, trying to keep her voice low. "The man couldn't tell a lesbian if she punched him in the nose."

Nàjma nudged Mel's leg under the table.

"Ouch! Why did you do that?"

"People can hear you. Are you trying to get me tagged?"

Mel leaned forward and said in a hushed tone, "Of course not. I was only trying to tell you he is staring at my breasts... and has a smirk on his face. Right in front of his wife, might I add."

"We both know the man has a lot more money than morals. No need to announce to the world what you are," Nàjma accused.

"Sorry," Mel apologized.

She wasn't sorry though.

"This is not the US, Mel. People here assume things and run wild with it."

"Like, if we accidentally kiss each other?"

"I'm not joking."

Mel saw her expression and back down. "I don't mean to be insensitive. You strike me as self-regulating and adventurous, with no one definite idea about the role of a woman and a certain type of social standing. You are making your own life with your own goals and dreams. I do know that it takes courage to do something different, and maybe when the right time comes...."

"Maybe," Nàjma conceded and softened her stare, liking Mel's assertion of her. "But, it's not like I want to spend my time defending my personal life in Liberia's justice arena. You don't understand. You have to be a Liberian to understand."

"I am."

"You are not. You are an American."

"If my father was Liberian, doesn't that make me Liberian?"

"All right," Nàjma said with a sigh. "One parent was," she held up a finger.

"Thanks for not holding up the middle finger."

That elicited a laugh.

"Come on, take me home before we get arrested," Mel suggested. "I almost want to kiss you in front of all these people."

Nàjma almost shot out of her chair. "Yes, let me take you home because... you are... you." She signaled for the waiter, paid the bill and was ready to leave in a hurry.

As they were walking out, Mel spotted Gbomai and waved. Nàjma found herself following Dr. Douglas' movements, and feeling something oddly, like affection.

___**********___

Two weeks after their lunch date, Mel was looking forward to a full weekend off in Monrovia. She had a brief flash of her and Nàjma sitting together, and smiled dreamily. Maybe there was something in her heart that knew it could be, a flutter of hope, a deep desire. Or just the sheer inevitability of what love can be between two human beings.

Spending whatever short time with Nàjma was all the way she'd imagined it would be. There were no pretension, no attempt to impress, and the woman (six years older) seemed to have an instinctive feel for when to stay silent, or when to respond. Mel tried to imagine living a life so free with her, but somehow failed. Where on earth was anyone really free? She thought about the evening Nàjma had driven her home from Sinker Circle.

Nàjma had parked in the driveway, but kept the engine idled. For an instant, Mel thought she would simply say "Thanks" and "Good night" and leave. But when she turned, their eyes met and held for just a beat too long. Before Nàjma realized what was happening, Mel had placed a hand behind her neck and pulled her toward her. She kissed her. Her lips, soft against hers. It took an instant for Nàjma's brain to register what was happening, and then she pulled away.

"I couldn't help it," Mel whispered, not the least bit apologetic.

She'd never been kissed on the lips by a woman before. As much as she'd tried to forget that little incident, Nàjma had found herself returning to it over and over, like a forbidden secret. She couldn't deny that she was drawn to Mel, not in an ordinary way like two girlfriends, best friends. It had something to do with the feelings of her natural heart. It was hard trying to sort through the mix up emotions that was crowding it.

Mel rarely had a weekend off and for that reason, Nàjma had offered to make dinner, jollof rice, Mel's favorite Liberian dish, and have her over on Saturday evening. She'd gotten a kick out of Mel fondness for fresh palm wine; sweet, not sour, or strong.

"When chilled, it tastes better than the best champagne I've had," Mel had said.

Nàjma was a genius in the kitchen, but watching her served dinner was like smelling roses. Mel eyed her with interest. The jollof rice had been delicious with just the making of what Mel loves; chicken, mixed vegetables and light tomato sauce. She was pleasantly surprised by the chilled palm wine served in a flute. Mel had sipped the wine, closing her eyes and hoping she'd shown her feelings. Nàjma simply smiled.

After dinner, Mel helped clean up and complimented her host extravagantly on her cooking and choice of wine, until she giggled, begging her to stop. Then they fell into small talks about their work.

Taking their wine glasses, they returned to the living room, nursing their wine and sharing stories from their pasts. As the evening wore on, the sky turned gray and finally black. Nàjma poured the last of the palm wine into their glasses.

It seemed as though they were out of stories at a point of a long, yet comfortable, silence. Mel tried her best to entice the woman into some kind of conversation, but she was watching the lit candle glowing from a bowl set in the middle of the table and thinking.

"What are you thinking about?" Mel asked.

Nàjma hesitated. It was a simple question, and she knew what the answer should be, especially if she wanted to keep her life from getting complicated. "Limitations," she sighed. "I recognize my limits."

Mel brought her fingers to the bridge of her nose and squeezed. "What limits?"

Nàjma drifted in an almost dreamlike silence. Her ideal relationship is, if they were careful enough, pretending to be just buddies around other people, it would be good enough. It was strange, Mel had never had previous relationships in this light. Two adults sneaking around like teenagers, hiding their relationship. Only, it was from the government they would need to hide their very personal adult relationship. It honestly seemed as if the world was conspiring against her.

Was it even fair to expect the woman to indulge in another kind of life with her, Mel thought. A life she had never imagined could be hers. A life without the rigid limitations others had set for her?

"Nàj?"

"Yes, Mel," Nàjma answered, torn between excitement and terror.

"There's nothing wrong with two consenting adults spending time together."

Her eyes steady on Mel's, her voice soft, Nàjma said, "Don't ruin this for me, okay?"

"Ruin what?"

"This. What we have. Don't ruin it."

"What do we have, Nàj? I should be happy with a buddy-pass relationship?" She paused, struggling to order her thoughts. "Well," she hesitated, then added, "Truth is, I enjoy being around you, even if it is a buddy-pass."

Mellody Douglas couldn't believe she'd said what she had said. She wondered if she had temporarily lost her senses. The fact is, Mel had never met anyone quite like Nàjma. For the first time in her adult life, she was nervous about being attracted to someone. Then again, she couldn't remember a time she'd enjoyed herself so thoroughly with someone.

"Buddy-pass?" Nàjma laughed. "I've never heard that one before."

"Oh yeah," Mel chuckled.

"We are more like," Nàjma searched for a word and could not find one.

"Like what?"

"Like, one is always chasing excitement, and the other is holding back."

"So," Mel furrowed her brow.

Nàjma said seriously, in a very hushed tone, "And, neither one would be happy without the other."

Chapter 40

NÀJMA MOORE HAD been walking about in her sleep all her life, now she'd been shocked awake by Douglas. She couldn't quite shake off the weird, but wonderful, mood that had wrapped around her since meeting the doctor. Perhaps it was simply the oddity of finding quick wit in a person so brilliant and beautiful. From the moment they met, she had sensed something that sets Mellody Douglas apart from others, especially those who had shown an interest in pursuing her. She was more than happy to accompany Mel to the lawyer's office for updates on the adoption.

They had hardly sat down when Grace announced, "The DNA matches! Ma Tarloh has every right to relinquish her child for the obvious reasons. Mel is able to offer a much better provision for Tapee's welfare. You're doing so already," she added.

Mel nodded agreement.

Grace cleared her throat. Then she smiled a smile that wasn't quite a smile. Her eyes seemed full of worry, her brow creased. The lawyer's attempt to dissect the situation was a nervous run-on explanation.

"They know about your work here," Grace alleged.

"Everybody knows Dr. Douglas," Nàjma said, looking at Mel, smiling.

"That's good, right?" Mel added.

"Right," Grace replied. "The senator also came up."

Mel sighed. There was a loud roaring noise in the space between her ears. It wasn't the sound of the ocean. "And?"

"There's some concerns... but I can handle those," Grace assured. "Here's the thing." Then the lawyer did that awful doctor's pause, that *search* for just the right phrasing to deliver to the patient bad news. Mel knew it only too well. "It's either Nàjma or Tapee," Grace said. "You'll have to make a choice and I'm serious, Mel."

Hearing the options, Mel felt as if she was sitting in a misty fog, in a bad dream. She couldn't focus or think. Her relationship with Nàjma was very important, and she wanted her son more than anything, all of him, not just the part where her humanitarian affluence aided his medical needs. As a doctor, she loves what she does. But Mel had also learned to smell the morning unfold, rather than see it. Now she loves the grassy perfume of the swamps, and closes her eyes when the wind chimes are being tickled by the Atlantic Ocean breeze. Only Tapee could have taught her all of that. Now she treasures and holds in her heart his giggles, every laugh, and every needy touch he communicates to her. She feels so lucky to have him in her life. At this instant an awful threat was forming, a storm brewing to force her into making a choice; Tapee or Nàjma.

Life can be more complicated than the plans that people make. The news was not too bad, but definitely not good. Bad stuff happens. Sometimes it makes no sense at all. Sometimes it's unfair. Sometimes it just sucks.

"Maybe I've been sending mixed signals," Nàjma whispered. She turned to Mel and said, "Mel, I can't do this. I shouldn't."

Mel looked at her, her chest was heaving. Nàjma's eyes were as far away as the moon. Maybe because she did not want to see the desperation on Mel's face. Poor Dr. Douglas. She'd always like the sound of Nàjma's voice. There were no doubts that she did not like the sound of what was coming out now. A little voice within her warned her not to push Nàjma into a corner.

Her words measured carefully, Mel asked Nàjma, "Are you as happy as I am?"

"I've never been happier."

"Then why? Why end whatever we have?"

Nàjma shifted uncomfortably in her chair. "I don't want to go to jail because I love someone who loves me," she said, nervously.

Sadness covered her face when she said this. But it wasn't about love at all. The adoption would not be possible if Mel's lifestyle is proven. Mel could lose the chance of becoming a mother, and worst, Tapee would lose every opportunity Mel had to offer. That would be too selfish.

Mel felt like her life was draining away. Tightness in her jaw, her throat burned as she swallowed back a tide of emotions. "So sodomy is okay for straight people and not gay people? That's what the law is saying," she challenged. "This is not fair. Tell me if I'm wrong."

"Mel, right now it's not about what's fair," Grace said. "It's about results. The other thing is, not you, but Dr. Moore could go to jail for one year."

Nàjma shifted her gaze to Mel.

Mel sighed. "I guess you're right," she said, "it is about results. But I don't feel I should have to choose one over the other."

Grace might as well have flung her words at a wall. It seemed Mel either didn't hear them or didn't believe it.

"It would be a risk for Nàjma," Grace stressed. "A risk. You are not aware of this, but in Liberia people can go to jail for homosexuality."

Nàjma drew in a breath and said, "I've been trying to tell her that."

"What?" Mel said, absentmindedly. "Tell me what?"

Grace looked at Nàjma. Nàjma shrugged.

"They are serious about that, Mel," Grace said.

"Meaning?" Mel said, frowning.

"Spending time in prison for homosexuality," Grace replied. "A jail in Liberia is no place for a human being, needless to say, a woman. Gay sex, voluntary sodomy, is illegal in Liberia and punishable by up to one year in prison. The legislation is even going further," Grace continued. "The law would penalize anyone who seduces, encourages, or promotes another person of the same gender to engage in sexual activities."

The thought made Mel's heart skip. "So we can forget marriage," she said curtly.

"Same-sex marriage is second-degree felony, punishable up to five years in prison," Grace informed. "Even the president supports that law."

Mel let out a low chuckle. "First of all, how could anyone prove anything?"

"What do you mean?" Grace asked. "Sex? Or marriage?"

"Well, let's go with the first. Sex."

"Truth is, I don't know," Grace admitted. "I don't believe that law has been challenged in the courts."

"Don't give her any ideas either," Nàjma muttered.

Mel looked at Nàjma and cut her eyes.

"Neither you, nor Dr. Moore, have admitted anything to me, but on my own, I've assumed you are more than friends," Grace pointed out bluntly. "I sensed the chemistry between you."

Mel liked hearing the *chemistry* part. "Your assumption does not prove anything," she said. "How could that stand up in court? Your word against mine?"

"You have a point," Grace nodded thoughtfully.

"Then we have no argument there," Mel said. "You can be my lawyer."

"I think you've mistaken my position in Liberia," Grace chuckled. "I'm having a heck of a time challenging a spousal rape charge in court at the moment. You can forget about gay rights here in Liberia. People really believe that law is there to preserve certain traditional values. Any type of gay rights activists would make an already bad situation for gay people in Liberia even worse. The United Nations human rights office has already expressed concern over the criminalization of homosexual behavior. Right now, I cannot be an advocate... as much as I'd like to."

"I didn't admit to anything," Mel said, looking at Nàjma.

Nàjma said nothing.

"Mel, I hate any law that discriminates against any citizen," Grace said. "Criminalizing homosexual acts between consenting adults violates individuals' rights to privacy."

"Who would write such a bill?" Mel asked.

"The senior senator from Bong County... Senator Taylor."

"Has she thought about sponsoring a bill to protect children? Because I see a lot of young patients, underage girls, who have been raped by men much older than they are. Maybe lawmakers ought to look at the real abnormal sexual activities, like pedophilia. Stay out of the consenting adults' bedroom and send those adults who sexually abuse children, to prison. Back home, offenders have to register. That way people get to know who they are."

"Mel, this is not the US," Nàjma said. "Why do I have to keep reminding you?"

"Well, Mel does have a point," Grace added. "But those changes will come very slowly, if at all."

Nàjma acknowledged this with hesitated nods.

"Let's get back to the adoption, shall we?" Grace encouraged.

"Sure," Nàjma said sharply.

Mel said, "There, something we can all agree on."

"We do," Grace replied. "Now, while the case is being decided, in no way should any *sensitive* actions between you two be known. I cannot afford to fight two impossible battles at the same time."

Mel started to say something, but hesitated, chewing on her lip.

"Mel?" Nàjma warned.

Mel looked at her. "How can something that does not exist have any actions?"

Nàjma held Mel's unblinking gaze and said to Grace, "I can assure you, Grace, nothing on our part would prevent the adoption."

"Agreed," Mel muttered, and give a tight smile.

An absurd observation, but an accurate one nevertheless. Mel had put a sneer into '*agreed*' that was so slight, Nàjma had almost missed it. From the little she knew of Mellody Douglas, it would take a shifting of the earth for her to agree to something she didn't want to do. However, the adoption was important.

"As far as the adoption is concerned, the last thing we needed was the DNA results," Grace said. "Everything has been put into place and all the necessary papers have been filed. We're just waiting for approval."

Mel let out a long breath slowly.

When you feel everything in your life has finally connected, it seems impossible that something bad could happen. It's the false sense of security love gives. Everything can be going great, and then, *wack*, you're blindsided.

God isn't cruel, nature is. God cares about good and evil, nature cares about balance. Mel wasn't a churchgoer, but *God-loving* instead of *God-fearing*. She cared about being a good person. Mel always argued one point to those condemning her lifestyle, homosexuality is not part of the ten commandments, but adultery is. So is stealing and lying.

"And, I'm *not* saying God doesn't mind me being gay," she had added. "My life doesn't speak for Christ, my lips don't speak for God. I'm serving human needs with the skills God has given to me. I am just being me."

Chapter 41

KATHARINE AND BOHN had been keeping Peace every weekend since RJ returned to the States. Now Grace had time to catch up on some things she had neglected. Visiting with family and friends was one of them.

"Tell me what happened," Yassah said to Grace as she walked through the door.

Grace sighed, as if the task of recollection of the breakup was a burden. "He asked for the breakup," she sniffed to indicate what she thought of it. "What can I say? Whether it's about my work or not, I don't know," her voice trailed away.

Yassah closed her front door, both women continued into the living room and sat.

"You do spend a lot of time working," Yassah accused.

"I do, and that's because I'm a lawyer," Grace alluded.

Yassah chuckled.

"I became a lawyer to make a difference. I cannot do that without hard work, or long hours."

"It's good what you are doing, Grace, but don't let your desk become life and death."

"I understand," Grace nodded. "But love is not losing its importance for me. I don't know why Alex feels that way. I have the right to work without feeling guilty. Don't I?"

"Of course. And, Alex needs your attention as much as those files on your desk."

Grace rolled her eyes, but she was listening.

"You need someone there so you can say good-night to, someone like Alex. He loves you."

Grace thought about that for a second.

After a long pause, Yassah said, "Are you okay?"

"I'm fine."

"You're fine?"

"One hundred percent."

Yassah did not want to argue with her. She gave the smile of a wise old woman and said, "That's all I want for you, to be okay."

"Well, I am fine."

For a while they talked about how well Peace was adjusting to his grandmother, then the conversation slowly drifted to Yassah and her relationship with the pastor.

"Grace, I never thought in my wildest dream, someone like that man would look at me."

"What do you mean?"

"Me," Yassah choked, like it came from deep inside.

It took a second for this to sink in.

"Yassah, you are as good a person as anyone," Grace said. "I think he's the one who's lucky."

"No," Yassah shook her head, "I am. Telling someone the truth, like my past, is the hardest thing. It's like giving someone you truly care about, bad news."

"I understand," Grace agreed. "I did not know how to tell Alex I was pregnant for another man. I broke his heart, and didn't think twice about doing it. Blinded by ambition, I guess. For some things, saying sorry is never enough. Poor Alex," she sighed. "I know no other words to express how I feel, when it comes to Alex and me, that is."

"He didn't walk away, Grace. He stayed."

"I know."

"So, what's the problem?"

"I don't think I need a man to complete my life," Grace said. "I've decided to dedicate my life to my work and my son. That's all I need."

"Your work?"

"Yes. I can do whatever I want, whenever I want. I can work as hard as I can to help the women, you know... do whatever it takes... for as long as it takes."

"And Alex can't fit into that life of yours?"

"I don't know. We've already tried."

"You do know," Yassah accused. "For whatever reason you are pushing

Alex out of your life, you need to think it through."

"There's nothing to think through," Grace chuckled.

"There has to be. You don't think Alex has forgiven you. Is that it?"

"What?" Grace baited.

"You heard me. You cheated, knowing you would get caught."

Grace said nothing.

"The bottom line is, you got another man's baby and he forgave you."

"Alex wants to own me, like the rest of them."

"You certainly have not forgiven yourself," Yassah appeased. "Is that it?"

"There's nothing to forgive," Grace shrugged. "Are you for real? My son is the best thing that has happened for me."

Grace would never admit to anyone the crush she had on Douglas the first day he walked into the office. It was only an infatuation, and Gia had sent an arrow straight to the heart of any possibility. She had her son, her career, a purpose, and a life she was satisfied with.

"You are forgetting something you taught me," Yassah said.

Grace stared.

"You've really forgotten?"

"Remind me, Yassah, please."

"You taught me that life has to be lived, day by day."

"I told you that?"

Yassah chuckled and said, "You used to preach it."

"What the hell does it mean? I told you, and I don't know what that means?"

They both laughed.

"You used to say, 'Make every day count, and make sure every person who matters to you, know that he does.'"

"I said that?"

Yassah nodded.

"That's deep," Grace cooed. "I do love Alex, I just don't love him the way he loves me."

"You don't have to love him the same way he loves you, as long as you love him."

"I didn't ask him to move out, he did that on his own."

"Maybe he wants you to ask him to move back."

Grace stared.

"You, and Alex, are stubborn. You both cannot have the last word.

Someone has to give."

Grace stared.

"Okay Grace, if you must have the last word, just apologize."

"For what?"

Yassah sighed and buried her face in her hands.

__**********__

Moments later after Grace left, as if designed, Alex appeared at Yassah's front door. The fact that they had missed each other only by seconds, Yassah wondered if they saw each other.

"I thought I had found the perfect woman for me," Alex started without saying 'Hello'. He sighed. "My God, Grace sees someone else to fit that same mold for her, and it's not me," he went on. "Your sister is so deeply in love with RJ, another woman's husband, she has forgotten about herself. How disappointing!"

Yassah understood it was a horrible emotional time for him. He hoped Grace loved him even half as much as he loved her. But this was a wish he knew would never be granted. His last hope was a desperate help from Yassah, the only person Grace would listen to. He told Yassah that Grace had a gift to care, a heart like no other, but she wouldn't let it serve her; it served a married man who was in love with his wife.

"Her heart has fallen so deep, she is drowning in it," Alex complained. "Don't let the smiles fool you, Yassah. Grace pretends to be happy. She's not."

"Maybe it's not about RJ," Yassah said.

"Really?" he said, with an equal mixture of humor and sarcasm.

It bothered Alex that Grace seemed to be nonchalant about their breakup. There was no one else he could named that had come between them. Douglas had to have been the reason.

"Try to understand Grace the way you want her to understand you," Yassah suggested. "Don't bruise your heart with *ifs*. The woman loves you the way only she knows how."

"By ignoring me?"

Yassah made no answer.

"The Douglas family gets more time than me," Alex whined. "That's an odd way to show someone you love them, if you ask me."

"It's her work, Alex. She's not ignoring you."

"Yassah, she has forgotten about us. I'm the one who's been buried in the process of her busy life. Look, I applaud her efforts to help the women, and I have nothing against that."

Alex's dispirited demeanor only reinforced the helplessness he felt. Yassah had no response to this statement.

"I'm worried about her too," Alex confessed.

"We both know Grace. She feels she doesn't need someone to take care of her."

"But she does."

"What if she does?" Yassah sighed. "Alex, you have to learn to wait until she asks for your help. That's what I would do."

"Then I'll be waiting forever," he mumbled.

Yassah shook her head. "You two are alike."

Alex gave an inquisitive stare.

"Really. You are just like her."

"Grace and I?"

"No, fufu and dumboy. Of course, you and Grace."

Alex chuckled. "And, you are the perfect pepper soup that goes well with us both."

"I am. So, you should try to fix it, Alex. It's not about Peace, or RJ, or the women. You're building a life together that matches the business you already have. Stop trying to kill each other. God spared our lives in the war, now you two want to kill each other?"

Alex listened.

"Are you going to call her?"

"She hasn't called me," he shrugged.

"It's a shame… you two work in the same office and you are not talking to each other. How do you think the staff feels?"

"They are too busy to notice… like her."

"Would you like me to ask Pastor Peabody to counsel y'all?"

Alex furrowed his brow. "Their ally? No, thanks. They flood his church and organization with enough cash…." Alex could not finish. "I'm sorry, Yassah, I really didn't mean that," he apologized. "I'm truly sorry."

"It's okay, Alex. We both know Julius is not like that."

"I know. I should not even think it. I am sorry."

Yassah smiled. "Why don't you call Grace? She says you've been avoiding her at the office."

"I'm not avoiding anyone. I do most of my paperwork at the school, and I'm with clients at the office... that's why she doesn't see me."

"Are you going to call her?" Yassah insisted. She paused just long enough for a 'yes' or 'no' answer. Alex remained quiet. "Okay, fine. But you can no longer call me to check on Peace. Call his mother."

Nice try, Alex thought. "You keep him most of the time, why would I call her?"

Yassah frowned at him for trying to appear unruffled.

"Alex, do you really want a life without her?"

The question scared him.

"Do you?"

"I'm not sure," he muttered.

Chapter 42

GRACE'S LAST STOP for the day was her first visit to Uncle Moses since RJ had come and gone. Moses Zarway had given her lasting friendship with family-oriented means. He had been her mentor and substitute father for the last fifteen years. The man had seen potential in her and he and his wife, Irene, had given her a chance when she so desperately needed one. Grace had to move out of her foster parents' home because of Mr. Johnston's midnight visits to the girls' bedroom. Moses and Irene Zarway recognized boundless ambition and enthusiasm in a young woman that was absolutely focused, and opened their home and life to her.

Grace Pupoh, stubbornly independent, wanted a good stable life and wanted to be dependent on no one for it. The Zarways pointed out the opportunities she would take advantage of to acquire skills to accomplish her dream. If the women were going to depend on Grace's skills, then they would have to help her get those skills. That's when Zarway suggested that his wife, and the other women, collect money for her law school tuition.

Uncle Moses and Yassah had been the only people she'd told about the pregnancy. He advised Grace to be honest with Alex. "Spinning lies in small areas seriously complicate things," he'd told her. He had learned from mistakes that had personally devastated his life and urged her to learn from his mistakes. "Fools learn from their own mistakes," he said, "smart people learn from other people's mistakes." Moses Zarway had indeed influenced her life.

Uncle Moses was lying in his hammock on the porch, his favorite place, enjoying the cool evening breeze when Grace drove into the yard. The old man lifted his head to see his caller.

"Where is my grandson?" he asked, seeing only Grace had come.

"I always know where to find you on a night like this," Grace greeted.

"What else do you do when you're not in that hammock?"

"I'm either taking my bath or sleeping in my bed," Uncle Moses said with a chuckle. "The older I get, the more I like to spend time in my hammock. I'm outdoors and I can look toward the sky. And while I'm looking at the stars, I can feel the eye of God looking down at me."

"God has one eye?" Grace joked.

Uncle Moses threw his head back and laughed heartily. "I've always liked that humor of yours," he said. Then he sat up.

Grace greeted him with cheek kisses.

"Peace is with his grandmother. He likes spending time there and I don't mind."

Over the years, their relationship had grown into a close father-daughter type. He was the rock Grace needed at that stage of her life when dealing with man-related concerns. Uncle Moses had not only the Y chromosome characteristics sending one down the masculine pathway, but also the tools to execute his sweeping ideas, and good judgment.

"You okay?" he asked.

"Yeah," she replied, keeping her face neutral. "I'm fine."

He grew quiet at her answer, working through something else in his mind. He'd learned to read Grace like a book, and wouldn't need to press hard for her to tell him what was troubling her.

"I heard Alex moved out," Uncle Moses said. When Grace stared with a quizzical expression, he said, "You two are good for each other."

"Alex doesn't think so," Grace said, accusingly.

Uncle Moses was familiar with the couple's history. The implications of her pregnancy were serious. But this matter, whatever the new problem is, could only be purely trivial to compare.

"Have you two even tried working it out?"

Grace sighed and said, "He's not talking to me."

"Are you talking to him?"

"How can I talk to him when he's not talking to me?"

"Then it's not just him, Grace," Uncle Moses said. "When two people live together, the stress flows both ways. This, I've come to believe, is both the blessing and the curse of a relationship. Not talking to each other hasn't helped, has it?"

"No," she mumbled.

"Just like self-control, *Reason* and *Will* is important in making any decision, whether it's about your work or your life. Verbal communication is important, mind you, but that alone is not powerful enough to transform a message." He looked at her, "Your behavior is."

My behavior? Grace calmly turned her gaze away out of embarrassment. But it dawned on her before the next word spilled out of his mouth, the father telling his precocious daughter to stop being a brat.

"A change in your behavior can start a change in Alex's heart," Uncle Moses encouraged. "A man has an ego too."

She turned her gaze back on him, and wondered, *Is he making it easier for me to make an ego-driven decision? Uncle Moses, what would I do without you?*

Grace had learned from Uncle Moses the three hardest thing to say to anyone; (1) I am sorry, (2) I was wrong, and (3) please help me. She hoped she would never have to say any of those things to anyone, yet a thousand reasons assailed her for the decision to approach Alex. The grand vision of a successful business, now not just with an invisible partner, but someone who'd helped start it, and a centimeter of romance between her and nothing. She had most of what she'd set out to attain, but a busy life was quickly becoming a free fall of insane living.

My ego for Alex's? Is that supposed to be my choice?

"Is that what I'm supposed to do?" Grace asked. "Feed Alex's macho ego?"

"Of course not," Uncle Moses replied. "You don't feed anyone's ego. We feed our body with food so we can live. Without food, the body dies. Our soul, like the body, is in search for a meaning. Something to tie to the pleasure we are looking for. What meaning does Alex bring to your life? What pleasure in your life is he tied to?"

Grace had a sudden inspiration to nourish her soul. She wouldn't admit to anyone that she'd never felt more alone since Alex moved out. She wanted him to come home.

"I don't go to church often, but I know God loves me," Grace confessed. "I do pray. I pray a lot. How else would I explain all that have been accomplished?"

"I believe God loves everybody, as long as you have a bond with Him. We go to church to fellowship."

"What's this *we* stuff? I've never seen you in church," Grace teased.

Uncle Moses let out a heartfelt laugh.

People swung lots of ways when it came to God and religion. Some people want the world to see how righteous they are, and others don't.

"How's work?" he changed the subject.

"Crazy and busy. I've been trying to get the case transferred to the Circuit Courts, but Judge Amos is not having any of that. You know why, don't you?"

Uncle Moses nodded.

"His hands are very deep in Boatswain's pockets and it's making my job tough."

"So? What do you do?"

"I think I've done just about everything that can be done," Grace shrugged. "I guess I need courage."

"Courage? Do you know what courage is?"

"I think I do, but what is it?"

"Courage is not having the strength to continued, and yet, you continue."

Not sure what he meant, Grace made a wry face.

"Going on when you do not have the strength to keep going," Uncle Moses explained. "The more difficult the obstacle, the stronger you are for tackling it. It seems you already have courage."

"I guess I do," she said. "I haven't given up. I'm not giving up."

Uncle Moses nodded. "Keep tackling the obstacle. You, Grace," he pointed, "will achieve something soon."

Chapter 43

LATE FRIDAY MORNING around 11:30 a.m., the Georgia Highway Patrol was investigating a fatal accident on the 285 highway in Tucker that closed all Eastbound lanes.

"The accident was reported shortly after 11:30 a.m. this morning, on the freeway just before LaVista in Tucker," said the reporter. *"The officer said 'A car crossed two lanes illegally without the use of his turn signal. The driver had realized he'd missed his exit and decided to make up by quickly jumping two lanes to cross over."'*

The news broadcast caught Paola's attention and she turned the volume up on the TV in the reception area.

The officer speaking to the reporter said, *"We don't know at this point what the driver was thinking, crossing over two lanes making his exit. The coroner's officials are en route. As of this moment, the three lanes of this highway will be closed as the investigation proceeds. It is unclear for how long,"* he added.

The reporter asked, *"What about the victims?"*

"The accident is still under investigation," the officer said. *"We cannot release names until we've contacted family members."*

Paola switched to a different local channel to see if she'd get better details. The headline read, *1 KILLED, 3 INJURED IN I-285 CRASH.*

"The driver in a car with Florida license tag was killed in a crash that sent three others to the hospital. The driver was pronounced dead at the scene," the reporter announced. *"The accident occurred at 11:30 a.m. near the East LaVista Road exit on 285 East when the 2010 Lincoln Navigator he was riding hit another car. The driver of the car, a male, we've been told, was transported to Grady Memorial in Atlanta."*

Gia rushed out of her office, with keys in hand and handbag on her shoulder. "Paola, I just got a call from the police… RJ was in an accident."

"The accident on the news?" Paola gasped.

"Please, get Kitty for me… call Osei… let him know," she choked.

Gia was out the door before Paola could press for more information.

As the premier Level One trauma center within 100 miles of metro Atlanta, Grady ambulances have been in many scenes, and Grady surgeons on TV during local disasters. RJ, along with the other victims, was taken to Grady, being a level One trauma center. Level One Trauma center provides the highest level of surgical care to trauma patients, which increases a seriously injured person's chance of survival by an estimated 20 to 25 percent.

RJ was in surgery, Gia was told, when she got to Grady. After the ER nurse updated her on the information she was able to tell, she escorted Gia to a waiting room. Gia thanked the nurse and slipped down into an upholstered chair in a corner. She could only imagine the operations going on to save her husband.

Not sure how much time had passed, Gia was startled by a warm touch of a hand on her shoulder.

"Gia," Osei said, leaning forward and keeping a respectable distance between them. "I came as soon as I heard. Paola called me. How is he? What's going on?"

"RJ was in an accident," her voice choked. "Somebody hit him… um… the accident on 285. Did you see it on the news?"

Osei shook his head, then asked, "How is he?"

"He's in surgery right now… that's all I know."

"Kitty is all right. I told Paola to call Ama if she needed anything."

"Thanks, Osei. All I can do is hope, pray… and wait."

"Have you called Mel or Mrs. Douglas? I can call them if you'd like me to."

"I'd rather wait until after the surgery… so I can have better details to give them," her voice quivered.

"He will be fine, Gia. RJ is not a quitter. He's a fighter."

"I know… I'm just… scared," she admitted.

All kinds of thoughts raced in Gia's head. *Really bad things happen in three's. The senator, Nana…. No, not my husband.*

The hours went by at an excruciating slow pace. She glanced at her watch every few minutes, and the hands almost didn't seem to be moving. Osei told jokes to lessen the worries. Other visitors and family members drifted in and out of the waiting room as hospital workers brought updates. Some crying, most looking worried. The TV screen flickered with never-ending images of the news on CNN.

Five hours later, a young female doctor appeared and walked into the waiting room.

"Mrs. Douglas?"

Gia got up, nodded, and the doctor walked toward her. She announced she was Vivian Pacey and reached out to shake Gia's hand. Gia tried to read her face. She didn't look like she was old enough to be a surgeon.

"Things went as well as could be expected," Dr. Pacey said, smiling that tired smile found on most ER physicians. "Surgery went well."

Gia's exhaled and waited.

Dr. Pacey explained all the procedures she had done to save her patient's life. The prognosis was positive, of course with the help of the patient's own will to beat the physical and mental challenges to recovery. The final tally of his injuries included seventy-two stitches in his scalp, twelve fractured ribs, a broken hip, two bruised kidneys and a broken collar bone. CAT scans did not show brain injury and as far as the test results, no internal bleeding. She cautioned Gia, which Gia already knew, evident of internal bleeding, if any, may not be identify for hours after it begins. Overall, things looked hopeful.

"Mr. Douglas is allowed visitors only for a few minutes in the ICU… one at a time," Dr. Pacey added, as Osei was now standing by Gia. "The nurse will let you know when he's moved out of recovery."

"Thank you, Dr. Pacey," Gia said.

The doctor walked away. Gia and Osei sat back in their seats.

An hour later a nurse came and got Gia and led her to the ICU. RJ was unconscious; his face puffy, arms and torso black and blue. There was a tube in his nose, another down his throat, a catheter led to a bag under the bed with urine the dark color of coca-cola, and twin IV towers dripped liquids into his veins. Electrodes were stuck all over his chest, sending reports of his vital signs to a monitor on a hinged arm on the wall at the head of his bed. A blood pressure cuff on one arm inflated and deflated automatically.

"Thank God he's alive," Gia whispered. "That's the most important thing."

"Oh, he's alive," the nurse said and patted Gia's shoulder. "He needs you now more than ever. Talk to him… you might be the medicine Mr.

Douglas needs right now."

The nurse stepped out of the room and Gia was alone with RJ. She gently touched his hand and lean in close to his face. "I'm right here, honey," she said, hoping he'd heard her voice. Tears came streaming down her cheeks.

It was beyond scary to think of losing him. Gia knew happy endings were hard to come by, but for once she was willing to prove it wrong. Esther in the Bible thought the same way. She would do what Esther did, pray... and pray... and pray.

The woman needed hope, because for the Christian, it is a certainty. But Gia thought of the idea of losing her husband and cried all the way home. That night, although Kitty slept with her in their bed, Gia felt lonelier than she had imagined living without RJ. She felt like someone who had been left all alone on the surface of the moon.

Early the next morning when Gia got to Grady, the nurse told her RJ was still unconscious. "Don't stop talking to him," she encouraged. "You can touch him too, he's not that fragile."

Gia walked into the room, saw the tubes that were stuffing life back into her husband, and her heart dropped. She reached his bed, touched his hand and whispered, "Whatever it is you are running from, forget it. I love you, RJ Douglas... more than a lot."

RJ remained motionless, except for his breathing motions.

"Kitty keeps asking for her daddy, she wants you home," Gia said, as if to provoke a response.

RJ remained still.

Over the next few days, Gia could never get used to the dissonant sounds of the ICU, the ventilators playing their musical tones and the monitors chirping ignored alerts. She watched the nurses take turns fondling with IV tubes and blood pressure cuffs, lab technicians drawing blood for labs, doctors scrolling quickly through the vitals and nurses' notes from the night before. One young medical student nearly tripped over the lab tech's cart that was hidden just inside the door.

All day the tones, beeps and alarms chirped away. Fresh hands were traded out for tired arms, and lines and tubes inserted in every possible way. As quickly as they came, people filtered away as the shifts ended in the ICU.

Each day Gia went home with a heavy heart, not knowing what to tell their young daughter why daddy wasn't home yet. Kitty would often look for RJ as soon as she wakes up, and would start crying if she didn't find him. She was his little shadow every morning.

Three days later RJ opened his eyes and saw his wife sitting in a chair next to his bed, staring at him.

"Hey, sleepy head," she said gently, as if her loud voice might hurt him. "Glad to see you can open your eyes for me to see them."

RJ coughed as he came fully awake, and it set off a sudden attack of pain in his sides. He held his sides. Gia furrowed her brows.

"Kitty… where is Kitty?" he whispered, trying not to move his head or even his jaw. Somehow, moving set off the pain receptors in his rib cage.

"Kitty is fine," Gia said, smiling. "She wasn't in the car, remember? You did not…."

RJ closed his eyes before she could say another word.

It had taken the medical team three days to reach the right balance of pain relief and consciousness. This miracle juice came in a timely manner, as the medicine drip worked on a regulated feed system from one of the IV towers. RJ soon felt the cold trickle of a boost moving through his arm and into his chest. All he could do was wait for the screaming nerve endings to be still.

"I love you, honey," Gia whispered, tearfully. "I love you so much. I am here, and here I'll stay."

RJ's eyes remain closed. Everything ache except for his heart. It felt good.

Chapter 44

RJ SPENT MOST of the time sleeping. He woke up sometime past midnight, in terrible pain, and saw Gia sleeping in a chair next to his bed. She woke up and called for his nurse, who came and filled him with more painkillers and then left.

"Where's Kitty? How is she?" RJ whispered.

"She's at home with Mom."

"I really hate...."

"Honey, please... you don't need to worry about Kitty, she's fine. She loves having Abuelita around, especially when she's getting spoiled. I bet she's having all the candies I wouldn't let her have."

"I know," RJ mumbled, forcing a smile.

Every time he tried to move, it felt like a knife sticking through his ribs. He groaned and grimaced. Gia couldn't hug or kiss him, his body being stiff and tender to the touch. She gently held his hand and smiled with concern.

"Mom and Mel will be here tomorrow morning," she informed. "Razaq is picking them up from the airport late tonight."

RJ smiled.

Gia had turned off the ringer on the phone on the nightstand even though she'd requested that no one call the hospital, not wanting the phone to wake RJ while he was able to get some sleep. So she gave him messages from friends and colleagues who had called her. Then she read aloud from get-well cards and note cards off flower bouquets delivered to his room. RJ tried to respond in the midst of his chemical-induced fog.

"Grace called," Gia said, hesitantly.

The fog lifted.

"Maybe because I haven't talked to Peace since the accident," RJ tried explaining.

Gia forced a smile and nodded.

"Thanks, honey," he said softly, then delicately squeezed her hand.

Gia brought it to her lips. "Get some rest, okay," she whispered and kissed it.

The hospital room was freezing. Gia got up, adjusted his pillow, did a soft forehead kiss, and gently tucked the blanket around him. A few minutes later they were both sleeping, holding hands. The nurse, checking in on RJ, placed an extra blanket over Gia.

—*************—

Katharine, Mellody and Razaq walked into the room, careful not to wake them. Their conversations were stilted, but Gia woke up to their whispers.

"Mom?" Gia got up and hurried into a hug. "So glad to see you."

Gia let go and Katharine hurriedly crossed the room to RJ. She leaned over the side of the bed.

"Hi, honey," she said, and gave RJ a forehead kiss. "Took us long enough, but here we are. RJ, you scared me."

"I was scared too, Mom."

"Hey," Mel greeted, pulling up a chair. She slid it closer to the bed. "And how are you doing, big brother? You just had to get all the attention, is that it?"

"Better than okay," RJ whispered. "Gia's been making sure of that."

Mel tilted her head toward Gia. "I think you almost deserve her," she said, looking at Gia, her eyes glittering with more mischief.

Gia squinted and said, "And you certainly don't deserve Nàjma. We all know that."

Katharine barked out a laugh.

"Oh yeah?" Mel chuckled. "I think I'm with the wrong family."

"You're with the right family," RJ said. "You're stuck with us because no other family would have you."

"It's good to see you two can still go at each other," Katharine added. Then she opened the curtains, and the fall morning sunshine speared through the window, brightening the room. "Now I can see you better," she said to RJ.

Mel retreated to a private meeting with RJ's doctor while Katharine inspected his injuries. The tube in his nose and down his throat were gone, but the catheter leading to the bag under the bed remained, now draining clear amber-colored urine. His face was no longer puffy, just his arms and torso were still black and blue, although much of it remained under the heavy bandage binding. Katharine's gaze went from top to bottom, inspecting her son's half-body cast that was promoting cure to his broken hip. She let out a breath.

"You should have seen him two weeks ago, Mom," Gia said, her eyes teary. "I was so scared."

Katharine reached for her hand and sighed. "I haven't prayed so hard in my life. I couldn't imagine loosing my baby."

"It's okay, Mom," RJ said. "Gia's been cheering me on. Thank God I'm over the hump."

Katharine squeezed Gia's hand slightly.

"Of course... anyone who sustains that amount of injuries is definitely looking for attention," said the familiar voice, as the door opened.

Katharine looked up with a concerned gaze.

Mel walked in. "He'll be fine, Mom," she said. "You know I can't let RJ get away with anything."

"You talked to his doctor?" Katharine asked. "What did he say? Did you check everything? Is everything alright?"

"Yes. Everything looks good, Mom," Mel said. "No need for concerns." She looked at Gia. "Looks like Gia can use a break so we'll step out for a bit. And Mom, that gives you a chance to breast-feed RJ."

"That's why we all agreed... Nàjma is too good for you," RJ fired back.

"We? Well... I think *we* should keep that little secret from her, don't you think," she said, and blew RJ a kiss. "Come on, Gia."

The two moved slowly down the corridor to a small family waiting room and took a seat.

"I'm just dying to tell you something," Mel whispered to Gia, without a smirk or a smile.

"Tell me what?"

"Did RJ tell you that Grace was a virgin?"

Gia gave her a tight smile, crease forming on her forehead.

"One hundred percent extra virgin," Mel quoted *extra virgin* with her fingers.

Gia gave a short, weak, laugh and asked, "Where did you get that?"

Mel smiled.

"You need to get your heart broken so you can become more sensitive to *us* women," Gia said, straight face. "Is that it?"

Mel ignored the jibe.

"I've always liked your dyke jokes," she laughed. "As tough as you are, you mean to tell me you didn't drill my brother?"

Gia continued to stare.

"Extra virgin," Mel repeated, trying to drill whatever point she wanted to get across.

"The only place I've seen that is on the bottles of olive oil. So what's your point?"

"You Italians think y'all own everything?" Mel chuckled. "Well... Grace was, and I'm sure there wasn't a label on her."

I was not a virgin when I met RJ, Gia thought. *So what?* She dare not encourage Mel's silliness though.

"Did he tell you this?"

"Noooo!"

"You didn't hit on her, did you?"

"Gia, please," Mel interjected. "Give me some credit. I'm not that bad, am I?"

"So how do you know this? And yes, you are that bad."

Mel rolled her eyes and said, "Nàjma told me."

"You can be a virgin, which I understand. One hundred percent is a *hundred* percent. You either or you're not. How can someone be an *extra* virgin?"

"No intercourse... no oral sex," Mel counted two fingers. "That's *extra*."

"Oh, well," Gia blew out a breath. "Like I really needed to know that. So why are you telling me this?"

"Because *she* wanted RJ, and not the other way around," Mel explained. "Had it been the other way, she would have said 'no.'"

"So?"

"Gia, RJ did not initiate whatever went on that night. Grace did. She had been keeping herself for someone or some reason."

"Who? My husband?"

"I don't think so," Mel shook her head. "If you've kept yourself that long, why would you give it up so easily to a stranger? By the way, she had a man. Nàjma told me Grace and Alex had been seeing each other since high school."

Gia shurgged.

"It was a mistake on his part, Gia," Mel went on. "A terrible mistake. That man loves you. He's been in love with you since the day he first saw you."

Gia's heart unwind, letting everything go, releasing all tight bindings. She needed to breathe. "I suppose so," she whispered and blinked through her tears. "Thanks, Mel." Her voice sounded drained of emotion.

"Thanks for what? And, why the tears? RJ will be fine. He was really banged up, but he'll be fine. I went over his charts and read all the reports, exams… everything."

Gia couldn't stop the tears. She tucked a strand of hair behind her ear and got up. "It's stifling in here… I need some fresh air."

Mel got up, intending to join her.

"I just need a moment, Mel… alone."

"Okay," Mel nodded. "I'd like to tell you something else though."

Gia met her eyes, but said nothing.

"You two made me believe that true love really exists," Mel said. "It's like you and RJ have this connection that can't be broken. I know, more than almost anyone, how much you two love each other. And even the darkest hours cannot take that away."

Gia felt her throat close. Then she exhaled.

"Come on," Mel said, placing a hand on Gia's shoulder, her voice gentle. "You go and get whatever you need, I'll check on Mom and RJ."

They walked the halls together, Mel turned into RJ's room and Gia continued toward the exit door.

Gia could not stop the tears. She felt like her heart would crumble if she didn't let them out. It was crumbling anyway. RJ was in a miserable hell of physical and emotional pain thinking she was angry at him. Did he still hope she would come to forgive him? *Oh, honey, I'm sorry,"* she thought, as she exit the building.

Mel walked in the room while RJ was explaining somehow, on Wednesday night, the day the church ended their mass fasting for his healing, just before midnight, he felt deep waves of peace flowing over his body. He actually thought he was dying.

"I've tried not to worry about my children's belief in God," Katharine said. "They will have to deal with God at some point in their life. Could've been the Holy Spirit, RJ," she added. "God promised to send us peace in crisis. Words of Christ Church members asked God to comfort us, and He did."

"I don't understand, Mom, but I'm grateful for their prayers. If that's what it took, I appreciate it."

"You don't have to understand it, honey. God's peace surpasses all understanding," she said and took his hand. "I cannot remember any moment in my life as terrifying as when I stood by and watched how your father was treated... and then your accident was even more terrifying. Honey, I knew the Lord was near as I talked with Him through prayers. There is always peace in God's presence.

"Mom, I pray God send that same peace to Gia's heart so she can truly love me again," RJ whispered. Tears crept in his eyes. "I love her too much to accept anything less... she is the beating of my heart. I see it in her eyes, struggling with whatever she's struggling with and it is scaring me."

Katharine squeezed his hand and smiled.

"Some things can't be fixed, Mom, no matter how you pray. I hope this isn't one of those things."

"Well, son, sometimes you have to try God yourself," Katharine said. "God is teaching you something and one day you will understand. Remember to learn the patience of an unanswered prayer. I cannot explain it to you, just trust God. Besides, you don't want the women in church pray *that* prayer."

She'd put emphasis on *that*.

"Why?" RJ asked.

Katharine's smile changed to giggles.

"Mom, why?" he asked again.

"Oh, it's just something silly," Katharine laughed.

"Mom, please tell me. What's so funny," RJ chuckled through his pain.

"Okay, I'll tell you," she stopped laughing. "Lynnette Vinton tells me the women in the church look at you with lust in their eyes... and they look at Gia with hostility. That ain't right, especially in the church."

"Oh, Mrs. Vinton," RJ snickered. "She's something else, Mom... but she's a good friend to have."

"She is," Katharine agreed.

Mel shook her head and rolled her eyes.

Chapter 45

A FEW MONTHS passed and Lonos' days had already melded into a routine. He spent the late morning hours, and the afternoon hours, watching Manor day-in-day-out. He studied Manor's schedule, or had tried to. Also, an hour or so was spent tracking those names on the pad and giving the men fair warning. He'd found seven out of ten and warned them.

CeRue Manor is a suspicious man by nature, and untouchable in the eyes of all. He watched Officer Lonos loiter near the club four days in a row, so he changed his schedule and made himself invisible, impossible to find, and hard to target. He made certain no one knew the security codes to his home nor the club. No one knew his schedule or the layout of his houses. The man had hired outsiders, imported construction crew to do the work on his homes and the club. Regardless, Lonos kept on stalking to where his heart led him.

Manor had become someone Officer Lonos had grown to loathe. He prayed that Manor's corpse would be discovered next, on the same beach he'd sent Bono and Seekey's. The only thing Lonos thought Manor was good for being that his flesh and bones, he hoped, would sooner, than later, fertilize the earth. He was sure no one would either care or remember him.

The trail grew colder with each passing day. With no witnesses, no mistake by the killer or killers, and only a handful of useless tips. The investigation hit dead ends at every turn, but Lonos was sure Manor had masterminded the killing of Johnny Bono and Matthew Seekey. The idea of Manor not paying for his sin filled him with dread. He knew he would not know peace until he had taken the news of the killer's confinement to the old woman.

To boost up moral, Bohn scheduled a meeting with Lonos to talk strategy.

Lonos gave details of his report filled with minimum progress and a lot of frustrations. When he finished he added, "Manor would even teach the devil tricks, that's how evil he is."

Frustration could be heard in his voice.

"The man is not stupid," Bohn advised. "He's not going to let anyone shove his neck into a noose. You will have to put it there. Put him in a dark corner, and never let him know who's hitting him. That's how you get CeRue Manor."

Then Bohn outlined his plan to Lonos in greater detail to some extent. He would tell him only what he needed to know to do his job, leaving the rest of the details unknown so he could honestly claim ignorance if questioned.

"Keep following Manor," Bohn instructed with quiet authority. "And do not make a pretense about it. I like what you're doing. I can see that he's becoming vulnerable with a stalker on his trail."

Lonos' head bobbed in agreement, almost smiling. "I'm sure there are evidences everywhere, but people are afraid," he said. "No one is talking. Too many hands are in his pocket so it's going to be difficult to nail someone like Manor in Liberia. I think he knows this."

"Don't worry about that because it doesn't really matter," Bohn replied. "Your job is to stalk him. Collect evidence when possible, and don't worry about how it's going to be used."

"Mr. Bohn, it's not just my gut feeling. I know he is responsible for Matthew's death. I will get the proofs."

Bohn knew better. The reality that most people in Liberia did not see that keeping a non-structural society alive was simply dreadful. There would always be zero progress. Zero. Corruption and disregard for integrity grew progressively worst. Compare to today's corruption, the charges of rampant corruption brought against the Tolbert government is a joke.

"Proofs are important," Bohn said, "but so is the gut issue here, which is his guilt. Collect whatever evidence you can. The authorities always look at the facts," he assured, then added, "Even phony facts."

Lonos did not know what to think of his boss' *phony facts* analogue. He did not ask, and Bohn did not explain. Lonos had a lot to learn at Level Clay, and it would take some time.

Like any place else, it isn't just about law enforcement in Liberia, it's about politics. Manor had been the biggest donor to every presidential candidate in the last election campaign, with expectations of political and non-political payback. Plain and simple, a deal with the devil. Some knew the man well, and others pretended not to know his dealings.

Not just those targeting the Executive Mansion, Senators and House reps were all equally gifted. Manor's funds turned their tongues golden with empty promises that made no sense. It did not matter though, because the reason they run for office is never motivated by altruism. After the elections, politicians shuffles through their elaborate dance of corruption, running the country right into the dirt. *USA Today* did a survey of the ten most corrupt countries in the world and Liberia was listed number one.

Every government's greatest resource is its citizens, and only less than fifteen percent of the adult population in the country was achieving its potential. Liberians were looking for hope while their leaders at every level were spreading false ones.

A good politician would work to expose people to opportunities they would never have. Like taking the young people out of their current environment of unskilled and unemployment, place them in a totally different environment with set goals, immerse them in a rigorous technical education and social refocusing programs. Remain focused on gauging their interests and ambitions to help them fulfill their goals. Liberia benefits when people are able to contribute to society.

That would be impossible as long as Liberia remains number one on the list of the world's most corrupt nations. Dirty politicians would continue to send Liberia ass-backward as long as they were re-elected to allow a scumbag like Manor to commit crimes and pay his way out of punishment. Worst, they jack the private sector by demanding bribes in their *box* system.

But not every Liberian politician is responsible for Liberians living in poverty. The honest, hard working politicians were few. They take care that they are not carried away with the error of lawless people and lose their own stability.

Lonos could see that Bohn had an avid interest in Africa, especially Liberia. He had hit upon many things concerning Liberia that mattered to him. It was a blessing working for Bohn, and it wasn't only about the increased in his salary. He'd learned more ways of how politicians in Liberia, and Africa, kept progress at a stall.

It had been hard enough following Manor or finding anyone willing to talk. An image of the killer getting away with the little boy's death, hurt. The bad feeling slammed into his gut with the force like a hammer blow. It filled Lonos with a dread like nothing he had ever known. That is, besides the image of the late Senator Douglas walking to the gallows. Although the senator's death was not his fault, guilt had landed on his shoulders like a pest. He squeezed his eyes shut.

"Headache?" Bohn asked.

Lonos sighed.

"It comes with the job," Bohn said. "Headaches. But as you do more assignments you gain experience, and soon, you don't notice them."

Bohn caught Lonos' gaze. The man looked tormented. Was he that angry at Manor? Or was it something else?

"Don't allow emotions to be involved in your work," Bohn advised. "It clouds your judgement."

"What about regrets?"

"It depends," Bohn replied. "Regrets can be loaded with danger. It's always a bad idea to go back. It's a waste of time. What you do is makeup, if you can."

Lonos nodded.

"Anyway, deliver these," Bohn handed two mailers to Lonos; two plain, white legal-sized envelopes, sealed and unmarked. "One is for Judge Amos, and the other is for Ms. Grace Pupoh."

Lonos took the envelopes, looked at them, and made a wry face.

"Don't matter who gets which," Bohn said, "same thing in both."

"Yes, sir," Lonos said, still looking at the mailers.

As he was leaving, Bohn said, "And, don't let either know who sent it, or who delivered it."

Chapter 46

"DON'T TELL ME you are falling in love with me," Adriana said, answering her phone.

"Aaaaaah… I'll never tell you that," Mel replied.

That provoked a laugh.

Adriana had felt a rush of love for the doctor. Mel was smart and had a body of someone who took very watchful care of their self. If Mel was playing hard to get, Adriana thought, her patience would pay off. "Okay, doc," she charmed. "What can I do for you? This is rare, you've never called me since the day we met."

The truth is, the doctor's beauty and brain had pulled at her heart.

"Well, there's a first time for everything," Mel said. "I need a favor."

Then Mel explained RJ's accident and the reason for her quick return to Liberia from Atlanta. She'd not been able to get a flight out of Liberia to South Africa, where her son had been left in the care of a nanny; the child is blind. Adriana was more than happy to accommodate the doctor. Not out of sympathy for the boy, but the opportunity to show off her toy, the Cessna Citation Mustang, and make an impression.

Mel arrived at the airfield looking like a model, wearing a cotton white shirt, designer shades, and jeans delightfully fitting. She walked with the easy grace of a woman who knows she is a knockout. Adriana led her to the plane and the pilot took their carry-on bags.

The private aircraft, approved for single-pilot operation, accommodates a crew of two and up to four passengers in a spacious club seating arrangement. Cowan sits with the pilot in the cockpit while his boss gets pampered with or without a guest.

"This is Dr. Douglas," Adriana introduced Mel to the pilot and Cowan. Cowan was reading a newspaper, or pretending to.

Mel waved her fingers and commented on the stunning display of screens in the cockpit; switches, instruments, dials, meters, and so on. Then Adriana showed her around. Behind the cockpit was a small kitchen complete with microwave, a sink with hot and cold water, a bar, drawers filled with Villeroy & Boch china and flatware, and an ice bucket where a bottle of Louis Roederer Cristal champagne was waiting. The bottle of Cristal Brut was paired beautifully with a box of Godiva 8-piece gold Ballotin assorted chocolates.

The woman has class, Mel admitted. *Something right out of my old playbook.*

And for dinner, Mel was informed that the flight attendant would be serving pan-seared tenderloin steak with a special sauce, (a mix of dry red wine, onion, beef broth, and heavy cream), with sweet peppers, corn and green onions served on a bed of romaine lettuce.

During the tour, there was one door to a cabin that Adriana ignored when asked, as if she would be giving away the most precious secret of her life. Mel did not insist, but she turned on the charm and chat up Adriana as if they were old friends.

After the pilot went through the emergency procedures and retired to the cockpit, he announced they would be taking off shortly. Everyone strapped in, he started the engines and they took off.

As soon as the seat belt sign was turned off, the flight attendant came over and asked if the women needed anything. Adriana wanted the champagne and chocolates served, and asked if she could have their dinner available soon after. The attendant politely assured her boss and walked away.

Ms. LeRoux felt a wave of satisfaction wash over her. She hadn't had this kind of evening often, keeping the company of a beautiful woman with no pretenses. No attempt to haggle over deals. No one trying to outsmart the other. She could get used to this contentment every now and then. That is, if Dr. Douglas would allow her.

Dr. Douglas, on the other hand, has always enjoyed the adventure of things going awry. Sometimes, just for the fun of it.

Adriana did not say anything about her business. She mentioned her mother who had passed away when she was ten. It has always been just her and her father, being an only child. And, she was daddy's little girl. She talked about growing up in Lichtenburg and then traveling to England to study at the University of Oxford where she'd earned a BA in

Economics and Management.

Mel filled in the conversation gaps with details about her son, the cause of his blindness and how excited she was about becoming a mother.

The attendant returned and poured champagne in two Waterford flutes. "Ms. LeRoux, dinner will be served in a minute," she informed, and put the box of chocolates down.

Holding up her glass, Adriana said, "Cheers." They tapped glasses. She wanted to know if Mel had a significant other, and soon. "So how does your partner feel about all these travels?"

"Partner?" Mel said, maintaining eye contact.

Adriana coolly returned her look. After all, it was an innocuous question. "Dodging the question, Dr. Douglas?"

Who wouldn't be flattered by the ardent attention of a beautiful and rich woman? Mel smiled and complimented the drink and chocolates.

"You are dodging my question," Adriana chuckled.

The flight attendant returned, served the food, and left.

"You are an interesting woman," Adriana continued.

"No, I'm not," Mel replied. "I'm nothing like my job. Now, that's interesting. It's amazing what the human body is made of, and how it works. Always surprising, never ceased to amaze me."

Adriana took a long slurp of her champagne before setting her flute down. She wiped her mouth with the linen napkin and said, "Helluva job. But I'd rather hear about you. Who owns your heart?"

Mel stared at her over her flute, making no comment.

After a few seconds, Adriana said, "I would really like to know."

"Why?"

"I like to know who I have to compete with," Adriana replied and took another sip. "As a matter of fact, aren't you tired of those commercial flights? Flying from Liberia, you could get to work quicker."

Mel took a sip, and savored the taste. "That is tempting," she said. "Flying from Monrovia to Johannesburg on a beautiful private jet."

"But?"

"But nothing."

"Then you have no one."

"I didn't say that."

"You have someone?"

"I didn't say that either."

"Then what are you saying," Adriana continued to pry, showing no signs of slacking off. *The woman has many secrets and not many answers*, she thought.

A silence descended between them.

"I need to use the bathroom," Mel said, rising from her seat.

Adriana pointed, and Mel made her way to the bathroom. She watched her go, wondering if she should join her. That wasn't a good idea.

Mel did her business and returned.

As Mel took her seat, Adriana muttered, "I didn't think it would be easy." Then she fortified herself with a last sip of the bubbly.

Mel smiled.

"Maybe we should watch a movie," Adriana suggested, because Mel was talking but not saying much.

"Good idea," Mel muttered.

The flight attendant loaded *I Can't Think Straight* in the DVD player, started the movie and left.

Two hours later, as the sun dipped below the horizon at Oliver Tambo International, they were touching the runway and screeching to a halt.

"My home in Atholl is only a few miles from here. I'd like to have you and your son over for dinner. Before I go back to Liberia," she added.

"Adriana, I'd love that, but…."

"But what?"

"The truth is, it's all work when I'm in South Africa. I don't even have time for lunch, let alone dinner. Usually I'm too tired to do anything else. I appreciate it though."

"How about when I get back to Liberia? You're not that busy in Liberia, are you? Sure you can make time for me. An hour or so? Just dinner."

Her words did little to penetrate Mel's temptation for lust. Even if she was tempted to accept the invite, better judgement prevailed. There was Nàjma Moore and Mel loved the possibility of settling down for a change.

"Adriana, I couldn't possibly give you anything close to what you want."

"How do you know? You do not know what I want."

"True," Mel mumbled, staring. "I guess so."

"Just think about it, would you?" Adriana said, eyes sparkling.

The corners of Mel's mouth curved upward. Adriana liked that.

Dinner was superb, the champagne and chocolates were delightful, it was a smooth landing and Dr. Douglas was happy to be getting off. Mel had indeed prepped for all of it.

Their embrace was long and unemotional.

"Ms. LeRoux, thanks for the accommodation," Mel said. "Everything was just wonderful."

"I don't give up so easily," Adriana whispered, and slowly pulled away.

__**********__

Two weeks later after returning to Liberia, Adriana asked everything about Dr. Douglas like a woman falling in love with a man. This made Manor seemed he was just an occasional penis, and that pissed him off. He couldn't believe after all these months, he was packing the wrong equipment to garner Adriana's attention, and Dr. Douglas might just have the right one.

"Adriana, what are you doing," Manor asked. "Now you want to sleep with the enemy?"

He understood the risk. When emotions dominate your mind you almost always lose the battle. He was already down that road with her. She, so physically perfect that Manor spent many nights having wet dreams thinking about her. Adriana had been manipulating men, or anyone for that matter, with an android combination of sexuality and anger since her young adult life. The woman was very good at it, and never thought of it as manipulation. It was as natural to her as breathing.

"What a beautiful enemy," Adriana smiled. "Are you jealous, Ce?"

"I'm just warning you," Manor said. "Adriana, you're making a big mistake to take such chances."

"You are warning me?" she scoffed. "Watch what you say to me, Ce. Don't let your tongue dig your grave. Enjoy life. There's plenty time to be dead," she finished with a devilish smile.

No one threatens CeRue Manor unless he or she was tired of living. There was something in her voice that made Manor decide not to argue. It wasn't because he and the woman were fused into one organism. He did not plan on making any mistakes. *She's just an egg*, Manor thought to himself, a rookie and a wanna-be. He plans on sitting on her until she hatch. You never get off the ride once you get on, Manor wanted to tell her. You learn to hold on in different ways.

At times Manor questioned whether the woman truly knew him as well as she'd led on. It was one thing to think she had total control over his sex plaything. But hand-holding one of the sleaziest of Africa's under-world was like playing Russian roulette. CeRue Manor had enough evil to scare all the good of the world away.

"I've never had a reason to question your actions," Manor said apologetically.

"So now you have a reason?"

"Adriana, what if she's snooping?"

"You can't be serious," Adriana said, eyes widened.

"I am."

"You think she's a spy?"

Manor furrowed his brow. "You can never tell these days."

"It's an honest question," Andriana chuckled. "Don't be so pissed off."

"You give her a ride with the cargo," he accused. "That was risky."

"And I thought you were jealous."

"I'm not jealous. I'm thinking about my business." Manor leaned down into her face. "Our business," he corrected.

Adriana slightly shoved him away.

"I'm not mad... just cautious."

"You think Dr. Douglas got nothing better to do than meddle in your business?"

Manor said nothing.

"I was hoping you were jealous."

Manor's chest puffed up. "You know very well you are the single most important woman in my life," he said, taking the woman's hand. It was as though the minute the words passed Manor's lips, his ability to bullshit on demand had clicked to a whole new level. "I mean... you wouldn't choose the doctor over me, would you? I know what you like," he said, smiling. Then he lowered his hand, along with Adriana's, down to his crotch.

Adriana stroked his sex plaything a few times and felt the tension when it moved. "Oh I know what I like, Ce," she whispered, "but not tonight." She pulled her hand away. "I'm not in the mood to be poked."

This surprised Manor. The woman had never *not* been in the mood for sex.

"I can get you in the mood," Manor coaxed.

"I doubt it... nobody makes me do anything."

Manor caught her gaze, there was not a trace of mirth in her eyes. Contempt filled his. *Bitch!* He swore in his mind. Then, a weird thought occurred to him.

Chapter 47

AS ALEX PASSED her office to go to his office, Grace thought of reminding him of the foolishness of his behavior leading to their breakup. He seemed in a hurry, again.

"Alex!"

He slowed.

"Good morning," Grace said, smiling.

He walked to the door, looking at his watch. "Morning."

"Alex, come in and close the door, please," she said, pleadingly.

He did, and remained standing at the door.

"You still not talking to me?"

"You've been too busy, Grace… like always."

She sighed. "Not so busy that I can't say hello. My goodness, Alex, we work in the same office. Don't you think we…."

Alex sighed and was reaching for the door handle.

"Wait, please," Grace pleaded.

He stopped.

"I hate us not talking."

"Really? I haven't noticed."

Grace put her defensive gear in check and said, "We miss you."

"We?"

"Peace… me. Okay, Alex, I miss you."

"Grace…." The desk phone rang, interrupting Alex. He glanced down the table at it. "Aren't you going to answer it?"

"No."

Even Grace did not believe she had said that. The phone kept ringing.

"Grace, answer your phone," Alex said and walked out.

The call came from Nàjma Moore, informing Grace that the adult literacy class had dropped low enough to be concerned. Then she launched into a gusty description about how the women had turned every class into a mock courtroom, arguing that spousal rape should not have a place in the public. Something that private should be done in front of family members, not a stranger. She'd tried to explain that rape is a crime, but the argument turned personal and heated.

"I'd suggest you talk to them about that, Grace," Nàjma encouraged. "They also need to know that their education is as equally important as standing up to their men."

"Thanks, Dr. Moore, I will," Grace replied. "We have a meeting tonight. I will address it. Thank you for making a difference."

Nine clients passed through their morning session. At noon, they closed for lunch exhausted.

As a busy attorney with a toddler and many clients, Grace had lunch either on the run or sitting at her desk. She sat at her desk, conversing with her three-year-old son on her cell phone while eating roasted peanuts with a bottle of Coke.

Staff members returned after spending one hour for lunch. No one monitored anyone's hours; everyone's standing was equal to the other.

Lutee walked into Grace's office, they *law* talk for a few minutes, then she disappeared to her desk to begin the next four hours of work. While Gbomai worked the Douglas adoption process (the paralegal had a huge network built on favors and whispers), Weyatta filed and copied documents and Kaifa, between classes, dropped off and picked up deeds and paperwork from various government offices. Grace had to be ready with her own assault for Boatswain. It seemed Judge Amos could not be compelled to refer the case and she was running out of steam. Grace thought long and hard about her ploy.

That, and she had to talk to Alex. She had already broken the ice. *It would be nice to have dinner in a day or so*, she thought as she punched Alex's number on her cell. While it rang, Grace pondered all scenarios why the relationship had crumbled after they had weathered the storm of her pregnancy. She could almost hear Yassah and Uncle Moses' analysis of her life without Alex. The call went unanswered after six rings and Grace hung up.

It was four-fifteen and Grace still had at least four clients sitting in the waiting area to seek her advice. She called Yassah and begged her to take Peace home, feed him supper and get him ready for bed. She would also be getting home later than seven. Her excuse was that she still had four persons she had yet to see.

__*********__

The rally started around eight-thirty with about sixty women crowded into the garage at Grace's house. They started by praying, then sharing and listening to each other's problems. Forty minutes after encouraging those suffering, Grace stood before them. There wasn't a sound; not a cough or a whisper.

"About this case," Grace said to the women, "we have too much to discuss. It's hard to explain. Since you all have become dull of hearing."

There was some low grumbling among the women.

"I've told you over and again... and now I have to tell you again how this court will treat you and how you ought to behave," Grace continued. "You need ABC, not words."

"We are learning our ABC," one woman defended.

"Not all of you," Grace corrected. "They tell me that the classes have dropped too low."

There was tension in her voice, and that got their attention.

"Most of you are not willing to learn to read. If you do not learn to read, you will not be able to know what is good and what is bad for you in the law."

"Learning ABC will make us lawyers?" One woman asked. "I'm a market woman. I don't want to be a lawyer."

"Where will all this learning go when our heads are filled," another woman challenged.

Grace chuckled at their pure innocence.

"What about the newspaper?" she asked the first woman.

"You read it to us," another woman answered.

"What happens when I'm not with you?" Grace asked her. When the woman did not give an answer, she asked, "When your husband beat you and the police writes his report, how would you know what's in it?"

There was silence. *Patience*, Grace kept telling herself. *Be patient, they will get the message somehow.* The point had hit hard. It showed on their faces, everyone staring.

"When someone abuses you and you hold your peace, staying mute and silent is not going to help you," Grace continued. "Keeping it to yourself will not help you. Your abuser will become worse. Know your rights… say something!"

"When you speak up, he'll only beat you again," one woman shouted.

"That's why we are a group," Grace said to her. "One woman cannot stand up to an abusive man and be strong… but many women can. So, stop being scared and stop being lazy. Learn to read and write, it is for your own good. Just because a skill is not needed right now doesn't mean it never will be."

Like scolded children, the women listened with rapt attention as Grace shifted and talked about the case, suggesting that every member of FW attend the upcoming court hearing.

"Leave your market if you have to," Grace insisted. "Filling the courtroom with all the women watching, Judge Amos would be terrified. It is up to us to let these people in our society… those who violate other's rights, lose their powerful influence because of their moral failures. Let's put them out of business!"

The women applauded Grace with gleaming smiles and fierce hand clapping. They all agreed, there would be no arguments about spousal rape in the classrooms, they were there to learn 'book'.

The evening was as fruitful as the morning, although Grace had not been able to talk to Alex, nor get the Boatswain case in front of another judge.

Chapter 48

THE OFFICE WAS like this, Grace or Alex would walk in and the staff would honestly smile. Grace arrived at the office before seven in the morning, not surprised that Lutee had made coffee and already buried in work. She greeted and was heading to her office when Lutee stopped her.

"Ms. Pupoh, I found this on the floor this morning. Someone must have slipped it under the door last night," she handed Grace a plain, white, legal-sized envelope.

Grace looked at the envelope, and then flipped it over. "It's not addressed to anyone," she noted.

"I noticed that too," Lutee replied.

Grace nodded, went to her office, put the envelope on her desk, went and poured her a cup of coffee, came back and sat.

The envelope was unmarked and sealed, and that made it suspicious. She opened it thoughtfully and took out the contents. There were two 5 x 5 photographs and one sheet of paper with jagged edges, torn from a composition notebook.

Sometimes good guys get lucky and Grace knew a thing or two about breaks. Sometimes they're for you and sometimes they're against you. It appears, Judge Zee Amos got caught fornicating with two girls, barely teenagers, and she had the pictures to prove it. An ass, and a fool.

Grace laid the photographs on top of the envelope, stood and walked to the door, closed it, then leaned against it. The first minute passed in absolute silence. She stared at her desk, assuming it had to be connected to the rape case. She walked back to the desk, picked up the sheet of paper and read what her anonymous informant had scribbled with blue ink, in large block letters:

IT IS LEGALLY AND ETHICALLY WRONG FOR HUSBANDS TO RAPE THEIR WIVES. WE ALL HAVE SECRETS AND MOTIVES TO AMEND. THANK GOD! THE INTERNET IS A GLORIOUS TOOL.

Grace kept the door closed until around eight-thirty, when the traffic increased in the waiting area. The rest of the staff came into her office, one at a time, for updates and assignments. She did not have a court hearing, but the morning was packed with client meetings. Grace performed adequately and appeared to be the same, like any regular day.

Late in the morning, Katharine called. She said RJ was doing better; he was still at the hospital, but wanted Peace to know his daddy would be just fine. Grace asked about the injuries and recovery progress, sounding proper and concerned, then asked Katharine to please keep in touch. That pleased Katharine.

Half an hour later, Lutee peeped from Grace's office door. "Judge Amos is on the phone," she informed.

"Put him through," Grace said. "Close the door please," she added.

Lutee closed the door. A few seconds later, Grace's desk phone rang.

She took in her breath, let it out slowly and picked up the receiver, "Grace Pupoh."

"Hello Counselor," Judge Amos greeted, "do you have a moment?" When Grace didn't answer fast enough, he said, "I'm personally contacting both attorneys on the Boatswain case."

"I have a few minutes," Grace replied.

"I suppose you haven't changed your mind about dropping the rape charge?"

"No. Why would I want to do that?"

"Just asking," Judge Amos said quickly.

"With all due respect, Judge Amos, we've been before you twice already. You have been given the law and know everyone's legal rights. No one should think anyone in any court stands above it. 'No' means 'no,' whether it's your husband or a stranger."

"Ms. Pupoh, you don't have to tell me about the law," Judge Amos interjected. "I know the law."

"I'm not trying to tell you anything, Judge," Grace said politely. Then, she felt challenged to refute the judge bluntly, showing by law he had failed to give justice to her client. "My client feels justice for her can only be obtained in the Circuit Court," Grace went on. "We've presented evidence in your court, and a list of witnesses that never seems to be enough."

"You can't tell me how to rule in my court," Judge Amos roared.

From the sound of his voice, Grace could tell his soul was far from calm. The Judge's mouth made sounds like teeth grinding on gravel.

"I'm simply telling what has happened in your courtroom, Sir. You called me."

"I did, didn't I?" he calmed.

She could hear his heavy breathing over the phone.

"You are not trying to use your power to bully me into dropping the charges, Sir, are you? Because others have been trying."

"Don't be ridiculous, Ms. Pupoh," Judge Amos barked. "I would do nothing of that sort."

"I didn't think you would, Sir. But, you called me... asking if I wanted to. I've made no indication to that."

"I'm aware, Ms. Pupoh. You don't have to remind me. I called you."

Grace waited to hear the reason for the call. There was a long pause.

"I'm calling to let you know the case will be referred to the Circuit Court," Judge Amos informed. "That's what you want for your client, right?"

Grace was smiling. She looked at the photographs. Her self-control was amazing. Now she was sure she might not have been the only one to have received the mysterious package. Someone had outsmarted the smart people and outmaneuver the people in power.

"Right?" Judge Amos asked again. "Isn't that what you want?"

"That's what my client wants, Judge," Grace answered.

"Ms. Pupoh, I see... you don't bluff," Judge Amos said, and hung up.

Grace had no principal suspect in mind. The package was clearly a blackmail to goad the judge, whether the informant had good intentions or not. She placed the contents back into the envelope, put it in the bottom drawer of her desk and locked it.

__**********__

The afternoon was nonstop calls and meetings with clients, mostly new. More land disputes came in. These were not just disagreements about property lines or clerical error that had created two rightful owners. Most were matters that had already been settled years ago before a judge, and with a final determination. Now ten or more years later, two or more separate entities feel they both have legal claim to the piece of property. Some claims were about properties that had been sold to two separate entities by the same person or relatives. Gbomai and Weyatta got through the stack of new client interviews while Lutee assisted Grace with the Boatswain case. If Tomah is to get the divorce granted, plus punitive damages, they would have to get all their ducks in order in front of Judge Bly Macavoi.

It was almost five before Grace found a few minutes alone. She checked in with Yassah, apologized for not calling sooner, and that she was not oblivious of her child, but her day had been hectic in a very good way. She promised to pick up Peace around 6:30.

Grace called the staff into her office around 5:45 p.m. When the last person came in, she looked at them and smiled, but only for an instant.

"Someone slipped an envelope under the office door this morning," Grace informed. "No one in this office better be responsible for that."

They studied her face, trying to decide how serious she was.

"What envelope?" Gbomai asked, looking at the others.

Weyatta and Kaifa looked at each other and shrugged.

"I found the envelope when I came in this morning," Lutee said to the others.

They still did not know what she was talking about. She had been trained to think like a lawyer, not a criminal.

"How about this," Grace said. "No one in this office has anything to do with the envelope."

Everyone nodded.

"That's good enough for me," she said. "Now, go home to your family and enjoy the rest of the day… or what's left of it." As everyone turned to leave, she added, "Thanks, guys. Everyone is doing a good job, and I appreciate each of you."

Chapter 49

IT WAS AS if he and Gia's life had been pulled at by a tidal wave. RJ's recuperation was slow, steady and excruciating, but he got stronger every day, week after week. The bruises from the car wreck were almost gone, but the soreness in the muscles and joints would take longer. While Gia was at work, and Kitty at pre-kindergarten, it afforded him the opportunity to catch up on the pile of papers covering his desk. Unless Katharine wanted company.

He ignored work, picked up the frame on his desk, and stared at his wife photographed during their shopping spree in New York, looking nearly flawless with skinny black jeans, a loose pale peach top, and towering black boots. The snapshot had been taken by a professional photographer who thought Gia looked too stunning to walk by and do nothing. He had snapped her, then introduced himself with an offer of a promising modeling career. RJ assured him she already had a job, his private dancer, and all they wanted was a copy of the photograph.

There had been no private dancing since the affair came to light, then the accident. Too many things had stopped since the affair came to light. RJ couldn't imagine any other way that they might fix the relationship. He had tried everything, and Gia kept pushing him away. He wasn't sure that he could be without his wife if she left him. Tears welled his eyes and he wiped them away. *Stop talking crazy*, he told himself.

"I made us some coffee," Katharine said, walking into RJ's home-office, holding two steaming coffee mugs. She handed one of them to him.

"Thanks, Mom," he said and took it. He sipped the delicious coffee which was laced with Coffee Mate hazelnut creamer. "Mmm-hmm, good coffee, Mom... just how Gia likes it."

Katharine smiled and said, "Tell me something I already don't know."

She sat in a chair near the desk and quietly sipped her brew.

Katharine could tell from the look on her son's face he was trying to keep up a calm exterior, trying to maintain self-control. It wasn't working. She saw the fear lighting up in his eyes, or maybe he'd been crying.

"What's on your mind, Mom? You're not watching *The View* this morning?"

Katharine put down her coffee mug and sighed. She knew her children so well. She smiled a knowing smile. "No, I can watch it tomorrow. Talk to me, RJ. Tell me what's wrong."

A comforting warmth filled his heart. It took him a minute or so before he pulled himself together and was able to talk.

"I've tried everything, Mom, I swear I have," he said. "It seems I can't get through to her. I've begged... I've promised... she knows it's her I'm in love with. She knows that having my family is more important to me than anything else. I want her, and no one else. I'm very, very sorry for what I did. Gia just can't get over what happened in Liberia."

"Well, what else *can* you do?"

"I don't know, Mom. Honest, I don't know. I can't pretend the kid doesn't exist. Peace is my son and I love him. It's just... just that my wife makes me feel like she doesn't want to be with me."

"You're taking too much on your shoulders, honey," Katharine whispered. "It's going to break you."

"Mom, I've already been bent to breaking point." He sighed. "I really have."

"Listen to me, honey. I know Gia loves you. There's not a doubt in my mind about that. Maybe she needs more time, that's all."

"How much more?"

"I don't know, honey. Are you sure you've done all you can?"

"I believe that I have. Maybe I haven't," he shrugged.

They talked for a bit longer, but RJ staring at the stack of paper on the desk was sufficient enough to dismiss Katharine. She finished her coffee and got up to leave. RJ was still sipping on his.

"Remember what I said," she coaxed. "Don't let this thing break you. It won't be good for you or Gia. Praying will do everybody good," she added with a familiar twinkle. "Have you tried that?"

RJ nodded. "Thanks, Mom," he smiled.

Katharine carried the coffee mug to the kitchen, then went to the living room with the intention of spending the rest of the day watching

TV, generally lazing around until Kitty gets home or RJ needed something.

Douglas hardly got any work done after Katharine left. He thought about his life, his wife, and their marriage. This wasn't some love story in a book, gushing declarations and love tokens. That was the stuff of fiction, this was his life, really. Real life rarely had happy endings, but he intended this would have one of the rarest of endings.

Time passed unnoticed. Gia got home, chatted with Katharine for a moment, and change from her work clothes into flow tank top and shorts. With RJ's high tech pieces of fitness equipment in the home-gym in their basement, she never underestimated the potential of her exercise mat in the bedroom. The formal Stanford University basketball player had always incorporated floor exercises into her hectic week schedule, even during pregnancy. Between taking care of the family, teaching at Spelman, and counseling clients at the office, there was hardly time to workout, so her every-other-day compound floor exercises gave her a full body workout that kept her in shape. Shape that whenever her husband, and other men, looked at her, a little tingle whispered across their skin.

She had just finished a session of compound exercise tailored to the floor mat—squats, push ups, and lunges—when RJ walked into the bedroom, excited to see his wife. His mind wandered to a game they used to play before she found out about the affair. Gia would incite a quickie, then dare him to finish before Kitty could walk in, or craw in, on them. They had been ten for ten, never getting caught.

A little tingle whispered across his skin as he thought about this, but he was sure it wasn't the anticipation of a quickie. He wanted to try another attempt at saving his marriage.

"I didn't know you were home already," RJ greeted.

"I've been home since an hour ago."

"Oh? I didn't even hear Kitty come in. Where is she?"

"Out in the yard with Mom."

RJ regarded Gia with an inquiry eye, and before the words came out she said, "I didn't want to interrupt you, that's why I didn't come to the study."

He nodded. *Oh dear, she reads me like a book.*

Gia turned to lie on her back, a sign she was finished with the conversation and wished to return to her workout.

"Honey?"

She stopped, looked at him and sighed.

"I'm not going to stop," he said. "Giving up is the last thing on my mind. In fact, I'll never give up."

She peered at him.

"What is it?"

She said nothing.

He screwed up his eyes and said, "Whatever it is, tell me. Let me know so I can fix it."

There was a long pause in which he could see her fighting with something. When she knew her voice would be stable, Gia said, sickeningly, "I never thought we would have secrets between us, RJ. And if Grace hadn't gotten pregnant, I never would have found out."

He was all too aware of the tarnished trust that had resulted from his affair. Osie had warned him that women have long memories, as it was being proven at the moment. His wife didn't have to keep reminding him of the stain attached to their marriage, but she did. Every time there was an opening, Gia headed directly for it, and would be doing so for a long time to come. RJ wasn't sure what to say. He had decided he wasn't going to use that word '*sorry*' again.

"It was a terrible thing I did to you," he muttered.

"You mean screwing her?"

He winced at the disgust in her voice. "That too," he admitted. "And, especially keeping it a secret."

"You really want me to believe you would have told me?"

It seemed she wanted to make the conversation difficult. She baited; he would bite.

"Yes," he replied. "And I almost did."

"What? Tell me?"

"Yes. As a matter of fact, it was our last night in Liberia."

She gave him a crooked grin.

"I swear, Gia, I wanted to tell you but the words couldn't come out. I was so afraid. Over the years, guilt and fear have hovered over me like a waiting avalanche. I've been miserable about it. There has never been a moment since that day, I haven't wished I could take that entire night back, every second of it."

"Well, nothing has meant so much to me as trust," Gia pressed. She hadn't said it with any hint of anger. She sighed, leaned back and said, "How am I suppose to feel while you're away on a business trip? While you're in Liberia without me. Or, while you're under extreme pressure because of your job or another family crises. How can I pass that?"

There's nothing more heartbreaking than a barrier to love when some-one is not willing to receive it. When his wife makes up her mind, she is as ceaseless as a cow chewing her cud. Of course she will have her way if he stops trying. But the thing is, RJ refuses to even think his marriage was in imminent danger of being swept away. He was far from giving up. Gia would not be *moving on* on him. That had never been an option. He'll make sure of it. Perhaps he had not done everything, or done *every thing* well. Just don't use the word *sorry* again, he reminded himself. She's heard it already, too many times.

"Because…" RJ huffed out a breath. "I'm betting my life on it this time, okay? I'm begging you to give me another chance. If nothing else matter to you, consider my plea. Please, Gia, give me another chance," he broke down.

Then RJ kissed the top of Gia's head, knelt on the floor beside his wife and held one of her hands. His gaze caught her eyes and he held on. "Please," he bleated. "Please."

The look in his eyes had love, affection, and a great deal of concern. Gia slowly reached out and took his other hand. They held on tight for a long moment. Then came the hug. They put their arms around each other, and RJ held Gia as if she would break. They stayed like that for a long time, talking a little bit, but mostly just holding on to each other. RJ held on to his wife's heart strings too, wanting never to let go.

"I wish I could take back that night," he choked. "I hate myself more for hurting you than you could ever hate me. I'm truly sorry."

"You already said that."

"I meant it each time," he avowed.

But the unexpected and gentle feel was like a wave of heat thawing the ice within her. Gia leaned back, not by much. Her gaze resting on his, simply watching her husband through eyes that had softened. Then she felt her heart open. The hurt lingered, but somehow she was able to welcome him in.

Chapter 50

THE SEEMINGLY UNIMPORTANT usually becomes critical in a criminal investigation. Lonos always went with his investigative instincts honestly. He was so good at observing and deducing things; his motto was *there's always a way to find things out*. He was no longer a policeman, but he was a private investigator, and Bohn thought of him as such.

Lonos peeked at his phone after it started to vibrate. The text message told him of Manor's precise location and he cracked a grin. It occurred to him, more vividly than it ever had, that he would spend every waking moment on catching Manor, then march with him triumphantly to Legion, the hangman, so all would be right with the world. Then, he would volunteer to drive Manor's dead body with squealing wheels, a fast ride to hell. He laughed out loud at the scenario.

Lonos was in a hurry to get to where he needed to be. He drove carefully, honking repeatedly, dodging pedestrians and swerving to avoid getting hit by other taxis. On the streets in Monrovia, people on foot are unforgiving even though they are truly the bullies of the transport playground. People and street vendors crowd the sidewalks and the streets, creating painfully slow traffics in all directions.

Lonos did not grimace as he swerved, almost hitting a woman ambling out into the street without looking. He tooted his horn, barely avoiding her. The woman waved at him, brazenly squawking indignation.

The fact that people seemed to think nothing of challenging something built with a solid mass of metal, or plastic, hitting their fragile body, rankled on his nerves. *Maybe these pedestrians ought to be charged money for jaywalking*, he thought. *That might probably fix half the painfully slow traffic problem.*

Lonos was hitting the gas on the old Toyota as it puttered into the yard and came to a stop. Manor heard the car long before he saw it. Knowing he had little time for Manor to see him before taking off, Lonos jumped out of the car the moment it stopped. These provocations were enjoyable to him and maddening to Manor.

"When I'm done with you, you'll wish to God you hadn't killed that little boy," Lonos barged into the subject, skipping any small talk that might waste precious time.

Manor gave him an icy look, but anger was coming. He could feel it, something resembling a flame.

Lonos pulled a pack of cigarettes from his shirt pocket and took one out. He lit up, then pressed the match flame out between his thumb and forefinger and flung it. He puffed his smoke and flicked the ash, all the while looking at Manor.

"You can run, but you cannot hide," Lonos wagged his finger.

Manor was his primary opponent, and this was a fight to the end. It was an intense battle of wits. Even more than that, a battle of wills. If anything, it was a mismatch because Manor had BIG-name people and a whole lot more money. Yet Lonos felt that this time Manor would lose. It didn't matter how many hands were deep inside of his pocket.

"You know, I could have you arrested," Manor threatened.

"Haven't you already tried that?" Lonos said with a smile of one quite comfortable in his own skin.

Manor's face screwed up in frustration. "I am so damn tired of you," he said angrily. "You should be minding your wife instead of chasing me." An intended affront about the officer's wife's affair with Chief Dolo.

Lonos forced a smile. The cheap shot had not provoked him at all.

"At least I know that my wife is at home," he said. "I'm not the one with the wife who's always away. Do you know what she's doing?"

Manor's face turned so tight, he looked as if he'd been shrink-wrapped. His lips compressed slightly, and there was a certain irritated look in his eyes. "I don't know whether to shoot you or cut you up myself," he said in a low, barely-in-control voice, fiddling with a ring on his finger.

Lonos pointed a finger at him, pulled an imaginary trigger with his thumb, and made a clicking sound with his mouth.

Manor stared at him with a stony expression. "Everybody has to die one day," he said through clenched teeth. "You are just running ahead of your day sooner than later."

Lonos also stared a pronounced stare.

"You think that you can appoint my day like you did Matthew Seekey?" Lonos asked. "I'm convienced that you had him killed. It was you who appointed his day to die, and I intend for the whole world to know this. I will find a way, Manor," he assured.

"You have nothing!" Manor retorted. "No proof. No evidence. Nothing! I am so sick of seeing you. Somebody will have to do something about you stalking me. And once I speak to the president, heads will roll."

"Yours would be the first," Lonos assured.

"Me?"

"Yep," Lonos said nodding. "You would be wasting your time because the Iron Lady wouldn't back you. She hates corruption. The sad thing is, she can't do it all by herself, and very few are equally willing. There are too many bandits that are loyal to corruption and greed, so the change would be very slow."

"Are you also blaming me for corruption?"

"I could, yes. But what really bugs me is the fact that you disrespect human life. Those who take your bribes will have to answer for themselves. You tried bribing me, have you forgotten about that?"

Manor was pissed. "You really think that you can nail me with some bogus crap? Slam me behind some prison bars?" He chuckled. "You are dreaming Officer Lonos. Oh, wait a minute. You are no longer an officer. I almost forgot. So, I would say *ass-hole* Lonos."

Lonos stared with a smug expression.

"Your threats are empty, ass-hole," Manor continued. "Keep threatening me and I'll squash you like a fucking bug."

Lonos barked out a vigorous laugh.

"I could call Dolo, but I bet that's what he's doing to your wife."

Lonos laughed louder.

Manor could go on, but the complete ridiculousness of the insults stopped him. Of course the man must not care about his wife, or he was bluffing. Manor took a deep breath.

"You're right, Lonos," Manor said. "There are a lot more people here who wants my money. There are even more who are willing to give me a lot of their money for whatever their heart desires."

This brought an instant reaction. Lonos' laughter died.

"Now that I have your attention, let me finish so I can leave," Manor went on. "I intend to keep giving those clients exactly what they want. Anything... everything," he said, scornfully.

"You are no god to give someone wealth, or take their life," Lonos barked. "You are no longer allowed to play with people's lives. Like every other human being, you are temporary and your time is up."

Manor chuckled. "I might not be your god, Lonos, but I am their god," he said. "I give them what our government isn't giving them. Cash. Lots of it."

"You are not going to kill another person, Manor," Lonos said, his voice hard. "I have my eyes on you and no amount of cash is going to stop me from following you. You didn't think that I could find you here today, but I did. Didn't I? Your foot, my foot; that's how it's going to be. I am your shadow."

"Don't be a fool, Lonos. If you come near my home again, or my office, I will shoot you. I don't want to see your face near my property."

"Your foot, my foot," Lonos repeated, then walked away.

Chapter 51

AT HALF-PAST ELEVEN after Adriana finished breakfast, she wandered to the back deck rather than staying in the room to wait for Manor who hadn't shown up for breakfast as promised. She had a sneaking suspicion that his wife might be in town. Chagrined, she sat on the lawn beach lounger, threw her feet up, leaned back and crossed her arms. Her back had barely touched the chair when Officer Lonos saw her, walked over and sat in the empty chair across from her. He had not bothered with even a hint of the usual formalities.

"I didn't invite you to sit," Adriana said through clenched teeth, uncrossing her arms.

She sat up. The woman had plenty of beauty, but Lonos could not see it.

"I thank you anyway," he said, scrutinizing her. "I could say it is nice meeting you, but why lie for no reason. I'm looking for your boyfriend."

She felt a hot flush work its way up from her neck to her face. "My fucking what?"

He stared at her in obvious bafflement. Pretty girls shouldn't use ugly words like shit, fuck, cock, damn, or bitch. She did. It would have been easier if she had been an ugly woman. But Adriana is a beauty with no soul.

"Your boyfriend... Manor. Remember him? I know he's supposed to meet you here today." Lonos looked at his watch, then stared off.

A waiter headed her way but Adriana signaled him away before the man reached them, then pushed the speed-dial button on her phone.

"If it's Manor you're calling, tell him that I'm waiting," Lonos spurted.

"You've got a nasty habit of showing up where you don't belong," Adriana snapped. "And that nasty tongue of yours, you need to learn to keep it in your head. I don't give a shit about this ridiculous childish game between you and Manor, but this is for your own good."

"You are the one with the nasty tongue, and...."

Before Lonos could finish, a rock-solid 6-foot-something man came out of nowhere. Lonos' eyes widened and he stood. *The man must be here to protect LeRoux*, he thought. He wondered whether Manor had sent him. His thoughts were interrupted by the sound of the man's rebuke.

"It's obvious Ms. LeRoux does not want your company," Cowan scolded.

The statement seemed out of context. Lonos stood for a moment without responding.

"He's not going away, you know. He's like a bad body odor. Just kick his ass," Adriana ordered.

Now Lonos had something to say for the woman's attitude. He suspected she was involved in unseen ways, but had kept those thoughts to himself. He said to Adriana, "Kick my ass, huh?"

Adriana rose from her seat. "Are you going to kick his monkey-ass or what," she yelled at Cowan.

"I need to kick your prejudice South African ass," Lonos said, now walking towards the woman.

"Hey! Hey!" Cowan barked. He stood between Lonos and the woman, leaned toward Lonos and said, "Where you think you're going?"

"You foreigners think you can come to my country and talk down at everyone? Try me," Lonos threatened.

Cowan turned to Adriana. "Ms. LeRoux, could you step away for a moment please."

Adriana did.

"Further than that, Ma'am."

Adriana took a few more steps.

Cowan requested more space until the woman was out of harm's way. Then a volley of jeering went back and forth between him and Lonos. As their argument reached the two minute point, Cowan wondered if his point came across clearly to the man.

After there had been enough debate, Cowan stood about an inch away from Officer Lonos' face and said, "Just tell the lady you're sorry."

There was no menace in his voice. It wasn't necessary. He had a way of sounding threatening without so much as a change of tone.

"There's no lady here," Lonos snarled.

Officer Lonos never hid his interest and had a cockiness about him. That could be ugly if Cowan too decides to prove his superior strength. He wasn't sure Lonos was throwing out a challenge.

"I say, she's a lady," Cowan said, with obvious sarcasm.

Defiance flashed in Lonos' eyes. It would not seem right for two grown men, antagonistic toward each other, don't actually fight. There were sharp intake of breaths. Tension stretched tighter and tighter. They waited for either to explode in anger. Cowan was dying to get to the part where he would make Lonos wished he'd picked on someone else. Lonos screwed up his face, thinking hard.

"Apologize to the lady," Cowan ordered, puffing out his chest.

Cowan had always waited and let his opponent take the initiative. It was a good way to get him off balance immediately, so that he needed only one well-placed blow to finish the fight before it got out of hand. This time he didn't. He stepped closer and grinned. As Lonos thought about whether to grin back or not, Cowan landed a punch just below the ribs. He didn't pull back. It must have hurt, but Lonos merely grunted.

"That's all you got?" Lonos snarled.

Cowan shrugged one shoulder and half-turned, but kept Lonos in his sights. He rolled up his sleeves to reveal thick muscled forearms and twisted his neck. Tension invaded his body. Cracking his knuckles, Cowan advanced, swung round and landed a punch on Lonos' jaw that sent him stumbling back. Lonos recovered and with a roar of anger, ran at Cowan. Cowan ducked, and as Officer Lonos lumbered past, tripped him. Lonos tumbled to the deck like a falling tree, landing with a thump that shook the deck, some witnesses would swear.

It all happened without Cowan thinking. In moments of combat, his mind seemed to empty and switch to another level. The motions were effortless, instinctive, and he could see Lonos' weaknesses as clearly as he could see the shape of him.

Cowan pressed his boot to the back of the man's neck, not hard enough to crush anything vital, but hard enough to induce fear. Lonos' arms flapped about trying to grasp Cowan's leg and his feet kicked aimlessly. It looked comical, but no one laughed.

Lonos felt he had no chance. Pure luck was falling ass backward and everything was turning out shitty. As soon as Cowan removed his foot, Lonos leaped to his feet and took off running. Cowan ran after him and brought him down with a football tackle.

With fights, his instincts were sharp and never failed him. Cowan held Lonos' arm in a grip that would leave fingerprint bruises. He felt in complete control of his body, confirming all the things that made him a good hired gun; ruthless efficiency, a heightened awareness of his surroundings, and instinct.

Ego can do terrible things to a man. Cowan punched the man's face, chest, and ribs. Then he finished off his opponent with a swift kick to the stomach.

Adriana felt her stomach turn at the sight of the oozing blood, but she quickly recovered. Their commotion amused her, she felt quite wild with relief. And, powerful. Cowan had given her a kind of thrill rush without touching her sexually. He'd performed his duties, displaying abs and biceps she longed to touch.

"Next time you see Ms. LeRoux, treat her like a lady," Cowan barked, then kicked Lonos again as he tried to stand.

Officer Lonos crumpled to the ground and didn't get up.

__**********__

It was a long day for Dr. Douglas. Every day seemed to be like that for Mel. She had an office hour starting at 7:30 a.m., and she was still around the hospital at eight and nine o'clock at night, sometimes later. She actually encouraged patients to call her any time if they had a medical problem.

Mel was at JFK a little past 5:30 in the afternoon, beyond tired. She'd been there since midnight to help victims that had been brought from a fatal car accident on the Monrovia-Kakata highway. She had noticed that the highway had no speed limit signs, nor other traffic safety signs. *One of the many important issues ignored by politicians*, she thought.

Her beeper went off and she made the call to Bohn.

"I know it's been a long day for you, sweetie," Bohn answered. "They're bringing in Lonos, can you please take care of him for me?"

"What happened?"

"Fist fight," Bohn replied.

Mel didn't bother for details. "Okay," she yawned. "Tell Mom that I'd be late and not to worry."

She located Lonos in the ER waiting area and approached. "Officer Lonos?"

Lonos lifted his head slowly, showing his battered face, embarrassed and hurting. His face showed that he'd been worked over good. A ring of crusty blood was still plastered to the hairline at his right temple, his lower lip cut and puffy, his left eye swollen shut. There was a massive bruise on his left cheek, plus half a dozen smaller lacerations.

"Come with me," Mel said, and led the way.

Officer Lonos followed slowly.

After the x-rays and exams, there were no broken bones, but the bruises and lacerations showed sufficient evidence that Officer Lonos had received an incredible whipping. Mel gave him ice packs for his bruises and Tylenol for the monstrous pain.

Yassah called Grace and gave her an abbreviated account of the fight Officer Lonos had with either Adriana's bodyguard or Boatswain, she wasn't sure who, and that he had been taken to the hospital. She was unsure of his condition too.

Grace call to Mel went to voice mail. She picked up her son from the day care early and went straight home. As soon as they got in, she secured the door for the night with the four locks; two she had added after Alex moved out, two dead bolts, and a chain latch.

Chapter 52

TOMAH HAD BECOME extremely nervous since Boatswain's last attack, and trying pitifully to look brave. Now that the case had been referred to the Circuit Court, they suspect Boatswain would probably be lurking nearby. Word travels fast, and they wouldn't be surprised if he was up to something else. She couldn't pretend as if she could come and go as she please.

As far as Boatswain is concerned, the type of woman an unlucky man could ever encountered is one possessing an enormous appetite for achievement. Even worse, a man-hater with the reputation for merciless ball-squeezing. When she is not pushing her obsession of wit and persuasion, she is not pleased. In his mind's eye, Grace Pupoh fitted that mold perfectly.

Macavoi is a woman of details, so Grace wanted to go over a few things with Tomah before the hearing. A lunch meeting was scheduled the day before. As they walked the main street, heading back to the office, Tomah stayed closed to Grace.

"Hey!" Someone yelled from behind.

Grace and Tomah turned around as Boatswain came walking toward them. Tomah wasn't shocked, but she was scared.

"Don't worry, he won't touch you," Grace muttered. "There are too many people here on the streets, too many witnesses."

Boatswain caught up, gave his wife a hateful stare and said to Grace, "You don't realize it, but education is your curse."

Grace furrowed her brow.

"You are fooling these women, talking about freedom," he continued. "Free from what? Their responsibilities? The role of the woman was clearly established by God, not me."

Grace wasn't sure if the man was giving credit, or offering an apology on the Lord's behalf. "Which role is that?" she sneered.

"The role of the woman? You should know... you *are* a woman. But don't be fooled by the fact that Liberians put a woman in the Mansion. That mistake has made all you women frisky. They say, 'when the head gets full, the womb gets empty'. You think having one child is enough? You should be having more children. Alex should keep you barefoot and pregnant... but he's not a real man. So you see, education is your curse."

Grace snickered. "And you think sexual terror makes you manly? I'm glad you've noticed that Liberian women are getting educated. We don't need *you*," she pointed at him.

"You don't need men?" Boatswain snarled, shaking his head like a bull. "Your education is what you need? Women will never be in charge. God put men in charge, so how can you change that?"

"Ellen is in charge... she's not just any woman. She's educated."

Boatswain cut his eyes. "That will soon change. No other woman will sit in that Mansion."

"It's not up to you, Boatswain," she pointed. "We, women, will get rid of your kind. That's what our education will do for us. See you in court."

Grace held Tomah by her elbow and proceeded to walk.

"She's fooling you, Tomah!" Boatswain shouted.

"Come on, Tomah, ignore him... keep walking," Grace urged.

"Tomah!" Boatswain shouted, "You can run now, but after the trial the law will put you back in my hands like a gift. Then, I will deal with you like I should have."

Confidence is inspiring, and yet so often misplaced. Boatswain had made his mark in so many ways in Liberia, why should the Circuit Court be any different? He also had Manor's status and money to back him. *Everybody has a price, Judge Macavoi would not be different,* so the man thought.

The women hurried away without looking back. Behind them they heard Cheah Boatswain laughing.

__**********__

Folks were certain in front of Honorable Bly Macavoi, the wheels of justice is always turning. In Macavoi's courtroom, she barked at lawyers, enforced deadlines, threatened perjurers with jail, and had actually dished out a few jail time. Even litigants pursuing frivolous claims were bounced out of her court. She'd graduated top of her class from Princeton and Howard University on government scholarships. Still a few years under forty, Macavoi had her eyes on the Supreme Court Chief Justice seat and well on her way to accomplish that. A rising star in the Justice Ministry, Macavoi had gone from Chief Prosecutor to Circuit Court Judge in a few years—on pure determination.

Beneath her agreeable smile is a fighter, a true believer in change. She had no political affiliate, belonged to no organized religion, showed no favorites and no preconceived notions about anything or anyone. She was open and fair-minded as she could possibly be. A few years ago, Macavoi was the government's prosecutor in the Heart-men case and had gotten the death sentence for all five perpetrators although the lineup included two influential men. Something she was very proud of.

Even as a lawyer, a strange curiosity attracted Macavoi to knowing the truth. She loves evidence and being thorough is her trademark. During the Heart-men trial, she'd used every piece of evidence from the local and international experts, every photograph, every willing testimony.

A judge is not the trier of facts (the jury is), except to preside over proceedings and maintain order, determine whether evidence is illegal or improper, and uphold the law. With her new position as Circuit Court Judge, Macavoi took the law seriously.

After evaluating the history of Judge Macavoi's prior decisions and biases on issues specific to the Boatswain's case, along with the strength of the evidence and the emotional issues, Diallo thought it proper to file for a jury trial in defense of the rape charge. For one thing, it would take more time, be significantly more expensive (Manor was paying), and could take a much longer time to be reached on a trial calendar. Even at that, it would be Judge Macavoi's discretion. Then again, juries can be swayed by emotion much easier than a judge. One thing bothered Diallo though, he wondered if the judge knew Grace had become a passionate and noisy voice for the Liberian women.

Grace objected to neither, and that bothered Diallo a bit too. That did not matter much, a jury trial in writing can be withdrawn orally in open court, if need be. A demand for a jury trial may be withdrawn at any time, with or without leave of court.

Judge Macavoi allowed the parties a temporary hearing, intended to result in some final resolution of the minor issues. Grace and Diallo met with Judge Macavoi at her office to address who gets temporary use of the marital home, and who pays temporary attorney fees.

"Did the rape take place during the marriage or before?" Judge Macavoi asked.

"During the marriage, Your Honor, " Grace answered. "Multiple times."

"Did both parties voluntarily cohabited after these rapes?"

"Yes, Your Honor," Grace answered. "My client had nowhere else to go."

"Where does she live now?"

"With friends."

"Why did she not go to these friends when the rape happened before? The first time, I mean," Judge Macavoi wanted to know.

"Mr. Boatswain is not an easy man to get away from, Your Honor," Grace said.

Judge Macavoi sank in her seat and sighed. She turned her gaze on Diallo.

"He did not stop her the day she left, Your Honor," Diallo informed. "She could have left before then… on her own will."

"She didn't just walk out," Grace threw in. "She was rescued."

"Enough," Judge Macavoi interjected.

Diallo and Grace looked at each other, eyeball to eyeball.

"Here's what we're going to do," Judge Macavoi said. "Mr. Boatswain can remain where he is, which is their home." She looked at Diallo, he nodded. "I'll order him to pay for his wife's accommodations while the case is in court."

"Your Honor, she's at a friend's house," Diallo challenged.

"She's not on vacation," Grace rebutted. "Mrs. Boatswain is out of their home because of Mr. Boatswain's abuse."

"My client will not make an issue out of this, Your Honor," Diallo said quickly. "He's always taken care of his wife. Why not now?"

"Fair enough," Judge Macavoi said, writing on her pad. "Any children?"

"None," both lawyers answered.

"No argument there," Judge Macavoi said, looking up at both lawyers. She smiled. "Now, Mr. Amadou, I'd like the list of your client's marital assets. All of it."

Diallo shifted in his chair.

"No fiction," Judge Macavoi warned.

"Yes, Your Honor," Diallo replied.

"Good," Judge Macavoi said and added, "as soon as possible."

Diallo nodded.

"My client acquired some medical expenses after we filed the divorce petition, Your Honor," Grace informed.

"Medical expense?" Macavoi frowned. "How come?"

"Mr. Boatswain attacked my client," Grace assured.

"After she moved out?" Judge Macavoi asked.

"After she was rescued," Grace corrected.

"Any witnesses?" Judge Macavoi asked.

"Neighbors, friends, family… we have witnesses, Your Honor."

"We'll get to those during the trial," Judge Macavoi said and scribbled more notes on her pad. "I guess mediation is out of the question," she said, looking at Grace.

"Unless Mr. Boatswain is willing to admit he raped my client," Grace said. She turned to Diallo, "Would he?"

"Out of the question," Diallo shook his head. "My client denied the charges before, and he's denying it now."

Grace turned to Judge Macavoi. "Mediation is out of the question, Your Honor."

"Well… see you all at the trial," Judge Macavoi said.

The meeting was adjourned.

Chapter 53

NINETY DAYS UNTIL the wedding and the engagement had yet to be announced, although Julius had already proposed with a ring. He had not rehearsed it before that evening at Sophie's Ice Cream Shop, where he had taken her for a treat. The way he asked was beautiful and thoughtful.

"Yassah," he said, "I've been in love with you for the last couple of years. I don't know if you are ready yet. If you are, will you marry me?"

Yassah smiled, utterly in love with Pastor Peabody and wanted to spend the rest of her life with him. She chuckled and giggled all at once. "Yes, Julius," she whispered, "I am ready to spend the rest of my life with you."

Julius Peabody was sincere and they care deeply about each other. Yassah wasn't sure they wouldn't be hurting some members' feelings, knowing how they felt about her. When the announcement is finally made, she imagine some members telling those who'd fainted, to please get up off the floor. What else to expect after hearing all the gossips.

"Pastor Peabody has become uncaring," Lynnette Vinton had protested thru gossips. "He is about to give himself up to sensuality... to a loose woman to practice every kind of impurity. That is no way to teach people about God."

"He knows better than to give the devil an opportunity," one of her supporters also added.

Some were open with the malice. One woman told Yassah, "Your sister should be ashamed of herself for trying to ruin RJ's life, the slut that she is. Now you are trying to ruin Pastor's life."

Sadly, ignorant controversies breed quarrels. And, being the Lord's servant, soon to be their pastor's wife, Yassah did not want to be quarrelsome, but kind to everyone, patiently enduring evil and correcting the opponents gently.

"Grace is not a slut," Yassah said to the woman.

"She sure didn't give that impression," the woman replied, "having sex with a married man. You know, not every secret can be sunk into silence."

Yassah prayed that God may perhaps grant them repentance, leading to knowledge of the truth, that they may come to their senses. However, it seemed hard to balance priorities with the pressure to defend the truth. She didn't bother telling them RJ was not married when Grace had sex with him. She didn't bother showing them the engagement ring Julius Peabody had put on her finger either. These women were a handful of lousy individuals in the church who criticized everyone, and all they did was point fingers.

The thing is, when you want to understand how to love, or how to be humble, or how to have faith, or even how to set your priorities, you ought to look at Christ and follow his example. It is written in the Bible, according to Bible students, that those who say they know God and read the Bible, ought to live in the same way in which Christ lived. There would be no cause for stumbling if you love rather than hate. Hate blinds the eyes and prevents you from seeing the beauty in others. You must acquire a sensitive heart to make others feel that there is something beautiful in them. That was what Yassah and Julius had discussed over the months.

Sunday service started like always; the congregation stopped singing, the choir sat down, then Pastor Julius Peabody walked to the podium, facing the assembly. The noticeable difference today was what he was wearing, a long black robe like a college doctoral candidate gown. He must have saved it for the occasion.

This robe had enduring good looks tailored in luxurious black wonder crepe fabric, with hand sewn black velvet panels and doctoral bars. It had fluting over the shoulders and across the back for controlling fullness and lined belled sleeves with deep cuffs. A purple satin pulpit stole hung around his neck; bright gold Latin crosses embroidered on both ends, trimmed with matching four-inch rayon fringes. Every piece of clothing Pastor Peabody was wearing seemed brand spanking new. All eyes were set on him.

"In case you didn't know this already, let me be the first to tell you. I have requested Sister Yassah Johnston to join me in holy matrimony. Thankfully she has accepted."

If his outfit had not grabbed their attention, his opening line did.

"I love Miss Johnston and Miss Johnston loves me," he announced, and smiled a bright smile.

A few members in the congregation mumbled, and most of the audience looked surprised. There was light applaud and some even said, "Amen". No one fainted and fell to the floor.

Then Pastor Peabody went into his sermon.

"Nobody in this church is better than any other person... in or out of this church. Nobody on earth is better than any other person in this country or any other country. When we choose to hate, that hate can return to us in the form of consequences... results we can never fully prepare for, like being alienated from others, or even angry with ourselves.

"In the words of Frederick Douglass, a former slave and a crusader for human rights, 'No man can put a chain about the ankle of his fellow man without at last finding the other end fastened about his own neck.'"

The pastor went on and told his assembly how each person was expected to live; whether you are a president, or a farmer, or the woman who wraps fresh fish in old newspaper at the market. He was shocked to see how people see other people in negative light just because life is a little more generous to them, when opportunity had come knocking on their doors and not the doors of others.

His voice got deeper and his rhythm got faster.

"We are obsessed with looks and things. What people do not realize is, it doesn't matter to God. Whether others are different in attitude, perspective, race, class, political pitch, or social standing, it should make no difference to those of us who call ourselves Christians. We should love others even if they are not our kind."

Close to the end, he talked about seasoning the life God had given each person.

"People are to be imitators of God. Walk in love as Christ who loved us and gave himself up for us, a fragrant offering and sacrifice to God. Love God. Love one another. There is nothing greater. The proof of your love for God is your love for others."

He preached against sexual immorality and other impurities. He discouraged filthiness, foolish talks, and crude joking. He encouraged that gossips be put out of their lives.

"Let no one fool you," Pastor Peabody preached. "An idolater, or anyone impure, has no inheritance in God's kingdom. Our speech, as well as our behavior, is to be a positive witness."

He urged each person to ask the Holy Spirit to guard their hearts and tongue from sin.

"Every life is a wonderfully made sample of God's handiwork," Pastor Peabody ended his sermon in a soft voice. "Every human being is an image-bearing likeness of God. Cherish the gift of life, brethren. Seize what has been handed you and make smart decisions. Life is, after all, a temporary situation. Tomorrow is made for some, not everyone. The best news is, if we confess our sins, God is genuine and impartial in forgiving them, and cleansing us from every unrighteousness."

Then he raised his hand and prayed, "Great praise, Oh Creator! We pray that our hearts are filled with love. Let the church say...."

"Amen!"

Chapter 54

IT WAS ALMOST 7:30 when Grace got to the office the following morning. She took the clipboard Weyatta handed to her and studied the names of new clients, six so far.

"I'm expecting my sister this morning," she said to Weyatta. "Please find a gap in this morning schedule."

Weyatta nodded. "How's eleven?"

"Perfect. Thanks."

Yassah was standing before Weyatta's desk at 10:30 a.m., politely inquiring as to whether Grace might be busy or not. Weyatta made her wait twenty minutes, then escorted her to Grace's office. Before Yassah sat, Grace offered her something to drink but she declined.

Grace never cared much about what people said behind her back, but when it came to Yassah, she was very sensitive. She knew where she wanted the conversation to go but could not be in a hurry. Then again, the resistance seemed impossible.

"Are the Johnstons coming?" Grace asked. Before Yassah answered, she said, "Do they even know about the wedding?"

"I called and told them."

"And?"

Yassah chuckled. "What do you think?"

Grace shrugged and said, "Sometimes people with a high opinion of themselves can surprise you."

"Well, you won't be surprised."

"They're not coming?"

"None of them are able to make it," Yassah jeered.

"They don't want to see you get married, and they don't want to be seen... the high and might Johnstons."

"And that is fine by me," Yassah huffed out a breath. "Julius knows who I am, and everything about me. They don't have to be here."

"Uncle Moses is going to give you away," Grace said, smiling.

Yassah's eyes widened. "Did you already asked him?"

"He offered. I didn't ask."

They talked about the Johnstons at length, with Grace careful not to make her feelings about them as dreadful as they truly were. Lord knows she had many reservations. Not just about the Johnstons, but with the members of Words of Christ Church as well, especially their attitude towards Yassah. Grace was happy to have been in church when the engagement was announced.

Lynnette Vinton and many others continue to talk, discuss and gossip that Yassah Johnston was simply ceremonially unclean to be their pastor's wife. It was remarkable how their pastor's eyes had left all Words of Christ Church *spiritual elite*, and had fallen on a sinful woman.

Lynnette Vinton's exact words to the other sisters were, "The woman has so many sexual blemishes, she makes Rahab look good."

And to that, another church sister added, "She would never be on our guest list for anything, much more get married to our pastor. And, in our church?"

They could not decide which was worse, Yassah marrying their pastor, or getting married in the church.

"I bet they are not welcoming you with opened arms either," Grace said, of the church members.

Yassah knew that if she sounded too religious, Grace would start preaching the deceits of so-called Christians. "Where do you think sinners go?" she asked.

"Le'Toit Club."

"No," Yassah chuckled, shaking her head.

"Where to? Hell?"

"No."

"Well, tell me. What did your *pastor* boyfriend tell you?"

"They go to church."

"Church?"

"That's what I tell the people in the church... those who call me the biggest sinner that has ever walked the earth," Yassah explained. "They don't recognize we are all far from perfection, those who go to church and those who don't go."

Understanding the logic, Grace said, "So the church is the hospital for sinners?"

"Yeah," Yassah replied. "It's certainly not a membership club for the righteous, even if Sister Lynnette Vinton thinks it is. She complains about how other members sing off key too, and those sometimes out of sync during the unison readings."

They both laughed.

"Mrs. Vinton thinks God must love her more," Grace joked. "In her mind, she's taking sinners by their hand and walking with them to the foot of Heaven, then introduce them to God."

Yassah barked out a laugh. "She doesn't know that God already knows those people?"

"Who's going to tell the Salvation Lady that?"

"One day I will."

"You?"

"Yes. Me. I will."

"I would love to be there," Grace jested.

Pastor Peabody had explained God's grace to his fiancé as such: Church members care for the poor, feed the hungry, provide clothing and shelter for the needy, but most of them do not understand sinfulness and the need for continual spiritual restoration. People have an unmerited favor with God despite sinfulness. Anyone who feels he or she does not have sins, they are deceiving themselves. The Bible calls you a liar.

"We go to church so God can heal our wrongs and help with our needs," Yassah explained. "We are *all* sinners."

"Are you going to start preaching to me now?" Grace was teasing.

Yassah smiled and raised both hands, "I'm only spreading the Word."

A quiet moment later, Grace said, with a serious tone, "It stinks... the way how people treat you even though you've made your life so beautiful. I'm so happy for you, Sis. I've never seen you so full of life... I mean, you look satisfied."

"I am. There is nothing more I can ask God for."

"Nothing?"

"Nothing. It's never good to be greedy with God. Don't dare ask for more if you already have what you need."

Grace caught her gaze and asked, "What about children? You've always said how important it is."

"Not any more. Not being able to have a child is no longer an issue.

All those backdoor abortions... I didn't know better." She sighed.

Grace smiled.

"Anyway, Julius accepts me for who I am... my past and all," Yassah said. "He loves me just the way I am."

"I love your attitude," Grace choked, obviously touched. "Important thing is we have a wedding to plan, whether they like it or not."

Chapter 55

CLEARLY A DISCIPLINARIAN, Grace's son behaved better than most kids his age. Before dropping Peace off to Katharine, she'd lectured him that there is a time to run and play, and a time to be quiet, especially through the church service. She did not want Peace attacking members' attention either. His only misbehavior in church was leg-wiggling. And, he did that a lot. Every time he wiggled, his knee got squeezed. One time he swung so hard, he hit the bottom of the pew in front of their's.

"Be still, child," Katharine whispered, then pinched.

Weddings and Church services hold a special fear for parents of toddlers. No one knows who put the wiggles in their tiny legs, but three-year-olds have a bad case of the wiggles, especially in places like church and weddings. Sitting still is no small task for a child. For this reason, RJ and Mellody never sat together when they were little ones. Katharine always sat between them to keep them quiet.

"How was Peace in church today?" Mel asked.

"Just like his daddy," Katharine replied. "I'll even go as far as saying, he is a little better than RJ was."

"Mom, that's an improvement," Mel praised. She turned to Nàjma and said, "You'd think Mom's fingerprints are embedded in RJ's knees from all those times she squeezed them in church."

"What about you?" Nàjma chuckled. "I can't imagine you being the quiet one."

"Squeezing her knee didn't help," Katharine interjected. "Mel got pinched."

"So that's why the church building is such an ordeal for me," Mel jested. "Now I know why."

"Please," Katharine said, cutting her eyes. "Pinching her wasn't enough. This child could never sit still, so Robert started keeping Mel at home with him."

"I liked staying home with Daddy."

"Of course you did," Katharine jeered.

Mel and Nàjma laughed.

"Something tells me you were very close to your father," Nàjma said to Mel.

"I was."

Nàjma had also learned Mel had inherited her father's sense of humor, among other things. "How come you never talk about him?" she asked.

In Mel's mind, the Senator's arrest, trial, sentencing, appeals, then the hanging, galloped by in a blur.

"I don't like to talk about sad things," she said. "What good is it?"

After the nightmare, not everybody had turned against the Douglas family. Being a doctor might have helped. But Dr. Douglas, along with her mother, shuffled along with their heads as high as they could hold it, and eyes dead ahead in the future.

Nàjma caught Mel's gaze and smiled. Tears were in them. "Are you working tomorrow?" she changed the topic.

"Nope. Didn't you hear?"

Katharine looked at Mel, anxious to hear. She was always happy to see Mel had a day off.

"While you all were at church, all diseases miraculously went away," Mel said, straight face.

Nàjma laughed. Katharine didn't.

"That's supposed to be funny?" Katharine said, frowning.

"Yeah, Mom. It was a joke," Mel playfully rolled her eyes. "Of course I'm going to work tomorrow… and that would be in South Africa. My flight is tomorrow afternoon."

"Commercially, I hope," Nàjma muttered.

"Did you say something?" Mel had sensed the irony.

"Thanks for driving us to church, Nàjma," Katharine said, and excused herself.

Mel knew Katharine had sensed a fight. "Let's go to my room," she said, taking Nàjma's hand and leading.

Nàjma hesitated, then followed.

"Sit," Mel said, pointing at the bed. "I promise I won't bite."

Nàjma sat on the bed, and began looking around the room with a steady gaze. Everything screamed teenager, sport-print beddings, sneakers, CDs, and books.

"This is Tapee's room, not mine. I'm sharing it with him," Mel explained. "He should have his own room... this is temporary. I don't know what's going to happen when my contract with WHO is over, but I don't plan on building a home here."

Nàjma furrowed her brow.

"Well, I certainly don't want your government in my personal life," Mel said. "Especially my bedroom."

"Are you moving back to the States?"

"Not for a while... but in the near future," Mel said. "Besides, when it comes to that, I'd still be spending my sabbatical in Liberia."

Nàjma got up. She seemed angry.

"Did I say something wrong?"

"When were you going to tell me this?"

"Tell you something that's a year away?"

"Something I thought concerned me."

"You?"

Nàjma turned her gaze away from Mel to the door.

"Then why are you always fighting me?" Mel asked. "Everything I try to do upsets you. I don't understand you."

Nàjma turned back to Mel, but said nothing.

"Look Nàj. When it comes to us, everything I say goes straight through your ears. I push, you pull. When I pull, you push. It has to be more than me going back home. Or, is it the trip with Adriana? Nothing happened... and that's the fact."

"So you did go on a trip?"

"I already explained. I needed to get back to South Africa because Tapee was there alone... with strangers."

Nàjma cut her eyes.

"Please, sit down," Mel pleaded.

Nàjma sat, taking her own sweet time.

They argued over motives and reasoned. Then their argument reached the thirty minute point, Mel wondered if she was making her point come across clearly. Their fight, if she could call it that, had run out of gas.

Silence hung for a long moment while both women stare into the distance.

"First thing," Mel said, breaking her slience. "When the adoption is finalized, I want you to stand as Tapee's godmother."

Nàjma took in her breath and let it out slowly. "Really, Mel?" she said, touching Mel's leg.

Mel felt her muscles tense and sat still. Nàjma's hand felt warm and good.

"I'd like that, Mel," she said, a smile edging her mouth. "I would really love it."

"Do you mean it?"

"Of course. It would be like getting a son too."

Mel took Nàjma's hand and held it. "Look, Nàj," she said, so carefully. "I'm in love with you, but I would never want you to do something that you don't want to do. This seems so natural to me. But, if I thought that you felt differently, I wouldn't have spent this much time with you. I know that I cannot turn you into someone you're not."

Nàjma laughed.

"Did I say something funny?"

"Someone I'm not?" she asked and chuckled. "Mel, we *are* friends."

"Friends get jealous when their friend asks other people for favors? Like, when they need to get to South Africa and that person has the means to get them there in time?"

"Well, not just friends," Nàjma corrected. "Best friends." Then she leaned in close and whispered onto Mel's ear, "I love you Mellody Douglas." She'd never felt more sure about anything.

"That's what you want to call us then? Best friends?"

"It has to be," she whispered, and sank into Mel. "Do you want me defending my personal life in the government's court or my church?"

"No," Mel smiled. "I understand."

"Really?"

"Really."

Nàjma kissed Mel's lips. Mel pulled her into an embrace.

As they held each other, Nàjma couldn't imagine wanting anything more than what was happening now, all regrets and reservations swept aside. Wanting more, she pulled back. "I really should be going," she said, trying to catch her breath.

"Really?"

"Really."

Chapter 56

LYNNETTE VINTON'S VISIT always seems purposeful when the conversation starts. "That woman can sure keep a secret," she criticized, referring to Grace. She'd dragged the *sure* too.

Katharine waited.

"I mean… where in the world did she hide that child? He looks so much like his father," Lynnette continued.

How in the world would Lynnette know what the child's father looked like? Katharine thought.

Nothing had been discussed with anyone outside the family. Then again, anyone looking at the child, and knows RJ Douglas, could easily tell Peace is RJ's son. Lynnette Vinton was no ordinary woman. She had that special nose for gossips and news. Katharine was tempted to remind her friend that nothing had been confirmed, but it will be useless. The child was a spitting image of her son.

Katharine stared at her friend.

"You know how I feel about RJ," Lynnette continued, now smiling. "I love him as if he is my son. That's a fine young man, Katharine. You know I don't say things I don't mean."

Katharine smiled, wasn't that the truth.

Lynnette loved RJ and never hesitated letting anyone know that. As for Mel, well, the girl had an inner beauty toward the needy, but that homosexual demon was a serious issue. That's how Lynnette always put it. Her sober criticism of that lifestyle had already been expressed to Katharine many times, and there was no need bringing it up again. As far as Lynnette was concerned, the natural couple, man and woman, is a thing of glory. Beyond that, homosexuality is just plain common dirt.

"Too bad he hadn't married the girl, even if she's country," Lynnette finished.

Katharine remembered her friend using the word 'country' once, while referring to her adopted son, Razaq. She'd expressed strong dislike for such prejudice, but Lynnette is Lynnette.

"RJ is already married, Lynnette," Katharine said, sensing the need to let her friend know she was more than happy with her daughter-in-law.

"Oh, I like Gia," Lynnette corrected. "I just think people ought to marry their own kind."

"And what kind is that?"

"Black people should marry black people…."

"And Liberian should marry Liberian," Katharine said with a shrug.

"Now, I didn't say that," Lynnette said, apolitically. "I love you like a sister, Katharine. Even better. I think you were too good for… well, you know."

"Robert?"

"You are a good Christian woman, Katharine… he wasn't. I know better… not to speak ill of the dead, especially when he's not here to defend himself."

The woman reprimanded herself before Katharine could. Lynnette was on the roll and Katharine let her roll on.

"Take Pastor Peabody for instance," Lynnette continued. "He keeps accepting all kinds of folks in our church. I don't know what he's thinking."

"Isn't the church the place where lost souls go to make their lives better?"

"Of course, but…," and Lynnette was lack of words. She looked at Katharine, shaking her head in both agreement and disagreement, if at all there is such a thing. "But does he have to court them too?"

Lynnette was now dragging Yassah Johnston and Pastor Peabody's relationship into their conversation. Katharine heaved a mournful sigh. Just like that, the woman had diverted the conversation from RJ's illegitimate son to their pastor's courtship with a worldly woman. Katharine gazed at her friend with sympathy, but Lynnette is Lynnette. The woman had a fetish to criticize everything and everyone, believing she was free of all sins just because she cared for the poor, ran the church women's ministry and carried her worn-out bible everywhere she went. The rumors about her sleeping with her houseboy hadn't gone away, but she didn't care. The houseboy had admitted it to friends, adding that they prayed after sex while he was still trying to catch his breath.

"That woman our pastor is so head over heels in love with has a past," Lynnette gasped. "How can he marry such a woman? I mean, a woman who has done too many bad things with men!"

Katharine's jaws dropped. "Oooh! Lynnette, what soul does not have a fault?"

"'As a jewel of gold in a swine's snout, so is a woman without discretion,'" Lynnette quoted the Bible.

Katharine simply stared.

"She seduced him with her swaggering hips and lewd ways. I think a pastor should do better... if you ask me."

"Nobody is asking you," Katharine said.

Lynnette gawked in shock.

"Let me tell you something, my dear friend," Katharine said. "I recognize your good deeds for others and I'm sure God recognizes them too. Are you sure your acts of kindness aren't to buy approval and praise from people or from God?"

Lynnette's eyes widened.

"I'm not condemning you, Lynnette. I'm simply trying to point something out to you."

"I'm listening," Lynnette muttered.

Katharine smiled. "We must be careful when we are doing good, or helping people in need," she continued. "We should never use our kindness of good deeds to buy acceptance and love from people, or from God. Salvation cannot be purchased, Lynnette. Ask yourself this... is there anything you can give God that He doesn't already have?"

"No," Lynnette muttered.

"Well... of course not," Katharine said. "Since this is so, Lynnette, what we all should do is learn that our good works can never save us. It can only show we are grateful to God for allowing us to do them. God still rewards each loving deed that is done; you know... especially those done with all your heart."

Lynnette furrowed her brows, her lips stretched into a flat line.

"Good works are not the means of our salvation... the *result* is," Katharine explained.

"We all study the Word, don't we," Lynnette said, disgruntled. She'd dragged the word *all* with more emphasis than needed. She had even rolled her eyes too. Katharine ignored it. "Well, the Good Book does say to correct one another."

"Yes," Katharine said and smiled. "The Bible does tell us to. But we don't always have to go all out on folks... maybe just a little dipper of chicken soup for the soul," she said, smiling a toothy smile.

Both women were quiet for a while. Lynnette shifted in her chair as they waited through this uncomfortable gap in the conversation.

Then Katharine stirred the conversation to Daughters of Christ growing membership and their new projects. "I'm happy more women are joining DOC," she said.

This grabbed Lynnette's attention. They talked about the organization at length until she was ready to leave.

Mel waited until Lynnette got in her car and drove off, and joined Katharine.

"How's the crow?" Mel asked, sitting.

"Mel," Katharine gasped. "That's not a nice name to call anyone."

"That's a nice name for her," Mel said. She could not suppress a chuckle.

Chapter 57

EVERY MAN HAS a weakness, and vengeance is Manor's. The news of Cowan kicking Lonos' ass filled him with supreme satisfaction. "Take a break from your job and come to Le'Toit for a treat," he'd invited Cowan. "I've asked your boss to give you the night off."

Cowan was escorted to the private lounge via a private valet entrance when he arrived at Le'Toit, after a mini search at the exclusive registration desk. Its level of comfort, and the quality of the furnishings and amenities, was beyond anything he had ever experienced in Africa. Cowan looked around the room, impressed.

Manor shook Cowan's hand vigorously and then abandoned formality and gave him a one-arm hug in his excitement. In a rush of words he said, "It was so good to see how you beat the shit out of Lonos."

Cowan abruptly pulled back.

"You amuse me, Mr. Cowan," Manor said, still excited. "You really do. When I first met you, I didn't like you one bit. You were always in the way and I couldn't get Adriana to fire you. Then when I got to know you, I wished I'd been the one to hire you."

Cowan looked at the man and almost burst out laughing.

"They don't understand life," Manor continued. "I do. Those who have, and those who don't have, makes the world go around. That's life. Until the world ends, there will always be the rich and the poor. The powerful and the powerless. Nothing and no one can change that. If it weren't for the evil qualities in people, I wouldn't have a business."

Cowan listened.

"People are not mad at me for what they think I do," Manor continued. "They are jealous of my success. They want what I have, but don't have the guts to go and get it."

"Quite a place you have here," Cowan said inquiringly. "So what does it take to get a membership?"

"Let's just say, membership is limited."

Manor didn't seem inclined to elaborate, and Cowan didn't push.

"Would you care for something to drink?" Manor asked.

"Club beer."

Manor smiled. "Really? I have American, European, or Japanese beer if you want."

"Club beer is fine."

Manor snapped his finger and a waitress came. She and Cowan exchanged glances.

"This is Peaches," Manor introduced the woman. "She handles all hospitality duties. Business won't be this good without her. She makes sure the customer's expectations are met."

Peaches didn't offer a hand or a smile. Not a word came across her lips. She stared at Cowan from head to toe, slowly undressing him with her eyes.

"Our customers like their privacy," Manor went on. "We make sure of it."

"Precisely," Cowan replied. "I like private."

Manor chuckled. "A Club beer for Mr. Cowan," he said to Peaches, "and I'll have water."

Peaches nodded and left. Manor's eyes followed the woman's behind as she walked away.

Moments later, Peaches brought in a large tray with a bottle of Club beer, two glasses and a bottle of Tasmanian Rain. The premium bottled rainwater originates from the remote Australian island which has the cleanest air on the planet, according to the World Meteorological Organization. This is important since Tasmanian Rainwater never touches the ground. As its name suggests, its water goes from the sky to the bottle to your mouth without ever touching the ground. The luxury 12oz bottled water cost drinkers eleven bucks.

After Peaches departed, Manor said, "I have a special gift for you for kicking Lonos' ass."

"Oh?"

"Yes," Manor nodded, smiling. He poured rainwater into his glass and held it up. "First, we drink to that bastard, Lonos."

Cowan did the same. The men clinked glasses.

Manor got up. "Follow me," he said, and led Cowan out of the private lounge.

__**********__

They spent a few minutes touring the facility. Le'Toit had a first-rate gym section; a large room with three showers, whirlpool, sauna, steam room, an exercise room equipped with the latest workout machines, and a relaxation room. In the walk-in closet, shelves attached to the walls were stocked with neatly folded white towels, white bathrobes, and workout clothing that looked like they had never been worn. Rows of athletic shoes lined one wall. Everything was in order by size.

Manor studied Cowan. "What do you think so far?"

"Pretty awesome," Cowan replied. "I'm impressed."

"Come, I'll show you where the bar is," Manor said, and led the way.

The bar came into view as they rounded a corner.

"Damn!" Cowan muttered to himself.

The space had been outfitted like a miniature Las Vegas casino. Its level of comfort and the quality of the furnishing and amenities was beyond anything Cowan had ever experienced. He looked around at the large open spaces. "How big is this place?"

"Enough space to hold a hundred guests comfortably," Manor replied.

The luxurious lounge walls were paneled in wood, rich browns hex-print carpeting, and three 100-gallon saltwater aquariums, strategically placed around the lounge on dark mahogany wooden stands. The aquariums were filled with the finest specimens of angelfish, clownfish, gobies, tangs, wrasse, dragonets, boxfish, puffers, triggerfish, butterflyfish, dottybacks, seahorses, rays and sharks. Live colors of corals, freshwater plants, and live rocks contributed to the beauty of the structures.

On one side was a high-end champagne bar. Another striking bar sat to the opposing side with six beers on tap, and thirty imported and local bottled beers on display. There were set-up for casino games; Blackjack, Craps, Poker, Baccarat and four Slots machines.

Le'Toit must have borrowed the motto: *What happens in Vegas, stays in Vegas*. Le'Toit housed more secrets than any building in the country, yet no one outside of Manor's guest list knew or spoke anything about the details of the club. Cowan wondered whether Bohn even had an idea about the inside of the place.

"Ready for your gift?" Manor said, with a conspiratorial grin.

Cowan shrugged.

"Come," Manor said, leading the way. "Peaches will give you whatever you need. When you are finished, she will escort you out. I have a date with my beautiful wife," he smiled.

Manor's precious gift to Cowan was a woman, but most would see a young girl, even a child. Trafficking the young and innocent boosted profits tremendously, as many of Le'Toit customers paid large sums of money to bruise the teats of their virginity.

__**********__

"Excuse me," Cowan said to the woman whose back was turned towards him.

She turned around to face him, like a tree branch would in the path of light breeze. Cowan met her eyes and then she looked away, nervously. He guessed her age to be around twelve and not a day more. He turned his back to her to avoid intimidation.

"I want to be your friend," Cowan said softly. "I promise not to hurt you. Okay?"

The girl remained quiet.

"I'm going to turn around so I can see your face. Is that okay?" Without a reply, he turned. Their eyes met. "Nod your head if you can understand me."

She nodded slowly.

"Good," he encouraged and smiled. His mirth softened her misery. "Why are you here? You looked like a child," he said softly.

"I was stolen," Ummu whispered. Then tears filled her eyes and she lowered her gaze.

Cowan felt sick. His heart broke at the depth of the child's distress. He took both her hands and waited until she looked him in the eye. "I will get you out of here, I promise, okay," he assured.

That was all the opening Ummu needed. She began talking and kept talking. The one-sided conversation was a discovery about CeRue Manor Cowan would not have learned anywhere else.

__**********__

The only person most important to CeRue Manor was the man staring before him in the mirror. His life support was women, money, more women and more money. He made a woman feel beautiful and wanted in a dangerous kind of way. But Manor had the demons of a man who had something to fear. He broke his wife's spirit and then patched it with her favorite treats, Swiss chocolates and expensive perfumes.

Lying is as addictive as any drug. As if his brain was wired to lie, Manor opened his mouth and the lies poured out. The man had always responded with a series of half-truths and outright lies. He told them all with equal practiced sincerity, and his wife had become accustomed to this.

Omolola had become sick and tired of her husband's indiscretion affairs, and had no energy left for any of their knockdown-dragged-on fights. However, Manor had somehow convinced her that no one listens to the whining of a spoil wife. But money can never fill an empty heart.

Manor picked up his wife for their date as promised, and drove her to Posh. They walked pass the bar and were instantly greeted by the maitre d' who escorted them to a private table set for two. Handing each a menu, the man said politely, "Mr. Manor, someone will be here shortly to take your order," and excused himself.

Moments later a waiter came, and Manor ordered them two glasses of champagne.

When the bubbly came, Manor said, "Here's to the woman who owns my heart."

This provoked a smile. Omolola wished it was true. She held up her glass of champagne, sipped and set it down.

The waiter wrote down their order and left.

Across from her, her lying husband smiled. Omolola wondered if he cheats because most, not all, men cheated. If a man could, he would. Their marriage had not been typical, and she doubts if not having children could have been the factor into the equation. She stared at him, forcing a smile. Before they left the house, Omolola had strengthened herself for the evening's event.

The waiter arrived at the table with their orders, placed an entrée dish in front of Omolola first, and smiled. She thanked him. Then he served Manor and said, "Enjoy your meal, ma'am… sir," and left.

The food was excellent.

Unexpectedly, Manor turned to watch Adriana LeRoux marching into Posh, wearing a dress that looked like it cost more than ten times any employee's yearly salary. Her makeup and hair were perfect, the jewelry tasteful enough to retain a wow, and the whiff of Channel No.5 trailing her. There was not a hint of delight in her expression. She looked at him, walked straight to the bar, sat down and ordered a drink.

"Excuse me, honey," Manor said to his wife, and stood. "I have to use the men's room. I'll be back in a minute."

Omolola didn't seem to have noticed her husband's carefully choreographed statement, but she did. His habits had taught her something was up; her husband must have seen a woman and was attempting to avoid an encounter.

The thing is, Adriana would declare war on any woman Manor woo, including his wife. She followed him into the men's room, opened her purse, strolled over to the mirror and applied her lipstick while she spoke.

"Tell me you're not sleeping with your wife," she said accusingly. "Because you are not allowed to screw her while you're screwing me."

"I'm not," Manor answered, "I swear. It's just dinner. You know we are having problems."

"And you're wining and dining her at Posh?"

"Just to pacify things until the time is right," Manor explained. "She wants us to have children, but she's always gone. Who is supposed to change diapers? It's just a matter of time."

Liars expect others to lie.

Adriana closed her purse, turned and leaned her butt against the sink counter. "If you lie to me, I swear I'll poison her food and make you feed it to her."

Manor laughed.

"I wasn't joking," she asserted. Then she stuck her finger down her panties and ran her middle finger over her clits until it was wet. "Here's something for you, Ce," she said, while running her scented finger in the space between Manor's nose and upper lip. "You'll smell me the rest of the night and I'm certain you wouldn't be kissing your precious wife tonight."

Adriana drew her finger away and Manor sniffed a good enough dose of feminine odor. She started to move past him when he pulled out his handkerchief and wiped his mouth.

Adriana stopped with her hand on the doorknob. "No need to do that," she hissed. Then, she walked out and slammed the door behind her.

Chapter 58

BOHN WAITED FOR Cowan at Vickie Spot, a small roadside restaurant off the main road in Logan Town. He sipped his Club beer while scanning a brief memo on Le'Toit club, the one Net had given him.

Manor understands the power of money and sex. Le'Toit club became notorious for gambling, drinking and the sleaziest of wild sex with innocent young girls. Everything and anything his clients wanted, they got plenty of; great food, drinks, Cuban cigars, drugs, scotch, and virgins. Most guests were usually more preoccupied with the stunning collection of young girls at their disposal, than the money they were losing to gambling and drinks. There were a lot of crude jokes and talk of women, disparagingly.

Net, Bohn's informant, had given his report not only on the activities in the bar, but details of some trafficking. A four-day weekend had cost him nearly $30,000 cash, about $10,000 of it for the girl. He had spent it grudgingly, although it wasn't his own money. Net swore to Bohn he did not touch her, pretending to be too drunk to do anything.

As Cowan walked in, Bohn folded the memo and placed it in his jacket pocket.

"He has hired smart criminals on staff," Cowan informed, as he landed hard in his seat. "A woman name, Peaches, runs things around the bar. She'd hired five of her young hooker friends from Vegas to tend the guests, wearing mini skirts and seductive smiles."

"It's a meat market for sleazy international child molesters," Bohn said, matter-of-factly. "They don't want to risk getting caught at home, so they go and prey on the young and innocent in small countries."

"Just Internationals?"

"Local bureaucrats go there too," Bohn said. "The same money they pay Manor to fill his pockets, he fills theirs with bribes, and some."

A woman came to take Cowan's order. He ordered Club beer and declined everything else resembling food. Until his stomach adapts, he wouldn't eat any cooked food sold by vendors at the market or a roadside eating place.

After the woman walked away, Bohn said, "Do you know during the war people couldn't find food or clean water to drink, but you could get a bottle of cold Club beer?"

Cowan stared in disbelief. His beer arrived and he took a gulp. "No wonder," he said, "this is one of the best beers I've had."

Bohn took another sip of his. "But, you can't feed it to children," he said, putting down his glass. "Clean water is always better."

Typical of Liberians, they celebrate with good times rather than mourn the loss of anything, even their country.

"By the way, how is Lonos," Cowan asked.

"Mel patched him up," Bohn replied. "Dude, you did a mean job on him."

"I was doing my job, protecting the man's daughter. He was very rude to her. Didn't mean to be that brutal, but Manor was in the lobby watching. Lonos is one tough guy. I mean, he handled that beat down like a champ. It may take the reality of death to soften him up. I like him."

Bohn chuckled and said, "He's tough and smart. I think he would be good for the team."

"I think so too," Cowan agreed.

"So, tell me... what did you find out about the place."

"Manor also trades rare diamonds, among other things," Cowan informed. "The kid told me she overheard him planing a trip out of South Africa with some red diamonds. Those are hard to find."

"Really? He's going to smuggle some red gems out of South Africa? The man's balls are bigger than I thought. Then again... a girl knows this?"

"Yeah," Cowan chuckled. "She's very smart. They kidnaped her while she was on her way home from school."

"Seems like a big part of his business is running abducted young girls from Guinea and Cote D'Ivoire," Bohn informed. "They run through the major cities along the only highway, primarily the northern leg from Danané to Monrovia; Sanniquellie, Ganta, Gbarnga, and Kakata."

"That's where the girl is from," Cowan said. "Guinea."

"Manor never uses his own vehicles to transport his merchandise, he rents trucks and vans, or burrow other people's cars. And, I think that's where the Senator got duped. They used his car, the strongest... and only evidence against him."

"So, linking Manor to anything is virtually impossible?"

"Nearly impossible," Bohn said, "but there's always a way."

"From what I gathered, Manor has all his goodies hidden in a safe in the private office upstairs. He keeps his backup files on a PS3 game console, some place in his private office. There are also USB flash drives... about four of them... color coded for each operation."

"Can Net get to them?" Bohn asked.

"I don't think so."

Bohn furrowed his brow, thinking.

"Most areas in Le'Toit club are off limits," Cowan said, "I had to damn near kill Lonos to convince Manor I can be trusted to take me there."

Bohn nodded.

"Maybe Dr. Douglas could," Cowan suggested.

"No!" Bohn said instantly. "I'm not going to put Mel in harm's way."

"Adriana likes her," Cowan baited. "Maybe she can get her into the place."

"I said, *no*."

Maybe his boss did not know that the doctor had once been escorted to South Africa by LeRoux on her private jet. He wondered if he should report it.

"Besides," Bohn added, "Ms. LeRoux has not even set foot in there."

What was I thinking? The man knows, Cowan thought, and said, "Okay. I didn't think about that. She hasn't."

"Find another way," Bohn said, more like an ordered.

"Le'Toit club has state-of-the-art technology. It's no challenge for us, but it's going to be tough. His files are on those disks, and only Manor goes to that area. No one else."

"We will get into Le'Toit," Bohn assured, and took a sip of his beer. "Tell me about the girl. What do you intend to do?"

Cowan supplied the information: "Her name is Ummu, she's twelve years old. From the moment they took her, nothing in her young life could have prepared her for all the things that assaulted her. Finding herself in an entirely unfamiliar world after the most uncomfortable long ride from Guinea to Monrovia."

Trying to imagine the child, a surge of fear flooding her, Bohn expelled his breath in a gasp, "Only twelve. How did they get to her?"

"She had taken a short cut home rather than walk on the main road with the other school children, a challenge she'd accepted from a class-mate. Ummu would be rewarded a bottle of orange Fanta and the respect from a boy, Kamara, if she reaches before him."

"Just being kids," Bohn observed.

"The thing is, she blames herself for getting caught," Cowan said. "All she wanted to do was prove to her friends that a boy could easily be beaten by a girl. She told me she mentally kicked herself," he chuckled. "Her kidnappers were old enough to be her father. There were three of them against a twelve-year-old girl, barely weighing ninety pounds. I told her she was brave and shouldn't blame herself."

"Put a grown man in that situation, and all his abilities of quick think-ing and good ideas would fail him."

"Ummu is a brave little girl, and smart too."

"So where is she now?"

"I've paid for room and board for her to stay at Moses Zarway's home," Cowan replied. "Grace's uncle. I told him that I work with the UN and I would be adopting the girl, but has to wait for my wife until the end of the year. I got her into B. W. Harris, a private school. I also gave her a cell phone so we can keep in touch daily."

"Nice story," Bohn nodded. "But what happens when December comes?"

"She wants to go home. I will have taken her home by then. I'd like to do that the first chance I get."

"That's good. But what about Manor? How did you get him to let go of her?"

"Manor doesn't see me as a threat. I paid him $15,000."

"Fifteen-thousand dollars? Cowan, Manor should be loosing money, not gaining fifteen grand. You know we cannot reimburse you for that."

"I know. And I didn't expect you to."

"That's honorable, Cowan," Bohn said admirably. "You know how to clean up a mess. Just, honorable."

Chapter 59

DISCOVERY WAS COMPLETED, disposition submitted, and the Boatswains' case had been developed and prepared by both parties. Mediation had failed, and no other attempts to settle; next was the trial.

It was twenty minutes past eight when Tomah arrived with her lawyer at the Temple of Justice. The line formed at the front entrance and moved slowly as everyone, lawyers, litigants and criminals, were searched for all banned devices. The Honorable Bly Macavoi held court on the first floor, Circuit Courtroom number two. Grace checked the docket with the clerk, which listed Boatswain vs Boatswain under *Final Appearances*. One other case shared the day's docket.

The old saying, that the law is a jealous mistress, had taken Boatswain to a different arena of supremacy. The legal ice his lawyer had him skating was very thin. In his right mind, Diallo would allow Grace Pupoh to preach to a female judge about rape and wife abuse. Of all people, he should know better. Grace could slash you with the tongue because her voice seems her most powerful weapon.

The eyes of the world were upon Liberia since it had elected the first woman president in Africa. Women's issues were receiving increasing attention as the Government was taking measures to promote gender equality in all areas. Efforts were being made to improve women's rights, not only specific measures to land ownership, but especially to sexual harassment; minors or adults engaging in non-consensual relations.

Sitting next to her client, Grace suddenly heard heavy nervous breathing. Cheah Boatswain had just entered the courtroom and Tomah's heart melted with fear. She looked at Tomah, it seemed there was no spirit left in the woman because of him.

"Don't look at him," Grace advised and held the woman's hand to steady it. "Keep looking straight ahead. Find a spot on the judge's table and keep your eyes on that spot."

Tomah found a spot to stare at. Her hands were still trembling. She pulled her hand away from Grace and pressed both hard against her lap until the quivering stopped.

The bailiff appeared and said his official words. Everyone rose, and the court of Honorable Bly Macavoi was now in session. The judge sat down and told everyone to be seated.

"The best place to start is at the beginning," Judge Macavoi said. Then she asked the defendant's lawyer if Boatswain had been made aware of the definition of rape contained in the amended rape law, and of the fact that non-consensual relations within marriage could be legally determined to be rape.

"He has been, Your Honor," Diallo replied respectfully.

"Both parties are aware that this case is a fault-based divorce, misconduct by one of the spouses is alleged as the legal basis for dissolution of the marriage," Judge Macavoi explained.

"Yes, Your Honor," Grace acknowledged.

"Yes, Your Honor," Diallo also acknowledged.

"This court requires proof of the alleged grounds," Judge Macavoi continued, directing her gaze at the plaintiff. "If the misconduct cannot be proven, or the accused spouse raises a defense to the claim, the divorce can still ultimately be granted, but on no-fault grounds. Husbands are not entitled to refuse to divorce, although a legal remedy could be sought after. Is that clear, counselors?"

"Yes, Your Honor," Grace answered.

"Yes, Ma'am," Diallo also answered.

Judge Macavoi looked up at Diallo. "It's not *Ma'am*," she corrected immediately.

"Judge," Diallo said right away. "Yes, Judge Macavoi."

"This court takes a spouse's misconduct seriously into account during the hearing, and also when making decisions about property division and the award of spousal support," Judge Macavoi continued. "I am not a *handpicked* judge, and I am no stranger to either counselors. The laws are on the books for a reason and I have the responsibility to uphold the laws."

Lawyers on both sides quietly reassured their clients.

"Before every case starts, I always say one thing about myself," the Judge continued. "Lying destroys trust. If there's no trust in your testimony, you'd have a serious problem in my court." She paused. "I *hate* lies, or anything resembling it."

Neither side made a reaction.

"You have been sworn under oath to tell the truth and nothing but the truth. I expect nothing less," Judge Macavoi ordered.

Diallo looked at his client and sighed.

Boatswain was looking at his wife and her lawyer; Tomah in close conversation with Grace, their two heads separated by inches. "Shouldn't we be talking as well?" he asked Diallo.

Diallo said nothing. Boatswain looked at his lawyer. Diallo held him with his eye and thought, *the man had bullied his wife and abused her before witnesses, what in the world could they talk about?* Grace had evidence, his wife's disposition, pictures and videos.

"Let's just wait until we know what they tell the judge," Diallo said, finally.

"Okay," Boatswain muttered, "that's what we should do."

―――**************―――

War is not a business of women, but Grace had come into court marching as if to war; with tongue like the pen of a ready writer. The plaintiff open first.

"The idea of accusing your husband or wife of spousal rape may seem absurd, but sex with a non-consenting mate is considered a crime. 'No' means 'no'," Grace began. "If you say 'no' to a person and he or she ignores you and forces you to have sex, it is rape. If you are raped, no matter by whom, you are the victim of a crime. This crime should be reported to the police and you are to be treated with medical remedy."

Grace turned her gaze on her client and said, "Even if you didn't fight back, it is still not your fault... you did not cause it to happen."

Tomah forced a smile.

"Now, let's get to spousal rape," Grace said. "Spousal rape is defined as a non-consensual sexual activity in which the offender is the spouse of the victim. This includes intercourse, oral or anal sex, forced sexual behavior, or any sexual act that leaves the victim degraded, humiliated, and, or, in pain. Even at the hands of your husband or wife, rape is rape. The law recognizes that now.

"On the night in question, Mr. Boatswain forced his wife to have sex with him by overpowering her and entering her by force while she said 'no' several times. She fought him off. That's rape."

Grace must have hit a nerve. Boatswain's face hardened instantly.

"Mr. Boatswain," she pointed at the defendant, "physically hit his wife, he bit her, and he tore her clothes off her body, degrading and humiliating her in every way. That's rape.

"Mr. Boatswain was violent before and during the sexual assault. His wife repeatedly said 'no'. He forced himself on her. That's rape.

"A woman does not surrender her consent upon entering the marital contract. Mrs. Boatswain never surrendered her consent upon entering her marriage. My client still had the right to say 'no' even if he was her husband. Thank you, Your Honor."

Grace sat down.

"Mr. Amadou?" Judge Macavoi called.

Diallo stood without notes, hands stuck deep in his pockets, completely at ease. He stated the factual basis for the case; she wants a divorce... she'll get one, but he took issue on the question of rape. He laid the blame on the law, giving women the opportunity to use the law to the disadvantage of husbands when their wives were mad at them. He questioned Mrs. Boatswain's lack of actions, "She could have gone to her family or friends if her husband was truly abusing her. We feel, Your Honor, that my client may have shoved his wife while he was under the influence of alcohol, but he did not rape his wife, or hit her."

Diallo finished and took his seat.

"Ms. Pupoh?" Judge Macavoi called.

The Judge's tone seemed challenging. She'd read the depositions of both Mr. and Mrs. Boatswain, Dr. Douglas' written statement, and had seen all the medical reports during discovery. She wondered whether Amadou had forgotten because he'd seen them too.

Egotistical men are always underestimating women. Diallo had given Grace an opening and she slipped in. She stood, shaking her head as if Diallo had lost his mind.

"Your Honor, we have witnesses and evidence to show Mrs. Boatswain was hit, kicked, punched and raped," Grace rebuttal.

It was a nasty shot to the groin. Diallo knew, even if people were afraid to testify, Grace had documents, photographs and a medical doctor on hand to testify. And, there were the dispositions.

Then Grace launched into a detailed account of the last beating in front of the neighbors and the confrontation with Boatswain the night before the trial. It was a spellbinding performance with the skill of a gifted storyteller. Not only that, she informed how Mr. Boatswain had tried asking others to persuade them in dropping the rape charge, including a family member of hers. Her voice faded and flowed, rising with indignation and falling with shame and guilt.

"He never touched her?" Grace snarled at Boatswain and Diallo. "You don't know the meaning of abuse. You have the opportunity today, Mr. Boatswain, to learn what hitting, kicking and punching is. The pictures of your wife's bruises would tell a different story to yours."

Cheah Boatswain began cracking his knuckles.

Grace checked the compiled list of eyewitnesses, individuals that would give an account of Boatswain's abuse toward his wife. Their testimonies were intended to help the judge believe the magnitude of harm the man had caused his wife.

"Your Honor, we call, Mrs. Ruth Somah," Grace announced.

Boatswain's intimidation and threats kept many from offering their testimonies, but wild horses would not have kept Ruth Somah from giving details of the day Boatswain beat and raped his wife. Somah placed her right hand on the Bible and pledged to say nothing but the truth.

"After the rape, Tomah told me she wanted to die," Somah testified. "Actually, she said to me, 'Being dead without her husband is a far better state than being alive with him.'"

She looked at Tomah as she said this, Tomah lowered her gaze. Some in the court covered their mouths with their hands, attempting to hide their gasps. The noise coming from the back of the room grew louder.

"Quiet in the court," the Judge ordered. "Settle down!"

"Sonofabitch!" Boatswain hissed. "Tell that old crone she's lying," he said to his lawyer through clenched teeth.

Diallo placed a hand on his client's arm. "Please, Mr. Boatswain, I've warned you about controlling your anger. The Judge will come hard on you and there would be nothing I can do. You have to be quiet," he urged him.

"I never liked that thing anyway," Boatswain sighed, referring to his neighbor.

Diallo took a deep breath. Irritated, Boatswain frowned at him.

"Tomah felt being tied to a husband had no happiness for her," Somah said, looking thoughtful as she continued. "I was not surprised about the things the woman said. I saw how Mr. Boatswain treated his wife."

"How?" Grace asked.

She was winning, Grace could tell she was winning.

"He treated her like one treats a stray animal," Somah replied. "When she accused him of having a girlfriend, he beat her. When he came home drunk and she complained, he beat her. He hit her even when there were no reasons. I saw this many times. I saw it with my two eyes."

"Let's talk about the rape," Grace encouraged. "Were you the only one there when it happened?"

Somah shook her head, "No," she said. "Beside me, there were many others there that day when he raped her. We heard screaming and crying. Lots of it. And that went on for a long while. Then when Tomah ran out of the house, blood was coming from here and here," she indicated her mouth and right elbow. "Her clothes were torn. We could see that she was not wearing any panties. Yet, one or two people seemed unconvinced that the woman had been raped. They would be the ones to gossip about her later."

"Mrs. Somah, let's stay with the incident," Grace said, politely.

"Yes… yes," Somah nodded. "Anyway, she ran over to the old shack behind Old Lady Musu's house," she said, and then turned her gaze to Boatswain. "Yes, that's true when they say life is cruel. So is he," she pointed, ending her testimony.

"Thank you, Mrs. Somah," Grace said and sat.

"Mr. Amadou," Judge Macavoi called, "Your witness."

Diallo got up and approached the witness quietly.

"Mrs. Somah, are you close to the couple?"

"What do you mean?"

"Are you friends with both, Mr. and Mrs. Boatswain?"

"I'm their neighbor, so that makes us friends."

Laughter erupted.

Judge Macavoi smiled. "Get to the point, Mr. Amadou," she said, politely.

Diallo nodded.

"You testified, Mrs. Somah, that Mrs. Boatswain wasn't wearing any underwear, is that right?"

"Yes."

"How do you know this?"

Somah remained quiet.

Judge Macavoi turned to the witness and said, "You have to answer,

Mrs. Somah."

"I don't know," Somah said and shrugged. "She was crying… saying that she'd been raped. So I assumed she wasn't wearing any."

Diallo smiled. "You also testified that you saw some blood," he reminded the witness. She nodded. "Where did you say the blood was?"

"Here and here," Somah pointed at her mouth and right elbow.

"Did you see blood anywhere else?"

"No."

"No blood coming down her legs?"

Somah looked at Tomah, embarrassed. "No," she murmured.

"Please speak up, Mrs. Somah," Diallo requested. "You did not see any blood coming down Mrs. Boatswain's legs that would have indicated rape, did you?"

Somah frowned. "No," she muttered.

"That's all, Your Honor," Diallo said and sat down.

"Any rebuttal, Ms. Pupoh?"

"No, Your Honor," Grace replied.

"Okay," Judge Macavoi said. "This would be a good time for a break. This Court will resume in two hours," she ordered and hit her gavel.

Chapter 60

COURT RESUMED PRECISELY two hours later, and Diallo handed over more documents to Judge Macavoi. Nonchalant of arguing liability, he would move to their strongest hand, Cheah Boatswain's medical record. His objections to Mrs. Boatswain's vaginal tear was that he had medical documentations to prove that his client was unusually well endowed, "for a short man," he had added.

Two witnesses for the defendant, both women, testified under oath that this was true. One woman said she'd ended the relationship because 'he was too big'.

Grace asked if her relationship with Mr. Boatswain was before, or after he'd entered into marriage.

After a long pause, the woman replied, "He didn't tell me he was married."

"You later found out that he was married, right?" Grace asked.

The woman sat quiet.

"You are under oath, so you may as well tell the truth. Was it his size, or was it his marital status?"

"I don't understand," the woman claimed.

"Why did you end the relationship with Mr. Boatswain? Was it because his penis was too big for you, or you found out he'd lied to you about being married?"

The woman sighed and said, "Both."

It was Boatswain on trial, not the woman. Grace ended the re-examination, "That would be all, Your Honor."

Judge Macavoi thanked the witness and asked whether Diallo had more to add. He did. The witness stayed with 'size' and 'lies', then he moved on to his client's medical reports.

"What my client suffers from is called, macropenis, an abnormally large penis," Diallo informed. "That's a legitimate medical term, I did not make that up."

Loud giggles came from the back of the courtroom.

"Quiet in the Court," Judge Macavoi ordered, stoned-face.

Silence followed.

"Go on, Counselor."

Diallo nodded.

"The Court has copies of the medical records, Your Honor," he continued. "So does the plaintiff."

Judge Macavoi acknowledged this with a nod.

"Penile gigantism…."

The courtroom erupted with laughter before Diallo could finish.

"Order!" Judge Macavoi shouted, hitting her gavel. "Mr. Amadou, we know that your client has a large penis, you don't need to remind us."

"Sorry, Your Honor," Diallo apologized.

"If what you have to say isn't relevant to his case, I'll hold you in contempt," Judge Macavoi warned. "Go on."

"Yes, Your Honor," Diallo replied.

"Get to the point," Judge Macavoi ordered.

Diallo took in his breath and let it out slowly.

"My client is being accused of rape, Your Honor, that's a very serious offense," he said. "We are not taking this lightly. He's fighting for his freedom."

"Get to the point," Judge Macavoi warned, forehead wrinkled.

Diallo nodded.

"The point I'd like to make here is this," he said, looking at the judge. "We've seen Mrs. Boatswain's medical reports… we know about the small lacerations she sustained, and Mr. Boatswain is sensitive to those facts. He is very sorry about that."

Diallo calmed. The courtroom silent.

"Your Honor," he continued, "I won't say that word again, but here's the thing. An average penis measures between five to seven inches… seven to nine inches is large, and well… anything over nine inches is, you can say, abnormal."

Judge Macavoi stared, no verbal warning.

Diallo felt safe to move on. "I'm not a doctor, Your Honor," he continued, "but realistically, the vagina can expand to deliver even an eight pound baby... no man on earth can claim to have an eight pound penis."

The court erupted with laughter.

Judge Macavoi struck her gavel several times against the sounding block, hard. "Order!" she shouted. "Anyone, I mean, anyone, who lets out a chuckle, will be escorted out of my courtroom."

Silence took over the courtroom immediately.

"Is that your point, Mr. Amadou?"Judge Macavoi asked.

"I'm not finished, Your Honor."

"Finish," Judge Macavoi ordered, now well beyond aggravation.

"Since the vagina can expand, it can be trained to take a larger... you know... penis," he said quietly.

"And your point is," Judge Macavoi said.

"My client did not rape his wife, Your Honor. What Mrs. Boatswain sustained is sex injury, not rape. They had rough sex one night... rough sex with your wife is not rape."

No chuckles, giggles, snicker or cackle escaped a lip. The courtroom remained dead quiet.

Diallo remained standing. He turned to Boatswain and smiled. He felt good. He might have discredited almost everything in Ms. Pupoh's pretty reports.

"Okay, Mr. Amadou," Judge Macavoi said. "You may sit down if you're finished."

"It wasn't rape, Your Honor," Diallo reasserted himself. "There was no rape... I'm done. Thank you, Judge."

Grace shot out of her chair before Judge Macavoi called for the plaintiff's rebuttal.

"Ms. Pupoh," the Judge recognized anyway.

"Thank you, Your Honor," Grace said, and then jabbed, "In this case, size does not matter."

Grace looked at the defense, then the judge, and then the audience. She had everyone's attention.

"You might want to consider what type of husband Mr. Boatswain was to his wife, rather than his abnormality," she continued. "A caring husband would invent a technique to accommodate his wife if he is well endowed," Grace rolled her eyes, clearly out of Judge Macavoi's view. "Mr. Boatswain was caring sometimes, when he and his wife had normal sexual activities. There were no sex injuries," she quoted *sex injuries* with her fingers.

"Those sex injuries that my client sustained," she quoted with her fingers again, "that are in the medical reports were because of rape, not because of regular sexual activity. Mrs. Boatswain was raped," Grace repeated.

"Rape, by definition of the law. Raped... raped... raped," she could not say the word enough. "Rape is a crime of sexual intercourse... with actual penetration of a woman's vagina with a man's penis... and here is the most important point," Grace said, and then paused. "Rape is sex, without consent... sex, accomplished through force... when that woman keeps saying 'no'...'no'...'no'. Saying 'no' constitutes lack of consent, no approval for the sexual intercourse. In this rape case, there was physical resistance, and there was force," Grace argued. "'No' does not mean 'don't'...'No' means, 'No.'"

Grace turned to the judge.

"We know what they're attempting here, Your Honor," she said. "The defendant is using his medical record to further humiliate my client. That won't work. My client has gone past humiliation."

"If you're finished, Ms. Pupoh, then you can do your closing. Mr. Amadou will get the chance to rebut when he does his closing."

"Gladly," Grace muttered, then said out loud, "Thank you, Your Honor."

Cheah Boatswain started to say something, Diallo told him to shut up.

__**********__

There was a long pause from Grace, but it was not because she was struggling to find words that would be truthful, yet soothing. She had caught her client's gaze and was smiling at her, reassuring her.

"Ms. Pupoh," Judge Macavoi said gruffly, as she tried getting the lawyer's attention. "A closing might be beneficial to your case, don't you think?"

"Yes, Your Honor," Grace replied and winked at her client.

"Well, get on with it."

Grace did.

"Sometimes the happening in our life comes in a way and at a time we would never expect," Grace said, looking directly at the audience, the pews were completely filled. "No advance warning. No time to prepare for it, by making things right. No new opportunities to prevent it from happening. But the truth to the matter is this... all of us are writing a story with our lives, one that will affect others now and in the future.

"For fifteen years or so," she said, now glancing at Judge Macavoi, "we were all under the cloud of gunshots and missiles. We all passed over the bodies of our dead relatives and neighbors… friends, and we were all taken to refugee camps to survive. We ate the same "hard time" food, made of whatever small animal that could feed our hungry children and fill our bellies. We drank the same dirty water to satisfy our thirst."

Grace paused. She had their attention.

"Now, these things took place for us to learn that when we, as a people, desire the type of evil as we did, ignoring the basic human rights of our weakest citizens, violating young children, indulging in taking bribes and killing as some did, we had to fall. Perhaps these things happened to Liberia as an example… we experienced things we never want to experience again. That is a lesson we must all learn."

Grace looked at the defendant, all necks from the defense table were twisted at her.

"We are seeking justice and the truth here," Grace continued. "We expect the law, and this court to serve out justice that is right from the law."

Then Grace delivered a condemnation of Mr. Boatswain's ethical shortcomings as a husband.

"Mr. Boatswain has been marinating in a hatred of his wife during their entire marriage, so intense as to surely amount to a personality disorder. He has developed a near-empty *partnership toolbox* rather than respect for his wife, prompting him to beat her disgracefully in front of their neighbors. That is the only abnormality that we recognize, and that should be the only abnormality the Court recognizes."

Boatswain might have thrown many punches, besides the first, but Grace was landing the heaviest blows. A hot-tempered client under pressure cannot be contained. Boatswain shot out of his seat.

"Sit down," Diallo whispered, quickly pulling him down by his shoulder.

"Mr. Amadou, another outburst from your client, and he will be very sorry," Judge Macavoi warned stiffly. "Another interruption in my Court, and your client will be spending the night in jail. Do you understand?"

"Yes, Your Honor," Diallo replied, unfazed.

"Go on, Ms. Pupoh."

"Thank you, Your Honor," Grace said, and she almost smiled.

Grace turned her gaze on Boatswain. He caught her gaze and his shoulders slumped.

"My client's goal is not to see her husband put into prison," Grace said, eyes locked on Boatswain. "Her goal is to survive… yes, survive. That is the best weapon an abused wife has… to finally put her own welfare first. Healing cannot begin until she speaks out against her attacker. Today in court, in front of all these people, Tomah Boatswain is speaking up against spousal rape, and against spousal abuse."

Then Grace ended by asserting that Mr. Boatswain must not escape punishment for violating her client's civil rights.

"The law is there to protect every girl and every woman against rape, whether it is her husband or a blood relative or a stranger. When a woman says 'No', she is saying to the man, he has no right to touch her body. He does not have her approval. Liability is clear in this case, 'No' means 'No'."

Grace sat down.

The judge asked whether Mr. Boatswain had something to say to the court.

On behalf of his client, Diallo said, "Mr. Boatswain only wishes to know why his wife is so set on seeing him in jail when all he did was take good care of her."

Tomah amazingly kept herself calm.

"You are doing great, Tomah," Grace whispered, barely moving her lips. "Stay calm."

"Is that your closing?" Judge Macavoi asked.

"No, Your Honor," Diallo said.

"Go on then."

"Thank you, Judge Macavoi."

Diallo paused again, as if to collect his thoughts.

"If Mrs. Boatswain has no interest in seeing Mr. Boatswain go to jail, then why are they pressing criminal charges?" Diallo accused. "This should have been a simple divorce proceeding, Your Honor. Everything had been on the table for months, and we could have resolved the case, if Mrs. Boatswain had disposed of the criminal matter. They would not settle. And, that's because this litigation is not about rape, it's all about revenge and getting back at a husband she no longer wants to be married to. People fall out of love. That's not a crime. Divorce is not impossible. But to accuse someone of rape, that's outright wickedness.

"We ask the court to see, beyond a reasonable doubt, whether my client is guilty of rape. There is no actual eyewitness to the rape… it's her words against his. All their so-called rape medical report shows is these two individuals had sex. Isn't that what husband and wife do? And, there's the medical records of my client's abnormality. Before the night in question, they had had many sexual activities during the ten years of marriage. She had the opportunity to leave, but she didn't."

Diallo turned his gaze at the plaintiff and said, "Mrs. Boatswain stayed with her husband because there was never a time in ten years, that my client abused his wife sexually. There was no rape... no one heard her say 'No' to her husband ... no one saw her fight him off. A man should not be sentenced to jail without parole, unless it's beyond a reasonable doubt, that he committed rape."

Diallo ended his closing and sat down.

Chapter 61

HEROIC MEASURES HAPPEN so fast one can hardly remember what happened. Other people have to tell you what you did after. Grace had been smart, and not *dumb* lucky. One of the first laws Johnson-Sirleaf passed after becoming president of Liberia was a law criminalizing rape and gang rape, making rape a non-parole offense in order to prevent abusers from returning to their communities and threatening the victims. The following year, the same law was expanded to include spousal rape as a recognized form of rape and as a crime. Women could change conflict into an opportunity, become the new empowered political faces and no longer be the face of the victims. Tomah Boatswain would be just that. The thing is, trials are not always about individual wrongs, sometimes they are used as a pulpit for a cause. And when you believe in change, hope is a mighty drug.

Applying legal principles and precedents established under the common law, Judge Macavoi's obligation was to make a ruling that is consistent and not based on revenge, but rather on the fundamental concepts of protection of the public, and fairness, deterring others from committing crimes and reforming the offender. Macavoi took into account the seriousness of the offense, Boatswain's background and prospects for rehabilitation, as well as the need to deter others from committing crimes. She would have to craft a decision to break new grounds, while being consistent with the principles laid down in the common law.

At five past nine, the bailiff announced, "All rise!"

Judge Macavoi made her entrance and took her place. "Please be seated," she said, looking around the packed courtroom. Macavoi adjusted her microphone closer. "In all the years I've worked with people, I've yet to meet someone whose life was all messed up because he, or she, did the right thing by obeying society law," she started.

Her tone was challenging. No one in the courtroom doubted what she would imply, rather strongly, that a society with no structure is a result of Africa's problem with war lords. Liberia needed change.

"After our civil war, today when Liberians' freedom is celebrated as an undeniable right to everyone... talk of conforming our lifestyle to love of country and respect for the laws that make us respect human rights is still often viewed as an infringement."

She sighed, and then shifted in her chair. No one's eyes left her.

"Anyone who speaks out against corruption and holds integrity to a high level is ruled out of bounds," she continued. "Why is that? It should not go unnoticed. Our society is increasingly marked with a recurring sense of meaninglessness and despair when it comes to life and liberty. Why is that?"

Supportive murmurs could be heard from the back of the courtroom. The judge struck her gavel and the courtroom gain silence.

"We must realize that a happy life, yours and mine, comes from a respect in the law of the land," she continued. "It is not in taking your position in society to bully civilian citizens, or anyone for that matter." Macavoi turned her gaze on Boatswain. "It is not in working with those who commit crimes and have the finance to run from facing justice. The laws are written to govern us, every citizen, serving as fences constructed to help us avoid reckless living. We are a civilized society."

Boatswain shifted in his seat.

"There are some of us who believe in our freedom and the freedom of others," she continued to look at Boatswain. Boatswain stared back. "We intend to get rid of those chains of corruption, the bondage of shackle that keeps Liberia behind the rest of the world. Next time you are tempted to break the law, or abuse another Liberian when you should be protecting your citizens," Macavoi pointed at Boatswain, "remember, that you are a police officer. Mr. Boatswain, remember the purpose of the fence. Choose to enforce the law rather than break it. We all benefit."

Boatswain lowered his gaze.

"You are not a man, Mr. Boatswain, you are a follower," Judge Macavoi provoked. "The things you do are wrong... you are breaking the law... the abuse, the bullying, intimidation... my goodness, the list goes on. Do you go to church, Mr. Boatswain?"

"No," Boatswain babbled.

"No, what?" Judge Macavoi barked, making a face.

"Show respect for the Judge," Diallo whispered to his client. "Say, 'No, Your Honor' and say it respectfully."

"No, Your Honor Judge," Boatswain replied.

Judge Macavoi smiled.

The man's macho ego was blistering. She knew a lot of women judges who would love this part, where a woman has absolute power over egotistical fools like Boatswain. Macavoi had not cared for it until now. In this case, the man sitting before her needed his ego deflated.

Looking straight at Boatswain's eyes, Judge Macavoi asserted, "*Your Honor* is enough. This is my last advice to you, Mr. Boatswain. Power, wealth and pleasure are good, but they're not the best in this life. God is the best, that's why we all should make time for church. It would be a good experience for you."

Boatswain nodded.

"Your wife has been willing to treat you with the utmost respect, while you enjoy treating her with absolutely no respect," Judge Macavoi said. "Why is that?"

Cheah Boatswain looked confused. He did not know whether to answer or not.

"Don't say anything," Diallo whispered. "Just keep looking at the Judge."

Boatswain sat quietly.

"Mr. Boatswain, you don't know the meaning of pain and suffering," Judge Macavoi continued. She hammered at the evil he'd committed against his wife, flogging her in front of neighbors, with no regard for her dignity. "She is your wife," her voice boomed. "You stood before God and others, taking an oath to love and protect her. But selfishness had made you ignore that oath. Shame on you, Mr. Boatswain."

Besides granting a divorce, it was the perfect case for the levying of punitive damages, and there was little doubt in Diallo's mind, the Judge's hand would be heavy. A jury trial would have put them into deeper waters. He thanked God he'd gone without the jury trial.

"The marriage is irretrievably broken," Judge Macavoi concluded. "This Court is satisfied with the evidence and testimonies of witnesses. The plaintiff has proven, beyond reasonable doubt, that the defendant, Mr. Cheah Boatswain, committed adultery and cruel treatment against his wife. Mr. Boatswain has a drinking problem, and the Court finds that his marriage has suffered because of his intoxication. Therefore, divorce is granted in this case on the grounds of a fault-based divorce, in favor of Mrs. Tomah Boatswain. Now, let's get to the spousal rape charge," she said and sighed.

Grace took in a deep breath and let it out slowly. They watched for five minutes as Macavoi flipped through the documents on her desk. The plaintiff, defendant, and everyone else, seems anxious for her to rule.

"This is a criminal matter, as far as the law goes," Judge Macavoi continued. "But, what do you do with he-say, she-say? The usual physical evidence used in rape cases is, more than likely, of little use in marital rape cases. All that proves is that this woman had sex with this man, which she had done many, many times in the past. It typically comes down to one person's word against another."

Macavoi paused and added, "Even though in this case, there is also battery. However, had the alleged rape taken place after Mrs. Boatswain had moved out of the home… it would've been easier to determine. Mrs. Boatswain never complained to anyone… a friend or relative, on a previous occasion of spousal rape. I see the pattern of physical abuse, but there's no pattern of sexual abuse. I have a problem with that. Spousal rape is really tough to prosecute, even for the best lawyers, since we have a 'beyond a reasonable doubt' standard."

Judge Macavoi went on to explain that rape in marriage is a serious and widespread form of violence against women, and must continue to be reported.

"Don't keep your mouth shut," she continued. "Any time someone forces himself on you sexually without your consent; this can be sexual assault or rape. Please, know that you have the right to say 'no' even to your husband. If he forces you to have sexual intercourse, he is raping you. The only way to make the judicial system work on women's behalf, is to report it. Tell someone. Tell someone the first time when it happens."

Macavoi saved her best for last. She lectured on the purpose of punitive damages, to punish wrongdoers and make examples out of them so they would sin no more. Boatswain might escape prison, but not punishment.

"No jail time," Diallo assured his client. "That's good."

Boatswain smiled.

After Macavoi flipped through more documents on her desk, she said, "Mr. Boatswain, we have to talk about damages."

Diallo whispered something to his client, and then said to the Judge, "We would go with what the Court recommends, Your Honor… mercy of the Court."

"I was hoping you say that," Macavoi replied. She turned to the plaintiff and asked, "Ms. Pupoh, what would you recommend?"

Grace looked toward the defendant's table. Boatswain shifted in his seat. Then she turned to the Judge and said, "Well, Your Honor, we figure Mrs. Boatswain is entitled to half of all the couple's marital property, and that he pays all medical expenses and legal fees, which includes attorney's costs."

Judge Macavoi searched among the documents for the list of marital property. "Let's take a look at what's been listed," she said, placing a sheet of paper on top of the pile.

Macavoi examined the document, reading it quietly.

The Boatswains had listed their non-marital properties, property each had acquired before the marriage; through inheritance or by gift from a third party. There was a valid agreement with the plaintiff and the defendant, the couple's main residence, a four-bedroom house, belonged to Mr. Boatswain before the marriage and Mrs. Boatswain entered the marriage with a full-size freezer that they'd used to make ice to sell. That business had afforded them enough money to purchase an old taxi that contributed a monthly income of $300.

During the ten-year marriage, the couple had accrued two new taxis, one Toyota city-traffic bus, and two small rental houses, all of which Mr. Boatswain claimed to have purchased with his money. The Judge thought otherwise.

"All marital property is subject to division," Judge Macavoi informed. "The Court has determined which property and debt are considered marital. Monetary value has already been assigned to some of the marital property and debt. Of those, they will be distributed between the two parties in an equitable fashion, which is meant to be fair, but not necessarily equal. Is that clear? That was done during discovery," she reminded.

"Yes, Your Honor," both lawyers agreed.

"Mr. Boatswain may keep the main house, one small house and one new taxi," Judge Macavoi said.

Boatswain nodded.

"Mrs. Boatswain may keep the other small house, one new taxi, the old taxi and freezer… in other words, the business… and the Toyota city-traffic bus. There will be no alimony payments. I'm also ordering Mr. Boatswain to pay all legal fees… of both attorneys, and all medical expenses of Tomah Boatswain."

Judge Macavoi paused.

"For punitive damage," she said, "this is what we'll do. Mr. Boatswain will pay Tomah Boatswain, ten thousand US dollars for pain and suffering. I think you should pay it," Macavoi said to Boatswain. "It's not unreasonable. That's for the sexual injuries she sustained on the night in question… your words, Mr. Boatswain, not mine. This court will make sure of it."

There were gasps and coughs and soft whispers as shock waves rattled around the courtroom.

Grace held Tomah's hand, looked at her, and smiled. "Don't say anything yet," she whispered.

Tomah nodded.

"The final judgment on this divorce proceeding shall then specify and restore to the requesting party, Mr. Boatswain, the name requested in the pleadings," the Judge informed. "The divorced wife, Tomah Boatswain, is legally prohibited from using the given name or initials of the divorced husband, Mr. Cheah Boatswain. Do you understand, Mrs. Boatswain, you can no longer be referred to as Tomah Boatswain?"

Tomah nodded.

"Answer, 'Yes', Your Honor," Grace said to her client.

"Yes, Your Honor."

"That means, make those changes on all legal documents," Judge Macavoi ordered. "You pay for those expenses, not Mr. Boatswain."

"Your Honor, I'll get this taken care of," Grace said.

Diallo glanced at Grace, their eyes met, and each offered a polite nod. The miracle of the trial was that the two lawyers would still be able to treat each other with a modest dose of respect, even discuss legal issues when necessary. Regardless of how nasty the situation had been at times, each was willing to rise above the gutter and offer a hand.

"Good luck, to you both," Judge Macavoi said, and then she announced, "Court adjourned."

Tomah's hands shook and her eyes filled with tears.

"Tomah, you've won," Grace said. "You're free from Cheah Boatswain. He can no longer touch you. What's your name?"

Tomah looked at Grace and said, "Tomah Chenoweth?"

"Good," Grace laughed. "You've passed the first test."

Tomah wept, and Grace embraced her.

Boatswain's expression ranged from puzzlement, to shock amazement, then to hatred. He had the best lawyer in Liberia and they had come to tussle, to fight dirty, and to win at whatever the cost. But he had lost his house, his cars, and plenty cash to his weak, pitiful wife.

"What happened?" Boatswain snapped. "An hour ago you were downright cocky."

"Not me… you," Diallo pointed.

Boatswain glared at Diallo. "That woman has no right to take my property away from me and give it to Tomah."

"She has every right," Diallo replied.

"Why didn't you object?"

"Because I couldn't! She's the damn judge… she has the final word."

"She must be drunk with their so-called women's liberty," Boatswain babbled. "Is she part of the frisky women club too?"

"Enough, Boatswain, I've had enough of you," Diallo warned.

"What?"

"You heard me."

"That judge has poisoned the well," Boatswain continued, "not just for me, but you too. Nowadays, a man cannot have sex with his own wife without the threat of rape. Is this then the life of every Liberian man?"

Diallo said nothing. He allowed himself to absorb Boatswain's nonsense because he had bigger fish to fry. Manor's reckless decisions lately, for instance. He stood, and with perfect composure, walked out of the courtroom, leaving his client behind.

Grace and Tomah were mobbed by a group of women when they walked out, mostly FW members. They wanted to know all that the judge had said and done. Had justice been given?

Grace wanted to jump up and punch the air. She contained herself.

Chapter 62

IBRAHIM RAJÉB, AKA Net, an overseas Nigerian investigative reporter for ABC news, had frequented Le'Toit club four times, and one of those times, he'd caught a US congressman in bed with an underage girl. He could hardly wait to tell the world a member of Congress was at Le'Toit club partying with a thirteen-year-old sex slave while on official business. Rajéb also had footage of drunken UN diplomats, other foreign government bureaucrats, super sport stars, and a few famous Hollywood used-to-be.

Thanks to the cool and great use for the latest miniature technology. Rajéb had tiny cameras that recorded on the sly; hidden in his pen, the button on his sport jacket, his key ring and even the dressy tie most complemented him for, all with built-in microphone and the ability to let him record on the built-in 4GB memory straight onto his computer a mile away.

The reporter informed Bohn he would have to break the story soon, he had already contacted the congressman for an interview before the story breaks. Put a US Congressman in a hot seat, and that would ratchet up the pressure on anyone, anywhere. The pressure was mounting with each passing day, so Bohn had to make a move soon.

Bohn phoned Lonos, and forty-five minutes later they were at Sugar Shack meeting in the back room for briefing.

"He is a rich man with a lot of stress," Bohn said to Lonos. "In the last few months morale has been low in Le'Toit club. And his big man, Boatswain, is having a fight on his hand. Once his divorce case had been transferred, there's no telling. Diallo, his lawyer, seems fed up because he's been spending more time with Manor than other clients, and the former super model is threatening divorce because Manor doesn't want children."

"He still has Adriana LeRoux," Lonos pointed out.

"Looks like Ms. LeRoux is no longer the bright spot in his crumbling business," Bohn replied. Then he shook his head and frowned. "Lonos, I'm afraid the clock is running much faster on Manor's wall. We have to get to those disks and everything else before time runs out. You will have to get into that club one way or another."

"How?"

"As a woman."

Lonos considered the suggestion for a moment, then he clenched his jaws and asked, "As a what?"

"Woman."

Lonos sighed. He remained patient as Bohn gave a dry summary of the reason things had to move along quickly, which wasn't much at all. Bohn never mentioned Net. At level Clay, Lonos worked on a need-to-know basis.

They both dwell on this for some time.

After half an hour of a dull narrative that was going nowhere, Bohn said, "Let's talk about you as a woman."

"Don't we have any other way?"

"Lonos, it's no big deal. It's not the end of the world wearing pantyhose and lipsticks for a few minutes."

Easy for you to say, Lonos thought. *You are not the one wearing it.*

"It comes with the job," Bohn said. "It could be worst."

Lonos did not want to think about how worst it could get. He sipped his beer and said, "I think I know someone who could make me look half a woman."

"Grace?"

Lonos nodded. *There's not much this man does not know*, he thought. "Yes. Grace."

"It has to be on Sunday, when only one guard is on duty and everyone else is suffering from a hangover," Bohn suggested, reaching into his jacket pocket. He withdrew a small pill tin box. "There are four pills in there, but you'll only need two." Bohn handed the box to Lonos.

Lonos took the box.

"They are just sleeping pills, nothing to kill him."

Lonos cleared his throat. "Is two enough?"

"Yes... only two. And, Lonos, you're doing an excellent job," he praised. "Good work."

"Thank you, sir."

"Look at it this way. There's a big upside and a small downside. Handle this one, Lonos, and you'll be moving up. Based on the progress of this," Bohn added.

__**********__

Manor could not get over the fact that the reporter, posting as a staid Nigerian businessman, had thumped a hole in his business, though a temporary one. But, the odds were seemingly stacked heavily against him, especially after that US Congressman had pressured Manor to rid any evidence of him being at the club. Lack of knowledge is no defense, the reporter had told the Congressman. Other important international and local guests followed. Big spenders slowed to a handful. The heat was on, but Manor did not care about what went on in America, as long as the guests would start filling the club again.

Manor thought of cooling things with his beautiful and fiercely supportive partner for a few weeks, since the last stunt she'd pulled at the restaurant. But a woman like Adriana is not easily brushed aside. The moment he found out she had landed in Monrovia, Manor called and asked if she had time for a quick drink. "Sure," she said, "why not?"

Manor arrived at the hotel an hour later and hurried to Adriana's suite. They carry on with small talks, a chuckle here and there, but the mood was pretty serious. The thought of Adriana screwing things up for him, while Le'Toit was loosing money, was troubling. Against his will, she had taken Dr. Douglas as a passenger on her private jet while transporting his medical merchandise. He had been furious about that.

Manor scolded and preached to his heart's content. Then he informed Adriana that he would be taking the merchandise out of South Africa himself. She was becoming a risk and he couldn't afford that.

Adriana could not keep from smiling, but only for a second. "You are taking them out yourself?"

Manor frowned and rubbed his chin. "Yeah."

"On a commercial flight?"

"Well, yeah," Manor answered. "Diallo is coming with me."

"Quiet an ego," she chuckled. "You no longer need me?" She narrowed her eyes and stared at Manor. "Seriously? You don't need me?"

Manor's gaze went from her face down to her breasts. He noticed the woman's erect nipples through her transparent blouse and salivated at the thought of screwing her one last time, at this very moment. He could almost feel the touch of her flesh.

"Are you hard of hearing?" Adriana yelled.

This startled Manor. Oblivious to what she was saying, he asked, "What? What did you say?"

Adriana rattled off as if she'd spent hours contemplating it. Manor absorbed the rattling and his mind was racing.

"Fine, I don't care," she snarled. "If you want to be a fool, then go right ahead. Get out!"

"What?"

"Get... out!"

Manor shook his head, sighed, then walked out, slamming the door behind him. He did not say goodbye.

The relationship had been fading slowly. At this point he didn't care too much, but he knew it would be impossible to just walk away from the woman. For one thing, her daddy is loaded with cash and status. And, Andriana is a snake. He couldn't afford to forget that. Galloping on a camel's back through the eye of a needle would be easier than putting her behind him.

Chapter 63

ONE DOWN, ONE to go. Grace had no time to bask after the Boatswains case, she was waiting for the final decision on the adoption. As of 2:00 p.m., nothing had been decided. Grace could not believe the delay. She should have received the final document since 11:00 a.m. Her cell phone rang. It was Mel.

"I'm heading your way... just wanted to know if you were at the office," Mel said. She sounded tired and frustrated.

"I'm still waiting for the decision, Mel. Maybe I'll have it by the time you get here."

Mel hung up before Grace said anything else.

At 3:15 p.m. Grace had not heard from Kaifa, and Mel hadn't arrived. She told Gbomai to make sure Mel wait for her at the office, and that she would be back as quickly as she could.

"Don't let her leave," Grace repeated as she walked out the door.

Four-thirty came early, Grace was still a no-show. Gbomai offered a few jokes, but Dr. Douglas was too tired to laugh.

"She knew that I was coming," Mel protested.

"That's why she insisted that you wait," Gbomai pleaded. "Please, Dr. Douglas, Ms. Pupoh will soon be back."

The office door flew open around 4:45 p.m. and Grace rushed in, huffing. "Look what I have in my hand," she waved the manila envelope.

"That better be good news," Mel smiled.

"It is," Grace said, catching her breath. "Ministry of Health and Social Welfare has provided it's case summary, granting you the adoption. It is in the best interest of everyone, especially Tapee. Congratulations, Dr. Mom," Grace handed Mel the envelope.

"You mean…."

"Yes, you are officially the mother of Tapee," Grace confirmed. "He's yours, a hundred percent."

Mel sighed with incredible relief. She felt very good. "Thank you, Grace," she said. "You have no idea how much this means to me. That little boy gives me more reasons to feel alive than anything else. Not even being a doctor, and I love being a doctor."

"I know, Mel," Grace smiled. "I know."

"I never thought that I would love anything more than medicine. My God," she sighed, "being a mother seems far, far more exciting."

"It certainly is," Grace grinned.

"You are amazing, Grace," Mel said. "Three months?"

"Well, I have a wonder suport team... my staff," Grace said, smiling. "They are the best."

Mellody understood arrogance. For someone who's incredibly smart, Grace should be arrogant. Mel liked that about the woman. "Amazing Grace," she muttered.

"Are you going to change his name?" Grace wanted to know.

"Only his last name," she said. "I'm not changing who my son is. I'm only changing who's responsible for his day to day care. Tapee Douglas... his last name is all that's going to change."

Mel got home around six, but not before calling RJ and Gia to tell them the good news. She even offered to pay for their return trip tickets to Liberia for the dedication. If anything, RJ joked that he could not have missed a trip to anywhere, where Mel is actually sitting up in a church. He wouldn't be sitting next to her though, he'd joked.

"I'm not the one who have broken one of the commandments," Mel returned.

Bohn took everyone out to celebrate, Katharine, Mel, Cecelia, Nàjma, Grace, Ma Torlah, Peace and Tapee. Kendejah was very nice and very expensive.

—**********—

The next day Katharine sat quietly in the backyard long enough to watch the sunset. It looked so stunningly beautiful and serene that it actually made her cheerful, spreading something good through her body. There have been lots of pretty sunrises in her life lately; three grandchildren, her reunion with Rufus Bohn, just to name a few. She would be looking forward for more.

Cecelia escorted Katharine's friend to the backyard. How people look on the outside is not always an indicator of what is in their heart. Lynnette Vinton's visit seemed purposeful, even before the conversation started.

"I'm a little disappointed, truth be told," Lynnette mouthed as soon as her rear hit the chair.

Katharine winched. "Truth be told?" she retorted. It took all of her willpower to keep from screaming at the woman.

Lynnette Vinton had personally petitioned against the adoption, based on Dr. Douglas' lifestyle, citizenship status, and the Bible. Mainly the Good Book, and what it had to say. She had applied enormous pressure, but to no avail. Grace took the hits, but sent back punches as well. This lobbying both fascinated and repulsed Katharine, to say the least.

To avoid being mired in *self-righteousness* seems impossible for the woman. Katharine hope her friend would one day, and soon, discover the real value of kindness. It wasn't just about raising a hand in the church when asked about members outreach ministry: How many fed the starving? Amount of cash given away. Or, Visits made to the bedside of sick people.

Servicing needs is to remind people of God's faithfulness to their needs, not mementos of the "good" we do for them. It's a good thing to have tangible evidence of God's help in your life. It helps others in knowing that God's provisions for the needy continues into the future. As followers of Christ, our good works should always be looked at as something done to encourage others of their confidence in God. The memories of what God does in one's life becomes a collection of building blocks of faith.

True, Lynnette Vinton headed the Women's Ministry and was wonderful. She visited and counseled with worried mothers, telling them that God was watching over their family. She stood with mothers by the beds of their ailing children. Lynnette Vinton even cried with them in their grief when their son or daughter died. She helped with funeral expenses too. *But Lynnette Vinton has no right to speak words that would pierce my soul*, Katharine thought.

"You do know what the Bible says about judging," Katharine said.

"I know what the Good Book says," Lynnette answered, shaking her head, rolling her eyes. "I read my Bible every day. I'm not a hypocrite, Katharine. When I speak of the gays, I know what the Good Book says. Homosexuals will *never* inherit God's kingdom. That's why I supported our government when they made that law. The death penalty is a bit harsh, but one year in jail is more than enough punishment. What they're doing is detestable!"

"Lynnette, what has that got to do with my child?" Katharine asked and gave Lynnette a few seconds to take in what she had said. Possibly even to understand. Lynnette sat up in her seat, bug-eyed. For once, she didn't know what to say, or do. "Whether or not you believe homosexuality is a sin based on your interpretations of the scripture, shouldn't there be issues surrounding the treatment of people and their intentions to do good?"

Lynnette stared.

"There are some Christian homosexuals, and there are those that desire deliverance from homosexuality," Katharine went on. "Rather than trying to be God and pass judgement on those individuals, a better option may be to offer prayers for those struggling with their sin... like every other sinner."

Lynnette took a quick, deep breath. She stared defiantly at Katharine and said, "Why you think I do these things, huh? The Good Lord wants us to correct. Yes, c o r r e c t... correct. It's right there in First Corinthians."

Katharine waited to hear more.

"Chapter five, verses twelve through thirteen," Lynnette continued. "God passes this responsibility on to the church family. It isn't my responsibility to judge outsiders, but it is certainly my responsibility to judge those inside the church who are sinning. God will judge those on the outside. As the Scriptures say, 'You must remove the evil from among you'. Evil people, that is."

"Evil people?"

"God wants his people to be pure, Katharine," Lynnette challenged. "He calls us to live holy lives. If we ignore blatant sinfulness in the church, then we fail to honor the Lord's call to be holy."

Katharine closed her eyes, took in her breath and let it out slowly.

"If we are trying our best to live for his glory, why can't others?"

"My daughter is not an evil person, Lynnette," Katharine said. Her face was a mask of disgust. "My baby has cared for more poor people than any church I know. That child works day and night for people she doesn't even know. This little boy means so much to her and you knew it. Yet, you did everything you could to stop her from becoming his mother. You called that doing the Lord's work?"

"I have nothing against Mel," Lynnette proclaimed. "It's not her I am fighting... it's the sin."

Then Lynnette broke down crying.

Katharine had no sympathy to give.

"Take the speck out of your own eye, then you will see clearly to take the speck out of another person's eye. Goodbye, Lynnette," Katharine said. "Go on now, hear?"

Lynnette got up. "I'm sorry, Katharine."

"You, go on," Katharine repeated. "I'd like you to leave... right now."

Lynnette took off as if the place was on fire. "I'm so, so sorry," she repeated, as she hurried away.

Bohn walked out the backdoor at the same time Lynnette was walking away. She was out of hearing distance when Bohn reached Katharine.

"I know enough about that woman," he said to Katharine. "I could give you some real dirt on that friend of yours."

Katharine looked up at him. He was smiling.

"No need to, Rudy," she mumbled.

Katharine had given Bohn equal amount of good and bad about the woman. Bohn thought: so what if she extends her hand to the poor and reaches out her hands to the needy? She supports the MaryMartha Orphanage, but at the same time, armed and dangerous with gossips and condemnation for everyone. Her negative attacks on others chipped away the value of her kindness. It's like venom and love, or topping a pile of shit with scoops of whipped cream.

"Miss Katharine, all due respect... that woman is scarier than a bolt of lightning," Cecelia said, pointing in Lynnette's direction. "Someone needs to stop her before she strikes again."

"Please, Kate, can I?" Bohn teased. "I would if she keeps messing with Mel. Mellody deserves better."

Chapter 64

GRACE WAS GLAD to see the final days of the trial draw to a close. It had held so much sadness, both physical and emotional fights and nervous tensions. She was ready to welcome a turning point in her personal life with its very own symphony orchestra. Alex could be back in her life, the burden to keep Peace's biological father a secret was over, and he would be sharing time with RJ or the Douglas family. FW membership rapid growth was encouraging, and she was looking forward to Yassah's wedding. God had been with her through the deep waters even though she had not frequently attended Words of Christ Church like others. Yassah told her when trouble comes, God promises His presence as long as she trusts Him.

All what Alex had told her was true, they were the facts. Love had everything to do with it. He loves her and had never stopped being her best friend. The thought of her making him feel unloved by her, lurched in her heart. She loves Alex also, but she wasn't in love with him. And, why not? Nothing speaks clearly of Alex's love than his actions toward her. He was caring, loving, and had always been considerate of her needs. In truth, Alex *was* the best partner life had offered her.

Grace had stayed awake all night thinking of the moment when she met Alex. In high school she was innocent and he teased her about that. Then he would kiss her belly till she laughed. He told her she was pretty and smart, and thoroughly likable.

All day at the office, Grace took phone calls, met people, made contacts, and swapped business cards with people she might probably see again—mostly those who had returned home from overseas.

She had not only survived the morning and afternoon sessions of a very busy day, Grace had vowed to let Alex know how she truly felt, what she truly wanted. She waited until the last staff left for the day because it would be an emotional scene.

As if on cue, the knock on his office door startled him from his paperwork. The office was quiet, supposedly closed and the staff all gone home. Alex didn't get up from his desk. He simply watched as the door swung inward.

"Alex," came a soft voice. A voice he knew so well, a voice that screws the clamp surrounding his heart.

"Grace," he murmured. He got up and walked around to the front of his desk.

Her movements were graceful and unhurried, she came closer. Alex smelled the freshness of her perfume before she reached him. Then she touched him, a whisper of fingers lightly across his cheek. "Please, Alex," she smiled a perfect smile, and their eyes lingered for a second.

He should step away from her but he couldn't. Her touch was a comfort and he needed to smother himself with it. He'd missed her to a great extent. His heart wrenched from his chest. His stomach twisted painfully. Alex needed to hold himself together, gather the battled pieces of his dignity and stand up to her.

"Grace, unless you feel differently, don't...."

"Oooh, Alex," her voice shook. "Please, don't be mad at me."

Oh boy! He didn't know what to say next. He drew in a sharp breath. Their relationship had gone through ups and downs, and he believed it was the natural consequence of couples that choose to stay together over the long haul. This was definitely one of those ups.

Grace brushed a thumb across his cheek and smiled at him again. "I love you, Alex Massaquoi, and I don't even mind being your wife."

Alex stared, and stared. He found he couldn't speak. His throat was too tight. He simply took her hand and kissed the back of it. "I love you too," he whispered.

Grace smiled. "I want you to come back home, Alex... please."

"Grace...."

"Things would be different," she interjected.

"Different... how?"

"Alex, I'll make time for us. I swear I will."

The persuasive look was designed, Alex knew, to drive him to such distraction that he couldn't think clearly. The twinkle in her eyes that went with her smile. She seemed more attractive, and it seemed odd that he had not noticed her brown eyes until now. They were quite pleasant to gaze into.

"And RJ?" He couldn't help asking.

"His son lives with us, Alex. I can't stop their relationship. RJ is Peace's father and we are his other parents." She paused. "Baby, it is what it is. I want to work on our relationship. I want you back in our home."

Our relationship, our home, our future, Alex thought. The ultimate word, he'd noticed, was *ours*. "That means our future is set? Are you sure?"

Grace nodded.

"Is that a 'yes'?"

His eyes were dancing and hoping she say 'yes'.

"Yes," she smiled. "Yes."

Had he not been manly, he would have wept for joy.

"I love you, Grace... no matter what," Alex said, and then gently kissed her lips.

"I love you too, Alex. I cannot promise you a perfect life, but I'll do my best to make you happy."

Alex looked at her with a glint of hope in his eyes.

Grace promised to be available for Alex, within reason, and then their movements for the evening were planned. They would allow Peace to spend the night at his grandmother's since RJ would be arriving from the States in the morning. Next, they would take a taxi home because they had a lot of catching up to do.

Rain started with the wind blowing into the city from the Atlantic Ocean. They stepped out of the office, embracing the light drizzles, and flagged down the first available taxi. Grace boarded, then Alex. The taxi drove in painfully slow moving traffic.

Other women were very much interested in Alex, but it was obvious he'd not found someone else. Grace thought about asking if he had kept his pants on while they'd been absent from one another. He would tell the truth, and she wouldn't want to hear it. Besides, she should not be the one to preach sex or safe sex. Who was the virgin that got pregnant with another man's child? *Don't ask, don't tell,* she thought and decided to savor the moment, every bit of it.

Grace turned to Alex. "Baby, I'm glad you're coming home," she whispered, and smiled a naughty smile as her fingers skimmed his forearm.

Alex could feel the blood rush through his ears, the way it does when they are lying in bed in a heated moment. Grace could count on her smile to get his attention. He smiled, not knowing testosterone is a man's greatest weakness, and a woman's most powerful advantage.

About forty minutes later, the driver maneuvered the taxi through the neighborhood using Alex's directions, then straight to the house. Alex paid, and as they enter the house through the garage, the driver noticed a private car and wondered why had they taken a taxi. He stopped, opened his door and ran before Alex shut the garage door.

"Excuse me," he waved Alex to stop. "Is something wrong with the car? I'm also a mechanic… I can fix it."

"No, we just don't use it every day."

"Why?"

"The traffic is terrible… and there's no parking when we drive to town," Alex explained, as if he'd owed him one.

"Then you need a driver," the man suggested.

Alex thought for a moment. "Do you have a cell phone?" The man nodded. "Give me your name and number… I'll call you if we decide."

The driver did.

Grace showered and towel off, then she went to the closet and looked for something to put on, finally choosing a negligee that dipped considerably in the front. She slipped it on and looked in the mirror, turning from side to side. It fitted her loosely. When she heard Alex clear his throat, she peeked at him standing in the door and smiled.

"I'm going to take a shower," he informed.

They heard the rumbling thunder and Alex walked to the bedroom window instead, to watch for the lightning. The next brilliant flash illuminated the sky with the promise of an all night rain. He felt himself fill with longing.

"I'll go make us something to eat while you take your shower," Grace encouraged and disappeared.

An hour later, they were sitting at the kitchen table eating dinner; fried ripe plantain and crisp fried fish.

Afterward, as Grace collected the dishes from the table, Alex said, "So why is RJ rushing to Liberia now?"

She turned her gaze at him and her face registered a disappointment that he had learned to recognize over the years. He fully understood why.

After a moment, she asked, "Really, Alex?"

Alex knew he had to offer something. He hesitated, aware there was more to her question than it implied. "I didn't mean it the way it sounded."

Grace gave a strange half smile in response.

"Let me do the dishes?" he offered, with a conspiratorial smile.

"I should let you," she replied.

Alex took the dish towel. "I'll do them... I'll be fast," he winked.

Fifteen minutes later, Alex was standing in the bedroom door, admiring Grace. She was lying on her side with her back toward him. He crawled into bed and was making himself comfortable when she turned and smiled.

"I would've washed those dishes in five minutes," she teased.

He kissed her.

"And, if anyone was waiting for me in bed, wearing this," she pulled at her negligee, "I would've been here in less than two minutes."

He kissed her again. "It's lovely, sweetie," he whispered, "but I love what's underneath it."

Grace slowly pulled the nightgown over her head and tossed it.

As the rain drifted across the roof and the wind strummed it peculiar sounds, Alex made her notice the music of the raindrops as it fell on the rooftop, and even on the trees outside. It was beautiful music, but they soon had forgotten the pattering of the rain, the wind and everything else, except for the urgent touch of each other.

Alex was good and effortless in bed. She loved the way he touched her, gently kissing her lips, cheeks, the hollow of her throat, her back, her breasts and everywhere. He knew how to hold her, how and where to touch her, how to wait, and then when to let everything on the inside explode. Finally, Alex stretched over her like a quilt on a cold rainy night.

Chapter 65

LYNNETTE VINTON THOUGHT to honor God by making reconciliation with her friend a priority before anything else. She reached the church before everyone did for the Wednesday evening prayer meeting, knowing Katharine would be attending.

"I'm sorry, Katharine," Lynnette greeted, embracing the woman in a bear hug. "I was just doing what the Good Lord wants us to do… correct each other. I did not mean to hurt you."

Katharine thought to tell her friend that it was not she, who Lynnette had harmed, it was Mel. But before she could, Lynnette said, as soon as they came apart, "As followers of Jesus, we belong to one another and our individual actions can impact the whole church and God's name."

Katharine stared unbelievably.

"Everyone doesn't have to sin, but one person's sin can affect everyone," Lynnette continued. "I was just tying up a loosed end, Katharine, that's all."

Katharine continued to stare.

"We can give God honor individually, but doing it together is something else," Lynnette went on. "It is better when we do it together. Don't you think God deserves our effort?"

"It's something else," Katharine repeated with a hint of sarcasm that Lynnette missed, because Lynnette smiled and hugged Katharine again.

It wasn't easy for Katharine to swallow her pride and accept the so-called apology. It was un-Christlike to condemn another person maliciously, and it would be un-Christlike not to forgive.

"Lynnette, no one will know what you mean when you say, 'God is love' unless you show it," Katharine said, and paused for a moment. "Lynnette, I would like for you to come to the dedication service," she invited.

"The whole family would be there, and you should."

"I will! Hallelujah, I will," Lynnette praised, smiling.

As if their worship depended on it, after they had reconciled, everyone fully enjoyed the Wednesday prayer meeting.

— ********** —

People in the church had whispered about Peace long enough, especially the family resemblance. Katharine had not known, but church members suspected it. Peace, when just a baby, no one noticed. Then by the time he hit six months, he started looking more and more like RJ, and less and less like Alex. People suspected. Rumors swirled, and Grace stopped going to church completely.

The rumor mill had become busy as usual, now that Dr. Douglas had actually been awarded the child, not just a child, mind you, a blind, crippled child. Those were the exact words going around. Rather than address the gossip, Katharine decided to cut to the chase and drag all the family's skeletons out of the closet.

"Pastor Peabody, would you please dedicate my three grandchildren instead of only Tapee," she requested. Katharine appeared purposeful at the moment. "This Sunday," she added.

For one moment, Pastor Peabody knew Mrs. Douglas wasn't going to let certain persons of ill-influence block her children's blessings. The church, which she'd been a dedicated member, had refused her husband's funeral to be held there, although they had faithfully paid their tithes and offerings.

Find me a family that does not have a secret, Pastor Peabody thought. "Sister Douglas, our church is a house of prayer for all people," he said. "I'll be honored. And, I have just the right sermon for this special occasion."

Katharine smiled an incredible smile.

"And, Pastor," she said, "I would like to say something before you preach."

The pastor froze and regarded her curiously.

"I'd like to talk to my grandchildren," Katharine explained. "It's important for them to love themselves if they expect others to love them. I love them so much," she smiled, "and I'd like them to hear that in front of everybody."

— ********** —

Before the usual Sunday service begun, Katharine invited all her grandchildren to join her at the podium; Tapee, Peace, and Kitty, for her new grandson's christening.

"Just walk up there like I've told you," Mel whispered in the boy's ear. He smiled.

Tapee had already attended two summer camps at GAB, (Georgia Academy for the Blind), and had private tutoring in South Africa and Liberia. Using a long white cane came easily, he led, and the others simply followed in his wake, order of age, oldest to youngest. He navigated to the raised dais, then to their grandmother. Katharine opened her Bible and read from Psalm 139:13-18, not in the exact order written, but in such a way to present her message.

"'How precious are God's thoughts,'" she began. "'More than I will ever know... too many to count.'"

The congregation shouted, "Aaaamen!"

"I've asked my grandchildren to join me up here so that I can tell each of them how precious they are to me," Katharine continued. Then she motioned each child to face her. The children shyly turned. "I love you, Tapee Douglas. I love you, Peace Douglas. I love you, Kitty Douglas. I love you all very much because God knitted each of you in your mother's womb in a wonderful and special way. You might have been made in secret from others, but not from God. He formed each little part of you Himself, one by one. Your name, and everything about you, is written in His books... even before you were born."

Then Katharine hugged Kitty first and said, "I love you, my princess." Peace rushed and hugged his grandmother before she could, and then Tapee hugged the tightest and longest.

Right after Katharine let go of the children, Pastor Peabody invited their parents and godparents to join them. Mellody, RJ and Gia, Grace and Alex, ambled forward. Then Nàjma and Yassah, standing as godmother for Tapee and Peace, joined the family. At this point, striking a nerve would not have mattered. Awkward or not, Katharine had indeed dragged all the skeletons out of the closet and placed them at the altar.

Pastor Peabody performed the baptism ritual of Christian christening, ending it with a prayer.

"Father in heaven, bless these children and this day of new beginnings. Surround them with your love so that they follow Christ's footsteps. Today, we ask that you smile upon them and their caregivers. And, Lord, may each life be lit with love through your kindness."

Then, Pastor Peabody invited the children to stand in front of him for the Prayer of Blessing. He raised both hands over the three small children, closed his eyes and prayed, "May God, who formed you beneath your mother's heart, bless each of you on this special day of dedication. May all who take care of you be blessed as they see the perfect gift of love, that each of you are. And, may the light of Christ, through God's Word, guide your little steps in the path of truth always as you grow up in wisdom, love and grace. In Christ Jesus' name, let the church say…."

"Amen!"

Parents and godparents quietly walked back to their seats. Katharine directed Tapee to take hold of the back of her upper left arm, just above the elbow. Then she proceeded to walk the children back to their seats; Tapee, a half step behind, then Peace and Kitty.

The regular church sermon followed.

Pastor Peabody's message was about dust, and how God had taken something so worthless to create something priceless, a human being.

"Fellow members, and you who fear God, the fact that God used dust to create us, humans, it is even more important that we should think twice about labeling someone as *worthless*. All people have their roots in God, the Creator, therefore all are equal. Neither race nor ethnicity is superior or inferior to another. Beware, prejudice is a sinful act."

Pastor Peabody went on to say why.

"There is universal agreement that prejudice is bad," he continued. "So, taking a stand against prejudice is like taking a stand against evil. For this reason, you must do something where prejudice is found, rather than join in. A mistaken opinion is usually based on over-generalization from known instances. Exercise tolerance and examine evidence. At least, be fair."

The congregation said, "Amen!"

He preached to the fact that what matters is not *where* people grow up, but *how* they grow up and that everyone *is* important to God. "What we become is more important than where we're from."

Pastor Peabody ended his sermon and prayed, "God, we are all in awe of you. You know us intimately. Thank you for creating each of us with such complex and care. Help us to love one another as you love us. Let the church say…."

"Amen!"

At the family dinner after the service, Mel said, "I can't wait to take my son to his first Broadway musical. I haven't been to one in a long time."

"Sure, he will enjoy the music," Nàjma interjected, "but it's going to be a struggle understanding the setting and the movements of the characters onstage."

"Not really," Mel said. "They have what they called, D-Scriptive."

"D-what?"

"It's a new technology that conveys the visual elements of the stage production through a small FM receiver. A recorded narration keyed to the show's light and sound boards, describes the set and the action as it unfolds onstage. Tapee would love it."

Everyone hearing this stared in wonderment.

"Technology," Mel shrugged.

"Tapee is lucky to have you, Mel," Nàjma said. "I'm so happy things turned out the way they did."

"No," Mel shook her head, "I'm the lucky one."

"Blessed," Katharine corrected. "Mel has been blessed with a son, not lucky."

"We both are," Nàjma said, looking at Mel.

Chapter 66

"YOU WILL HAVE to get on that plane with me tomorrow morning," Manor said to Diallo. "That's the only flight to keep us on schedule."

"On schedule for what?"

"You'll see."

Diallo shrugged. He never insisted on knowing the details of Manor's business. His gut feelings told him if he knew half of it, he'd feel dirty on the inside. Lawyering was his business to mind and he made a shipload of money doing that.

"I can tell you this though," Manor continued. "By the time I complete this deal, it will be my last. I'll have a shit load of money... we can retire," he grinned.

"You mean a shipload," Diallo corrected, ignoring Manor's possible early retirement.

"Like I said, Diallo, a shit load."

"I take it you already have the tickets? So when is the flight?"

Manor was explicit in his instructions: "We'll board British Airways to fly out tomorrow morning at 8:25 a.m. to London, from there, to South Africa. Don't be late, Diallo," he finished.

"How long are we going to be there?"

"I'll let you know after we get there," Manor articulated, then he waved his lawyer off.

__**********__

After a seductive call from Manor to his pissed-off business partner, his driver obediently carried Adriana to his home. Adriana was pleased to rendezvous with Manor and he felt as lucky as a star. No one was arguing. Their relationship, business or otherwise, started to cool now and they did not have much time together. Whatever time they had, it wasn't wasted on talking. In fact, the bed was the one place Manor and LeRoux was never competitive. She had an unusual sexual obsession and he was immune to love.

Adriana had the tight look of a woman under a great amount of stress but holding it together. Or, maybe a slight regret. She had lied to Cowan about a headache to meet with Manor. Another thing, she'd never met him at his residence. They always meet at RJK resort, her suite. He had actually brought her to his personal space.

"I want to apologize about the other night," Manor greeted, while gazing deeply into Adriana's very cold, very unimpressed killer eyes.

Sometimes you have to fight fire with fire, or with the best wine money can buy. Manor offered her a glass of champagne. Adriana sipped and tasted the creamy bubble finesses and almond-orange notes of the drink, Ace of Spades. She smiled when Manor held up the brilliant pink gold bottle. Then he escorted her to the master bedroom, and pointed to the luxury shower, a meticulous design, ultra-violet bonded glass enable crystal shower enclosure.

She took a quick shower, then emerged from the bathroom to find Manor waiting in bed, wearing nothing but cool white sheets tangled around his body. He smiled a promise of pleasure.

The fornication was more of a quickie than a tango. Manor and LeRoux had more champagne afterwards.

Unknown to her, Manor had furtively slipped Rohypnol (roh-HIP-nol) in the bubbly and Adriana could not have seen it, smell it nor taste it. The date rape drug sometimes called the Forget Pill, had knocked her out.

A few hours later, Adriana opened her eyes, barely, her hand outstretched toward the empty half of the bed. *Ce must have gone to the bathroom,* she thought. Before she realized it, a massive black-dressed figure loomed at the edge of the bed, hand clutching a strange-looking pistol with a square-shaped barrel. He leapt forward and with a flick of his wrist, quickly planted the end of the barrel against the side of her thigh. He pulled the trigger. The contact point on her immediately shot to painful excruciating burning flesh. Adriana screamed.

She managed to turn her head and saw another black form of a man staring at her. Their gazes met briefly. She tried to yell, *Ce! Help me!* But the words wouldn't come out. The bogeyman took aim with the Taser and fired again.

In her last second of consciousness, throughout the pain and the burning and the panic and the fear, Adriana's thoughts went on the heart-man.

__**********__

At 3:35 a.m. the tan Renault city-passenger traffic bus headed out of Monrovia passing through Paynesville onto the Monrovia-Kakata highway; then from Careysbury to Todee District, to Kakata and beyond. The paved highway offered the best bet for making time and nothing to worry about.

Cowan knew exactly the time of the kidnapping, when Adriana's phone signal disappeared from the network.

__**********__

It's hard to imagine anyone packing red diamonds between sweaters, trotting off to the airport, and hoping it would remain a secret. The man was obviously smuggling them.

It was just a routine baggage inspection, but there was nothing ordinary about the contents of the suitcase. The South African customs agent who examined it discovered 20 pieces of rare red diamonds. The diamonds were estimated to be worth as much as 1.8 million dollars, yet the passenger indicated nothing to declare to customs authorities.

Meanwhile, another custom agent managed to dump every single thing from Manor's carry-on bag onto the conveyor belt. He watched helplessly as very personal possessions rolled by in front of suddenly interested strangers. Manor vented with language no one ordinarily would use within three miles of any church, and launched at the agent. The airport security team grabbed their infamous passenger. Manor kicked and screamed while two policemen cuffed him and whisk him away.

__**********__

"We know everything," the officer said. "You can either cooperate with us, or we let the chips fall where they may."

Manor felt a pang of fear. "I've told you everything," he said. "I've been set up… I want my lawyer."

"Okay, in that case, let me tell you what's going to happen," the officer said. "In a few minutes, a male officer will come in here and take all of your clothes and jewelry… your watch… rings… everything, and he will subject you to a full body cavity search. You will be given other clothes to wear. You will be taken to a holding cell in this building. After that, an agent from another agency will remove you from this site and take you to another facility for further interrogation. Do you understand that?"

"What other agency?" Manor asked.

"I have no information on that," the officer said. "You are a smart man, you read the papers, you know what happens to smugglers. There's no point in holding out."

Another officer caught his gaze and said, "Mr. Manor, we are trying to help you here, for your own sake. Who is your contact in South Africa?"

Manor didn't say anything. Silence, being the best show of strength.

After waiting a full minute, both officers left. Manor sat in his chair, wondering what was taking Diallo so damn long. No matter what, they were not going to break him.

A black male officer came in with a large paper bag in hand and dropped it on the table. In a deep South African accent he said, "Are you carrying any sharp object? A needle or anything like that?"

"No."

"Are you currently infected with the HIV virus?"

Manor cut his eyes and replied, "No."

"Take off all your clothes and jewelry and put them in this bag," the officer ordered. "Here is a marker. When you remove your things and placed them in the bag, seal it with the tape and sign your name on the tape."

Manor took the bag, tape and the sharpie. He waited for the man to leave, the man remained.

"When you are finished, lean over and hold the end of the table," the officer continued.

This sent a tasteless chill down Manor's back, within an inch of his life. His Adam's apple took a hard barb. He'd never stood naked before any man. Another man cannot be over his body, it is against the rule of nature. Against his will, he followed the man's instructions.

Manor was now naked and bent over.

"Spread your legs," the officer ordered.

Manor's legs barely move apart.

"Wider."

Manor moved his leg, but no more than an inch.

"Wider," the officer ordered. "Wider! Wider!"

Manor looked over his shoulder and looked at the man staring at him in a way he'd never been looked at by another man, like an object to be processed. The officer did processed Manor, shoving his gloved hand into Manor's body cavities. First the mouth, then he greased up and invaded the rectum.

Manor disassociated his mind from his body, refusing to believe what was happening to him. Another man was actually touching him. He wanted to cry and pee and vomit, all at the same time.

The officer finished, handed Manor a pair of jeans and a white T-shirt and ordered him to dress. He left Manor in the room, taking with him the bag with Manor's things. Manor got dressed and sat quietly, feeling abandoned, alone and helpless. He was cut off from the world he rules; where he gave the orders, he shouted the commands and he demanded whatever, whenever. It has always been CeRue Manor who accomplishes which he intents. He liked seeing the fear and respect for him on other people's faces. It was the other way around now.

Ten minutes later the door opened, two immigration officers came in, a white man and a black woman, both wearing business suits. Manor asked if he could use the bathroom. They declined to answer, but worked swiftly to put cuffs on his hands, then connecting the chains from hands to feet.

They quickly led him away.

The officers walked with Manor, one on each side, to the elevator. In less than a minute, the elevator made humming noise and the door opened. The male escort slightly shoved Manor to get in. The elevator took them three floors up and stopped, and Manor was led to an office.

It was a small room, bare walls painted white, like the inside of a large closet. The overhead light bulb had no fixture. In the middle of the room, behind a small folding card table used as a desk, a man sat in a white plastic chair waiting. He had a pad and folder in front of him, with a Bic ball pen in his hand. The officers led Manor to the chair opposite him. Manor sat and the man looked up. Staring at Manor was the bland face of an interrogator with dark interested eyes. The two officers walked out and closed the door. That's when Manor noticed the door had no knob or handle on it.

Manor asked, almost pleading, "Can I see my lawyer now?"

His voice sounded strange in his ears, like someone else. Manor was *asking* rather than *demanding*.

"Of course, after you've answered a few questions," the man replied. "You give us a little and we give you a little, okay?"

Manor nodded.

"Name?"

Manor gave his full name, nationality, marital status, and occupation, and then asked, "Why you need all of this?"

"I ask the questions," the man asserted. "You don't say anything unless you've been asked. Do you understand?"

Manor nodded.

"That was a question," the man said. "Answer 'yes' or 'no.'"

Manor answered, "Yes" and screwed his face.

"When was your first trip to South Africa?"

"This is my first trip."

"You are lying," the man accused.

"I'm not lying."

"That is not an answer to the question," the man asserted. "Let's start again. When was the first time you traveled to South Africa?"

Manor sat mute. A few minutes went by. The man was also silent, staring at Manor, eyeball-to-eyeball. He began drumming his fingers on the table top, an attempt to intimidate.

"When was the first time you visited South Africa," the man articulated sternly.

"I swear, this is my first trip," Manor replied.

"You are lying," the man accused.

Manor said nothing.

The man scribbled something on his pad. Still looking down at his pad, he asked, "Have you been to South Africa before?"

Manor said nothing. He began shivering and knew it was a bad sign. He needed to use the restroom and was afraid to ask.

The man looked up at Manor, forehead furrowed. "We could be here all day, for what it's worth. Nothing happens until you cooperate," he said. "Have you been to South Africa before?"

"Yes," Manor mumbled, his voice hardly audible.

The man sighed and leaned back. "When?"

Manor studied the man's face and said nothing.

The man leaned forward, "When?"

Manor startled to the sound of the door opening before he could make an answer. The same immigration officer that brought him, entered.

"How long?" the immigration officer asked.

The interrogating officer said, "He's not cooperating. He's hiding something, that's why he's lying."

"I'm not hiding anything," Manor pleaded, calmly.

"Then why are you lying?"

Manor sat mute.

The officer tapped the table, staring at Manor. He turned to the immigration office and said, "Take him to the cell."

"Can I call the Liberian Embassy?" Manor pleaded.

The interrogator declined without answering. He had not even dipped into the depth of his creativity to get the man talking. The agent had gone through the official channels, now he was forced to use the unofficial ones. He gestured urgently that Manor is taken away.

Chapter 67

LONOS SPENT DAYS in preparation, knowing that mental preparation was even more important than physical preparation. His imagination of Manor reminded him of the importance of the mission. His feelings of dressing as a woman did not matter. He'd prepared his manhood.

Finally, it was time to get ready for the mission, turning into a woman advertising herself for the night. He drove to Grace's house.

Lonos gaze followed Grace from her closet to the bed, holding a hanger with feminine garments. He wondered if he would dress like a woman as easy as talking like one. To stay in his disguise would be a tedious experience, but he'd had enough practice sessions.

"You know, Officer Lonos, you have a better shape than most women I know," Grace complimented.

Lonos chuckled. "I'm afraid your skills may not be enough to make me look like a real woman," he said, "you need a miracle."

"We'll see," she replied. "To make it work, I'm dressing you in jeans and a blouse. Put these on and I'll be back to help you with the blouse," she handed him the pair of jeans.

Grace left the room and returned ten minutes later. She helped him with the blouse and arranged a cap to cover all his hair, then took a step back to survey her work.

"How do I look?" Lonos asked.

"Like a man dressed as a woman."

"Not even as an ugly woman?"

"Not yet," Grace chuckled. "You need something down the front of your blouse."

She went into the closet and thought of all the items that could be used, returned with a handful of cloth materials, and dropped them on the bed.

Lonos watched as Grace cut and sewed a pair of nylons into two pouches. Mischief danced in his eyes.

"What are you making?" he asked, knowing what they were.

"These will confirm you are *all* woman," Grace said, smiling. "But you still have to work on your walking and talking like a lady."

"Like this?" Lonos swagger.

Grace laughed. He laughed.

"Be shy and naughty at the same time," Grace advised, and set the finished pouches down.

Lonos picked up the pouches, one in each hand. "Do you think these are big enough?"

Grace looked at him. "Men are always concerned with size," she chuckled. "Why?"

"Women too," Lonos pointed. "Let's face it, it's all about size when it comes to both men and women."

"I guess you're right," Grace laughed. "But it's not that serious when it comes to us women."

She took the stuffed pouches and sewed them closed. Lonos watched her stuff them down the front of his blouse into the bra. The bra was too big for them.

"I knew they were too small," he laughed.

Grace unfastened both pouches and added more padding until the bra was tight enough to hold them in place.

"Do you think I look like a woman now?" he asked, squeezing both breasts.

"One more thing," Grace said. "I need to do your makeup and hair."

She applied some foundation, eye liner, added lashes and eye shadows, rouge and lipstick. She put a wig to cover his cap and styled it. The wig was firmly in place by the time Grace was done.

"Let me see how I look," Lonos said. His jaw dropped at the same moment he stepped in front of the mirror. He was beautiful in form and appearance. "I see why all those women come to you, Grace. I cannot recognize myself!"

"Hope no one try to hit on you before you reach Le'Toit club," Grace joked.

Lonos ignored it. "I'm not concerned about that. I don't want anything to go wrong."

"Why? You never worry this much about your work."

"This is not about my work," Lonos narrowed his eyes. "I'd hate to let the old lady down. I don't want Manor to get away with killing that little boy."

Damn that man. Officer Lonos had always comforted himself with a deliriously inspiring fantasy involving a pleading, broken Manor being dragged to a pole to face a firing squad or the hangman's noose. Even turning the man over to the devil, if only dreams could come true.

"You think he really had that little boy killed just to get his organs?" Grace asked.

The heart-man was both mythical and factual, creating a magmatic fear in the country. The heart-man did not discriminate when it came to the victims, age or gender.

"The evidence is on those discs, Grace. I've got to get my hands on them. I believe those discs have information about the senator too. Senator Douglas had to have had some type of connection to Manor. I think Manor set him up, but I don't know why."

"Really? But Lonos, we know that the senator wasn't a heart-man."

"True," Lonos nodded. "But there has to be some connection."

Grace stepped back to inspect her work. Her eyes traveled over Lonos, making certain she did not miss even one of the details that proclaimed him a female. "Now, you look like a woman," she said, nodding approval.

"Thank you, Grace," Lonos said, and went out the back door.

__**********__

It was early Sunday morning, the streets were dead. Most people were either getting ready to go to church, or sleeping off the booze and wild sex from last night's orgy. Lonos' biggest fear was getting noticed by a broke policeman.

All was quiet and still at Le'Toit. Lonos veins pulsed with adrenaline as he stared at the building, a beehive of criminal activity that had seen more drugs, death, and perverted sex than possibly any building in Monrovia; before, during and after the civil war.

He strode to the side door where a security guard saw him, thinking Lonos is a woman, and waved. The security buzzed, releasing the security lock. Lonos opened the door, walked in, and stood before the desk.

Sitting behind his desk, peering sensually at her, the man smiled. The guard may not have been the sort of man who needed money in his hand, but like most men, he may be the sort of man whose morals sways when faced with a pair of breasts. His mouth lifted on one side like it was caught on a hook. Lonos leaned over the desk, pleased to see his gaze. The man moistened his lips with his tongue, and Lonos' heart plunged into his stomach. But he felt confident, as if he could get this man to do almost anything, given the right words and the amount of cleavage.

"Is CeRue here?" Lonos coaxed. His voice was a little deep, yet not masculine enough to identify his sex.

"Mr. Manor is not here," he said, admiringly.

"Oooh. He told me to meet him here today... this morning." Lonos glanced at the office door upstairs. "Are you sure?"

"He's not here at the moment, but I am in charge. Perhaps I can help."

Lonos sighed. "I'll just have to come back," he said and began to walk off.

The man rushed out from behind the desk and stepped in the way. He was taller and stood close, which meant he could see straight down Lonos' blouse. Lonos let out a seductive giggle.

"I'm sure I *can* help," he smirked.

"Well…what exactly are you in charge of?" Lonos asked and tried a simpering pout.

"It is a job you're trying to get, isn't it?"

Lonos nodded, pretending to be embarrassed.

"Come, sit down," the security guard said. He stepped out of the way and pointed at his chair.

"Thank you," Lonos said. He coughed and sat. He coughed again. "Do you mind if I have something to drink?"

"Of course."

"Will you join me?"

The guard hesitated. A voice in the back of his head told him to say *no*, but it was small and easy to ignore.

While the guy was thinking, Lonos added, "Only if you don't mind. I hate to drink alone. It's not good for a woman to drink by herself, especially when she's with a guy."

The security guard's eyes dipped to Lonos' breasts again. Her large bosom rose and fell with her breathing. He pressed his lips together. "I think you're right," he said and smiled.

His mind had gone numb and he was only vaguely aware that he wasn't thinking straight. He couldn't. Lonos, which he thought to be a woman, had scrambled his wits and stolen every last sensible thought.

"I'll get the drinks if you tell me where to get them," Lonos offered in a sexier voice. "A man should not serve when a woman is around."

The guard laughed. "I'll get the drinks... a fine woman like you should be served. What would you like? Wine? Beer?"

"This early?" Lonos teased, winking.

The security guard laughed again. "Since its Sunday, let's have some wine," he suggested.

Lonos nodded and the man left.

Lonos quickly removed the small pill box attached to his bra. It was easy to hide the sleeping pills between his fingers.

"Let's establish an understanding before anything," the guard said, returning with a wine bottle and two glasses on a tray. Lonos nodded. "I can get you hired as long as Mr. Manor doesn't find out you made your appointment this morning. In fact, don't tell anyone. Not a soul."

"Of course," Lonos winked.

The guard unscrewed the cork and filled both glasses.

"Is that CeRue's office?" Lonos pointed at the door upstairs.

With his eyes off the glasses, it was easy to slip the sleeping pills into his glass. He nodded and answered, "Yes."

Lonos handed a glass to the guard and sipped her own.

The guard sipped the wine. "This tastes different," he pulled a face.

"Maybe because it's not cold enough," Lonos suggested and drank the contents of his glass. "I like warm wine... it makes me tipsy," he laughed.

"Really?" the guard smiled. "Now, what type of work are you looking for?"

He refilled Lonos' glass with a smirk. Lonos' gaze flicked to the door.

"That's Manor's office, no one goes up there but him," he informed.

"No one?"

"No one."

"Not even you?"

The man laughed. "You want Manor's job?" he joked and sipped.

"Of course not."

The guard shrugged. "So, what do you do," he licked his bottom lip, leaving a distinct shine behind. "If I help you, then you'll have to help me. We *are* friends, right?" he mumbled sleepily.

In the next moment, before Lonos thought of an answer, the guard wrapped his fingers around Lonos' wrist. Lonos gaze met his.

"What did you put in my drink?" he frowned.

His grip tightened and burned. Then his grip loosened, he let go, and fell asleep.

Lonos crept upstairs to the office, then to the door and tried the handle. Locked. He hurried back down the stairs, rummaged through the desk drawer to find a key. The drawer contained paper clips, coins, pens, a ruler, and a few unused sticky pads. He checked under the desk, everywhere. Nothing. He thought of breaking the lock. Unless....

Lonos poked the guard's shoulder. The man snored loudly, but didn't wake up. Lonos checked his pockets for a hidden key, but found none. He thought some more. Then Lonos hesitantly put his hand down the man's undershirt and touched his cool, clammy skin. It was worth it, because he found a key attached to a leather strip pinned inside his undershirt. Lonos took the key, hurried up the stairs, and inserted it into the office door keyhole. It clicked open and he went inside.

Despite how well things were going, a head of nervous sweat surfaced on Lonos' forehead. Breaking and entering is a true art, and Lonos knew his limitations. The place also had a security system connected to Manor's phone. Why hadn't he thought about that. He took a moment to inhale, then exhale. Reporting failure to Bohn would be out of the question because he took pride in his work. He should work very fast. Seconds later, he moved in.

Manor's office was sparsely furnished and lacked many of the normal bits and pieces of a busy businessman. He kept no computer nor paper files here. He kept his private office private, but those who had entered were left with the notion that nothing confidential, or worth much, could bleed out of the place. And, the man had a lot to hide.

In the office were a sixty-inch L-shaped desk, antique black with Hansen Cherry top, a genuine leather traditional executive office chair, a set of office guest chairs, and a kneeling chair. Set into the opposite wall across from the desk was a door. A closet, most likely, or a private bathroom. Nothing unusual about that.

Lonos carefully nudged open the closet door. He quickly discovered a twin-size bed, neatly made, and matching nightstand. He pulled out the top drawer. "Shit," he muttered, noting a few puzzling items; packages of unopened needles and syringes, elastic straps, snort straws, bits of paper, plastic baggies, drug vials containing liquids and powder substances. He quickly snapped some shots with his phone.

He was startled for a moment when he saw a slender line of light coming from the top of the wall. *Is there a camera in here?* His eyes raced to the top, where he saw it. The camera lens in the wall was next to the molding, a pinhole lens, designed specifically for secret recording.

Lonos raced back to the office. *Where the hell is the video recording machine?* He opened the desk drawer, found a button, hit it, and the bottom drawer slid open. His gaze closed on the small infrared portal at the front of the machine. The video recorder was controlled by a special remote, its function buttons overridden. His blood ran hot with the possibilities, this sort of arrangement suggested sex videos of underage girls. He thought about putting a bullet into the damn thing, if he had a gun.

He went into the small connecting bathroom. It had a modern drop-down ceiling, marble floor with pebble design and cream painted walls. The shower was a one-piece fiberglass unit with handles on three sides of the wall. Fresh towels hung on a towel rod outside, next to the mahogany cabinet sink. The toilet paper looked new, so did the soap.

Lonos pulled the door to the vanity and found it strange that it was locked, and there wasn't a keyhole. He shook his head. As he was about to leave, he froze. Set into the wall, to the side of the vanity, where it opens, was a button.

"Shit," Lonos swore again. "Where could those disks be?"

Manor's money got him every type of gadgets there is. *What could be so valuable here to go to all this trouble?* He could not take his eyes off the button. Lonos is a very curious man, and people attempting to hide things came close to irritating him. Secrets made him sick. He believed in the principle of full and fair disclosure with his whole heart. Putting action to that belief, Lonos took a deep breath, pointed his finger at the button and pushed it in.

The lock on the cabinet housing the sink, clicked. He took another deep breath and pulled the knob on the door. Lonos saw what was in the cabinet and swore under his breath.

On the top shelf was a PS3 console, five security tapes and four USB disk cases. The first two cases Lonos picked up were heavy, each housing an external SATA 2.5" HDD hard disk external enclosure, with 750 GB memory. Each of the other two cases held eight 64 GB USB flash disks. No video game in sight. The bottom layer had about 100 piles of $100 bills, about 20 per stack, filed in rolls of ten. The cash was neatly bundled with thick rubber bands.

Lonos quickly tossed every item on the top shelf into his handbag. He picked up a pile of bill and did a quick inspection. The bills were old and new mixed. For one ridiculous second, he thought about the eighth Commandment before stuffing all twenty cash piles into the bag. He almost forgot the stack of *girlie* magazines.

Officer Lonos put his bag straps over his head, then across his chest and walked out, quietly closing the door behind him. He hurried downstairs. Walking toward the front door, he thought of kissing the sleeping guard's forehead, but smiled instead. The man should have been overwhelmed by his ruse, but it was the thought of the flash drives in his bag. They felt like Manor's balls and he wanted to squeeze. On those disks were everything needed to keep CeRue Manor and his accomplice in prison for a long time.

Chapter 68

"I'M NOT GOING to prison, Diallo, I'm not," Manor declared.

Those were not the words of suggestions, but the demands he'd expected when he bailed his client out of detention. They had just checked in and had not quite settled down at the Peech Hotel, a fabulous little hotel set in a tree-filled upscale neighborhood where Diallo had booked them two rooms at $200 a night each.

Diallo took a few moments to gather his wit.

Manor groaned and buried his head in his hands, but did not offer any more comments. He did not want his lawyer asking him why they'd kept him so long, that would lead to questions about the activities he'd gone through while in custody. Diallo might think less of him as a man, and Manor couldn't face his pity. The man's pride was larger than his fear of prison. It was difficult to imagine Manor doing jail time anywhere; assuming he had been set up, he hadn't broken any laws, and there would be no reason he could end up in jail.

There was a long heavy pause in the conversation. Finally, arms stretched, regarding his client sitting across from him, Diallo said, "Are you doubting my skills?"

Manor looked up. "I don't give a damn about your skills," his voice rose above Diallo's. "Diallo, focus! You are getting damned close to loosing your number one client here." Then he fixed Diallo with a wide-eyed stare. "I'm getting out of South Africa by any means necessary."

"Of course. That's why I'm here."

Relief flooded Manor's face. "I'm glad you see things my way," he nodded.

"I do," Diallo said heavily, sucking in air through his teeth.

Having a client like Manor, Diallo should be used to living his life on a knife's edge. His mind ran back through the years, looking for that better place and time, the *good old days*. But for some, the past harbors mostly overpowering memories. Deep in the past, there was the cruel hand that money had empowered to do many immoral things. At times he wished Manor would have found another puppet. Diallo thought about his wife and there was a ghost of a smile on his lips. Cecelia meant more to him than he'd ever let on. He felt a deep longing for his wife, and more of her tender love he'd ignored over the years, chasing money. It would be nice to finally start a family.

A knock came at the door and Manor nodded to Diallo, who quickly rose to open it to a young man about fifteen.

"Tomorrow a taxi will pick you up from the court and bring you back to the hotel," the young man said. "Madam has arranged it."

Diallo raised his brows.

"I thought we were going to her house," Manor said, joining Diallo at the door.

"She will meet you here," the young man assured.

Diallo asked, "At the hotel?"

The young man nodded.

Manor took a twenty dollar bill out of his pocket and handed it to the boy.

"Thank you, sir," the young man took the money and left.

Evening crept up and calmly smothered daylight and the activity that went with it. Manor wanted to make sure he would not rot in a South African prison, or any other prison for that matter. While Diallo worked quietly on his motion for the hearing in the morning, Manor made several calls, bending ears to more wheeling and dealings in a few hours than he'd done his entire life.

"Come on, Diallo, we're leaving," Manor ordered, after making his last call.

Diallo looked up from his paperwork. "I'm not finished. I have to be on my A game when we face the judge."

"Don't worry about that."

"What?" Diallo shoved his legal pad away and rubbed his temples.

"Come on, we're leaving," Manor said, now picking up his bag.

Diallo gathered his things and followed Manor hurriedly to the check-in desk. Manor paid for the two rooms they did not use for the entire time booked, and called for a taxi.

"Where are we going?" Diallo asked.

"Never mind where we're going. You'll see when we get there."

Diallo sighed, letting out his frustration.

The taxi drove them some fourteen miles, southwest of Johannesburg, to Soweto. Manor paid the driver, the taxi slowed to a crawl and they jumped out.

"Come on, Diallo! We have to hurry," Manor said, and picked up speed.

The two men ran passed a few houses and turned onto a narrow side street, lined with zinc shacks built close together. Each had shuttle windows, behind which the poorest of the population lived. They leapt over potholes as they ran. Mud splattered over their shoes and up their legs, but that didn't slow their progress. Diallo followed Manor into the yard of a house where a woman was standing in the doorway with a candle in hand. She wore nothing but an oversized shirt, the top revealing an immodest amount of her extraordinarily large breasts.

"Get in!" she shouted, waving her hand.

They were glad to. It was a perfect hiding spot until all arrangements were completed. The woman was a friend of Manor's mistress, she owed him no allegiance.

"I'm tired of this," Manor said, panting heavily. "I don't know how long I can do this."

"South Africa is not my favorite place to play hide-and-seek either," Diallo said, between gasps of air.

The woman chuckled and said, "Come, I've fixed you something to eat. I knew you would be hungry."

They ate the food so quickly, they couldn't have chewed properly, let alone tasted it.

"I want to talk to my lawyer in privacy," Manor said to the woman.

She walked out of the dining room.

"I've arranged for us to fly out of South Africa tonight," Manor broke the news.

"What about court tomorrow?"

Manor smiled a conspiratorial smile. "Who's going to court?"

Diallo looked at his watch. "Adriana is flying us out?"

"Of course not."

"Then who?"

"You ask way too many damn questions," Manor said. Then he chuckled, "I forgot that you're a lawyer."

"What about the diamonds they took?"

"There's plenty where that came from," Manor shrugged. "The only thing is, I cannot come back to South African any time soon."

Diallo nodded, too stunned to speak.

About half an hour later, the woman came back to the room. She turned her gaze on Manor, a frown tucked on his face. "What are you thinking about?" she asked.

He shrugged and looked at his watch.

"They will be here soon," the woman assured.

"I think I can get us to the airstrip myself," Manor said, looking at Diallo. He rose, walked over to Diallo and spoke a few words, so softly that only Diallo could hear them. Then he picked up the bag. To the host, he said, "Thanks for your help. Here's a note, could you give it to Madam? The instructions will tell her where she'll get paid for her troubles."

The woman took the note and nodded.

Manor made for the window, tossed the bag through it, and climbed out. Diallo followed. The two men were gone. The woman could hear their feet scrambling against the zinc walls and then the thumps as they landed. Her ears followed the noise of running feet until it died out.

"We need to be fast," Manor said. "This way. We will get a taxi from the main road."

Diallo thought he heard voices, or was his mind playing tricks? The footsteps were certain. Manor heard them too. They ran down a thin alley blocked between two old buildings. The deep shadows swallowed them as the footsteps came closer. They stopped. When the footsteps retreated, they pick up running again. At the other end of the alley, they paused, looked right and left, then turned right into another dark, narrow lane and stopped.

"Where to now?" Diallo asked, running alongside. He had shortened his strides not knowing where to turn.

"Wait," Manor whispered. He took a moment to catch his breath and try to organize his thoughts.

Two men ran down the adjoining street. One man pointed to the alley where Manor and Diallo hid in the shadows. Manor tapped Diallo's shoulder and pointed back the way they'd come.

"Are we going back?" Diallo whispered, and gulped in some air. If they had not slowed down, his heart would have burst through his ribs.

Besides, fear made his legs weak and his body began trembling.

"Come on," Manor demanded.

They had not gotten far when another two men blocked their exit. The first two men advance from behind. They were trapped. Diallo sank to the ground, put his head on his knees, and burst into tears.

"Mr. Manor," one of the men called. "We're here to escort you to the plane. Why are you running?"

Diallo's sobbing eased immediately. Manor heaved a heavy sigh of relief. Diallo drew in a long measured breath because his heart was still racing even though his body had stopped. Manor could feel Diallo's fear, like an echo deep within him. He grew angry with his lawyer.

"Be a man," Manor scolded.

"I don't crumble like that, no matter what you might think," Diallo said.

Diallo thought about asking Manor some questions about how he'd provided the escape, but he said nothing. His answer could lead to more questions. He wanted to press Manor for details of the final plan of their escape. The thing was, no one had tried to arrest him. It was Manor the authorities wanted.

Manor and his lawyer were rushed away and taken on a quick road trip. They got out of the car, hurried into a building, and then out the door. Safely away from the building, protected by total darkness, the men led them to a sleek private jet, engine running and waiting. They stopped at the bottom of the jet's staircase.

Diallo's quandary, legal or otherwise, was having to choose between his client and his wife. "I can't stop thinking about Cecelia," he complained.

Manor looked at him with disgust. "That's the problem with you married men who let love control your conscience," he scolded. "It makes you weak."

Diallo would have laughed, except it was no joking matter. He had been the man's tool for too long, and nothing more. No one had to tell him. He'd done things on Manor's behalf without thinking twice, because his head was stuck too far up the man's ass.

"Manor, it can't be for money that you're involved in smuggling these diamonds. You've made more money than any African president I know."

"This time, it's not for money," Manor spat.

"What for?"

"Revenge."

"Revenge?"

"Look Diallo, this is no time to start asking stupid questions. Are you coming or not?"

Diallo thought long and hard. Should he continue to run with Manor, or should he remain and insist on not boarding that plane. His instincts were for the latter. He was really thinking about his wife. He hesitated for a second, tried to shake it off, and said, "I'm going nowhere with you, Manor. I'm going home to my wife."

His lawyer's words had not pleased him. Manor's face grew angry. "Suit yourself," he said, offering a nasty smile. Then, he hoisted the bag over his shoulder and climbed into the private jet.

After the takeoff checklist was completed, the pilot lined the jet up on the runway and applied power. The jet engine roared and he steered it straight down the runway. The plane's wheels spun up speed, and the moment it reached the proper speed, he tilted the nose of the jet, generating a lift. The jet rattled and vibrated a little, and seconds later, the nose of the plane tilted up and everything got quiet and smooth as they lifted off.

Sixty seconds into the flight the engine failed, and the pilot could not continue safely. Twenty seconds later, the giant bird took a nose-dive and crashed, bursting into flames upon impact. Skidding aflame 200 yards from where it had fallen, the engine flew out travelling another hundred yards.

Chapter 69

"COWAN, WE HAVE proof," Bohn said. "It was Manor who had her snatched. They found her Blackberry in his things at the airport in South Africa, and it has a series of missed calls and texts from various individuals trying to contact her with growing degrees of urgency, especially Daddy."

"Damn it!" Cowan swore. "I was hoping her daddy wouldn't know she's missing until we get her back. Her Blackberry was never going to be of use to Manor anyway. Sir, she's still in the country... alive."

"In Monrovia?"

"No, sir."

"Where?" Bohn asked. Before Cowan spoke, he said, "Never mind. Team up with Lonos and get her back... asap."

Underestimating is for idiots, so Cowan never underestimates. He'd taken a job and damn if he'd not executed it at the highest standards of performance. Cowan had acquired the world's smallest global positioning 16 satellite real-time tracking system, the WorldTracker SMS (GPS Tracker), only 2.5 by 1.7 inches, and planted it in Adriana's purse, unknown to the woman. Using cutting edge 3D mapping technology from Google, the SIM card in the device sends SMS messages through a server, allowing the user to use Google Earth to track the target live. The location data are reported to a cell phone without the use of a computer or website—no need of the internet.

A phone call from Bohn had sent Lonos speedily to meet with Cowan. The men had not seen each other since their fight, and Lonos still had a bruised ego. Cowan had to break the ice somehow. He looked up. His expression wasn't mocking, but frank. "I might as well put my head on the chopping block and save Mr. LeRoux the time and effort. But before I do, I'm going to get Adriana back."

Lonos kept his face impassive. He had not come to make friends. Bohn had ordered him to meet with Cowan and follow orders.

"You do what you get paid to do, Lonos, it was all business," Cowan said of their fight. These were not instructions nor an apology. As apologies went, this was as close as Jay Cowan was ever going to give.

Looking at the man, Lonos remembered every pound of Cowan's fist, every spray of blood, every snicker. Most of all, he remembered the cold ruthlessness in Adriana's eyes while she watched her bodyguard tried to murder him; he called them, *killer's eyes.* Cowan had nearly killed him. Yes, he was rude to the woman, giving her a taste of her own medicine, but surely that should not have warranted such a brutal beating. While this beating went on, everyone stood around too shocked or too scared to stop Cowan.

Lonos was collecting a paycheck from Bohn and duty was calling, so he had to put personal feelings aside. Lonos remained impassive.

"Look, what happened, happened," Cowan went on. "The fate of this man's daughter depends on us putting our efforts together. And, I mean pronto."

Cowan's phone buzzed and he picked up right away. "Cowan," he answered.

"If my daughter is dead, Mr. Cowan, so are you," Mr. LeRoux snarled at the other end. "You are a dead man as sure as my name is, Pieter LeRoux."

The phone went dead before Cowan said a word.

"Ms. LeRoux put her little finger in the fire and hope for something good," Cowan mumbled.

"Mr. LeRoux?" Lonos inquired as to the caller. Cowan nodded. "What did she expect? Fire burns," he shrugged.

Cowan's phone buzzed again, an incoming message flashed. He checked his SMS text message, then Google Earth map. "Come on, Lonos, we're going to Salala to get Mr. LeRoux's precious daughter."

"How do you know she's in Salala?"

Cowan held up his phone, showing Google Earth high resolution satellite image of Liberia with a little red dot blinking, off and on, off and on.

"Right on Salala," Lonos noted. "What if they relocate?"

"Geofence sends alert if they do. I'll get another text message of the new location."

"So, you get a signal whether they're indoor or outdoor?" Lonos asked, impressed.

"Yes, sir," Cowan answered. "It's water-resistant too."

"Come on, partner, let's go," Lonos said, then added, "I want a rematch after we get Ms. LeRoux back home."

"Think you can handle another knuckle sandwich?" Cowan joked.

"Cowan, this time, it's you who are going to get the country blow."

"What's a *country blow*?"

"You'll find out," Lonos laughed.

The men shook hands, boarded the car and sped off.

—**********—

Cowan's job was indeed never boring, which he appreciated. He liked international assignments, especially the people. Interviewing them, investigating them, but never arresting them; that was their local authority responsibilities. Foreign people never failed to fascinate.

Liberia, being a small geographic area, where two-thirds of the country's population lives in small towns and villages, would not justify each town's police force. Things happened, but not like in Monrovia. In fact, Cowan had hardly seen a patrol car beyond the boundary of Monrovia. He cared less because the matter did not warrant legal permissions, and he *could* police his heart out as much as he wanted to.

After driving a rough fifty-something miles, Cowan and Lonos entered Salala. With a few taps on his cell, he was able to bring up satellite images of their target. Cowan zoomed in on snapshots of a rural road, then a narrow dirt road leading to a spot bordered heavily by mud huts. The exact match of the GPS appeared to be a spot in the middle of the small village.

"They got her tucked away in the middle of the village," Cowan whispered to Lonos. "We are getting her out without alerting the neighbors."

"Or her purse," Lonos pointed out. "Maybe they got her purse."

"My gut tells me it's her," Cowan assured.

Lonos nodded.

"So here's the deal," Cowan continued. "I don't give a damn about the kidnappers, all I care about is the girl."

"I care about the girl, *and* the kidnappers," Lonos countered. Cowan looked at him. "They might be the same ones that killed that little boy and I promised his grandmother I'd find them... the heart-men."

"Lonos...."

"I know, I'm working for Bohn, not the Liberian government. Cowan, you don't understand. I gave that old lady my word."

Cowan thought it over for a moment. "Fuck it," he sighed. "Okay, let's talk strategy. How do we approach, control and contain?"

"I'll approach and get the layout of the place," Lonos suggested. "Anyone seeing you might spook the kidnappers."

Cowan furrowed his brow. If only Lonos knew, he had a great deal of experience spying on people and their activities.

"Look at your size, man… you'd look like a giant among my people."

"They might not *all* be your people," Cowan said with a comical smile.

"Okay, we both go."

"Let's get this done," Cowan said crisply.

And just like that, the two-man task force taking on the kidnappers was ready to get the party started.

Chapter 70

IN INTELLIGENCE OPERATIONS, it is the habit of military police officers to explore, secure and mobilize; Lonos' repertoire. Cowan, former military, makes warfare his specialty. Lonos' idea, Cowan's plan; they would execute as a team.

Cowan took inventory of the village, seeking out the hideout hut while quieting planning the most effective approach. Nearby was a patch of pepper blossom a few steps away, and there was no fence cutting off one's neighbor. The sounds of the night—chirping of bats, shrill chorus of insects and snoring sounds of unidentified animals—plus a full moon shimmering its pale light upon the village, evoked the mood.

They sneaked up close to the hut, and practiced patience. Then, Cowan peeked through the cracks in the wooden window. Inside the hut were sleeping mats, wooden benches, baskets, and cooking pots. He counted three sleeping bodies, none resembling a woman's. Both men assumed the crouch position.

Lonos nudged Cowan. "How many?"

"Three," Cowan said, holding up two fingers.

Lonos chuckled.

For a moment, Cowan smelled jasmine, the notes of Chanel No 5, one of the most famous, and expensive, perfumes in the world. Anyone living in this village simply cannot afford a bottle of Gabrielle 'Coco' Chanel fragrance priced over a thousand dollars. Perfume can make that necessary difference, and non-verbally convey a lot. He wondered what the woman was feeling, being stuck in the same outfit, or worst, in living quarters with dirt floor. Soldiers are used to low standards, the lady is no soldier. The spoiled brat had screwed up, but she was also too tough to crumple. Cowan could count on her for that.

They approached the door and Cowan examined it for the lock.

"No locks," he whispered. "They just have a nail bend into a hook." He almost laugh.

A millisecond in time, Cowan used his penknife to unhook the nail and push the door in. It creaked. All three bodies remained on the mats. Lonos crept in first, then Cowan.

Cowan pointed to his eyes, then at the sleeping bodies, meaning, *Keep an eye on them.* Lonos nodded.

It took a second to spot Adriana, standing in the corner away from the kidnappers. She had managed to untie her hands, not her feet. She was blindfolded, Cowan noticed, and thought, *How the hell did she do that?*

He drew near and she felt his presence. Rather than scream, Adriana swung her arms to fight off the would-be attacker. Cowan was quick: He grabbed her with his strong arms and twisted her around until she was caught in his embrace, her back to his front, her arms locked by her sides where she could no longer hit him. He held her, and whispered softly against the top of her head, "It's me, Cowan. I've come to take you home."

Emptied of all her energy, Adriana slumped against him and began sobbing.

"I want you to keep the blindfold on until I get you into the car," Cowan whispered, mindful that the surroundings might spook her.

The ice-princess nodded and held on to the man like they were two long-lost friends.

"Ms. LeRoux, I want you to listen to me, okay?"

Adriana conceded his request with a single stiff nod.

"Keep the blindfold on," he repeated. "I want you to wait here in this spot and I mean, don't move. Do you hear me?"

"Y-y-yes."

"I'll be right back," Cowan whispered.

Lonos moved close enough to the woman's silhouette, without touching, as Cowan had planned.

"Well... well... well," a man's voice whispered. Cowan turned and saw the three men standing. He detected a French accent. "Manor a dit que vous viendriez ici," one man said in French.

"He did, didn't he," Cowan replied.

Amused that Cowan understood, and perhaps spoke French, he chuckled. "Oui... Oui."

Cowan concluded they were rookies, sleeping on the job. *This should be easy.*

Former military, the brains, equally respected for his brawn, now a current private mercenary. The kind of man who would do whatever it takes to earn the money. As of this moment, failure was not an option. Failure has consequences. Besides, it would be unethical, a break in mercenary code. Faithful to the finish; perform with endurance and finish strong.

The three men approached Cowan, while he stood between them and his subject. There was a thought. He signaled Lonos to stay put.

Cowan watched one man pull the Taser out of a leather holster around his waist and move toward him. Simultaneously, he pointed the Taser and pulled the trigger, while the other two kidnappers jumped Cowan's back.

It's true what they say: 'The bigger they are, the harder they fall.'

Cowan magically disarmed the trigger man, pointed it at his chest and within seconds, the man was now on the ground, entire body jerking crazily. He dropped the Taser and grabbed the men on his back, one arm each; he swung hard, flapping their bodies to the ground.

Cowan picked up the Taser, pointed and fired into the first man's exposed forearm, then the other. The men shrieked. He fired again, then stood over them, holding up the Taser like a gunslinger. "Whatever you can do, I can do better," he muttered.

You would expect Cowan to purse his lips and blow the smoke from the end of the barrel. Cowan wondered, *How many unfried brain cells could they have left?* He pointed and shot each man once more.

Suddenly, with an ear-splitting roar, a big man appeared out of nowhere, fists clenched, face enraged. About half a second, Lonos found the man's gaze locked on him, the target. The big man charged, but Lonos quickly sidestep, and as the man move forward, hit him with every ounce of strength across his back. The man fell and Lonos kicked at his body several times, aiming for his ribs, while he was trying to curl up. Lonos grabbed the man by his hair, lifted his head until his shoulders were half off the floor, then slammed him back down. Lifting, then slamming, the man's head with every word, "I…should…fucking…kill…you!"

"We don't murder on the job," Cowan yelled, "but… if your subject's life is in danger, that's another story."

Lonos stopped. He looked at Cowan.

"I swear I counted three," Cowan shrugged. "Where did he come from?"

"The back. He probably went to take a leak," Lonos concluded and released the man's hair.

Cowan took Adriana in a fireman's carry, carried her to the car, and lay her on the back seat. Lonos followed.

Suddenly, with an irritated roar, the big man Lonos assaulted, leapt to his feet and charged. Cowan and Lonos got into the car a split second before he threw a brick at the front windshield. The glass spiderweb, but did not break. Cowan started the car and sped off before he actually reached them.

__**********__

Update implies progress: Cowan phoned Bohn.

Bohn picked up his phone on the first ring, mindful not to wake Katharine. He climbed out of bed and went to the kitchen.

"Beauty's with the beast," Cowan said by way of greeting.

Bohn interpreted that as code for Adriana's been successfully rescued. "Manor is dead," he informed. "He tried escaping from South Africa authorities on a private plane. Sonofabitch crashed... blew up."

"Lonos would be glad to know this. What about his lawyer?"

"Arrested."

"The lawyer needs a lawyer," Cowan chuckled. "Private plane, you say? Was it LeRoux's?"

"Her private jet is still at Springs Airfield. Cowan... get the man's daughter home," Bohn said and disconnected.

__**********__

The next day after Bohn's briefing about the plane crash, Officer Lonos steered his old jalopy through slow-moving traffic, then into the parking lot of the Monrovia Police Department building. He saw the police chief standing next to his Ford SUV, headed his direction and parked three spaces from the Chief. Lonos got out and approached Dolo.

"Did you really think you could have gone on forever?" Lonos provoked. "Pretending to serve and protect the Liberian people?"

"What the hell are you talking about?"

"If I were you, I would resign and look for me a lawyer," Lonos said sharply. "Taking bribes, suppressing evidence, covering Manor's dirty work... prostitution, trafficking. They have a lot more on you, buddy. The sad thing is, you don't have the kind of dough Manor has."

Dolo looked nervously at Lonos. "They? I have no idea what you are talking about," he said slowly, his voice nervous and at least two octaves higher than normal. He was struggling to stay calm.

"You already know what happens to heart-men," Lonos said coldly. Then he made hand gestures of a noose hanging its victim, and sticking his tongue out to the side of his mouth.

"How dare you! Are you accusing me of being a heart-man?" Dolo's nostrils flared with anger.

"Yes," Lonos replied. "The surgically precise cuts on Matthew Seekey's body," he said pointedly. "You, impeding my investigation, and then taking me off the case. Firing me without warning. It got me thinking about a little joint op you and Manor had a few years ago. Remember Senator Douglas?"

"Shut the hell up!"

Lonos leaned against the hood of Dolo's precious SUV, simply to provoke. The one no other officer is to touch, or even ride in. Dolo treated the government issued vehicle as if it was his private ride.

"Dolo, your gods are dead," Lonos announced. "The gods who have blinded your mind with bribes. What are you going to do now? Dead gods can do nothing for you. Manor and his disciples... they all went boom!"

"You are nothing but a *doeko*," Dolo stared. "How would you know this? This is all bullshit."

"Oh, it's true. Manor's dead. I wanted to be the one to break the news."

"You're lying," Dolo muttered.

"You'll see," Lonos assured. "Now that I've told you, I'm going to see the old lady," Lonos finished and walked away, not looking back.

Chief Dolo watched as Lonos got in the old jalopy, started it and drove off, sporting both broken taillights. He couldn't believe the news, too shock to get behind his steering; his knees rubbery, his eyes wet and unable to stop the tears, his neat uniform shirt now stained with sweat at the armpits. Dolo wiped perspiration from his forehead, got his cell out of his pocket and punched Diallo's number. It went straight to his voice mail. Ten attempts gave the same result.

In the sickening business of illegal trafficking, did you expect happy endings, a small voice asked.

Chapter 71

IN HER PRACTICE, Dr. Ricciola had never encouraged any of her clients to surrender to God their marriage problems. Misunderstood or overlooked perhaps, but spiritual guidance could very well be the secret to saving a troubled marriage. She considered it on the advice of her mother-in-law, the family spiritual advocate. Gia agreed to save what was left of their troubled marriage, and RJ was more than willing to join her for counseling with Pastor Peabody.

The five-mile distance from the house to the church took forty-five minutes because of traffic. Neither one said a word in the car until RJ brought the Toyota Landcruser to a halt at the back entrance to the church.

"Here we are," he muttered. He got out, walked around to the front passenger door and opened it. Gia got out and he escorted her to the building, then to Pastor Peabody's office, walking slightly ahead to open the door, then following to catch up as she walked through.

She acknowledged her husband's courtesy with a softly spoken "Thank you" each time.

The office door was open. Pastor Peabody had been waiting for them, (he had arranged to be alone at the church) and seemed ready and willing to give all the time they needed.

"Hello and come on in," he waved at them when they reached his office door. He got up.

RJ ushered Gia forward, then he followed. Pastor Peabody shook their hands and pointed to a sitting area designed with a loveseat, two matching chairs, and a coffee table between them. "Sit anywhere," he offered.

Gia sat on the loveseat and RJ sat next to her.

Pastor Peabody pulled the coffee table to the side, making room to accommodate RJ's long legs. "I normally don't have anyone this tall come to my office," he joked and sat in the chair opposite RJ.

"Not too many six-footers in Liberia, I guess," RJ chuckled. "Thank you for seeing us, Pastor Peabody. Gia and I appreciate this."

"We do, especially on short notice," Gia added.

Then RJ told him why they needed his counsel.

"Marriage is a partnership affair," Pastor Peabody started. "Your happiness depends on the two of you to be of the same mind, having the same love, being in full accord and of one mind. You cannot be self-conceited, or see yourself as a rivalry. Count your partner more significant than yourself and do it with humility. Each of you must look not only to his own or her own interests, but also to the interests of the other."

Gia had preached this message to many of her clients. In his mind, RJ set check marks at every point made. There were no misgivings about any.

"When your thoughts for yourself are lost in your thoughts for your wife or your husband, there is a great measure of love in the marriage," Pastor Peabody went on. "That love feels the sorrows your partner feels, that love gives support where it is needed and that love is quick to take delight in every aspect of your partner's life. A marriage filled with that kind of love is a fulfilling partnership."

RJ could almost pat himself on the back. If this was an exam being graded, he would get an A plus.

Then Pastor Peabody said, "What causes quarrels and what causes fights among us is our passion of "me" coming first."

RJ's A suddenly dipped a notch. His wife had accused him of only thinking of himself when he 'screwed' Grace and their marriage.

"That's the core of the war within us," Pastor Peabody continued, "me... me... me. Our desires are for self-serving reasons only. We crave things, and to obtain what our double-minded heart desires, we do things selfishly. We are easily tempted because we are drawn away by our own desire... easily enticed by those idols.

"Fornication, like adultery, is a form of an idol," he stressed, "an idol of unlawful sexual intercourse. It stabs a person's conscience and steals the worth of the most precious thing you have to offer... your body. It steals the worth of a marriage."

Gia heaved a painful sigh. She turned and looked at RJ, while he stared ahead, too afraid to know what expression his wife had on her face. He brought his fingers to the bridge of his nose and squeezed. She sensed his nervousness. Then RJ felt her reach out for him and he took her hand.

"If there is any potency in your faith today, God will give you happiness again," Pastor Peabody encouraged. "RJ, do you have anything to say to your wife?"

"Yes, I do," RJ assured.

Apologies can be hard to make because it takes a spirit of humility to admit your mistakes. RJ had messed up and had apologized to his wife privately. Now he must apologize to Gia in front of a man of God. He stared at the floor, thinking about the dilemma of his own making. When he finally spoke, he acknowledged the pain he'd caused his wife. He repented in the brokenness of her trust and the change of life-direction marked by longing for something more than what he had available to him in his relationship. He expressed his longing to save his marriage by willingly acknowledging his selfish violation of their love, first toward Gia and then toward Grace. He realized that he deserved nothing and pleaded to save his marriage without a demand of any kind.

RJ told the story of how he and Gia had met the first time, at a Christmas party. Then he told about the news about her pregnancy, their wedding, and then the birth of his daughter. He had kept those memories alive in his heart because they meant so much to him. As he finished, his wife could feel herself falling in love with him again.

"I love you, Gia," RJ said, closing his atonement. "You are the love of my life. I intend to fight for our marriage until my heart stops. I'll love you for as long as the life given me."

Words well chosen can open a frozen heart. His apology was felt a thousand remorse deep. Gia smiled a tearful smile.

"Pray to God that as He has forgiven you in your own sins, Mrs. Douglas, you consider your husband's regret," Pastor Peabody encouraged. "He has begged for forgiveness."

Gia nodded.

"When darkness falls on your life, Christ is the pathway," Pastor Peabody continued. "It's good to use His example… to find forgiveness in your heart."

Gia smiled.

"You and your husband need more than a new start," Pastor Peabody went on, looking at Gia, and then RJ. "I pray God gives each of you a new heart. As sinners, which we all are, we need a fresh heart."

RJ caught Gia's gaze and they both smiled.

"Shall we pray?" Pastor Peabody suggested.

Gia answered, "Yes."

RJ nodded.

"Why don't the three of us stand and hold hands… let's make a circle," Pastor Peabody suggested.

Everybody stood up and held hands, making a small circle.

Eyes closed and heads bowed, Pastor Peabody prayed a long one.

"Our Lord, our God, how excellent is Your name in all the earth! Heavenly Father, we surrender to you our conflicts and our burdens. Thank you for reminding us that you are our rock and our answers. Help us never to forget that.

"I asked that you heal this beautiful couple's love life. May both be willing to release any un-forgiveness harbored to each other, or to others, or to themselves. Cleanse them of all anger or resentment, Lord. Help them to see each other through the eyes of love... Your love. I pray all effects of their mistakes be undone in all directions of their future. Renew their love, gracious Father, so that they have harmony, romance, friendship, respect, honesty, and great love for one another.

"They are ready for you to bring the holiest vibrations of love and healing between them. Where they are afraid to love… where they have built walls of any kind in front of their hearts, may they be healed and set free. Let this bond be a channel for God's love and healing. As lessons come and challenges grow, let them not be tempted to forsake each other. Bring them together in heart and mind, as well as body. Let RJ always remember that he has the most beautiful woman in his wife, and let Gia always remember that she has the most beautiful man in her husband.

"We surrender ourselves to you, Father, as RJ and Gia surrender their marriage to you. May it serve your purpose, may it receive your blessings and carry your power always. May they never forsake each other. Bless this union once more with a peaceful and loving home… with patience to be more tolerant… to know and see only the things that really matter… to surrender all habits of thought or speech or deeds that breed discord.

"We thank you, Father, for giving us this opportunity and ask all this in the name of your son, Jesus Christ… Amen."

RJ and Gia said, "Amen."

RJ released Pastor Peabody's hand, and continued to hold his wife's hand. He pulled her toward him, leaned in and kissed her lips softly. "I never stop loving you, honey. I love you and I am sorry for hurting you so badly," he said. And at that, he broke down, his sobs coming out in heaving bursts. "I've asked God to forgive me. I'm begging you to forgive me, and give me another chance to do right by you."

Gia cupped his face in her hands, the way she always does to make sure she has his undivided attention. They were eye to eye. "I know," she whispered, her voice loaded with passion. Then tears filled her eyes and ran down her face. "I was angry and disappointed, but I never stopped loving you. Forgiveness is a tough word, honey, but I'm willing to try."

RJ began to cry even harder. Then he did the bear-hug-lifting thing she'd always enjoyed, and began kissing her. Holding his wife in his arms was more natural to him than his own heartbeat.

In times of grief and sorrow they held each other, and she took his grief and made it her own. When he cried, she cried, and when he hurt, she hurt. She had been there for him when his dear Nana passed, and when his father was an accused killer, and when other shameful family secrets came out. Gia never judged, she made him see things clearly when they made no sense. She was every reason and every hope he had for the future. They were linked in a way that few things are, and it was impossible to think of her not being a part of him; there cannot be one without the other. He prayed they would always be together.

Gia pulled back a little. "Honey, we are in the church," she reminded him, a little embarrassed.

"Oh," was all RJ could say, feeling hopeful again.

Pastor Peabody permitted himself a smile. "May God help you through the aching times, Mrs. Douglas," he encouraged.

"Thank you, Pastor Peabody," Gia choked.

"Keep Christ as the head of your family," Pastor Peabody encouraged, "because He is what we need when a relationship we cherished falls apart. No matter what our situation, as Christ-followers, we know where to find help."

Later that evening, for the first time in months, RJ and Gia were lying in bed together wanting each other the way they used to crave each other's touch. Cool sheets, dimmed lights, the delicate upsweep of her breasts, the male-smell of him, eager hands, skin against skin, their lovemaking was as sweet as the first time. They lay back later, still entangled, Gia's leg flung over RJ's hip, his arm beneath her shoulders, breathing each other's breath, softly touching each other's body.

"I'll never, ever, hurt you again," RJ whispered. "I'd rather die than do anything that selfish."

His eyes welled tears when he finished. He blinked and the tears rolled down the side of his face. Gia felt something tickled her skin and turned toward him. He caught her gaze.

She touched his face softly, then whispered, "Hey, Flaky, we are going to work it out."

RJ let out a sigh of relief.

Love before the storm, she thought. *Because of Peace, our life will always include Grace.*

Then Gia turned her back, sighed and waited for sleep.

Epilogue

TIME HAS A funny way of dimming the edges of reality until only something blurry remains. Then when that happens, people go back to a more normal routine. Like clockwork, tomorrow pushes itself on the calendar and time moves everyone along. Ups and downs spell come and go as the earth mindlessly spins around the sun, confirming new beginnings.

It was a moment of thanksgiving. The women, old and young, and their friends, relatives, and neighbors had begun to arrive at the banquet hall at Words of Christ Church. Everyone was in a hugely celebratory mood.

As one big family, the women planned a good hospitality for the woman who had taught them to love themselves. They had prepared an amazing meal for the special occasion, a royal entertainment: a feast of two sheep, one goat, one cow, one hog, and fifty chickens. Some people ate more meat that day than they'd had their entire life. They prepared jollof rice, collard greens, palmbutter, fufu and dumboy with goat soup, roasted meat, roasted fish, boiled plantain, cassava and eddoes to go with the fish and shrimp gravies. The aroma of pork and beef ribs filled the air. Four kinds of bread filled the serving tables; rice bread, cassava bread, shortbread and cornbread. Tomah had even made her specialty that day, her contribution was a gravy dish made with liver that went with the shortbread and cornbread. Just non-alcoholic beverages were served.

Yassah Johnston and Ruth Somah greeted everybody at the rear entrance of the church as they arrived. Yassah had happy smiles for everyone, especially Julius Peabody, who had come to support.

"Girl Power!" Pastor Peabody observed, and smiled broadly.

Yassah grinned right back.

Julius leaned forward and kissed his fiancé on the cheeks before joining the attendees.

The party started around three o'clock in the afternoon. After Pastor Peabody offered the opening prayer, it was a howling start. They got a lot of laughs and playful jeers from members and non-members alike, even husband-supporters.

Ruth Somah opened the meeting with a burst of thanksgiving for Grace's services. Then she sought to open the eyes of their hearts to even more exalted victories, the improvements in each woman's life since they met Grace. When Ruth cranked up the volume to express the importance of Grace's service, not one low mournful note sneaked out. To question whether or not to stand up to those who violate your rights, education had proven a great tonic, a perfect remedy in the fight. Women's right is worth fighting for.

"Thank you, Sister Grace, for the encouragement and the hope we find in learning to read and write. One is completely helpless when she cannot read," Ruth finished.

Others gave testimonies of the lawyer's services. Shyly, Tomah first thanked God, and then Grace, for helping her escape a life of slavery from her husband.

When all was said and done, Yassah said the closing prayer: "Bless our children to be like trees, grown up in their strength, that they are the cornerstone for Liberia. May our farms grow full and our markets be according to the farms. Help us, God, to work hard for each other without complaining. May we be happy with one another."

The meeting adjourned. Everyone got up to leave when one woman joked, "Change is good… but dollar bills are better!"

This brought out a burst of laughter.

__**********__

On the first Saturday in June, Grace and Yassah designed a wedding ceremony with an expression of worship reflecting joy, celebration, culture, and love. Each guest had a clear impression that the couple was making a solemn, eternal covenant with each other before God and their families.

There was beauty in the church. A hundred white lights sparkled, palm branches and flowers everywhere, smiles and tears and music. Words of Christ Church filled with family and friends. Five minutes to the start of the ceremony, the choir began to sing and the ceremonial candles were lit.

The bridal processional began with Pastor Cyrus Wleh, the officiating minister, then Julius Peabody. Alex Massaquoi, standing as the Best Man, escorted the beautiful Matron of Honor, Ms. Grace Pupoh. A four-year-old Flower Girl from the MaryMartha Orphanage, and Ring Bearer, Peace Douglas, followed. Peace looked as handsome as his father, and every bit a Douglas. That's what his proud grandmother had said while they were getting dressed.

Pastor Wleh announced, "All rise for the Bride!"

Yassah and Uncle Moses began their march, her arm eloquently looped with his. Moses Zarway, dressed in a three-piece black suit and white bow tie, ambled proudly with Yassah, beautifully dressed in a white silk knee-length dress, holding a bouquet of white and yellow roses. All eyes were locked on her. Staring straight ahead, she smiled radiantly until they reach the front.

Then Pastor Wleh called the assembly to worship.

"Dearly beloved, we gathered here in the sight of God, and in the presence of these witnesses, to join together this man and this woman in holy matrimony, an honorable estate, instituted by God. It is therefore not to be entered into unadvisedly, but reverently... discreetly, and in the fear of God. Into this holy estate, these two persons come now to be joined."

After reciting an opening prayer, the congregation was seated.

The Minister asked, "Who gives this woman to be married to this man?"

Uncle Moses proudly said, "I do!" and rejoin the couple.

The charge to the Bride and Groom was read. Julius and Yassah, facing each other and smiling, recited pledge and expressed wedding vows. They exchanged rings, lit the unity candle, and the pronouncement was made.

Pastor Wleh recited the closing prayer, and right after said, "Julius, you may kiss your Bride."

Pastor Peabody gladly did. He kissed his bride softly on the lips, and he was a terrific kisser. Gentle and firm and just right. That was a part of his charm, and a part of the attraction. Everyone was completely amazed. Well, mostly everyone. Lynnette Vinton, holding the biggest gift, shifted and pouted through the entire ceremony.

Pastor Wleh announced, "It is now my privilege to introduce to you for the first time, Pastor and Mrs. Julius Peabody."

The familiar wedding rituals and cultural traditions transformed into meaningful celebrations; dancing with relatives, family or strangers, consuming large amount of the finer foods, fine drinks and humorous embarrassing toasts. Rather than tossing of the bouquet, Yassah simply handed it to Grace.

The newlywed loved every minute of it.

Julius Peabody toasted to his bride, telling the guests he never had the privilege to pick and choose, as people thought he had. Yassah Johnston was simply the direction where his heart went. Teary eyes, his bride smiled at him.

Then the bride and groom danced in the magical glow of the candle lights, Yassah resting her head on his chest, and Julius wearing a bright smile.

Whether Lynnette Vinton liked it or not, Yassah Johnston daringly entered the matrimonial state wearing white.

__**********__

Peace took a bit of time to adjust after RJ had returned to Atlanta. One night he finished his Goodnite prayer and as Grace tucked him in, he whispered so softly, "I want my daddy." It nearly broke her heart.

She looked at him and saw pain in her baby's eyes. It's obvious he misses RJ, holding on to a wallet he'd bought him. RJ's picture is in it.

Grace mindlessly pushed the strange looking stuff animal out of the way, a 12-in green pig with red mustache, and sat on the bed. Peace grabbed it quickly and pulled it close to his chest.

"I'm sorry, baby," Grace said with a smile. "I was just getting it out of the way so I won't sit on it."

Peace held on, a frown tucked on his face.

"We know you'd miss your daddy, that's why he said you can call him any time."

He was silent. Then he smiled.

Grace looked at her watch, it read eight o'clock, which meant, it was one in the morning in Atlanta.

"Peace," her voice was soft. He looked up at her. "It's too late to call Daddy right now because he's sleeping."

"But I'm up," he whined.

She chuckled at his innocence. "It's one o'clock in the morning where he lives. It would be rude to wake him up just to talk if it's not an emergency."

"Momma… can I call him in the morning? Pleaseeeee?"

"Of course, we can call him as soon as you wake up. I think that would be a good time to call."

Peace dropped both wallet and pig, and opened his arms. Grace leaned in and got the sweetest, tightest hug ever. Her son gives the best hugs, that's why it felt like her heart was melting.

Now that Peace was tucked in for the night, Grace thought of nothing to do except wait till Alex gets home so that they go to bed together. He had called ahead to say he would be home a little late, and he already had dinner.

Twenty minutes after she had sat at the kitchen table, sipping on hot Lipton tea and reexamining her own actions over the years, she heard the back door open and closed. Seconds later, a voice followed.

"Grace?"

It was Alex, holding his school bag in one hand and a paper-bag package in the other; her guy, just in the nick of time.

"Where is Peace?" He asked, pulling the surprise out of the bag. A pint of vanilla ice cream from Sophie's Ice Cream Shop, Peace's favorite.

"In bed," she replied. *He really must have lost track of time*, she thought. It was past the boy's bedtime.

Alex was smart enough not to intrude on her thoughts. He put the ice cream in the freezer and said, "He can have it tomorrow. I tried to make it home early, but couldn't. Sorry."

Grace smiled.

"Okay, what's wrong?" He asked anyway. He knew her so well and knew something wasn't right.

Everything that had happened had somehow directed her heart to Alex's love. He cared about Grace when the burdens pressed her against all odds, and when the responsibilities distressed beyond belief. His heart was really touched by her grief. He cared enough to be near when she had wronged him. He saw in her what she had not seen in herself—a need for others. "No man is an island, Grace," he'd said, time and again. Alex wasn't afraid of hurting her feelings, he was always truthful rather than pretend to protect.

The gentlest, kindest man she knew, going back to high school and before, a true friend. Who didn't like Alex? A teacher who encouraged his students to love and value themselves, and offered tutoring to the ones desperately in need to bring failing grades up. Alex, who freely gave bus fares and registration fees to struggling students. Alex, a pretty-girl watcher, who'd remained faithful to the woman who'd promised to be a virgin on their wedding night, but now has another man's child. He'd forgiven her too.

"Hold my hand, Alex," Grace whispered, "hold it tight."

He did.

"I don't have the slightest idea why I'm starting to cry. But I guess, it's because I'm the luckiest girl in the world."

Slowly and firmly, emphasizing each word, Alex said to her, "I really do love you, you know." Then he kissed her.

__**********__

After Manor's bust in South Africa, Famatta Kpan and LJC could not withhold from the world the biggest news ever to come to Liberia since the hanging of the last five heart-men. The LJC front page headline read: **Ce MANOR—FLATten.**

For a number of days the newspapers and TV were filled with sensational stories about CeRue Manor. The LJC front page displayed pictures of Manor and his lawyer, and several articles, chronicling all the events, Manor's bust at the airport, his arrest, the escape attempt, and the plane crash. It too would soon be yesterday's news.

Sunday morning, rather than drive, Grace took a taxi to her office to pick up a few documents she wanted to go over at home.

"Drop me right here," she said to the driver.

He wheeled at the curb two buildings down and stopped. Grace paid and got out.

Standing at the curb right in front of the office building, was a woman staring at Grace as she walked toward the building.

"Good morning," Grace politely spoke when she reached her.

"Morning. I'm Omolola Sanusi," the woman introduced herself, "CeRue's wife. It's you I've come to see."

The formal super model sported large sunglasses, smudged makeup and a bad case of nerves. Grace extended her hand and they shook hands.

"Mrs. Manor, please come in," Grace said, pointing to her office door.

Omolola squared her shoulders, adjusted her grip on her designer bag strap and resiliently followed, as in moving to keep composed. Grace ushered her in, then to her office, and to a chair across from her desk.

Meeting her for the first time, Grace guessed the woman at late twenties, early thirties. Obviously African in descent, but spoke with a British accent. The oversize sunglasses covered half her face, but it was obvious she had been crying. Tear tracks stained her cheeks, while a hoarse rasp thickened her voice.

"What would you like me to do for you, Mrs. Manor?" Grace asked, before the woman sat.

"Please, call me Lola," Omolola said, and sat in the chair across from Grace's desk. She removed her sunglasses.

Up close she was a wreck—drawn skin, bruised eyes, worn-down expression—like a woman taking the news of her husband's death very hard.

"Can I get you something to drink?" Grace offered.

"White wine."

"Sorry… I was thinking… maybe coffee, tea or a soft drink. Coke or Fanta?"

"No, thanks," Omolola shook her head. Her hands were shaking badly. She placed her bag on her lap, laced her fingers together and rested her hand on top of the bag.

"Okay," Grace sighed.

"I need a lawyer," Omolola said, staring directly at Grace.

Grace's cell phone rang before she could register the woman's request.

"Excuse me, Lola," she said, and then answered, "Hello?"

"Thank God, I got you. Grace… I need a lawyer," the anxious voice greeted. "And, I mean right now… asap."

Grace recognized Diallo's voice and sighed. Perhaps she should have let it go unanswered.

—**********—

Cowan's phone buzzed and he picked up. "Cowan."

"Don't forget, Cowan," the voice greeted. "Remember the country blow I promised you? One day I'm gonna deliver. Might be today, might be next year, but I'll do it."

"Lonos, get back to your training!" Cowan ended the call with a grin.

—**********—

After Bohn met with his team and got possession of the spoils, he and Katharine flew to London for what would be a vacation, but not after he put a report together for RJ. He had accomplished something rarely achieved in Africa. He had changed the direction of a life, not just any life, a gangster's.

Africa's underworld is made up of war lords, dictators, and gangsters like Manor; men who do not value human life. The Net, a new scheme Bohn drafted had been tested and actually worked. The man's steps had been directed to phony authorities and then into the hands of mercenaries, all paid with his own money. Manor's Lieutenant General was next.

Bohn inserted the first USB flash drive into his laptop. *Removable Disk (O)* appeared on screen after a few seconds, listing all files in alphabetical order. He selected the first of ten video folders, pressed 'play' and plugged in his earphones. CeRue Manor introduced himself and explained what he was doing. This was a record listing all his personal assets, employees, associates, and clients. His network of clients extended from Africa to every other continent except Antarctica. Manor got them whatever they needed as long as they had the cash. Lots of it.

When Bohn disconnected the last disk two hours and forty-five minutes later, there were some things he had never expected, but glad to have seen them. The recordings detailed prostitution, smuggling of diamonds, guns and other banned weapons, legal and illegal drugs smuggling, gambling, trafficking medical merchandise, human trafficking, those embedded in his operations, as well as his clients. The discovery hit hard, and Bohn gazed at his laptop screen. The one thing he was certain about his business was, even when you've reach the expected endlines, there are a billion loose ends waiting.

He reread the files on the brothel posing as a massage parlor for uppity men, but didn't know how to, or how much to tell her. The senator had been a regular at the place until he and Manor had fallen out.

Katharine walked into the study, caught Bohn's gaze, and stared at him for a few minutes, waiting. She reached out and touched his arm, "Well?"

Brilliance failed him miserably. Bohn spoke slowly, stopping occasionally to scratch his forehead while he tried to set his story straight. How does he spin fact into fiction for the woman's benefit. After five minutes, it was obvious he wasn't willing to share whatever information he had with her.

"It's okay, Rudy," Katharine smiled. "You don't have to tell me the details of everything. I understand. Just one thing though."

"One thing?"

"Would you tell me if there's anything in your report about Robert?

Would you?"

"Of course."

She sighed. "Is there anything in there about him?"

He nodded again.

"Tell me. I'm sure it's something I already know. And, if it isn't, I still would like to know."

"Did you know Razaq is his biological son," Bohn said, hesitantly. "Did you know that?"

"I already knew that."

"How?"

"Sometimes pets grow to look like their owners, not adopted children. From the first day I saw Razaq, he looked more like Robert than RJ and Mel did."

"That didn't bother you?"

"It did. It hurt, but I love all my children the same. Sometimes I feel I love Zaq more."

"Really? Why?"

"For one thing, Robert did not like having him around. He didn't think I knew. I didn't ask, and he never offered a confession. Why have children if you don't want them?"

Bohn listened.

"It wasn't the child's fault," Katharine went on. "And, that little boy stuck with me as if we were joined by the hip. It was like forming an alliance," she chuckled. "He stayed here with me until he finished high school. I couldn't leave him with my mother like I did Mel and RJ. Zaq did not want to stay with Mama or Beulah. That's my baby," she sighed. "Since he's been away for college, he calls me every other day or so." She thought for a moment or two and said, "Anything else?"

"Uh?"

"Besides Razaq, did you find anything else? Anything at all?"

"No," Bohn lied. "That's it."

Katharine took in her breath and let it out slowly. "Thank God," she whispered, as if a weight had been lifted off her shoulders.

—✳✳✳✳✳✳✳✳✳✳—

Back in Atlanta, RJ and Gia were finally back on tracks, happy to welcome back the life they'd started a few years ago. They will push away the despair of his affair, his near fatal accident and work on building a happy family together—his son, their daughter and another child on the way. Like her pregnancy with Kitty, their second child together was conceived in Liberia. Celebrating the wonderful news, Gia joked, "Honey, you absolutely cannot go to Liberia without me, and when we do go, no sex. Three times is a charm!"

"Three equals trouble too," RJ added.

They laughed.

Gia had not known how she was going to trust her husband again until Pastor Peabody had suggested they armed their marriage with faith, meaning God's presence. But the enemy of trust was still out there somewhere. However, having the presence of Christ in their home will take care of that. All the good people they had in their life; caring family members, wonderful friends, and having God, the best company in their home. Faith in God and each other will keep things sweet and strong. No matter what happens, she now depended on God, not her or RJ. The kind of trust that will triumph over any wrong. This time around, she and RJ were on the same page, they were going onward together with a spiritual peace.

As for RJ, learning to acknowledge God in a personal way was not bad. It wasn't like the way someone like Katharine, or Pastor Peabody, or Lynnette Vinton for that matter, showed their faith. He attended church on special occasions—watch meeting night, Easter service or accompanied Katharine to satisfy her. He now realized neither his financial success, nor their intellectual accomplishments, nor had their physical attraction and attributes saved his marriage. God had allowed this impossible task in his life to teach him what his mother had always prayed for—one day her children will get to know God in a personal way. He'd learned, only your trust in God makes an impossible task become possible.

It was almost ten o'clock when he took sleeping Kitty off Gia's chest and carried her to bed. Standing in her bedroom doorway, admiring his little princess as she slept calmly, accompanied by Mono, the monkey stuffed animal Abuelita had given her, and the half dozen Angry Bird plush toys she and Uncle Zaq had collected together. Of course, the only one he had bought her was a 12-inch green pig with red mustache, and she had given it to Peace. RJ had bought it only because it wasn't a bird. Peace had gotten attached to the thing and the bottom line, it made RJ happy. He blew her a kiss, closed the door and returned to the living room.

Gia was still sitting on the sofa. He sat next to her, placed his arm around her shoulder and sighed. RJ could not imagine life without her. The night was quiet, everyone asleep and it felt as though they were the only two people left in the world.

"Honey," he said, holding Gia's hand in his.

A gesture meant more than words. She squeezed his hand trustingly. "What is it?"

"It's been a rough ride these past months," he said.

"It has," she agreed, now looking into his eyes.

RJ studied her eyes as if he was reading their future in them. They told the truth.

"I've thought about all the things that have happened," he whispered. Gia bent her head to catch his words. "I am responsible for derailing our lives, and I will be responsible for letting it run smoothly from now on... with God's help. Everything will be alright."

Gia stopped his words with kisses. He'd said it as if it was that simple.

They went to bed and the beautiful night ended like every other night.

Nine months and twenty-six *labor* hours later, Ricci Jenkins Douglas entered their world with a distinct and mightier cry, announcing his arrival.

READ ALL THE HEART MEN NOVELS
BY OPHELIA S. LEWIS
__**********__

THE HEART-MAN IS inhumanly alone. Relatively old like the boogeyman, he is a frightening imaginary being, accept his traits are far from imaginary.

Heart men
ISBN 13: 978097360965
eBook ISBN 9780975360996

"I am REALLY ENJOYING *Heart Men*..."—**Richelle Howell** (*Reader*)

"Overall, **HEART MEN** is an INTERESTING read...I ENJOYED RJ's PASSION for life, his LOVE for his family, and his tenacious search for the TRUTH...I certainly enjoyed his story. It held my interest from beginning to end."—**Damali Griffin** (*Imani Literary Group Book Club Member*)

"This is a story that has NEVER BEEN TOLD...I was pleasantly surprised to find out it is a LOVE STORY more than anything..."—**Manseen Logan** (*Bella Beau Marketing & Publicity*)

"I just finished reading **HEART MEN** here in Ghana on my Kindle...I LIKED IT A LOT...It seems that there are so many TABOO SUBJECTS in a society, and this is one not just in Liberia but everywhere...—**Tim Nevin**

Also available in eBook and downloadable formats. Read excerpts from all the books at www.ophelialewis.com

MONTSERRADO *stories*

HUMAN HISTORY DISCLOSES the anger and despair that too often mar the lives of people. This is Lewis' second collection of short stories, beautifully illustrating real life challenges, great story line, and a sweet voice sure to woo readers. The stories provide a view into Liberia society one cannot get from the headlines, written with perfect cultural rhythm that will bring readers to Liberia with the characters.

In **Good Father**, a cassava farmer, hard-pressed to provide for his family, questions his teen son's dream of becoming a football star. His encounter with an American coach, and a heart-to-heart conversation with his old father, ensues the love a father feels for his son. The fate of two strangers collides in **Sweet Mother**; Sundaymah Boye, a rape victim of the war with no desire for improving her life, and Nick Anderson, a thirty-something African-American who is losing his life to cancer. What each has to offer is priceless. A vital moral lesson pervades in **Firestone**, when a 15-year-old boy is caught breaking and entering. He is taken to the path of opportunity rather than prison. In **Believe**, divine power unites with human effort, as Youwah Saytue's faith is tested by the threat of a lethal African black mamba.

Montserrado stories
Paperback | 150 Pages | 2012
ISBN-13: 9780985362508
eBook ISBN: 9780985362546
Available for all eReaders

Books by Author

ORDER THESE BOOKS direct from **Village Tales Publishing** and save 10%
www.villagetalespublishing.com

MY DEAR LIBERIA (RECOLLECTIONS) is a collection of timeless narratives that is an integral part of Liberian tradition...sure to stir souls, energize minds and heal hearts since the civil war. Lewis serves as a common voice, shinning light on a part of Liberia's history, when people cherished the ordinariness of everyday life.

My Dear Liberia (recollections)
Paperback / 70 Pages / 2004
ISBN 10: 0975360906
ISBN 13: 9780975360903

Journeys
(a collection of poems)
Paperback / 100 Pages / 2007
ISBN 13: 9780975360910

Poetry that is readable and enjoyable. Readers peeking into Lewis' world will find a poet who teases love, sings love, and dances love. Yet love's sprinkles of sadness are never absent. If love brings people together, if love celebrates life, here, between the covers of Journey lie examples of some perfect lyrical narratives that should warm many hearts.

The Dowry of Virgins (and other stories)
Paperback / 178 Pages / 2011
ISBN 13: 9780975360927
eBook ISBN: 9780975360972
Available for all eReaders

IN THIS COLLECTION of seven imaginative short stories; themes represented in the work are of African and Liberian cultural influence. It seeks to explore, within African setting, the emotions of ordinary people when they face extraordinary situations. The emotions range from love, hate, greed, envy and fear. Lewis placed these ordinary people in unusual situations and let the characters decide for themselves the outcome of the story. In essence, her stories are generally, character-driven. Look for the twist in every tale in this collection!

LEWIS' UPCOMING BOOKS

Clay Ashland: a novel

Soloman's Porch

I'm About To (juvenile literature)

Where In The World Is Liberia (Children's game book)

Visit author's website for details at www.ophelialewis.com

About the Author

Photo by Portia Langley

Ophelia S. Lewis has created more enduring fictional characters than any other Liberian writer writing today. She is the author of the popular heart-man novels, *Heart Men* and *Dead Gods (HM2)*. Ms. Lewis has also written two collection of short stories, *The Dowry of Virgins & Other Stories* and *Montserrado Stories*; a book of essay, *My Dear Liberia*; and a collection of poems, *Journeys*. These books provide a view into Liberia society one cannot get from the headlines.

Lewis has also written two children's book; *A is for Africa* and *The Good Manner Alphabets* (How to be a super polite kid).

Ms. Lewis writes full-time and lives with her family in Georgia.

Follow author on facebook, twitter @ophie2020, or her website at www.ophelialewis.com.

www.ingramcontent.com/pod-product-compliance
Lightning Source LLC
Chambersburg PA
CBHW060812030726
47503CB00002B/455